THE WORLD WAS ALL BEFORE THEM

Designs for a Happy Home

The World Was All Before Them

Matthew Reynolds

BLOOMSBURY CIRCUS

LONDON · NEW DELHI · NEW YORK · SYDNEY

First published in Great Britain 2013

Copyright © 2013 by Matthew Reynolds

The moral right of the author has been asserted

Bloomsbury Circus is an imprint of Bloomsbury Publishing plc
50 Bedford Square, London WC1B 3DP

Bloomsbury Publishing, London, New Delhi, New York and Sydney

A CIP catalogue record for this book is available from the British Library

ISBN 978 1 4088 1796 4
10 9 8 7 6 5 4 3 2 1

Typeset by Hewer Text UK Ltd, Edinburgh

Printed and bound in Great Britain by CPI Group (UK) Ltd, Croydon CR0 4YY

www.bloomsbury.com/matthewreynolds

For Kate

They hand in hand with wandring steps and slow,
Through *Eden* took thir solitarie way.

Milton

CONTENTS

TWENTY-FIVE HOURS
IN OCTOBER

Brakelights flared and 0.47 of a second later young Dr Philip Newell too pressed the brake pedal of his VW Golf 1.6 Tdi Bluemotion, built 26 months and 13 days before, in Wolfsburg, on the river Aller, the arrow-straight Aller, where perch dart and poplars flutter, though Philip had bought it only the other week. The precision-engineered silver machine slowed slightly from 80mph to 74 and then, as Philip saw more red lights reddening ahead of him in a long, quadruple array curving right to follow the road uphill, slowed again when he pressed the pedal further down, feeling the metal of it push back against his foot, against the skin and muscle and metatarsals and proximal phalanges: 60, 42, 35, 30, then a judder down to 20 – at which Sue, sitting next to him, pulled her eyes back from the misty distant late afternoon sky, and looked forward, and glanced across towards him, and looked forward again at these things that were stacking together ahead of them, agglomerations of metal and rubber and plastic, slowing and settling, nosing each other's rear ends – they were bullocks, snorting mist, glaring with red eyes: yes, a herd being pushed backwards, pawing at the ground with heavy black hooves as, in a slow glide, the engine disengaged now, Philip and Sue, in their own metal and plastic box (with fabric trim), slackened to 10, 5, 0, perked up to 10 again for a moment, then dropped to a more definitive halt.

There was silence.

Then: 'Phhhhu,' said Philip.

'Mmgn,' said Sue.

All around, there was the air, chilling and thickening as it was rotated out of reach of the sun. There was the land which, leftwards, fell away and mapped itself out into fields, hedgerows, copses, lanes and roads, lines of telegraph poles and sequences of pylons, a farm-house with corrugated iron barns held close around it, a slab of cottages, and, in the soft fawn blur of the horizon, a scattering of sparkles as the daylight drained. On the right, beyond the other carriageway, where other cars speed irritatingly along the channel of the road, each one swelling as it approaches, its headlights dazzling, until, snap, in a moment, it has passed, and is receding and is gone; beyond this intensely frustrating, flowing carriageway rises an embankment strengthened with honeycomb-pattern slabs of concrete through which plants grow, thistle and dandelion, rye grass and meadow grass, wall barley, common couch and cock's foot, buttercups and poppies, though they are not flowering any longer, they have gone to seed: only the occasional red clover raises its fingers to the sky. On the crest of the embankment, a fence of metal posts and barbed wire holds back a mass of nettles, their leaves blackened and shrivelling in the cold. Behind them are the cathedral shadows of a wood where beeches loom, where fallen leaves of dun-colour and taupe and sulphur and skin-pink are changing, becoming slimy, fragrant, soft, returning to the ground where worms contract and surge, sucking their way through the earth, where ants and mites and beetles thrive, where cylindrocarpon and penicillium extend their filaments, where azotobacter and acromobacter flourish; and where, under a tipped-up, rotting trunk of maple, woodlice scurry and earwigs writhe. An early fox pads by, ears up, head a-twitch. A late mosquito drifts staggeringly towards its burrow. A pipistrelle flits. High up, a sparrow fluffs its feathers for the night, rolls its head this way and that, and lodges its hard, tender beak within the warmth. Further off, at the end of a slender branch, dangles a single stubborn apple, already gleaming in a glint of moonlight, even though it has been hollowed and part-ingested by a maggot housed within.

Yet none of this is seen by Philip and Sue, for they are sealed within their own particular micro-environment where: bang! the ball of Philip's right thumb hits the steering wheel which judders while the reactive energy of the impact makes his hand bounce back towards him. Because he really wanted to get home. He needs to rest. Because although the first two weeks had gone OK it was still really demanding. Because the reason they had gone OK was that he'd been fully awake, and alert, and wholly focused. Adrenalin prickling in him non-stop through the day. Now that he was at last a proper doctor. Now that it was finally at last just him being put face to face with a patient and being allowed to, no, obliged to do the utterly weird things that doctors do. Like for instance stick your fingers up their arse. Or listen to the clank-thud of their heart. Or inject alien liquid into their blood vessels – if that was the right path to take, of course, only if it was right. Because there's the rub. You can misdiagnose by missing something. Or you can misdiagnose by seeing something that isn't there. Or also you can simply have a brain-out and put the wrong word in the prescription, depomedrone not depoprovera (!) Or you can miss a contra-indication. Or you can . . . or actually you can just not feel up to slowly and carefully unpicking and thoroughly considering those many cases which are a tangle of body and mind. In which doctoring is as much about talking as handing out medicine. Or more. He sees a mother and a little boy sitting side by side in two orange plastic bucket chairs in the consulting room. He sees himself, listening, nodding, answering: he is projecting receptiveness and wisdom and concern. The little boy is bored, his eyes are sleepy, he is rocking back and forth on his hands which are squeezed beneath his thighs. The mother is speaking, she is fluting anxiety and self-blame. She drags a hand across her eyes, over the pink, hawk nose and the high forehead. She pushes her hand up into the clump of blonde hair, grabbing it, pulling it back. The eyes that look up at him are blurred and narrow, pouched in sagging blueish skin. She wants the treatment to be reconsidered. She doesn't want to criticise Dr Adam Hibbert, of course not; but she thinks that now she is in a calmer place. And now she, Janet Stone is in a calmer place, she has more time to give to Albert. And now she has more time to give to Albert she can do a better job. Because – suddenly her scratchy voice breaks through and Philip hears it in his head as he shifts his foot from brake to accelerator and nudges the car forward, letting it roll a little before resignedly rotating his foot back to touch the brake once more: 'What I can't get over is I can't stop thinking that because I wasn't there for him, because I was so crap, he is being stuffed full of chemicals. And doctor' – she says, staring at Philip pleadingly – 'they've turned him, those pills have, into a different person.' She sniffs. She hangs her head. Now she is looking at the chessboard of brown and mushroom-coloured carpet tiles. She says, resolutely, woefully, one word at a time: 'He's getting medicine instead of a mum.'

Which was great. It was really great that she had come to that perception and was showing that resolve. But that didn't mean it was necessarily true. And whether it was or wasn't it was going to take a lot of time, a lot of careful management. Which meant he really needed to get home and rest. Because OK, Janet and Albert Stone would probably not be back in the orange bucket chairs already next week. But someone would be. Someone equally problematic starting at 9 tomorrow. And all he asked was a moment of calm by himself at the end of the weekend, just to sit, and turn the pages of the paper, and check something or other on his phone; just to relax, and breathe, so as later to have some chance of going to sleep. Which was something that presumably never troubled Dr Adam Hibbert. Dr Adam Hibbert who felt no anxiety, slept the sleep of the innocent and the worthy every night. No, actually, the fact is Dr Adam Hibbert doesn't need to sleep at all; he is always on the go. Far away, on his completely exciting and worthy sabbatical somewhere up the Khyber, Dr Adam Hibbert is even now conducting amputations as the bullets whizz around him.

Philip breathes in decidedly through his nose. He lays his hand upon Sue's hand which, he now notices, is resting elf-like upon the jean fabric over his thigh. He realises that Sue's elfin hand is sending little sonar-blips of tranquillity across his hip towards his spine and up it to his mind. She in her turn feels, ever so slightly, his touch; but she doesn't really notice it because she too is thinking, she is thinking of the gallery, of the big last room where Al Ahmed's sun will be, that amazing, sumptuous, profligate idea of a haze of threads created from the shredded fabric of a whole wardrobe of Fortuny gowns. For the big last room of the gallery would be darkened, gloomy like the sky around her here. So the shattered fabric would emerge glimmeringly from the atmosphere, not trashily shine out. So it would seem diss-, no, what was the word: immanent. Although actually, here, now, you can't really properly see the blackening air since their car is illuminated by the headlights of the car behind. And that one must be illuminated by the headlights of the car behind it, etc; and it will be the same for the cars in front, so that they are all enclosed in a sort of tube of myopic brightness. But never mind because still, peering through that circumambient gleam, you can just about imagine Al Ahmed's sun floating there high up and distant and sublime. Which was, she supposed, with a sudden slide of disappointment, how it was going to figure in the gallery, winched up out of reach. Whereas what she would like, what she personally would like, would be if you were allowed to touch it. If you could miraculously, outrageously reach out and grab and hold some of the precious filaments in your fist. Or if you could push your face into them so that, not only so they stroked your cheeks but so you caught the smell of them whatever that would be. Or if – get this – how about if also you were allowed to stick out your tongue and touch with that, or taste with that. Because how many people have ever actually felt a piece of fabric with their tongue? She was standing on a box, she was at – where was that place in London where the loonys stood? – well anyway she was standing there with a megaphone holding forth. Try it! Taste a shirt today! And what was kind of sad but also kind of brilliant was that if people did, if anyone actually did that tiny thing, or if you could put on a show where people were allowed to, encouraged to, and then to think about it – then they would be surprised. It would make a difference to them.

Because there is so much to notice that we usually do not. So much to nourish us! Even now, even here in this stretch of what was officially a waste of time, what was officially deeply, horribly frustrating. What was there, well, for instance, there was Philip sitting there beside her. She lifted her hand away from his knee and moved it across, and down, and folded it into her other hand which was lying on her lap. She let herself sense his presence on the far side of the air between them, his condensed energy, his twitchiness – the way his head would settle rigid . . . and then jerk, the change of mind, the shift of gear, the altering angle of his arm. His fingers fluttered against the steering wheel. He pushed himself back into the seat. He scrunched his shoulders and let them fall. Always the same, even in bed at night, the tossing and turning. Whereas, with her, all that moved in her were her lungs, breathing, and the air through her nostrils and her pipeways. No: that couldn't be completely right. There was the heart, and the blood. There were doubtless all sorts of chemical reactions too. Actually . . . actually maybe this could be the thing! This could be something to offer up to Omar next week. If you could catch it in a piece . . . this unceasing activity that went on in people even when they were still. Marc Quinn's head of blood. No – the thing to do would be . . . how could you . . . what was wanted was some way of capturing, no, registering the fleetingness, the inside movement, the movement that was always going on inside. Such as for instance maybe an ECG.

'Do people's heads' – she asked – 'use different amounts of energy, depending on who you are? If you record people's brainwaves can you get an electronic signature?'

Philip smiled a familiar smile. Such a Sue question. 'Don't think so,' he replied. 'Maybe someday but I don't think we can at the moment. It varies. When you think more, that's activity, you can pick that up – there are jagged peaks. It's more intense when you're concentrating, trying to solve a problem. When you relax the waves stretch out.'

'Did Einstein's brain,' – she continued her enquiry – 'use more energy than everyone else's?'

'I think only if he used it more.' Philip moved his feet, set the car going forward a little, let it freewheel. 'But with him he probably didn't. Things just occurred to him. Popped up.'

'If you could measure a great physicist's brain, do an ECG just when he was about to have a really great idea . . .'

'It really wouldn't show any different. I doubt it would. It couldn't. It'd be like any old idea, like thinking, um, like thinking what to get someone for their birthday.'

'Oh.'

'Or what to have for breakfast.' He made the car slow, stop.

'Basically your brain uses the same as a lightbulb. It doesn't vary much. If you spend all day thinking really hard it's not going to make you thin.'

'So that's true, lightbulbs in comic books. Sort of.'

The car nudged forward a little bit then settled to a halt yet again.

'You know actually it's E-E-G,' Philip couldn't stop himself adding: 'Not ECG. ECG is the heart, cardio. EEG is Electro-encephalo-gram.'

Sue let her mind be filled with the sounds that the stereo was sending out to bounce around them, a beat and some kind of electronic interference making a sort of tune, swelling and spiralling and soaring and falling. What instruments were they? You couldn't tell, no instruments, electricity. You could hook a machine up to a brain, amplify it. Which would give you the music of thinking. Which must be a bit like whalesong. Pathways of flashing lights as the ideas travel down them; and the sound to go with it. Fill the whole gallery so people are inside the pathways and the sound, inside the experience of experience. Or get these cars to hoot one after another: that would be like a message passing along. Or flash their lights. Morse. The train was like that too. Every morning travelling in and every evening coming back she was like an idea. The rattle of its arrival; the shrieking of brakes. You could have a track running round the gallery, interlocking, an enormous endless spaghetti junction of trains. Not in a landscape but in some body-like environment, curvy and enveloping. And the trains tiny, much smaller than usual, specially manufactured, nipping here and there like mice, unstoppable. That would surprise the punters, wake them up. That would be a change from Al Ahmed. It was definitely worth developing. Take a bit of time on Mon and Tue. Frame the concept properly. Because Omar had said he wanted something fresh. Because she had definitely got the impression that now, now that she had settled in, learned the ropes, he wanted to see what she could offer. And here it was. Come Wednesday, she would pitch it. Yay! She smiled. She became aware of herself once more, that she had a body, that she was sitting in the car.

They seemed now to be moving more persistently. She raised her head and looked out, around. Still high darkness to the right: trees. Still to the left a sweep of land, fields, a scattering of lights in the distance. Still couldn't really see.

'It's a crash,' Philip announced.

'Is it?'

'On the other side. This was all just people slowing down to look. All this just because of people slowing down to look. It's bananas.'

'It must have been bad.'

She gazes across his hands on the steering wheel and sees on the other side a fire engine and two police cars each lit up by the others' lights. They are framed by the slender arch of a footbridge. From the warmth with Philip inside his car Sue looks out into the cold and sees, beyond the central reservation, someone standing, in a luminous jacket, signalling cars past in the other direction, one by one. There is an ambulance with its back doors open. Now Philip is accelerating: Sue's head swivels correspondingly, peering to see, in the darkness, with cars easing past in front of it on the other carriageway, a wheeled stretcher being pushed along, its steel frame glinting, and beyond it, lodged under the far corner of the foot-bridge, a big stopped lump, a conglomeration of shadows, something compacted, its tyres in the air.

So they sped past, on the other side, not having witnessed the crash, the panicked shrill screech as the car slid on its roof over the coarse asphalt, still going at 50, heading towards the . . . no – before that, the bang of its hitting the springy steel barrier on the central reservation which sent it bouncing in a cartwheel, once, twice, as, inside, for the solitary driver, only 19 years old, the world had gone slow and quiet, giving him leisure almost to enjoy the unusual visual experience, the horizon rotating, trees turning like the hands of a clock, until bang! – he was upside-down and the roof had crunched into the top of his head and he was sliding sideways at insane speed with this terrible noise all around him until . . . no, before that, the first hint of a wobble as he, Toby Knight, heading back to uni after a cool weekend away, moved out into the fast lane, not really going that fast, only 85, or so it seemed until the steering wheel jerked to the left and he pulled it back but now he is veering too far the other way so he straightens and the car drags left again so he pulls again and it is too, too fast, it is zigzagging, it is like slithering on ice and, bang! – he hits the springy steel barrier on the central reservation which sends him cartwheeling until . . . no, even before that, six weeks before, the intrusion of a two-inch, flat-headed nail which had somehow sneaked in between the treads and been pushed in through the vulcanised rubber, through the layers of textiles and steel ply, penetrating the whole carcass. There it had lodged, solid and secret, until the particular combination of pressures, heading downhill, at 85, on a slight curve, stressed the vicious sleeper-cell, and angled it, and tweaked it, until, pfuff, there was a sudden rush of air and the tyre sags and bells and wobbles and the steel rim of the wheel jars into the road surface and the tyre rips and there is no grip now and the car is heaving to and fro as the driver struggles until, bang! – he has hit the springy barrier on the central reservation and is cartwheeling and sliding and collides side-on with the edge of the concrete pier of the pedestrian bridge at which Toby's upside-down head is jerked sideways and hits the door pillar next to it and bounces back and his neck muscles tear and his vertebrae are dislodged and the delicate brain tissue crashes against the hard internal wall of the skull, so that membranes are compressed and blood vessels perforated and the grey matter begins to bruise and throughout the whole beautiful, intricate brain the shock-waves spread a microscopic anti-net of broken connections, a spray of less-than-hairline cracks. There he is, his head against the roof again, his consciousness glad that it has all come to an end, that it is quiet, this black and white world he is in now, even if there is a sensation of wrongness coming from his neck, even if he seems to be having to try very hard to keep seeing, seems to be having to make an effort to continue even being. There are sounds in the distance, what are they? People calling, footsteps running? Or the song of morning birds?

Passing by, 27 minutes later, Sue says to Philip: 'He must've had to be cut out.'

'One or two people touch their brakes, then everyone has to, then, bang, there is a traffic jam.'

'It's hard not to look. We were just looking. Well I was.'

'There are three thousand five hundred deaths from crashes each year. Ten each day. Nobody cares. We all keep driving. Too fast. I keep driving too fast, that's the weird thing. I'm completely aware it costs the NHS billions a year, think what we could do with that, think about the sport and good nutrition for young children we could fund with that. We've all decided it doesn't matter. Society has decreed' – Philip pressed on – 'that a nought-point-something chance of getting killed by a car each year, that that's OK. We've made that judgment. And yet still each time anyone sees one it's like oh no what a tragedy.'

But even as he protested, Philip's thoughts were circling his image of the scene of the accident like swallows swooping and sighing, and then following his image of the ambulance as, its doors clammed shut, it eased into motion and trundled away, lights flashing carnivalesquely but making no noise. Inside, what would there be? Neck brace, blood pressure cuff, ECG, oxygen mask and fingertip oximeter and IV. The paramedic having raised a vein and gingerly slid in the needle and attached the tube. The paramedic now sitting beside the patient steadying his head and watching, watching for any signs of flagging life. Speedily but carefully the vehicle would drive along and up and round and here and there until they reached the DI, the high, square, tiled carriageway porch of A and E, the bright harsh light, the inevitable jolt and rattle as the stretcher trolley hits the ground and trundles up the slope and onto the pavement and over the ribbed mat at the entrance and then it is into the glide of the smooth polished concrete floors inside and is drawn along by the imperious rhythm of the hospital where, once it has found its bay, a staff-grade will sweep in to assess, with a nurse to assist. Pulse, pupillary reflex; focus on the head and neck, fingertips caressing, assess GCS, off for an X-ray,another ECG hooked up, consultant brought in to consult. Surgery? High risk of secondary injury. Control bleeding. What is the ICP? Craniotomy? But now the tense, bright, messy, high-tec scene is fading from Philip's attention which is returning to the slow-motion rhythm of the road, the pulling out and tucking in, the passing and being overtaken. To the left the moon makes zigzag lines of quartz among the granite of the clouds.

Through Sue's mind, the lights of the road traverse, stretching her thoughts this way and that, pulling them apart from the moment of the disagreement. Ahead are pair after pair of red lights, all almost the same, dull as though resentful, except for the occasional differ-ent setup, a configuration of sparky LEDs, lozenges of glitter around empty eyes. Beside them are the diamond headlamps of the other carriageway streaming forward into their future but back into her past, following this journey she is taking with Philip in reverse, perhaps for a mile or two before branching off, perhaps for longer, perhaps even, one of them, all the way back, A34, M what was it, M something else, A this or that, another A, a B and then other roads, and others, not to mention the roundabouts and traffic lights and roadsigns and verges; not to mention the towns and villages and isolated houses; not to mention the fields and woods and copses and hedgerows, the barbed wire fences and electric pylons and telegraph wires, the contour lines and public footpaths and sites of special scientific interest. All that stuff would be the same for them, for whoever it was, in that car, taking the same road (only backwards); the same environment passed through. But some things would be different: the pedestrians, the other cars on the road. The weather would have shifted a little, and the light. Wind dropped, probably, as the evening enveloped what for her and Phil had been the afternoon. To be blunt about it, she thought, as she surveyed the ideas that had come into being in her mind, time would have passed, that's all. No, because actually time had passed. Not 'would have passed': it had. Her mind felt stuck as she tried to merge the landscape she could remember into the landscape she was imagining, and to spread that imagining out onto the world behind. So time had passed, so what? Well, a person might have cut their finger. Or died. Or split up with someone. Whereas, on the other hand, that blade of grass was still that blade of grasss, unless it had been trodden on. That stone was still that stone. Though actually with many of the people too it would be much the same. With many of them nothing really would have changed at all.

The car that she was following, in her mind, back the way that she had come, turned. It turned into streets whose names she maybe could remember. Black Rock Rise, then something else, then Ocean View. It turned, this small white hatchback, in at an open gateway on the right between jagged stone walls. But her mind travelled on, on to the next driveway which sloped down between amoeba-shaped patches of luminous green lawn and divided around a pond. She followed the rightward branch towards a burgundy front door and then – whoosh – she was in through the letter box and floating on in through the hallway corridor to the sitting room with its thick cream carpet and fuchsia suite, its several mahogany occasional tables with their glass surface-protectors upon which Betty's collection of Russian dolls shone plumply; its frilly lamps, both table and standard, and its flesh-coloured walls crammed with gold-framed photographs of seabirds soaring and diving and perching and pecking and nestling and roosting, chubby, with their trademark look of shock. There was the picture window, beneath which the hillside sloped gently away until a sketchy fence marked the boundary of the garden; after which there was an area of tundra where the coast path passed; after which there was nothing except the cliff-edge and some air. From the cosy eyrie of old Mr and Mrs Newell you saw, if you did not look down, no land at all: an endlessness of gas and liquid; the sea, slate-dark, choppy, crisped with white, as Sue imagined it now, seeing herself sunk in the soft pink armchair nearest the window, looking out; and the sky a million swirling wisps and mists and accumulations of paleness and grey. With her legs folded up, she had been watching a thicker, blacker raggedy slab of cloud move towards her, darkening the air and sea beneath; but here was Betty, come through from the kitchen, picking up the two cups she must have left a moment earlier in the serving hatch, easing herself carefully forward, the cups held stiffly out ahead of her, one in each hand. She bent her knees to place the cups on the low table in front of the window and set about sitting down in a chair identical to Sue's on the other side of it. She gripped the armrests; she leaned her whole body backwards; she bent at the hips and the knees, keeping her weight always on the hydraulic pillars of her arms, until she had lowered herself gently into the cushion.

'Bloody back,' she said. 'It's such a nuisance. But the best thing,' she said, struggling to lean forward, 'is to keep mobile.'

Sue pushed Betty's cup across the table.

'Thank you dear. What I hate,' she said frankly, lifting the cup, then pausing it beneath her lower lip, 'is to think this is a taste of things to come.'

Sue must have looked at her enquiringly.

'Old age.' She sighed the words.

'Anyone can slip a disc,' offered Sue.

'Yes,' said Betty, gratified. 'Yes they can.' And then: 'Well, I've brought you a cup of tea.'

'Thank you.'

'No sugars, that's right, isn't it?'

'Yes, that's right.'

There was a pause. And then:

'This is so amazing,' said Sue.

'Better than the pictures, I always say.'

'You must spend, do you spend whole afternoons just sitting here? I could.'

'Oh no, not whole afternoons! But it is' – she carried on after a moment, making a concession – 'nice to know it's there. You know, you can just glance out and see it, see the weather coming in.'

'Do you ever feel . . .' Sue had said then, turning, reaching for her cup of tea, looking up, 'that you're sort of dissolving into it? Your spirit going out into it, and it comes into you, so that you sort of rise up out of yourself. Fade away?'

There had been a pause.

'That's how I felt, a bit like that, just then,' Sue had said, stubbornly.

'Ken appreciates it for his photography. He lurks here, like a hunter. Twitchy' – Betty's voice was warm at the thought of him, of his energy. 'That's what they call them, you know, birdwatchers: twitchers. And he is, when he's lying here in wait. The perfect hide, he says it is. That's one he got from here' – she says, turning carefully in the chair, angling her head, then her shoulders, then lifting up her arm to point – 'a black-headed gull, though you can see it's more of a brown head really. Mostly all the ones in flight he got from here. Not the ones on the cliffs, obviously, or the shoreline, because you can't see them out of this window, can you? It'd be a miracle.' She chuckled briskly, glancing into Sue's eyes for an answering smile. 'He goes down into town to get them developed. There's a place there that does them properly, Dawton's.'

'He hasn't gone digital?'

'Doesn't hold with it.' Betty gulped the end of her tea and eased herself forward to plonk the cup on the edge of the table.

Then she leaned back upright, stiff and straight, and looked at Sue out of her deeply lined grey face with her shining blue eyes.

'I didn't want to move up here yet. It was Ken's idea. I liked it down in the town where Philip grew up . . . But, you know Ken a little bit now, don't you? So you know he does always want to get things organised well in advance. This bungalow came on the market and he said: it's ideal, we'll be all set up. But for me it was a wrench. Because down there, in town, in those streets, that's where our whole lives had been. I mean our whole lives as a family: I lived in Haston before that. But down in town' – she smiled puckishly – 'that's where Philip learned to walk! We'd go out, toddle along. Do a bit of shopping. And then we'd be at the sea. He was fascinated by the pebbles. One of them would catch his eye. He'd be standing there, you know wobbling a bit, with his little arms stretched out as if he wanted to give the whole world a great big hug. Then he'd set off and I could see he'd be making for a particular pebble. One of those great round ones, you know how big they are. He would bend over, and lift, and lift, or try to lift, and then . . . whoops, over he tipped, and his face'd go into the beach and his nappy would be in the air. It was' – there was that warm tone again in her voice, but she did not laugh – 'so funny.'

After a moment she went on: 'So to tell the truth I don't feel quite ready yet to just sit here and doze and fade away.' She looked stern. 'Give me a few years yet.'

'A few decades,' Sue had said emphatically, wincing as she realised the meaning Betty had taken from her words. But now, as she winces again at the recollection, it leaves her, and she sees that she and Philip in their VW Golf Bluemotion are nearing the end of their journey, nosing along Dartham Street where the shops are, then Turnpike Lane, then over the little bridge which marks the edge of the old town, then right, beside some ancient, patient willows. They passed along Helium Avenue with its meandering edges and its ornamental planting, of privet, beech, rhododendron and even the occasional palm, designed to screen the dedicated parking places that fronted each pastiche Victorian property. Then they were into the heart of The Willows, a signature brownfield development where every home boasted magnolia-painted walls, recessed down-lighting, half-height tiling to the ensuite, and a multi-point security system to the front door, together with all the high-spec energy-saving measures that today's environmentally-conscious home-owners feel entitled to demand. In vehicular motion, Sue and Philip negotiated Elysium Crescent (Georgian) and traversed Parnassus Row (Tudorbethan) before turning into their own patch, Eden Grove, a terrace articulated around three sides of a rectangle to give the impression of converted stables in a country house, or perhaps an array of traditional paupers' cottages. On the roof at the centre of this array was a little angular belfry from which no sound ever came. Philip parked in their allotted space in the central courtyard. Having unfolded themselves out of the vehicle, lifted the tailgate, shut it, and swung their bags over their shoulders, the pair of them were guided by low-level lighting towards the frontage of no. 12, the two-up-two-down individu-ally designed quality residence which was their place (rented) for the circle of the year. The slammed car doors had left a silence in the air; above them, the cold stars shone.

Indoors there was the usual hanging of coats in the hallway alcove and kicking-off of shoes. There was the clomping upstairs (this was Sue) so as to chuck knickers and T-shirts into the round wicker Habitat laundry basket in the corner of the bedroom, and to hang up her grey Diesel cargo pants and black Reiss zip-up top, and to lay Philip's jersey and jeans on the slim blue ottoman at the end of the bed for him to damn well deal with; and there was the going-through to the open-plan sitting-room-kitchen-diner (this was Phil) and pulling open the clattery door of the fridge to extract a little bottle of Becks, and levering it open, and slumping with it on the shiny brown soft faux-leather sofa in front of the sharp-edged gleaming square pine occasional table, thumbing at his Desire to check the week ahead and monitor his Pocket Empire and scroll through the last few days of Pulse updates, statins safe to give to patients with abnormal LTFs, BMA to resist rationing role, even though in some cases, Philip thought, a bit of rationing probably wouldn't go amiss. He could hear the tumble and splatter of water upstairs as Sue showered, and so kept pressing here and there on his touchscreen: plunging pass rates for CSA / echinacea 'no use for colds' – but hang on, when you looked into the figures there was a measurable advantage, so predictable the spin in the reporting / 27–floor home for Mumbai billionaire incorporating its own hanging gardens and multi-storey car park / Nobel Prize for Chinese dissident Liu Xiabao but he himself does not know it yet though his wife may be able to tell him tomorrow in prison, grubby tiled walls, pale blue cotton pyjamas, slop bucket, one hour of exercise, if that, metal cot, the slamming of the door / oh look Cher from yesterday already on YouTube and he watched again the marionette movements in rubik cube trousers and heard again smug Cowell saying: 'I see the future here' / defuse Taliban child – dumb bombs – flesh-ripping ball-bearings – a carnival of gore – as young as 11 – significant psychological damage – cured with volleyball and cricket – shrapnel – tearing epidermis dermis hypodermis releasing an inflammatory response which floods the damaged site with neutrophils which clear it of debris via phagocytosis except not the lump of metal itself obviously remove with tweezers disinfect debridement risk of tetanus: administer metronidazole followed by anti-tetanospasmin though what are the chances of sourcing that in the borderlands of Pakistan?

Dr Adam Hibbert would know.

Philip became aware once more of the room around him. The rumble of the fridge; the whirr of the Virgin box as it updated itself; the cough and sigh of the boiler; the whine of the extractor fan upstairs. Beyond all that, was there also the whispering of ash and elder in a breeze outside? He rose and plugged the phone into its wire on top of the microwave and moved to the room's door where he turned and lingered, looking around before putting out the light. In the capsule hallway was the saffron gleam of streetlamps filtered through the milky panes of the front door. He double-locked that door and climbed the carpeted stairs, jogging lightly up them with a little skip halfway. Round the tight end of the landing; in through the bedroom door; and there she was; there was Sue, in the bed he too was going to sidle into. There was her pale face in profile on the pillow. There were her eyelashes. There were her delicate porcelain cheeks – no, soft . . . they were linen / no – silk / no – milk, no – . There she was with her body snug under the duvet and her face in the cosiness of the pillow, aware of him (was she aware of him?) but not looking up: that was trust; that was intimacy; the having her just lie there, knowing he was there; knowing he was there moving around the room, in his clothes, while she lay there warm, with nothing on (probably), with her mind drifting and her body just there gently lying. He lifted his jersey and T-shirt over his shoulders; T-shirt in the basket; jersey added to the pile on the chair. Belt unbuckled; trousers pushed down; socks drawn off in the same movement, his thumbs hooked under the rims of them. Socks in the basket; trousers on the pile. In his boxers he went back onto the landing and turned into the bathroom: smooth floor, chilly. Never liked the look of his face in close-up, the pores, the incipient stubble, the sebum gleam, the desquamation of the stratum corneum, perpetual attrition of the boundary of the body, softening, flaking, tumbling, floating; a continual disintegration into dust. Tap on; facewash; hot-water; splash; dab dry with a towel, don't rub. Contacts: bin them. Toothpaste; buzz in the mouth dislodging colonising bacteria streptococcus mutans not in fact ultrasonic; rinses / spit / done. And then he breathes in deeply and out deeply and pads softly through to the bedroom once more where he sits on the side of the bed, lifts himself slightly to ease off his pants, turns, slides, is under the duvet, is wriggling into the warmth where Sue is, touching his chin to the back of her shoulder, his tummy to her bum, his tibia to her heel. She stirs and he stirs; and he shifts and she murmurs; and she reaches out for the light, clicks it off. In the intimate dark, with the front of his thighs against the back of her thighs, and his fingers on the giving flesh of her tummy, and the back of her skull pressing into the cartilage of his neck, his internal pudendal artery dilates and his corpus spongiosum and two corpora cavernosa begin to swell. But her body stays still and her hand moves over his hand, squeezing the tips of his fingers between the tips of hers and the springy lump of her thumb muscle; for her mind is anticipating the morning, the alarm, the getting up, the economical, almost-automatic movements, the leaving the house in the dusk, the three segments of the short walk to the station: the Willows; then the asphalt pathway between chicken-wire fencing held high by concrete pillars, with bright lights over as the daylight strengthens around; then /

but in any case (he thinks) it is late; and he is tired after the being-with-his-parents and the long drive; and as, in his brain, the alpha waves slow and stretch and lose their regularity, so, in his mind, as the bumpy higgledy-piggledy theta waves take over, his thoughts slither and jump and he is with his father halfway up a verdant slope, his father's wide body in its old waxed jacket, plodding ahead of him, jabbing the ground with a straight old shiny beech-branch stick, each foot in its thick scratchy sock in its old leather boot lifting and landing /

while she is completing the third segment, the lane of old houses along the canal, and is into the driven atmosphere of the station at rush hour, the queue at AMT, four people before her; that's 70, 140, 210, 280 seconds, more than four-and-a-half minutes! – the man in front of her, cheap pinstripe, shiny over the shoulderblades, looks round, catches her eyes, his skin is grey though he can only be thirties, his eye slides off towards the big wall clock in the distance, then he shifts from foot to foot and wriggles his shoulders as all around a tannoy announcement booms distortedly /

while his father's ash-coloured hair whips this way and that across his grooved forehead; the sparse eyelashes flutter and the narrowed eyes water in the wind. What is that on them? Xanthelasma? /

while from the platform she steps up into the train, pushes her way determinedly to a seat, and the world starts to pass her by on either side, the station is behind her and the town is behind her and fields spread out on either side and a meandering river flows through them so cold and natural and smooth /

while rib of beef, the cladding of juicy fat, the crisp skin; a nice bit of cheese with two or three glasses of red wine; trifle with custard and, whoosh, up goes the LDL, arteries claggy, look out for angina and/or leg pain during exercise, stifling the blood flow, a yellow lump breaks; and then /

so cool and smooth with the summer light dappled through willows, soft squelch of the mud among her toes, the water up to the top of her thighs and she launches herself in /

while Philip's throat tightens as he slithers down the familiar clattering helter-skelter of panic into the blackness, howls echoing, spiders' webs wrapping him, bats flapping in his face; but he wakes with a jolt and opens his eyes and can see the ceiling through the gloom; can discern the scratch of light outlining the blackout blind over the window. He breathes in, and holds; and out, and lets his muscles droop; and in, and holds; and out . . . here it is safe: he turns and presses his cheek against Sue's back and lays his forearm over her waist and hip /

while she now is into the quiescence of deep sleep, the heart heavy and slow; the breathing heavy and slow; the blood pressure low; her muscles baggy and slack, the body collapsed, each bit of it weighing down into the mattress /

while here it is safe, and warm, and they are covered; they are breathing; all the delicate activity of life is going on here, the two of them side by side. He is able to see a little into the darkness. He is touching her and the sheet and the duvet-cover and the pillow-cover and the air. The molecules of their atmosphere, of sweat and farts and sperm and mucus and conditioner and body lotion and the remains of kedgeree and Becks and toothpaste on the breath can all dissolve into his olfactory epithelium and be understood. Here it is safe, and warm, and their skin is intact, for the 13.5 tog microfibre duvet will repel flesh-ripping ball-bearings; and he sees Sue walking towards him, once, in spring, not knowing he would be there: she is stepping speedily forward by the side of a busy road, her glance jumping hither and yon, until, like a grasshopper, it lands on him, on him. She is standing under a cherry tree blossoming in spring; and her face blossoms into a smile.

There they lay, the air passing through his mouth and her nose, along their tracheae and bronchi and bronchioles to their alveoli, inflating their pulmonary trees, permeating their respiratory surfaces; and out again, and in. Their hearts pump; their blood circulates; their stomachs continue to digest, their colons to propulse, their skins to perspire. In their brains, electricity ebbs and sparkles and eddies and flows. There they lie, upon a sheet of paymaster cotton nurtured to woolly blobs in the dusty fields of Tennessee, nourished with potassium, phosphorus, nitrogen and lime. There they snuggle, under a duvet of polyester microfibre, manufactured in hilly, thrusting Zhejiang, and shipped from Shanghai past Vietnam, Brunei, Sri Lanka; past Yemen, Eritrea, Libya, Morocco, Lisbon, Vigo, Quimper, to South Shields. There, upon a mattress constructed in Leeds, upon a frame made of Swedish pine, upon a carpet of tufted polypropylene, upon floorboards cut from Estonian pine, they lie; within walls of silica and alumina and lime and iron oxide and magnesia and polyisocyanurate and aluminium foil and gypsum; behind windows of glass sandwiched with argon and held in place with PVC that keep in the warmth and out the chill which settles now over the land outside: a square of patio and, beyond that, a margin of dandelions and sticky willie and grass; and, beyond that, a line of ash trees and a scattering of elders; and, beyond that, the railway which, in the morning, will speed Sue to the city and her workplace but which now lies still and silent, save for the very occasional passage of slow processions of night freight; and, beyond that, more elders, nettles, gravel, dandelion, until: Kidney Meadow, where the numb grass bows as the dew gathers upon it; where primrose and buttercup and willowherb and flax all hunker down against the coming cold; and where, beyond hawthorn, bramble, ash and willow, through the silent river, the endless, un-translucent water flows, at a rate of $10.3m^3$ per second, carrying perch, roach, bleak, a ripped Tesco bag, carp, chub, a diaphanous condom, barbel, snails, a bulbous pouch now empty of rolling tobacco, worms, leeches, a slithery shoe, fresh-water shrimps, crayfish, the shed skins of damselfly larvae, and a large amount of indeterminate material formed from lilies, reeds, rubber, pennywort, algae, bread, bark, grass, dead fish, and moss, and polystyrene, and willow leaves, and . . . and irises, and dead swans, and dandelions, and . . . and cardboard, and . . .

As an owl wheeled over the roof of 12 Eden Grove, Sue and Philip slept.

As Dr Adam Hibbert, among the hills of southern Khyber Pakhtunkhwa, stirred in the morning light, they slept.

As a cat tiptoed along the wall of their back patio, they slept; and they slept still as it sprang.

As old Mr Newell woke and rose and got out of bed in his pyjamas and went to the bathroom and peed and came back and sat on the edge of the bed for a moment with his head in his hands, they slept.

As Venus rose once more into the sky, they slept.

As, in the DI, the ventilator attached to the lungs of Toby Knight puffed and sucked and puffed and sucked, Sue and Philip slept.

As dew came down upon the land and the trees and the buildings, they slept.

Until they woke; after which, having risen and dressed and eaten, Philip waved goodbye to Sue who had risen and dressed and eaten too. He watched, coffee in hand, as she strode across the courtyard away from him through the grey light, and vanished; and then, 10 minutes later, it was his turn to begin his journey, though as he now walked, what, 800 yards to his workplace, she was zooming 54 miles to hers. Having passed the fourth, shiny, Victorian-style lamp-post on Parnassus he turned into Elysium, then down Inglenook Passage which opened onto Felicity Place where he took the Monet-style little footbridge over the villagey pond and pressed on, into the narrow entrance way of Lily Walk which spat him out halfway along a street of the old town. Here the houses are bigger, and there is more space between them, and the paint on the windows is flaking, and the front doors are of varying design. Here the walls are crusted with lichen, bushes bulge over fences, cars squat casually by the side of the road, and streetlamps look their real age. Seeing the black edge of the health centre at the top of the street, he accelerates towards it so as to arrive urgent and slightly out of breath. His hand pushes at the wire glass and hides, for a moment, the year-old faded notice that reads: 'If you are exhibiting flu-like symptoms please do not . . .';

and then he has lumbered in, around the awkward corner to reception where Sushma looks up with her face blank and enquiring for a moment until she registers that it is him and not a patient and flowers into an encouraging smile. 'Morning,' she says, turning to see if there is post or paperwork for him, which of course there is. Then he is off again, along the strip-lit, windowless passageway, left, right; stop; struggle with your bunch of keys, drop it, pick it up, open the door, and get yourself into the little room, Dr Adam Hibbert's room, which is yours, Philip's, for the circle of the year. The metal and chipboard and laminate desk with its lockable drawers. The heavy, black, worn, gleaming couch with the roll of covering paper at the foot of it. The laminate lockable cupboard and laminate shelves on metal brackets, bearing books left behind by Dr Hibbert: *BNF*, *Oxford Handbook of General Practice*, *Gray's Anatomy* (38th edition), *World According to Clarkson*, *Wisden* 2003. The three orange plastic bucket chairs, on a chessboard of mahogany- and mushroom-coloured carpet tiles. The grubby white desktop, purring already, portal to the practice EMIS web, and email of course, and the blessed internet, gateway to the world, and the better little Skype window that lets him glimpse Sue from time to time during the working day, and the clip-on camera through which she likewise can glimpse him. He clicks into EMIS for his appointments. All new to him except Stone, A right at the end. Can they have been to their referral already? Surely not. He clicks open the notes to make sure that it is them. Yes, and there is his record of last time: 'Ongoing treatment for ADHD. Discussed reduction or cessation of Ritalin dosage, ref. Paediatrics'.

Still five minutes till the first patient. He scanned the notes: last seen, of course, by Dr Hibbert for an asthma check-up, could be anything. He clicked open the *Guardian*: Rooney targets move to City, you amaze me; American pays drug addict to have vasectomy. He started Skype and minimised it because on the one hand obviously patient confidentiality but on the other it is nice sometimes to simply know when Sue is there online. Now a window opens in his head and shows him Sue on the train, or rather his imagining of her on the train: the little tensed figure, black tight jacket and trousers, thighs crossed and her ankle doing that thing he could never manage, winding round behind the other ankle so her legs are in a plait. She would – he thinks – be angled away from everyone, looking out. Or looking down at her phone or her notebook. She would be scribbling or sketching. Or she would be watching the passing world, her mind empty and open, her pupils oscillating as trees and birds and houses snag them and let go.

But if by some miracle Albert and Janet Stone had been to Paediatrics already he should have heard from the consultant. They appear in his mind, walking away from him along a corridor: Janet's floppy dungarees, the white T-shirt underneath criss-cross denim straps, the shining polished floor, light coming in from the left, wide swing-doors with booming, muffled, high-pitched noises echoing around. Albert's thin arm lifted, his hand in hers. But only for that little moment because, as they came towards a place where people were, he would, with sudden sulkiness, pull it away. Philip remembered Albert in the bucket chair in front of him in the consulting room, when Ms Stone had stretched her hand across towards her child as she began to talk about his father, and the boy had shifted, his cheek twitching, the mechanism of arms and legs reconfiguring as he turned away from her, lifted himself up off the chair and moved towards the window to look out onto the tiny pebbled courtyard through the blind's metal slats. Nothing to see there. Ms Stone had glanced up into his, Philip's, face as though to say 'Is it OK for him to stand there?' – and: 'You see how things are?' At which he, Philip, looking back, had done something with his eyes and eyebrows and mouth and cheeks to signify: 'Yes that's fine' and 'Yes I do.' So she had talked on, reaching out to him with her worries: the dad who was sometimes there and sometimes not but made it crystal clear there were more important things in the world than her and Albert. But who somehow still always managed to get them to accept him back in – only the instant they felt they could rely on him he bloody upped and went. At which the chemical-electrical responses of Philip's brain had permeated him with feelings of engagement and resolve. For here was a case where doctoring absolutely was not just pills and sympathy. This was complex. This was about the whole person, no, about three people. This was going to be a challenge.

A rat-tat on the door interrupted Philip's memory and he jumped himself back into the present; called 'come in' and at the same time checked again the name of this first patient of the day. As the door opened and a foot and a face appeared, Sue, 36 miles away already, was thinking that, to be fair, the problem about working in an institution, about being subordinate to other people – which was that you had to give time to things that, if it was just you, you wouldn't bother with – this minus could also sometimes be a plus, or partly. So that, although Al Ahmed as a type, going by what he mainly stood for, wasn't her thing at all, it really had been educative tracking step by step through his career. Alright, she had groaned when Charlotte had asked her to do a trawl to gather material for the catalogue. But if she hadn't had to do it then she wouldn't have got to know about Al Ahmed's early interventions in the iconography of the veil – slim white shop dummies bare except for their heads which were wrapped in the rich, patterned Fortuny cloth as though their faces were mummified but the rest of them untouched. Or the really intense, wall-hung pieces that were in dialogue with Arte Povera – rectangles of fabric stretched over a frame like a canvas and slashed in the manner of Lucio Fontana. Or the lighter-hearted but actually rather magnificent work to do with freedom: toy boats, with beautiful billowing opal and emerald and ruby-toned Fortuny sails, that had been released a mile or two out from Sumqayit on the Caspian Sea and left to wash up where they would on the coasts of Iran or Turkmenistan or wherever, depending on, well, literally depending on the wind or the currents but metaphorically depending on the so-many factors that need to mesh to create freedom. Lots of them had sunk, of course; and most of the ones that had been recovered were bedraggled or damaged; but a few were not. A few arrived somewhere pristine.

So that – but they were getting to the outskirts of the city now, grey warehouse walls up close against the track – so that there really was a lot to admire and learn from in Al Ahmed, even if he was, well, what was the problem with him? The problems were: he was too masculine, he was too grand, he was too much held up to be admired. And probably actually that wasn't even his fault, or hardly. It was the fault of the Art World which had done its relentless Art World thing, valued him and interpreted him and turned him into a commodity, basically shrink-wrapped him in this super-high-class supermarket that was the International Art World, so that he could be safely exhibited by people like Omar in galleries where everyone would gather round and admire. Instead of being really affected. Instead of being needled and tantalised and awakened in the way that she, Sue, really liked to be, and really wanted other people to like to be too. But now the train was slowing and she needed to be ready for the off: phone stowed, bag grabbed, stand and edge into the aisle. Beyond the window she can see bodies escaping, hitting the platform, speeding away. And now just – can I squeeze past – thank you – she is one of them, striding among the other striding people, their steps forming for a moment a rhythmic synchrony, then shifting into syncopation, then disintegrating into non-relation. The ticket barrier. The concourse with its high roof, lights, strange shoddy arrangement of low shacks, La Croissanterie, Pret, Phones4U. Human beings pinballing here and there. Out onto the street with its colder, fresher air, and noise: Scaffolding Alarmed / 07832 99 . . . edge round it; smell of paint; the lower overall-legs of a painter, himself a painting, splattered in baby blue. Cars Parked Here Without A . . . a cyclist skims past, lycra, thighs pumping: looked at from behind he seems to have no head, how slim the bike is, carbon fibre. There is a group of people in front and she slows, joins them in their waiting to cross the road; but cars too are slowing, stopping; green man: go. Round a railing and into a triangle of parkland, pressing on through the space and quiet of it, poplars lining the edge of it, beginning to thin now, to show their bones. Another railing: left. Cross and right down the quiet road along the back of the warehouse. Left and right and left. And there at the end of this street is the white concrete and greenish glass of Spike, expanding as she walks toward it. She waits again to cross. There is the sloping line of windows, the cut-off top front edge of the building which forms one side of her workspace. Anglepoises on inside. A van pushing past, Open Reach, then a blue car. There at the end of the sloping line of windows is the protruding jaunty cube of Omar's office, dark. Over she goes and across the pavement and in through the glass doors to the economical white entrance hall, Oisin at the white concrete desk not looking up.

'Hi Osh,' she calls gaily, sweeping through, still proud that she can push open the metal door marked 'Staff Only' and go on up the stairs and along the corridor which cuts through the middle of each workstation. There is Caro turning her wide welcoming face with a smile; and there, as she walks along, is Elmer, so slim and concentrated, not turning but just lifting a hand in salutation as she passed; and then she was in her own space, sliding into her Aeron chair, dumping her bag, clicking the mouse and about to type her password only there was a slip of paper on the keyboard: 'Omar meeting at 2, CH.'

'What's this?' – she called, standing up and looking over into Charlotte's cubicle.

'He rang earlier from home.' In her buttoned tweed jacket, Charlotte revolved slowly: 'Or from somewhere.' There were her knees in thick, blue-grey tights.

'Is it . . .'

'He won't be in till then.'

'Is it the Wednesday meeting brought forward?'

'Dunno.' Charlotte's face, looking up, smiled briskly. 'He sounded a bit cross. Apart from that, I'm afraid there's no information I can give you.'

Efficient Charlotte would have everything prepared for all eventualities. Whereas she . . . if it was going to be the Wednesday meeting she needed to . . . because she had counted on having some time. What she ought to be doing this morning was working on the Al Ahmed catalogue but she could push that back. She settled down again, logged on, saw Philip was online but he could call her if he wanted. She needed to . . . she opened a doc and contemplated the white virtual page. She typed 'ECG'. She typed 'Trains'. She thought: how is that going to, the train thing is too much of a . . . She was going to delete 'Trains' but instead pressed Return again and again and again, pushing that wrong word down to the bottom of the screen, away from the focus of her thoughts. Because what you wanted was something that developed coherently from room to room. So that if you had mainly sound in the first room you needed . . . But who was this looming from behind? Oh it was Caro who was now standing there expectantly. She was holding a box file. She was wanting to talk through ideas for the merchandise. Damn!

Sue turned, stood, pulled a chair close to hers. She and Caro greeted each other, sat down; and at once they were politely harmonising their expectations for the encounter, establishing clear though implicit parameters. Then they were into the harmony of the meeting, two professionals speaking and listening and responding; inclining their bodies side by side to study the drafts and mockups; raising their heads and leaning apart so as to read each other's faces. They talked through the choice of postcards. A natty idea of a Fortuny swatch stretched over a little balsawood frame that you could slash to make your own miniature Al Ahmed. And then the usual books etc. And some actual Fortuny cushion covers and scarves. It was all fine, as of course it would be. Caro was good. And yet . . .

As the aftermath of Caro's presence faded from the workspace, Sue found she wanted to howl. The feeling had been erupting slowly inside her during the mild conversation and now it was about to overflow. Because merchandise was actually the worst. Because merchandise was where the whole thing became so obvious and so upsetting. Because people had had, or at least people ought to have had, the amazing, fracturing, possibly life-changing experience of encountering a work of art. And then what did they do? They bought a catalogue that told them how they ought to have responded. That . . . OK of course people wanted to have some knowledge. Only natural. No, more than natural, necessary. Sometimes you simply couldn't open yourself to the artwork in the right way unless you had a grounding. But what so often happened was that the experience was totally stifled under the too-big heap of information. So that, say, when you were talking to someone about something, about some show that they had seen. They so rarely told you what it was really like, how it had seemed to them. Instead, they told you stuff about it. Captions were the same, of course. And even postcards, even actually postcards could be dangerous. Because the risk was, with a postcard, that you thought you were buying a reminder of the thing that you had seen; but actually you were buying an impediment, a sort of veil. An interloper like a cuckoo. Because the postcard was not in fact the same as what you had seen; it came to take the place of it. Because the needling, tantalising, fleeting but so important actual experience went skipping away, and all you were left with was a little bit of cardboard. And maybe you would look at it and think: what was so special about that? You would search in your memory for the thing that had made you buy the postcard in the first place and you wouldn't be able to find it. Because somehow, insidiously, the postcard would have got inside there too. It would have got inside your brain and located the experience and smothered it and kicked it out.

By now she was up and walking, hugging her coat tight around her, walking quickly along the white corridor, skittering as though unconcernedly down the steps. She wanted out, into the air and the bustle and the noise. And as she pushed open the heavy glass door of the building, Philip, 54 miles away, was pushing the light, hollow, plywood and veneer door that opened into the so-called common room, i.e. just the room where the kettle and coffee were, also the venue for the weekly practice meetings. Sara Kaiser was there, greeted him. She was standing by the window, a cup held in both hands in front of her just below her chin, her head bowed towards it. Philip moved to the table, switched on the kettle, picked up the jar of instant to unscrew the lid. Her stance was reminding him of something. Cold daylight shone on one of her cheeks; the other side of her face was in shadow. He let a second heaped teaspoon of instant pour into his mug.

'If we had a machine,' she said, 'we'd only drink more and it would be bad for us. So it is in harmony with our vocation as healers that we have only instant coffee on the premises.'

'Ought to be QOF points for it.' The kettle had boiled already and he poured as she laughed her loud laugh: 'Oh yes.' The spoon tinkled in his mug as he stirred. 'A sensor' – she continued – 'connects the kettle to our computer system so our usage can be monitored.'

'And costed.'

'And costed.'

'An Imbibing Incentives Scheme, soon to be rolled out nation-wide.'

'Or rather not to imbibe.'

'Like antibiotics: just say no.'

Philip felt at ease. An OK morning and now he was happily chatting. Sara had been warm to him from the start.

'Can I ask, did Dr Hibbert, Adam Hibbert, did he ever mention Janet and Albert Stone, mother and son? Did they ever come up?'

'No,' she said quickly. Then she said earnestly, in her deep voice, looking at him with her wide, dark eyes: 'You know we don't gossip about patients.'

'Well I wasn't . . .'

'If you're having a clinical concern' – now the tone was bossier – 'then you can raise it at the practice meeting.'

'Yes of course I didn't mean to.' He was sitting on the little tatty foam sofa. He leaned forward, started to leaf through the brochures, X-Chem contamination control, OptiCap Ph-independent in vitro dissolution.

She was moving towards him. She was settling into the wooden armchair which had squeaky black-plastic-covered padding. He looked up, took in the mass of her leaning forward in a monkish brown dress and knotty cardigan. She said: 'Is everything OK?'

'Yeh. Yeh it's fine.'

'You know,' she said. She started to lean back but stopped herself by hooking her hands around her knees. 'Something to bear in mind is that patients often when they see a new doctor lay it on a bit thick. They have another go at trying to get what they want. Which is not necessarily what they need. For example antibiotics, as you say.'

Philip now had unhunched himself and felt that there was friendliness between them once again.

'I had one, each time went from me to Adam, to George, to Isobel, to Paul – and then, when none of us would give them to her – she changed practice!' Sara Kaiser was looking into his face, offering a smile for him to respond to. He gave a hint of a chuckle back.

'Also' – now her eyes slid away – 'there isn't always one right path. You know that too.' A quick glance up at him. 'Each of us tries out different things.' Now looking solemnly at the floor. 'Follow your instinct and your training. If Adam said one thing and you think another, that's OK. Maybe he's right, maybe you're right. You can only do your best. Just like he tried always to do his best. Like we all do.'

As he listened, Philip felt the presence of Ms Stone in his mind: didn't see her, exactly, but re-encountered the impact of her as, two weeks before, she had been sitting upright in a chair in his consulting room, staring straight ahead. 'The ritalin did help' – this shadow-figure of Janet Stone began to enunciate as Sara Kaiser finished speaking – 'it has made him easier to handle. But that isn't necessarily a good thing, is it. What he used to be like – he was really responsive. He'd hear something, birdsong or the phone ringing and he'd imitate it. He'd sit down to do a drawing and then after a minute he'd stop, run upstairs and do something else, be on his bed being a downhill skier, jumping and swerving. And it was annoying' – the voice pressed on – 'I can see why the school didn't like it. I'm not saying he wasn't a handful. I found him a handful meself. I mean I basically wasn't coping, at times I totally wasn't coping – that's why I . . . but what I can't get over is I can't stop thinking that that was really him, that because' – and here her voice was thickening, the sobs were about to come – 'that because I was a crap mother he is being stuffed full of chemicals, and they've turned him, those pills have, into a different person.' She had sniffed. She had dragged her hand across one cheek to wipe away the tears.

'I hope you have a happy afternoon,' Sara Kaiser's voice broke in. She was all the way over at the side of the room by the sink, rinsing her cup. She posed it upside-down on the draining board and moved towards the door.

'And you,' said Philip, vehemently. He was bewildered. Sara Kaiser swept out and the door swung to. But Ms Stone was still there vividly in his mind, rubbing her hand across the other cheek, lifting her head, shaking it like a dog emerging from the water.

'So he seems to have lost his appetite?' – Philip had asked.

'Yes.'

'He strikes you as being subdued?' – Philip had continued, following procedure, piecing together a history.

'Yeh that's right.'

'Have you noticed any other changes, for instance anxiety or physical twitching?' The whole scene was running on replay in his mind.

'He does have a bit of a twitch in his face . . .'

'I'd like to talk to Albert himself now for a bit, if that's OK?'

'Do you want me to . . .' – she had begun to ask.

'No that's fine,' he had replied: 'You can stay. Albert?' Sitting in the common room he saw again the boy as he had stood in the consulting room, his face at an angle so it was half in shadow, half gleaming in the window's slatted light.

'Would you mind if I asked you a few questions about how you've been feeling?'

The boy had twisted his head very quickly, just a little each way.

'Would you mind coming to sit here, nearby? It's easier to talk.'

The boy had sidled over, edged into the chair, sitting with his hands under his thighs, see-sawing on them gently.

'Thanks. Do you sometimes find, at lunchtime or teatime, you're not hungry?'

'Mmm.'

'Do you sometimes feel worried about things?'

That movement of the head again.

'He doesn't rush out to play like he used to' – his mother had filled in – 'I don't know if it's he's feeling flat or he's worried. That's the problem, doctor. I don't think I can tell any more how he's feeling inside.'

'OK. Thanks Albert. That's very helpful. We're going to see if
we can make you feel a bit better. Now Mrs Stone . . .'

'Ms.'

'Sorry.'

'Or Janet.'

'OK. Do you know what dose he's on at the moment?'

'One capsule each morning, when he gets up.'

'OK I'll just . . .' Philip had risen and, still bent over, had nudged
around the desk to where he could see the screen; had tapped, and
– 20mg. Huge!

'Albert, would you mind if we just . . .' – he had said, moving
back – 'found out how much you weigh?'

So they had done; and it was while they were doing that that he
had asked Janet whether it had been the psychiatrist in the hospital
who had prescribed that dose; and she had answered:

'We never went to no hospital.'

He heard it again: 'Never went to no hospital'; 'Never went to
no'; 'no hospital'; 'Never went to' and his heart started thumping
again as it had thumped back then and his throat tightened as it had
tightened back then. He must have blushed; he must be blushing.
Because the guidelines were granite strong for suspected ADHD.
They had to be. Always refer for specialist assessment. 'So it was
only Dr Hibbert who . . .'

'That's right. He was very certain of it.'

The memory stopped when it hit that rock and dropped Philip
back into the common room in the present on the tatty foam sofa.
There was the window, the ceiling. His body was trembling still, his
breath quick and uneven. He looked for the clock on the wall and

saw that it said: 2 pm. He took a slow, deep breath, lifting his ribs and his shoulders. He shut his eyes. Then he opened them, and rose, and moved towards the door at pretty much the same moment as, 54 miles away, Charlotte's head popped above the dividing half-wall and said: 'Ready?' Sue reached for a pen, a piece of paper; she stood, folding the piece of paper in half and then, as she walked along behind Charlotte's loud steps, in half again, before she stopped and turned to pull the glass door shut behind her. Omar Olagunju, in his neat dark blue suit and soft lilac shirt and olive tie, turned, said 'Charlotte, Sue,' and nodded them towards the two grey Aeron visitors' chairs that were located in front of his wide glass desk. He leaned forward as they settled into the springy mesh: his arms were laid out in front of him, his hands clasped in a double fist. Behind him, and to the left, two bare grey walls. Behind Sue and Charlotte, and to their right, the wide metal slats of blinds half barring the floor-to-ceiling windows.

Omar said: 'Al Ahmed has cancelled.' He let the words sit there for a moment. And then: 'Obviously I'll need to tell everyone before long and there will need to be a press announcement but for now I want to keep it tight, between the three of us.'

'But' – Charlotte stuttered – 'we've been working for . . .'

'I know. It's unbelievable.'

Charlotte had her hands on her knees now, was breathing deeply, leaning forward: 'Why . . .'

'I don't know. I haven't spoken to him. He hasn't had the courtesy to speak to me. His principal assistant says he is unwell. Implies some sort of breakdown. He says Al Ahmed is withdrawing from all engagements. Speaking to no one. He says Al Ahmed apologises profusely and promises that if ever he exhibits again it will be first of all with us.'

'Would it help' – Sue said – 'if we . . .'

'Yes' – Charlotte came trampling in – 'if we made clear that we can offer a very high level of support; that really he can simply be an inspiring presence, we can create the piece, have it created, like we did with . . .'

'Of course I've said that. Jesus I've been fighting this for a week!' Omar actually banged the table. The flat of his hand came into contact with the glass of the table, jarring it. 'It's over.' He was looking at them both, looking from one to the other. 'I'm sorry to spring it on you. It's a shock, I know. And a waste. Of all our time. And a terrible disappointment to me. I feel personally let down. But I assure you there is nothing to be done. What we have to do now is leave it behind. And think forward.'

There was a pause. Omar kept shifting his gaze from one of them to the other. Charlotte was calming herself.

'One thing' – put in Sue – 'is that Caroline is about to order the . . .'

'That's right: Caroline will have to be the next to know.' Omar turned to the slim monitor at the leftward end of his wide desk and tapped for a moment on the keyboard. 'But Sue,' he said, turning back, 'can you delay her for a few days without saying why? – say . . .'

'I'll say Al Ahmed wants refusal.'

'OK. Good. Only a little lie.'

Charlotte was sitting up straight again. She said: 'So what are we . . .'

'For myself, I simply cannot see a way forward. I think it very likely that for those three months we will have to go dark. As Director of this Gallery I cannot approach another high-profile artist in this circumstance. It is too late. We would look desperate. And it would be insulting to them, it would look as though we thought them second best. And anyway they will all already have made their arrangements years ahead.'

'We could spin that to our advantage,' Charlotte said constructively. 'We don't deny that a crisis has happened but the line we take is that we're not prepared to compromise on quality. And then, come the autumn, there will be extra publicity for the Art and Language retrospective.'

'Nevertheless it is a grave step. Ideally we would not be taking it. That is why I asked you both last week, when this . . . eventuality was starting to seem unavoidable, to do some thinking. About innovative ways we might use the gallery. In case, if this happened, as it has done, there might be a different pathway. Not just to think outside the box, but – to blow the box sky high.' He swirled his hand as though with a fly-whisk. He looked smilingly from one of them to the other.

Sue felt cold. A pulse was throbbing in her throat. Her mind was clear. This was her chance, grab it! – so she said: 'We could . . .' but Charlotte cut in: 'I was thinking about up-and-coming artists. If we turn ourselves into a studio, recreate a studio show, really fresh . . .'

'No!' Sue almost shrieked. Then, abashed: 'Sorry, that's a good idea. Obviously. It could work. There's a pool of talent we could draw on. But' – her stomach swooned. Now she was going say what she thought. 'I think we should try something more radical.

How about we . . .' – oh, if only she had had longer, just a clear afternoon – '. . . put the punters centre stage, get them to focus on their own experience. Let's say we don't show them anything that they can think of as having been created by an artist. No actual works of art at all, not even videos, not even really installations.'

She paused. She glanced. There was no immediate positive response.

'And instead' – she was speaking it slowly, thinking it through – 'they walk in, and there's a room, with . . . a heartbeat. Let's say, there must be such a thing as a portable ECG: let's say we strap on an ECG to each person as they walk in. And then they go into the first room. There's a heartbeat. They're not sure if it is their own or not. Or when there are two or three of them in the room they'll have to really listen to see if it is actually two or three heartbeats superimposed. Or . . . not.'

Still no enthusiasm but at least no interruptions.

'In the second room, . . . it'll be the brain. Instead of sound there will be vision, a projected brain trace on the wall or all around them. And we'll have put electrodes on their heads so there'll be the same uncertainty. About whether it is theirs or not. And in the third . . .'

But Omar was speaking: 'I welcome this contribution, Sue . . .'

Sue wanted to press on: 'We can call it The Whole World, because what they experience . . .'

'I welcome' – Omar's voice was flat, his face still – 'this contribution, Sue. Let's keep it in the air. Other ideas?'

'OK another idea,' she said, now frankly floundering: 'Postcards . . .'

'I think,' said Charlotte, 'I might be able to get Elton Barfitt.'

'Now that . . .' said Omar; but Sue was saying 'they don't do gallery shows.'

'I think,' Charlotte said with an air of authority, 'that could change.'

Was Omar going to . . . why wasn't Omar probing her on that?

'Elton Barfitt are a name,' said Omar. He paused, still holding the floor with his expression: he was thinking; he was reaching a decision. 'And, when it comes to it, that's what we need, a gallery like us. Sue,' he said, pointing his narrowed eyes at her, projecting his penetrating voice, 'I appreciate your idealism. Your verve. I really do. We need you here to keep on goading us, keep us up to the minute, keep us . . . live. But, when it comes to it, we have to recognise our limitations.' He stopped to think again. He brought his fingertips together and touched them to his lips in a filmic pose. And then he said: 'I can't . . . I'm going to hold myself back from this; leave it to you, Charlotte, and you, Sue, the two of you together, to take forward. You need to be very careful. Your negotiations with Elton Barfitt will require tact and sensitivity. But at the same time we need an answer quickly.' He leaned back in his chair, looked past them towards the slatted window, then gave them one final moment of focus: 'Keep me informed.'

The meeting was over. Charlotte and Sue had risen and were easing out through the glass door; they were in the brighter light of the main office. Then Charlotte's mouth was near Sue's ear, murmuring: 'Let's keep going, walk straight out, get a coffee.'

As Sue and Charlotte carried on walking, Philip, 54 miles away was dabbing clorhexadine on a painful crimson swelling around a little pus-crimped puncture.

'I thought,' said the patient, as Sue and Charlotte were trotting down the stairs, 'it might, you know, come out by itself.'

'Now I'm going to put in some local anaesthetic,' said Philip, ripping the bag around the syringe and piercing the ampoule of lignocaine 1%, as, 54 miles away, the glass doors swung shut and a little bit open and then decisively shut again behind the two women.

'It'll sting first before it takes effect,' said Philip, sliding the needle into the tissue, pulling back a little on the plunger then pressing it gently, firmly.

Charlotte leading the way, the two women turned left along a cobbled street.

Philip injected the other side of the swelling too.

Sue and Charlotte parted to circumvent a lamp-post in the middle of the narrow pavement then recombined with syncopated strides.

He waited for, what, three, four minutes as they walked.

It was very much stuck in the adductor pollicis muscle between thumb and index finger, right down at the bottom where the metacarpals met.

Now right into an alley.

'What I'm going to have to do,' said Philip, as the two women turned again, 'is push it. Because if I pull it'll just get worse stuck because of the barbs.'

And here they were.

'OK. This might hurt. Ready?'

So that, as the two women were stepping down through the door of the little pub, Philip was pushing the tiny metal eye; and as Sue was noticing the stone floor, wooden benches and velveteen stools, the patient, a Mr Stephenson, sucked in his breath; and as Charlotte strode towards the illuminated promise of the bar, the sharp, bloody tip emerged through the epidermis, and as Charlotte exclaimed 'What are you having?' the whole big, strong, steel, lurid fishhook lay in the palm of Philip's translucently gloved hand.

'Just fizzy water thanks,' said Sue.

'Well I need a whisky after that.'

'Alright then . . . gin and tonic.'

They took their drinks to a small round table and perched there, shrugging off coats, laying purses and phones on the tabletop between them, the two women: Charlotte with a blonde bob and pale tweed jacket but a blue blouse under and no pearls; Sue with crew-cut dark hair, and straightforward grey jeans and a black, felt, square-cut jacket, breast pockets like the top of a boiler suit, practical and plain.

'Shall I tell you a secret?' Charlotte confessed: 'I'm not completely sure I can get Elton Barfitt. I don't know them. I don't even know if they're free.'

Sue was struck by the chubbiness of Charlotte's face, the pinkness of her cheeks. She said: 'So how are we . . .'

'I simply love their work. And also I really didn't want the gallery to go dark. Omar would have taken that decision right then. Did you see how he reacted to your ideas you were putting forward?'

'Well it felt like you both . . .'

'He would have said the same to mine if you hadn't . . .'

'Sorry.'

'It was like he was a stone,' Charlotte declared. 'Letting them wash over him. Not open to them at all. So I thought what can I say that he would go for. And what should pop into my head but Elton Barfitt? There's no harm in it. The worst that can happen,' she carried on gaily, 'is they say no. But I would so love it if they didn't. I would so love it if I can persuade them.'

'Why' – Sue was still in the turmoil of the meeting – 'does he ask me to come up with things if he doesn't ever like them. Why did he employ me?'

'Because, well I think,' Charlotte said, 'he wants to feel they're in the mix. You know, that they could be his sort of thing. I think,' she opined from the height of her eight years' experience of working with Omar, 'he wants to feel radical but in fact he is a very conservative figure.' Charlotte had finished her double whisky already and was turning her head towards the bar.

Sue said: 'But Elton Barfitt aren't going to do anything conservative.'

'But did you hear how he talked about them? It's the name. It's simply the fact that they are famous. He came up through the time of the YBAs so he thinks that value and celebrity go together.'

'Which makes it all the more . . .'

'Plus,' said Charlotte, rattling the ice-cubes in her glass and lifting it to drain the last drops of dilute drink, 'with Omar I'm sure there's a financial consideration.'

Sue allowed herself a little bit of a guffaw: 'Those suits . . .'

Charlotte smiled. 'Can I get you another?'

Sue shook her head and then waited as Charlotte arose and went across to the bar. How good The Whole World might have been. People would have come in, opened their ears, opened their eyes. Been so . . . alerted. They would have loved it, she was sure they would. It was such a fuck fuck fuck. But then her vehemence exhausted itself, and the alcohol softened her a little, and she ended up thinking: still, there will be other chances.

'Running a gallery,' said Charlotte, returning, 'it's basically like, or it can be, basically like insider dealing.'

'So you think he's been quietly buying up some Al Ahmed?'

Charlotte smiled appreciatively. 'He's bloody sharp. Has to have been to have got where he is, given, well' – Charlotte seemed to lose her way for a moment – 'given who he is, and especially where he started. Walthamstow: would you believe it? Then Aberdeen for Chrissake; then the break to Bristol and now here. He's created himself.'

The two women reached for their glasses, drank. Charlotte checked her phone. Sue looked around: nobody. Only an old bloke with a pint bent over the paper which was spread flat on a large rectangular table in the darkest bit of the . . .

'So: Elton Barfitt,' she said.

'Are you really OK to work with me on this? I know it's not what you . . .'

'No, it's alright,' said Sue. 'It's my job. And anyway I do like them.'

'To me,' Charlotte announced, 'they are really among the greats. The person I do know – because I'm not actually being completely cavalier, I do have some idea – the person who I hope can get us access was the publicist for their last project, you know the one in the Sahara?'

'To do with air-conditioning.'

'Yeh, roughly,' Charlotte admitted. 'So they were sitting there, on this big, double gold throne. In the middle of the desert. In like forty-five, fifty degrees. And, yeh, surrounded with air-conditioning units and, like, micro-spray sprinklers, so they used up all this electricity to create a bearable environment, because of course all the air-conditioning went off into the air and the water-droplets evaporated pretty much as soon as they left the nozzles. And they were dressed like Restoration fops, in wigs and silk . . .'

'I remember, it was wild.'

'Though apparently,' Charlotte leaned forward to whisper, 'so my friend says, they had a military-grade cooling system going on inside the wigs, with lots of little tubes, so actually it wasn't as wacko as it seemed.'

'Still, said Sue, 'it was a very strong piece.'

'Yeh,' said Charlotte. 'It was, wasn't it. I'm glad you think so. Because, to me personally they are probably the artists I most relate to, that mean the most to me.'

Sue decided to leave that one floating in the air. 'So,' she said: 'Say you do get through to them tomorrow. Or whenever. What will you . . . ?'

'Spur of the moment.' Charlotte grinned. But then her face relaxed: 'No actually shall we sleep on it? And confer first thing tomorrow? I've got an inkling of an idea . . . but I want it to mature.'

'Sure,' said Sue: 'But we can't in the office.'

'Oh no of course. I'll say I'm working from home. And you can . . .'

'I'll ring you on my way in.'

'And can you . . . ?'

'Yeh,' said Sue, conspiratorially: 'I'll take care of anything that comes in for you tomorrow.'

'That's it then.' Charlotte had her hands on the tops of her thighs; was pushing her stool back, standing up, reaching for her coat. Sue gathered their glasses, slid two fingers down their sticky interiors, deposited them on the bar. Then the two women were sweeping out of the door; Sue was licking her fingers clean; they were out in the bluster of the world outside, stepping along the pavement while Philip, 54 miles away, was sitting, relaxing, breathing deeply in . . . out . . . in. Maybe 30 seconds till they knocked. And if . . . Deep breath. Just wait and see . . . now here were footsteps. A brisk tap tap on his door. The face as it opened . . . but this was not Janet, not Ms Stone, nor Albert.

'Do come in,' he offered encouragingly as he rose, stepped backwards and around his desk to check the name which now turned out to be a Mrs Grace Hanworth, the receptionists must have changed it at the last minute. But no, here in the pile were old paper notes for her as well, so it must have been at lunchtime.

'Welcome Mrs Hanworth!' – he exclaimed to the figure who was already sitting neatly in one of the orange bucket chairs, watching him with pale, greenish eyes. A bit of jaundice in them?

'Am I not who you were expecting?'

'Oh no, just – checking the list,' he explained: 'Sorry.'

'Yes I am Mrs Grace Hanworth,' she said. 'I don't come here often. I try not to come here at all,' she elaborated, watching him.

'Well, I think that's a good plan.' He is walking back around, lowering himself into his own orange bucket chair, resting one elbow on the front edge of his desk, giving his attention to the patient. 'So long as it doesn't result in anything getting missed. You're right that lots of people come to the doctor when they don't really need to. But also, sometimes' – he is speaking in a measured and yet jovial tone – 'you have to see a doctor to be sure it isn't serious.'

'Oh but something has been missed already,' she said. Her face seemed to harden at that moment as he watched her, her eyes lost their focus. There was a pause. She was looking – nowhere. He was noting her face, sunken (query cachexia?); a bit parchmenty too. Her neck was swathed in a scarf of swirling red and purple; the rest of her was wrapped in a long woollen cloak of pale brown. Coming to herself again, she said: 'It's nobody's fault.'

'And what . . . ?'

'People usually say that they are riddled with cancer. Which is so' – she took a little breath, lifted her eyebrows – 'ignorant. Because to be riddled is to be aerated with holes. Whereas cancer . . . what shall we say?' Now her eyes were lowered, she was contemplative. 'Cancer congeals. Clots. Infiltrates. Gluts. Overruns.' She spoke the words softly. Then she lifted her eyes and smiled a little smile. 'In my own case,' she said, 'it completely blocked me up.'

Dr Newell waited attentively.

'I'm sure the details will be there for you in my notes,' she said carelessly. 'Cancer of the small bowel. Quite a rare one! But only adenocarcinoma so not so rare as all that.'

She shifted her body, trying to get comfortable in the slippery, un-ergonomic chair. She came to rest slumped somewhat to the side.

'Initially' – she was speaking in half-profile – 'the patient refused treatment. Social evils, she had always believed, should be resisted with every possible resolve. But something like this' – her hands opened suddenly like claws – 'this was physical. It said to you: step back from the world of people. You are part of the natural world. Like a wounded pigeon. Like a broken blade of grass.'

There was a moment's quiet.

'And also,' she said, turning, lifting her torso upright, meeting Philip's eyes, 'the patient was a bloody-minded independent old bitch who simply didn't want to put herself into the hands of so-called experts.' She grinned cheekily.

Then her face went blank.

'But after a while, as you can see, she changed her mind. There was a risk of a blockage. Of the duodenum tearing. Of all the sludge in one's stomach spilling out into the torso and filling it up and swelling and getting infected and – ugh, it was disgusting. The insertion of a bypass seemed a sensible and straightforward oper-ation. And so it proved. Just a bit of plumbing really. It has done its job and I have since been able to concentrate on other things.'

'I'm glad to hear it.' Dr Newell paused; and then he set about speaking in a manner designed to project both calm and concern. 'Mrs Hanworth. I'm sure you can appreciate, and I hope you don't mind me saying, that yours is quite a complex case, with a history.

And I'm – I'm new to this practice. So, if you would like, I think it might be worthwhile our taking some time to go through things in detail so we can see how best I can help you. If you would like. And do please feel that we have all the time in the world, there is no pressure on time.'

'So you see, I am not a fanatic,' she began to say as he looked at his watch: 5.58 already. 'I am not ideologically opposed to the undoubted advances made by western medicine. I understand that there is no given boundary between the natural and the artificial, no difference, really, between antibiotics and peppermint tea. However, I also believe that it is wholly misguided to subject oneself to a series of intrusive, uncomfortable, expensive treatments in the desperate endeavour to delay what cannot be averted. In struggling to prolong life' – she was looking past him now, straight ahead of her – 'you destroy it. Because life is not mere existence. Life is not measured in days, hours, minutes, seconds but in sensa-tion, action, understanding, illumination. You should not rage, rage against the dying of the light.' She had relaxed now and was looking at him again, looking into his eyes warmly; and there was almost a smile in her voice as she continued: 'Enjoy the sunset. The evening is part of the day. Imagine a sonata with extra alien notes stuck in the final bars to make it last a few more minutes at whatever cost of dissonance and disproportion. No.'

'I completely appreciate that point of view. I sympathise with it.' This was one of those moments when you had to remember that the normal gestures of fellow-feeling were very ill-advised. In normal life, someone speaking to you like this would be a relative or close friend. And you would reach out and touch them, give them a hug. But as a doctor you could not. All Philip's sympathy had to be concentrated in his voice: 'Nevertheless, as I am sure you know, there are things that I might do, or that a nurse might do, to help you live out the rest of your life more comfortably.'

She reached out to him somehow with her eyes. What can it be about a microscopic adjustment in the iris, and a flicker in the muscles under the surrounding skin, that sends out what feels like such a strong message; that prompts Dr Newell to smile a little, the muscles in his shoulders to soften, his pulse to slow a pip or two.

Then she takes her eyes away.

'I don't think I want to be comfortable. I want to be aware. To understand. Not in the sense of theoretical understanding, of knowing what is happening. But of sensing. I want to watch and listen and taste and smell and feel the decay of me. I want to be in my body the way I have always been in the world: open to it. This is the great gift that . . . dying slowly like this can bring. You feel yourself unravelling. It is so arrogant, isn't it, the way well young people stride about the world. Thoughtlessly. As though they were strong. As though they were individuals. But I am dividing. It is as though I am holding myself cupped in my own hands and I am falling to pieces there, slip-ping through my fingers. And that is true. That is how we are in the world. We are pieced together out of lots of different bits. It's magical – I don't deny it. It is amazing. But then we disintegrate back into what we were made out of to begin with. It is a great gift to be able to be in this, open-eyed, as it is happening.'

She had finished. She had said everything. Her gaze was now resting on the floor.

'I wish everyone' – Philip said helplessly – 'could be so wise.'

She took a deep breath in, lifting her head as she did so, looking around her, seeing him as though for the first time. She spoke briskly: 'I am feeling sick. I have been feeling sick for weeks. I retch. I don't manage to hold much down. Under all this' – she was referring to the clothes that wrapped her, the cloak, the scarf – 'I am skin and bones.' A smile flitted over her wrinkled face. 'And lumps.'

'Are you suffering from swollen lymph . . .'

'Yes,' she said sharply, 'but I don't mind that. I am even a bit interested in that. The new shapes I am developing. Some of which are really quite surprising. It is the nausea I want taking away now. I am bored of it.'

'It is a horrible feeling. But I think we should be able to reduce it considerably, perhaps even get rid of it altogether;' and he moved into clinical mode, suggesting metoclopramide for starters, gently introducing the idea of a suppository, warning her of side effects both likely and possible, explaining how the medicine worked. He proposed that she return in a week or so for a follow-up.

'Thank you Dr Newell,' she said. And then: 'Really, thank you. But I would rather not. Or rather: let's say that if there's a problem I will come back; and if there is not, I won't.'

'That's your choice, of course,' Philip admitted, smiling with professional warmth. 'Although' – he adopted a more admonitory tone – 'I hope you won't take it the wrong way if I say that sometimes it takes a doctor to see if there is in fact a problem.'

'As things seem to me, Dr Newell, I am currently, from a medical point of view, almost nothing but problems. The question is which of these problems I am content to live with, and which (if any) not. It is not a medical decision. It is personal. I am determined, above all, to continue making it for myself.'

'No that's fine, absolutely of course. Before we wrap up, would you mind if I just check through with you some other possibilities. Shall we start with pain?'

'Yes, I do have pain. I am content to have this pain. I open up a space within my body, between me and the pain, and I watch it. I picture its origin and the path it follows. This interests me and gives me a feeling of control. Alternatively, I abstract myself. I sit straight and calm and breathe. I give my attention to the rhythm of my breathing. I let my mind float up and away. It wanders in the cool air like a cloud. Or it takes me back into the past. You can understand, Dr Newell, that I have a great deal of past. I am now at the end of a lot of things. When I was young there was the Empire. There were English gentlemen. Absurd, isn't it? So much has changed since then. So much has got better.'

He murmured indistinctly in reply.

'Do you ever' – she continued – 'go for walks in Kidney Meadow? When I was a girl, nightingales nested there. That's something that has not got better. In fact, it has got very much worse. In one summer, when I was a girl, I counted sixteen varieties of butterfly: now there are four. Even the sparrows are dying. Even the bees. I walk along the river. Dead fish, floating. So it does not feel so very terrible that I too am being poisoned. It does not feel out of place.'

It seemed that she had come to a stop. After a moment, she stirred, lifted herself carefully from her chair and took the stick that Philip, having risen too, was holding out for her.

'It has been very nice to meet you Dr Newell,' she said, courteously.

'Yes indeed. Do come back as soon as you wish.' He was pulling the door open. She walked through it and methodically away.

The phone was ringing. Before he could speak as he picked it up a thin shrill voice leapt out at him: 'Dr Newell can I go now?'

'Jackie I'm so sorry it . . .'

'Dr Newell, I know you are – new. Next time, spare a thought.'

'I'm sorry I couldn't . . .'

'It's sodding seven o'clock.' A click and a buzz.

He sat. He should be completing the note on Mrs Hanworth but instead he sat. Her watery eyes: what colour were they? – He saw again their pallor and the hint of jaundice. Well, it was admirable. It was pig-headed; it was admirable. He should have asked about . . . shit, what had he been thinking of? – he should have asked about her family; he should have given more information about nursing care. But she had been so . . . armoured. Well, it could wait for another time.

Because inevitably there would be another time. With her tumour growing. With it, the chances are, fingering its way into her liver. The vicious brutal primitive little cancer cells breaking off and floating round, looking for trouble. Millions of them being neutralised in the circulation; millions more to take their place. One plus one plus two plus four plus eight. Snagging in a lymph node, and another, and another; spreading between the pleura of the lungs. And what good is medicine against that? A chute seemed to open in his mind and his being went spiralling down into a pit. His stomach knotted. His face drooped. Tears gathered in his eyes; but then he shook himself, and lifted his head, and pulled himself up and out of the clinging blackness. He put finger to keyboard. Dismissed the QOF prompts. Finished the note. Logged off the computer. Gathered his bag and his coat. Then, locking his door, he was away, down the corridor; reception; out of the front glass door, locking and double-locking.

As he scurried off along the pavement, shoulders hunched, Sue was nearing the end of her return train journey, speeding through the thickening gloom. As he crossed the Monet-style footbridge she was waiting by the soon-to-open carriage door; and, as he turned into Eden Grove, she was striding the asphalt pathway between chicken wire held high by concrete pillars. Having entered no. 12 he switched on lamps and drank a glass of water. He opened the fridge and pulled out a beer. Then Sue's key was in the lock and as everywhere outside went dark the two of them were indoors in the light together.

SIXTEEN HOURS IN FEBRUARY

His father was floating towards him. His father rotated as he floated towards him through the mist blowing up over the cliff-edge. He held out his arms towards his father who was floating over verdant damp mossy grass towards him. The siren of an ambulance sounded in the distance. The siren of the ambulance sounded louder, louder. His father floated away, up, caught in a billow of the wind; his father was wearing undulant robes like Noah which made him mingle with the mist. The intrusive siren was becoming purer, sharper. Philip became aware of the skin of his body touching the sheet over the mattress. Philip became aware of the underside of the duvet-cover touching the skin of his body. That sound again: it was only the call of a bird, nothing but a bird. See-saw, see-saw, see-saw, see-saw. Hi there. Hi there. Hi there. Wake up, wake up, wake up. Light was illuminating the thin blue curtains, leaking around their edges, sending a narrow shaft across the centre of the room. Ohmigod what time was it . . . but as Philip lifted his shoulders and craned his head to look for the bright green digits of the old clock radio, as his latissimus dorsi muscle pushed and his rectus abdomini muscle pulled, some spark of electricity in his brain sent him the happy news that it was Saturday. His head flopped down into the pillows and his eyelids drifted shut. What was that bird? He was a child again on a walk with his father. Little bird, black on a branch outlined against the blue and white piebald English summer sky. Great tit of course. Calmness came into his head again. He let himself sink back into the slow dawn of receding sleep where his head was heavy; where his eyes were egg-cups filled with mercury; where, with its slowed pulse, and lowered blood pressure, and softened muscle tone, and loosened ligaments and tendons, and unpressured cartilage and intervertebral discs, his body was laid out on the sheet on the underblanket on the mattress, massy and slack. He enjoyed the drag of gravity upon him. That great tit's call again, high-pitched and insistent, careering around the elaborate entrance channels of his ear, oscillating the tympanic membrane, traversing his ossicles, doing something mysterious in his cochlea so that it then sounded, sounded, sounded in his mind, a great tit rejoicing at this first moment of possible spring, singing 'it's warmish, warmish, warmish, we didn't die in the winter, winter, winter, didn't freeze, and tumble from our perches, and hit the ground feet up in the frost or snow, to be scavenged by a fox, no no, no no, this is going to be my nest, my nest, my nest; look there's a snowdrop, snowdrop, snowdrop; gosh and a crocus, crocus, crocus.' Oh, and there were other chirps and twitters, of other birds, what would there be, robins, blackbirds, blue tits, each doing its own thing; no but also all doing the one same thing of saying 'life, life', contrib-uting to the 'beep-beep, beep-beep, beep-beep' of the landscape's ECG.

Philip stirred. The hairs on the backs of his fingers touched some bit of the surface of Sue. His skin touched her skin. The lovely curve at the top of her hip. This was the tenderest time, the waking together, or the not-quite-yet waking together. He eased onto his side, his knees bent, facing towards her, his weight resting on the flesh of upper arm and thigh. He let the backs of his fingers touch her skin again, halfway up her chest at the side. Didn't want to wake her! He imagined a cocoon of something – rays of light or strands of silk – growing out of him and wrapping round her. That was it: his ribcage would unbend and the ribs would sprout, unfurl-ing like the tendrils of ferns, curling round and wrapping her. She seemed to him so tranquil, lying still and neat, with her impulsive intakes of breath and all-but-silent exhalations; but in fact, inside her, her brain was sparking, her eyes were flickering and, on the edge of consciousness, the meeting with Elton Barfitt was re-enact-ing itself in her mind. The gateway opening and shutting. The courtyard of – what must it have been, some Victorian factory? Grass between the flagstones. High walls on every side. Windows that were semicircles: strange. Grey clouds speeding overhead. In the echoing building she was walking on the smooth concrete floor with a geometrical receding perspective ahead of her. Char-lotte was beside her. They were following some assistant or PA who was wearing white Green Flash tennis shoes with a charcoal eight-ies trouser suit that gave her an almost triangular torso. The PA stopped and stood to one side and there were Elton Barfitt, sitting.

Their strangely waxy facial skin, the light gleaming on it softly. They really did look identical. After a decade of plastic surgery. The dark skin lightened; the light skin darkened. The sharp nose rounded; the snub nose sharpened. One set of cheekbones bulked up; the other scraped away. Hair dyed. Eyebrows plucked. Which had been the woman, which the man? In their identical black lycra jumpsuits the two bodies moved as though they were magnets in the same network of forces. This limb repelled that; that limb repelled this. One mouth was moving and saying: 'It's not about prestige.' The other mouth opened and said: 'We don't care about prestige.' The tick-tock, unstoppable, alternate, horribly disappointing speech continued at its transgendered tenor pitch:

'It's courtesy.'

'I.e. a lack of it.'

'Pure and simple.'

'No respect.'

'Not even elementary tact.'

'No courtesy.'

'Good-'

'-bye.'

The faces became Greek tragedy masks and an amazingly focused jet of air came out of the open mouths. 'No,' it howled: 'No! No!' as it hit her bang in the middle of her torso and pushed her backwards: she was spiralling and there was darkness and the wind was saying 'No! No!' and she landed somewhere with a thud.

There was a leaf on her tummy. No, there were some fingers on her tummy. She tensed for a moment at the horror of it but then sensed that actually she was in a bed, she was warm, she was waking up, these were Philip's fingers, lovely Philip who was there snug beside her in that same one bed that was shared by the two of them. Sluggishly her arm drifted across, her fingers found his fingers and the two sets of fingers interwove themselves with one another. Really she needed to talk to him about it.

His heavy body was moving and there was his hard head laying itself on her chest. He must have wondered what was going on: she must have seemed so preoccupied and really she owed it to him to come clean.

His skull was pressing at the bottom of her throat and her right nipple was being prickled, tingled, she could feel it becoming solid, the sherbet sparkles of sensation spread, there was a tickling underneath her tongue. She really needed to sit down with him and say: this is what I'm doing, it's a risk but I'm happy with that, I'm committed and I need you to be as well.

But now his fingertips were tracing the outline of her hip, finding a winding path down the centre of the top of her thigh. Because actually it was probably going to get quite hard over the next few months, she would probably go quite manic.

And now his tongue was sliding over that lumpy right nipple, and his teeth were nibbling at it, and the palm of his other hand was giving some attention to the neglected soft other nipple, and she stirred and her breath became a moan as endorphinergic and morphinergic mechanisms spluttered into life.

Softly his lips moved over her tummy's tender skin, making the cutaneous receptors tremble; and probably actually – the words were going blurry now in her mind – she would be glad of – blurrier – some rea.sur.nce.

Their faces were nuzzling and their mouths, chewy and bitter from sleep, were meeting and their lips were scuffing each other's cheeks and lips and necks. Hearts thudding, the valves snapping open, slamming shut.

She grins. She wraps her arms around his shoulders and hugs him to her, feeling her body seem to soften and proliferate as, in his body too, arteries dilate and tissue swells, and all the beautifully adapted and various receptor neurones fire in happy harmony making brain cells iridesce and swirl and jive.

In the dappled shadows the bodies cling and thrust and arc and stretch. Toes splay. Arms prop shoulders from which a torso slopes. Two legs spring into the air. A head flaps from side to side. Fingers tense, hips grip and ankles twine. Forehead bows to forehead and hair touches in the air as eyes look longingly into eyes, thighs vie, lip lips lip and . . .

But, damn, dammit! – what was this?

Anxiously he began to get the impression that his vas deferens was initiating its rhythmic squeezing too soon, too soon . . .

But phew she too seemed to be surfing the waves of neuromuscular euphoria, so that as, sweating, panting, he bowed his forehead to her chest, she gripped him tight, her sharp nails stabbing; and then they were grinning and kissing each other's noses, cheeks; and then they lay entangled for a moment, breathing; and then they rose, one after another, went for a piss, came back and settled into bed again.

His head was on her chest and her hand was in his hair and she was full of warmth and tenderness towards him and he felt safe.

In her mind she saw an image from some months before: his face turned towards her smiling, his cheeks plumped up beneath the sparkling eyes, the whole of him emanating happiness that she was there.

In his mind he saw the outline of her body burnished in shadowy light: shoulder and upper arm and breast and the little lynchet undulations of her ribs. He felt a trickle of something electro-chemical down around his ilium and was wanting her again, wanting her longer and better in some epic desert scenery to theme music by Ennio Morricone.

Then his mind switched and tranquillity came through him. He was remembering when he had said that he was going to have to move here for a year and she had said straight off: 'I'll come.' And he had said: 'But the commute and it'll be pretty dull there.' And she had said: 'That's OK'; and then: 'It'll be interesting living in a nowhere place.' Then she must have seen anxiety still trembling in his face; seen him thinking that she couldn't really mean it, that she would get bored and give up after a month or two or, worse, would get bored and want to leave but wouldn't because she would feel under an obligation. She had leaned forward and taken his hand between her two hands and looked up at him so sunnily: 'We'll have one another.' And in his chest had been the thrumming of a harp.

Now they were lying side by side, calm, supine, holding hands.

'We should go for a walk later,' she was saying.

'There's George's party.'

'Not till the evening.'

'Listen. That's a great tit.'

'How do you know?'

'Just do. It's one of the easiest. Don't you?'

'We never went to the country.'

'And we never went to a city.' He snorted–giggled. He nuzzled her shoulder as she, smiling, draped her arm across his neck.

'I'm going to get the paper,' he said. 'Stay there. I will bring you green tea and the paper.'

He was up, stepping into trousers and pulling on a top, not bothering with contacts but hooking his little wire glasses over ears and nose. So irritating that you couldn't have a paper delivered but the thing was to pretend you weren't getting out of bed at all: nip out and back with the snugness still around you.

Now he was down the stairs; jacket on; there was a flyer on the carpet – he saw the letters 'Birth of the . . .' but he was opening the door, out into the air. Warmish. Damp. Snowdrops in the planters but he was across the courtyard of Eden Grove now, not thinking, not noticing much, just being in the rhythm of the walking, hands in his pockets, face trying not to feel the air. Left along Parnassus this time. No one about on the tidy street. Oh, but there was someone. Washing his car. Washing his car at 9.30 on a Saturday! Philip's mind was livelier now, despite himself. It was moving ahead of him, seeing the end of Parnassus and the awkward artificial joint that connected it to Fountain Street at the edge of the old town where the paper shop was. And Mrs Hanworth's house which he had visited when she had had a fall. It was really amazing that nothing had broken: there might well have been secondaries in the bones by now. Even so she wouldn't last much longer. Don't think about it, don't think about patients on your days off, allow yourself to relax. George

was right it was always better to live some distance from the practice: remember that with the next job.

Here is the newsagent, the bell clanging as he goes in, the paper,
a euphoric Arab crowd, one pound seventy. Now he was hurrying
back: one eye on the street one on the news. 'Standing down', cross
the road, 'handing power to the military', mind that lamp-post, 'a
new dawn', it was definitely warmer, 'in the name of Allah the
most merciful . . . fuck off'. With a smile he slid the lump of newspaper under his arm and, supporting it at its bottom edge, he strode
along. Such amazing things going on over there – their whole
world changing. They were risking their lives. While he . . . though
at least he was doing something good. And at some point he could
always go off somewhere like Adam Hibbert. That would be nuts
and bolts medicine, rehydrate someone and save their life. Or just
simply properly clean a wound. Whereas so much of what he did
here was basically reassurance. Or marginal. Securing an increase of
0.2 Quality Adjusted Life Years at a cost of.

And yet, as he crossed back into the tidiness of The Willows, he
felt a swelling of revulsion at the sort of thing Adam Hibbert was
doing, bringing the glories of western medicine to the Third
World. What was off-putting was the way it was made to seem
like an adventure. You could jet in, make a difference, and jet out
again, patting yourself on the back. That was clear in the email
they had all got from him: 'Job done!' – and the pictures of epic,
sunlit, mountain landscape with Adam in the foreground, sweaty,
tanned, in military-looking gear, grinning, eyes squeezed against
the light, his arm across the shoulders of a man whom he had
helped, who was wearing a white robe and brown waistcoat and

white pill-box hat, and who was so thin he seemed hardly to be able to bear the weight of Adam's arm.

That's just me being prissy, Philip thought as he turned into Eden Grove. Oversensitive, i.e. basically a coward. Because Adam Hibbert was really making a difference. If you added up Quality Adjusted Life Years he would be light years ahead, in a whole different category like a billionaire, a plutocrat of good. Whereas he, Philip Newell, all he did was spend his time mildly ameliorat-ing the lot of e.g. a dying old lady who wasn't even that nice. But as soon as he said that to himself a countercurrent of feeling flowed through him. He remembered her stern, watery, greenish eyes, her brave head in profile with the patchy, blotchy skin sagging from it in wrinkles and folds, her delicate, scattered, white, white hair. There was a tenderness and a dignity in helping her. It was actually something wonderful.

Now he was finding his key and his mind switched to thinking about how he would nip in quietly, and quickly make the tea for Sue and a coffee for him, and then with the two cups in one hand and the paper in the other glide up the stairs to where she might be dozing again all snug and dissolute and warm. But as he opened the front door he could see a figure at the kitchen end of the living room, dark against the window. She was there, in her dressing gown, with her back towards him, looking out. His body smiled at seeing her but he also felt a swoon of disappointment that the lingering longer in bed together was now not going to happen. She could be so brisk sometimes.

She turned. She switched on the kettle which boiled at once; and then she reached for the cafetiere: so sweet of her. He chucked, meantime, the paper on the table, and in one movement took off his jacket and threw it on the sofa. A square-cut wooden chair screeched on the lino when he pulled it back to sit on; now he was yanking at the plastic round some bits of the paper as she put a coffee for him down beside it. The newsprint spread across the table top. She was still standing, leaning against the edge of the sink, the window behind her, her arms crossed in front of her, keeping the fabric of her dressing gown tight around the root of her neck, her cup held in one fist.

'I want to go to that,' she said – nodding at something on the table. It was the flyer he had seen as he went out. 'Birth of the Earth,' he read. 'Our planet is sick. But just as, in the case of the legendary phoenix, life bursts from the ashes, so in this case too the environmental emergency may release a greater spiritual benefit to us all. Come and discover what is happening and why and what you can do to help. It might just be time for you to change your life. Change your life and help to save the world.'

'Why?'

'Curiosity. It's on a boat, did you see? I think it must be moored in Kidney Meadow.'

'It says,' he said, looking at the small print, 'follow the signs.'

'A treasure hunt,' she said. 'I'll make us some brunch and we can go for our walk and end up there.'

'Alright.'

As he settled into the paper it seemed to him suddenly so very nice that Sue, that another human being, simply wanted to do something for him, with him, make a plan, make him coffee and make him brunch – OK he mainly did the cooking during the week but that was because of her long commute, only fair; whereas this was spontaneous and warm; this was because of love. He sipped his hot coffee and scanned the page, reading of a moment of historic significance, of a revolution carried out by ordinary people, of something in our souls that cries out for freedom. Each phrase sparked a little image or opened a tiny pathway in his mind; while Sue, watching him, was thinking that even just reading a newspaper lifted you away from where you were. That maybe the web wasn't such a big change. So that really there had been something faddish, overblown, about Elton Barfitt's idea, the pile of body parts, a mixture of obviously artificial prostheses and imitation bits of real limbs. The idea being that after Butler, and especially now with the web, there was no difference, really, between a plastic limb and one that was made of flesh and blood and bone: neither of them was actually You. Because, these days, You was a disembodied entity that could manifest itself in many different forms, avatars, performances. But that idea was *so* false, it struck her more forcibly than before now she thought it over again. She sensed her own body, her skin warm with a sheen of dry sweat on it, a little bit tacky if you touched it or niffy if you smelled it, all swaddled in this dressing gown which, now she set about sensing it, was touching her in a million different places with its towelling fluff.

Next there would have been a gallery full of projections, of light waves which would focus into an image here and there on the walls but which would also permeate and illuminate the air, bouncing off floating bits of dust and rebounding off the punters so that they too seemed to be laced with immaterial information. After which . . . but she became aware again of Philip reading the paper, lifting the big pages and lowering them, smoothing them, letting his eyes dart across them, lifting, lowering, smoothing, until his attention was drawn into a story; at which he would lean forward so that his head was accurately positioned above it, and reach from time to time for his coffee. Watching him, she was thinking that she simply couldn't work out, even after going over it and over it, whether Elton Barfitt had all along been toying with them, with her and Charlotte, or whether they had at first really been keen to do a show and then really had suddenly got offended. She moved around the table. She touched a finger to Philip's cheek as she squeezed past him and he raised a hand to halt it, pulled it to his lips. Because it had seemed to be going so well. She moved onwards and settled in the slippery, faux-leather armchair by the door. They had seemed to believe, and appreciate, what Charlotte had said about how much she loved their work, how much it meant to her. Why shouldn't they – it had been true. And they had really seemed to agree with the idea of just for once exhibiting in a gallery, because choosing a not-tremendously-prestigious place like Spike would be a way of showing how thoroughly they did not care. It had felt like such a real intellectual connection. It was only at the last minute, at the moment of what should have been absolutely trivial practicalities, that everything had gone wrong.

'What's magic,' Charlotte had said, 'is that we have a slot this summer, a clear three months.'

At which they had totally cramped up.

'How come?'

'It's just . . .' – but the terrible hostile double sniping had begun: 'You've had a cancellation?'

'You want us to fill in for who, for Howard Hodgkin?'

'Anish Kapoor?'

'The Prince of Wales?'

'To get you through a sticky moment?'

'Plug a little hole in your calendar?'

'Be the Elvis tribute band?'

'The Paris Hilton Lookalike?'

'The I-Can't-Believe-It's-Not-Butter?'

'Another nourishing dollop of so-called "Art"?'

'No! No!' – Charlotte had howled. They quietened. She tried saying she had thought they didn't care about prestige – but that had only set them off again:

'It's not about prestige,' they had cried out in their terrible duet: 'It's courtesy.' Etc. Etc. And that had been that.

Well, nothing she could have said would have changed it. There was no other way of handling it. They were just fucking twats – that was what the matter was. Sue felt so sad, horribly sad, that these people whom she really had admired, who had seemed so principled, who must, after all, have put themselves through so much pain for the sake of their art, should end up just like the rest of them. Conceited. So fucking focused on their reputations.

Which had left her and Charlotte, a weeping Charlotte . . . but there was Philip stirring, rising . . . which had left her and Char-lotte in their quandary. Philip was moving towards the sink with his cup. Why hadn't she told him? She watched him, his shirt tucked into his jeans, the belt around his waist. Because – well, this was obvious: she'd known why all along. Because she didn't want to risk him not reacting as she wanted. For him to feel anxious and for her then to get irritated. She didn't want to feel a jot of difference between them about something that meant so much to her.

Or maybe. He was rinsing his mug under the tap. Maybe it was actually more because the gamble might look different when it was in the open. If she told it to someone who was not Charlotte. He was filling the mug with water, lifting it to his mouth, drinking. Maybe it would look plain stupid. Maybe it was all – but the thoughts left her as she landed wholly in the world again. She called: 'Going to get dressed.' She pushed herself up off the chair. She was standing. She was walking out.

After coffee and green tea; after the paper. After brunch and after chat about this and that. After more coffee and green tea. After they had pulled on their coats and shut the door behind them. After they had exited The Willows and turned right, and crossed the railway, and taken the narrow muddy path, they were wandering through Kidney Meadow hand in hand. There was the sky. There were trees. There was a lot of green. There was wide, reedy grass beaten down in clumps and dotted with wet. And there were bright little nettles with furry leaves, not yet ankle height.

What was odd was how much of everything was dead. Tangled above the low, green layer were the brown-ish and white-ish remains of taller plants, stripped of leaves, scrubbed bare, slim trunklets bent and broken and jumbled, tens, no, thousands of them, all around.

'Like skeletons,' Sue said.

She noticed – there – a solitary, ruddy-brown, dead plant, about head height, its slender branches pointing acutely to the sky, punctuated every inch or so by amber scrunchies of shrivelled foliage.

'You gruesome girl,' said Philip.

It was like something made of oxidised copper, she thought; an intricate ancient candalebrum. And what were these geometrical constructions like the frames of bust umbrellas, a few seeds still clinging to them, gleaming like flattened pearls?

'Burnet saxifrage,' said Philip.

'It's a junk-yard,' said Sue.

'Listen,' he said: 'What's that?'

'Yeh, yeh,' she said 'Great tit. But shall I tell you a secret?' She popped up on tiptoe to reach his ear, and whispered: 'I think it's better not to know its name.'

'Can you see it?' – he asked as she swung down and away from him again, though their hands still held.

She looked; they both did, lifting their heads, squinting at the network of black branches. The cloudy sky behind was surprisingly bright. There it was, the little eyelash beak a-flutter, the amazingly loud, shrill whistle blaring out.

'Do you see,' Philip said, gathering Sue to him with one arm and pointing with the other. 'Can you see the black stripe down its front like it's split in two?'

'Yup.'

'And the mossy greenness of the back.'

'No. I can't see that.' She looked a bit longer: 'I don't think you can either.'

'Yes I can.'

'No you can't against the light. It's just a silhouette, apart from the bright yellow and black.'

'I can.'

She was wriggling against the hug of his arm, pushing him. 'No: you know it's there and so you think you see it. See? That's why it's better not to know. That way' – she had broken away from him – 'you can see what's really there.'

'But it is really there.'

'I mean: that way you see just what you really can see.'

'But knowing what to look for helps me really see it.'

'That's true. That's definitely true.' She was standing apart from him, speaking forcefully but full of happiness and trust. She was about to carry on her declamation but he put in:

'That's how I make a diagnosis.'

'That's right. You've said it. It's political. Your way of seeing pushes the world, including people, into a structure of knowledge that defines them and gives you power over them. The other way, my way, which is actually fundamentally left-wing, democratic, tries to have each new sensation fresh, each time.'

'Be astonished at the taste of a cup of tea,' he said, smiling at her. Sue could be such an egghead.

'So I'm afraid,' she said, 'you are one of the oppressors.'

'Whereas you are delighted by the lovely ring of the alarm clock every morning.'

'I am,' she said. 'I really am. I leap up every morning with a happy smile. You've seen me. Or you would have seen me if you weren't such a slugabed, lying there groaning.'

'When they invent the intravenous coffee machine I'll be just fine.'

Hand in hand, they wandered on, through a place which, a century before, had been the town dump and which now grew russett apples and bramleys, crab apples and damsons, comice pears, greengages and sloes, though all that could be seen of them in this present moment of late winter and early spring were the battered trunks and branches. On these bare structures perched here a black-bird, there a magpie, here a threatened sparrow, its feathers fluffed against the cold, and there a wood pigeon with its swollen, elegant, pinkish front, its neck sunk in its shoulders. A squall of long-tailed tits came scattering across, cheeping and spluttering. High up, a standard robin sent its delicate, skyey doodlings through the air.

They passed a grizzled hawthorn with its coating of lichen like little cabbages, some grey, some fierce cumin yellow; and then they were out into the open part of the landscape, the part which flooded in winter, the water permeating the topsoil and pooling on the underlying clay. The wind whipped them and they leaned together as they walked. Ahead a convoy of huge railway poplars marked the line of the river. A gull swung overhead with its kukri wings; another soared higher; a rook flapped raggedly across.

So, on they walked, over the mud, which was over clay, which was over chalk and flint, which was over gault, which was over Jurassic slate, which was over carboniferous limestone, which was over much else, down to the distant core.

And on they walked, under the atmosphere where currents swirled and undulated in the upper air, forming clouds in blotchy, cellulitic bands.

They reached, Philip and Sue, a lock whose thick wooden valves had stood two hundred years against the flow. They nibbled a bit of chocolate, kissed, rubbed each other's hands. They watched a boat go through, then crossed between wiry railings, then turned to follow the towpath back along the other side of the river. Now they saw a laminated bit of paper nailed to a wooden stake: 'Birth of the Earth', with an arrow. Philip checked his watch and they walked on.

The path ahead was sunk into a narrow muddy groove, barely a foot wide: how strange, Sue thought, that people should follow so precisely in one another's footsteps. She and Philip erred to this side and that on the flat grassy verges, holding hands. To their right, a tangle of hawthorns and brambles, then low-lying grazing fields; then a muddle of other indistinct trees; in the distance, a shadowy line of hills. To their left, the greenish muddy river, its water swirling, gleaming under the bright white sky. Beyond it, the flat expanse over which they had come just now, infrequent dots of humans wandering, the tinier specks of birds fleeing across. And beyond that, the houses, little lumps, half-hidden.

Now they were nearing a great, grey-skinned poplar with massive, upward-pointing branches and sprays of higgledy-piggledy twigs. Around and beyond the base of it were the white, prone sections of a tree that had been felled and left barkless; dotted in among them, people. Sue and Philip saw the splotch of a blue coat, and a red one; other duller figures stood here and there.

'Must be it,' said Sue.

Philip checked the time again and they approached. 'There's the boat,' he said: behind the trunk of the still-living tree and the group of eight or ten people they could see part of the roof of a long barge, with a wind turbine lifted high on a pole, its rotors turning idly. One of the people had weather-beaten features, dreadlocks, stiff combat trousers, heavy boots, a little dog, springy, melancholy.

Another had a round, fresh, open face, big cheeks, blonde wisps: she was the one in the bright red coat. There was an elderly couple, he patrician, brusque; she shorter, intense and still. But now someone was walking towards them. Oh it was, oh god – a patient. In jean dungarees, with a loose brown cord jacket over, out of her rugged, pink face, with a hunk of yellow hair pulled back, she began to speak:

'Dr Newell.'

'Hel . . .'

'I'm Janet – Janet Stone' – she said, seeing the struggle in his face and helping him.

'Hi,' he said. Bits of recollection began blocking themselves into place: ADHD. His suspicion of Dr Hibbert. His raising the matter at the practice meeting and his being pooh-poohed by George Emory. God that had been embarrassing. And Sara Kaiser had sat there quietly, lifting her wide eyes for a moment to look at him with an I-told-you-so expession, nodding her head while Dr Emory patronisingly explained 'we can't go back over every imperfect piece of procedure. There's no point. The question is, how is the patient doing now? And under your care,' he intoned in his dried-plum voice, 'I am sure the little boy will do splendidly. General Practice' – and here Dr George Emory had actually wagged his finger – 'is an imperfect art. Often it's pretty seat-of-the-pants stuff. I sometimes think' – he had added, after a moment's pause and a little smile – 'that so long as we don't actually kill someone we are doing pretty well.' So that had put him, young Dr Newell, in his place, with his fresh face and his suspiciousness and his frankly adolescent naivety.

Janet Stone was speaking again: 'I wanted to thank you. Because . . . well, have a look!' She pointed over to the side of them, past the usual tangle of bramble and hawthorn, to where part of the felled trunk lay. A little boy stepped daintily along the top of it. His arms stretched out wobblingly like a marionette's; and then he had jumped over a ragged, up-sticking obstructive bole and landed again, his legs narrow as a robin's. Then he had jumped again and was on the ground, and was somersaulting, and was on his feet again, kerching! fists clenched, a speedy, tough, martial arts hero. Then he was running, running, in an arc, in a circle, and again in a narrower circle, and a narrower, and a narrower: he was spiralling; he was water going down the plughole; he had flopped and was lying flat on his back, his limbs stretched out.

'Look at him. He's so happy again now. Spontaneous. He's himself again. It's down to you, doctor,' she said, actually reaching out and grabbing Philip's upper arm so that he felt a muffled pressure through his jacket. Looking up into his eyes, she said again: 'Thank you.'

'Oh well it wasn't . . .' He was embarrassed, baffled. Surely all he had done was refer them? He asked: 'How's school?'

'Yeh. OK,' she said, letting go of him, turning, finding Albert with her eyes again. 'Sometimes he does get in trouble. But they haven't complained or nothing.'

'And the . . . behavioural therapy. Is that being helpful?'

'We're not doing any of that, doctor. But don't worry. We're fine. I've got him on a simple diet. No stress. Regular bedtime. We didn't like the medicine and we don't want any therapy. We just want him to be able to be himself. And he is. And that's . . . ace. And next to that, if he messes the odd thing up, it don't matter. He's just being him.'

'What's he doing now?' Sue put in. Albert was stalking on stiff legs, his torso bent forwards, his head pointing to the ground.

'Birds,' said Janet Stone. He's being a wader. Oh' – he had switched pose and gone galumphing off, legs bent, his fists at his armpits, his elbows flapping awkwardly – 'it must be that magpie's set him off, do you hear it?'

They both, Sue and Philip, became aware of a faint industrial clatter in the air, a pile-driving clank–clank.

'How wonderful,' Sue said, 'that he's so responsive. I've never seen anything like . . .'

'Yes,' Janet Stone said decisively. 'It is.'

People were moving towards the boat.

Sue asked: 'Are you coming to this too?'

'I'll stay out here with Albert,' Janet said: 'Heard it all before.'

'It's really good to see him so happy,' said Philip, pleased. He signalled farewell with his smile and the two of them, he and Sue, joined the queue to be handed on to the deck. A man stood with one foot on the bank, one on the gunwale. He had a shaved head, the pepper-specks of follicles darkening the brownish gleam. He wore a rough, orange, woollen smock-like top, and baggy yellow trousers.

'Welcome,' he said, as he took Sue's hand in one of his and placed his other hand under her elbow, supporting her across. He was lithe, practised.

'Welcome,' he said again to Philip, his arms hovering near him in case of a slip. Sue found her way down narrow steps into the bowels of the boat; inclining his head, Philip followed. The interior was bigger than they had expected. It was wider than a canal-boat, in fact twice as wide. Portholes on either side let in good light. It was possible to stand up straight. The floor was polished, narrow planks. Slim shallow beams spanned the ceiling. An assortment of wooden chairs were lined up in rows, pointing forwards, as though for a lecture. The occasional stool. A bench. In front of them, a couple of rugs, and cushions. Room for maybe twenty people. At the end was a white projection screen, with a small wooden table to one side. The two of them took their places on chairs some-where in the middle. I can't believe – Philip was thinking – I can't believe they're not engaged in a programme of behavioural therapy. There was a scraping of chairlegs as the patrician couple found seats in the row behind.

'This is a very practical setup,' said the woman in a jovial tone.

Because even if things seem OK for the moment they're not necessarily going to stay that way and they need to have resources. What can the clinic . . . .? Tremors went through the floor as the guy with dreadlocks thudded past, his dog skittering and snuffling behind him, all the way to the front where he went down awkwardly on one knee and then reclined on a cushion, his legs stretched out, his dog rotating and then flopping down, pushing its head into his tummy. But then maybe they didn't go to the hospital. They didn't go to the hospital! That must be it. They didn't bloody go this time either just as in fact they maybe hadn't gone for Adam Hibbert! Yes, which would make what Adam did maybe a bit more understandable. The woman in the puffy red coat slipped in nimbly across the aisle from him and looked around smilingly. She put a hand up to her face and pushed a wisp of hair behind her ear. There was tightness in his throat and at the top of his chest as a spurt of anxiety went through him. But it wasn't his, absolutely wasn't his fault. The calm clipped voice of his trainer from a couple of years before came into his head. 'Patients are responsible adults. We advise but we can't compel. It can be very frustrating. When they are dead-set on doing something that is bad for them and you can't get them to change their mind. When you agree a course of treatment with them, or think you have; and then you never see them again. That's the most frustrating of all. Because you just don't know what's happened to them. Until maybe they turn up in A&E.'

But now the lithe man with his shaved, tanned head and bright, Buddhist clothes was edging round them, pulling shutters across the portholes. Calm, said Philip to himself. Leave them be. There is only so much you can do. One by one the circles of light went out. He became aware of Sue again beside him and turned his head to look as shadow spread around them. Her head was moving slightly as her eyes flicked here and there.

The lithe man was at the front now.

'Thank you,' he was saying, in a soft, probing voice. 'Thank you so much for coming. It's good of you to be here' – his eyes were looking round the room, trying to fix each one of them in turn – 'and good I hope will flow from it.'

He was half sitting, propped against the edge of the table.

'My name is Ash. I want to start with a moment of reflection. If you would gather your attention here into this space. You may find it helps to fold your hands in your lap. To breathe deeply. Slowly.'

Again the searching eyes were touching each one of them in turn. 'Become aware of your body. Here. With all its sensitivity. Make your mind present here too.'

Philip's hand reached for Sue's, found it; and then he did indeed become aware of his fingers squeezing hers, the flexores digitorum contracting, skin slipping over skin, the resilient flesh compressing as phalanges interlocked. He was wanting to say: Christ Sue what have you brought us to? Nudging her shoulder against his arm, she seemed to receive and accept the message.

'Because your mind too is sensitive on many levels' – Ash was pressing on. 'Sensory, rational, sympathetic, imaginative, spiritual. I would like all that energy to be focused here in this place. We need it. The earth needs it of us.'

Philip was a thoughtful and humane modern doctor. He did not believe medicine and technology could cure all human ills. He believed in treating the whole person. But this sort of New Age bollocks really was too much. Still. Try to look upon it as amusing. The prickles of his irritation softened and a feeling of forbearance spread. Sue must be interested in it from an Art point of view. It was warm here and the chair was OK and they had been walking for a while. And anyway it was a local thing and they'd been complaining that in The Willows there was no feeling of community. But that was partly because wherever he looked he saw a patient, or a potential one. Can't really relax with the footie down the pub when you've recently been intimate with the fat man's piles or the loud girl's genital warts. As actually here too with Ms Stone and Albert. What were they doing here? At least they had stayed outside.

'I'm sure you all know these pictures,' Ash was saying. 'Our beautiful earth.'

It was the familiar image, the great stretches of blue sea, the continents arthritically swollen and twisted, the swirls and striations and speckles of cloud.

'The glaciers that are receding. 1978' – a valley filled with choppy grey ice. To Sue it seemed like actual stormy water swirling down, as though someone had clicked their fingers and some rapids had flash-frozen. Cryogenically stilled, the arc of the water's energy held there ready to leap again when the switch was pressed the other way. But actually really it couldn't be like that. Actually really this must be the look of slow and grinding movement. Millennial pressure.

'And here it is last year.'

Definitely shorter, thought Philip.

'A warmer sea makes bigger storms. New Orleans. Here's the hurricane.'

Its ammonite swirl.

'And here's the damage.'

Tranquil water dotted with the tidy roofs of houses. The roofs like rafts. Or like the tops – Sue thought – of palatial dwellings for future civilised beavers.

'You've seen these images,' Ash continued matter-of-factly in his soft voice. 'And I am sure you have responded. You have turned down your thermostats. You have replaced lightbulbs. You have installed loft insulation where appropriate. You use the car a bit less often and you make sure the tyres are fully inflated when you do. You switch off appliances at the wall instead of leaving them on standby. You put less water in the kettle. You'd be amazed' – there was a chuckle in his voice – 'how many people haven't, all over the place, not only middle America. A couple of weeks ago I was down south, Maidstone, where apparently it is still the 1970s. They barely have recycling. They all drive everywhere. The town is mainly multi-storey car parks. In that kind of place you have to start from basics. You have to say: no it's not a hoax. If we do nothing, this' – the map came up – 'is what the UK will look like in 2080. A bigger version of the Outer Hebrides. Can you see Maidstone?' The voice was harsher now. 'No you can't. It's underwater.

'But that was there,' he carried on, his posture relaxing, the voice settling back down to its tranquil norm. 'Here I know I am with friends. So I would like to share with you . . .'

He paused; smiled; his gaze rested on Philip for a moment and then, as soon as Philip was feeling uneasily as though something were expected of him, slid to rest on Sue's pale face which smiled brightly in reply.

'. . . to share with you some concern about the quality, the depth of our response. Each of us has made these little tactical adjustments. Now we watch the news, waiting for governments to make their little tactical adjustments. What is it to be? Wind farms? Tidal arrays? Nuclear? James Lovelock's tubes in the sea to bring up nutrients and make algae bloom, thereby absorbing carbon dioxide? Let's paint' – now the voice was sing-song – 'our roofs white. Let's pray for the development of carbon capture. Nuclear fusion. Artifical photosynthesis. Let's float enormous reflective umbrellas in the sky. Make artificial clouds. It's all quite fun. But what I wonder' – the voice had dropped now, gone back to its flat meandering original tone – 'is whether we are really hearing, really properly understanding, the cry of the earth.' His head bowed. Quiet. Water lapping at the edges of the boat. A see-saw and chuckle of birdsong, great tit and robin. But it was as though Ash were listening for something beyond what their ears could hear.

'Look at this place.'

Philip shifted, crossed his legs: it was, what was it, in the Gulf, Dubai, that artificial island.

'Palm Jumeirah. Look at it. A logo in the sea. For people to live on. Here are the houses.'

A close-up. Lego blocks crammed together. A road, a line of houses, an artifical strip of sand. One tree per mansion.

'Here are the sort of people who have bought these houses and enjoy living in them.'

A stocky, white man, curly straw-blond hair, blue polo shirt, white shorts, hairy upper legs. Eye-sockets in shadow but his chubby cheeks shine. Beside him a tanned, slim, oval-faced, younger woman, long straight black hair, a slinky sort of dress. Cat – Philip thought – and cream.

'Here is one of the 100,000 Indian and Pakistani and Bangladeshi slaves who worked 12–hour shifts in the desert sun or through the night to construct their luxury residence.'

Blue overalls. Red helmet. Trim Charlton Heston moustache. 'Many died.' One eye open, its chestnut iris gazing out, a gleam. The other eye narrowed, seems to be looking askance. A human being – Sue thought – saying: here I am, a human being. She slid her hand out of Philip's grasp and folded it in her own other hand upon her knee. Behind the Indian or Pakistani or Bangladeshi slave were skyscrapers and lights, the night, a candlelit terrace, a western couple, his hand on her hip. Adverts. Such glassy smiles.

'I can find no image of the slave-servants who do the cooking and cleaning. It appears that there is twenty-four-hour maid service with no actual human maids.'

A white illuminated rectangle. The whirr of the projector which – oh of course it must be behind the screen.

'It is easy to scorn them. It is easy to say: that's very bad but it is over there. A long way away. Geographically but also spiritually. It is easy to say: those are the corrupt, and those are the exploited, and it is very bad, but here things are better, here we are lucky, and can manage to live in reasonable equity. And that is doubtless true.'

He bowed his head. All still.

'And yet when I look at this man and woman.'

The cat and the cream again.

'And ask how they can fail to see this man.'

The eyes.

'I ask myself what I fail to see. When I look at these obviously misconceived places to live.'

The Lego blocks.

'Large lumps of concrete designed to separate people from one another. Designed to isolate them from the natural world. Air-conditioned. Built on artificial mounds which even now are sinking. In a place where there is no natural fresh water to drink. With the result that every drop of drinking water has to be artificially desalinated. With the result that residents of Dubai have the largest carbon footprint in the world, much larger even than Americans. To enable people to live in these enormous bunkers surrounded on the one side by concrete roads which reject life, which are like endless gravestones stifling the earth. Surrounded on the other by artificially constrained sea which even now is thickening with algae and filling with shit.'

Again that acid in the voice.

'When I look at these isolation units I wonder about me. I wonder how isolated I, too, am, even in this fragile boat which gets cold when it is chilly and hot when it is hot, which bobs up and down in the currents and wanders here and there, which is visited by birds and home to insects and snails and waterweed and lichen, and which is open to anyone like you . . .'

A pause, the voice subsiding to a slow pulse, the eyes moving from listener to listener in time with it.

'. . . people . . . here . . . who come . . . in the name . . . of our suffering earth. Because even I, even here, find it hard sometimes not to think of myself as just myself. An individual. Walled off from the world by this . . .'

. . . he slapped the back of one hand with the fingers of the other and the sound of it ricocheted around . . .

'. . . and this . . .'

. . . he slapped the side of his head . . .

'. . . the skull and skin that shut me in. Or that would shut me in if it were not for these . . .'

He raised his hand to his face again but gently now.

'. . . my eyes that see; and nose and mouth and ears that smell and taste and hear; and all the tender nerves . . .'

Now he was gently touching his hands together, running finger over finger, dabbing a fingertip against a palm.

'. . . all these that bring the outside in, that mean I am like a living sponge in a warm rich sea, or a jellyfish, permeated by the world around. Only it is not "the world around" it is the world all through me.'

His arms were extended but relaxed on each side of him as though the air were water and they were floating in it.

'Togetherness.'

He put the word in the air and watched as though it too were floating there.

'Togetherness must be our key. Togetherness with one another. Togetherness with the world.'

Head lowered, arms down, all quiet.

'Togetherness is a concept. But more importantly it is a feeling. To develop that feeling we need to use our bodies. We need to teach our bodies to trust. Look at me standing. I trust that the world will stay still. I trust, even though we are upon water, that waves will not tip me to the floor. And watch . . .'

He reached out towards the weather-beaten dreadlocked guy, and wiggled his fingers, at which the guy stood up, bulky in his tapestry jacket, and then kneeled, sitting on his heels, his hands on his thighs in front of him. Ash turned so that he had his back to this kneeling bulky figure. He stretched out his arms on either side again, a crucifix.

'I trust,' he said.

Then he was rocking on his feet, forward, back, forward, back, back, back a bit further, staying straight but leaning backwards like a mast being lowered until: there it was: the centre of gravity had gone out far enough and he was falling, so quick suddenly until

– ah, the bulky man had caught him safe. Sue lifted herself from her chair a little, hands braced on knees, so that she could see the big man holding the torso of the lithe man like a baby. Then Ash's feet slid back towards the rest of him so that he would be able to stand again.

'I had to make an effort to trust this man Orpheus,' Ash said when he was standing again, in the middle at the front. 'I was vividly aware that that was what I was doing. I could almost feel the crack my head would get from the floor if he failed me. We must learn to feel that that is how we trust the earth. The earth, every second of every day of every year, is our saviour. And if we are to trust it . . .'

. . . his voice sharpened . . .

' . . . we must earn its trust as well. We must stop poisoning and heating and digging and scratching and exploiting. We must care for the earth as it cares for us.'

He moved backwards a little.

'As one first small step,' he said, 'I would like to invite you, any one of you, all of you, to come up here, one by one, and experience this moment of trust. To be baptised into togetherness with the earth. Who would like to be first?'

He looked here and there among them, smiling.

'Who would like to take the lead?'

'I will!' – called out the blonde who had been wearing the red puffy coat. Now it was slumped in the chair beside her. She stood with alacrity. Brown tight woollen top and jeans. Perkily she edged sideways out of the row and walked freely, happily, to the front. She stood side-on. Orpheus made way for Ash who kneeled behind her. She turned her head towards the audience, grinned. Her body was side-on and her face was front-on like an Egyptian fresco. Then she turned her head back so that it was again in profile. She rocked forward briefly — and then all of a sudden she had tumbled backwards and was in a heap in Ash's arms. Letting herself lie there, she murmured a just-audible contented sigh. Then she was scrambling up and moving back towards her place. Her face was pink and her hair was scattered across it.

What was Sue . . . ? Philip experienced a curdling sensation in his stomach and lungs as Sue rose and turned away from him to walk the other way around the chairs to the front. She had not spoken but moved decisively as though it were obvious that she was to be next, as though it were simply her turn to do this straightforward thing that to Philip seemed so embarrassing. There she was. She was looking at the wall in front of her, the line where it joined the ceiling, the circle of the blocked porthole. She was aware of her body, the pressure of her heels and the balls of her feet through the soles of her shoes on the floor. She was aware of her head balancing upon her neck in the middle of her shoulders. She tried to imagine the space behind her, a perspective pyramid of lines drawn from the outline of her body to the place where Ash's arms were waiting. She was still.

Philip said to himself: 'Is she not going to?' but then she was wobbling, tipping, a tree trembling and creaking and then crash it was down, she was down. Now it was Philip who lifted himself from his seat, as she had done earlier, his hands braced against his knees, the better to see her lying there, her head on the shoulder of the lithe man, her forehead — he was sure — touching his chestnut cheek. But then at last she was rising and finding her way back towards him. 'Your turn,' she said as she sat. But he would not.

'Go on,' they heard the elderly woman whispering vehemently behind them.

'I can't. My joints,' the elderly man replied.

'Well, I will,' she asserted; and so she did, simply and gracefully.

Is it only women? – Philip was wondering; but then someone else from behind them came forward, a man; then someone else and someone else, until almost all the small audience had participated in the experience of togetherness. Philip felt himself become more rigid, his whole myology tensing as he resisted the atmosphere of joviality that now seemed to permeate the room.

'Is that everyone?' Ash asked, centre stage again. 'Thank you, those of you who accepted the impulse to togetherness. And to those of you who did not . . .'

. . . his eyes were pointed, of course, at Philip . . .

'. . . I hope you soon do become able to hear the call, to allow yourselves to trust. For . . .'

. . . phew, those eyes have moved . . .

'. . . we all know that we are animals. We know we have soft skin. All of us like to feel the breeze upon it or the sun's warmth. And yet so much of the time we shut ourselves away. In houses, upon carpets, behind double glazing, in air-conditioned offices, in cars. All the time witnessing the world outside, if we bother to lift our eyes, through glass. Which means not witnessing it at all. Which means not recognising who we are, creatures among other creatures upon this natural world. Here is a human eye.'

Aargh, thought Philip. Then: oh, just another projected image.

'Here is the eye of a rabbit.'

Yes, that's what it is.

'And a cow.'

Ditto.

'And a rat.'

Again.

'Which would you say is the most tender? Here is a hair on the back of a human hand.'

Indeed.

'Here is a cat's whisker.'

Several cat's whiskers in fact.

'Here is the horn of a snail.'

Where the eyes are, Sue thought knowledgably.

'Which would you say is the most sensitive?'

Cat's whisker, said Philip to himself: would you like me to put up my hand? / Sue was interested: there really does seem to be a lot in common.

'Here is the epidermis of an onion.'

Cells like sandbags.

'Here is the skin of a fish.'

OK, pretty much the same.

'And here is human skin.'

Definitely not, thought Philip. Must be another vegetable. Why is he doing this? I could blurt out and say that's not human skin. I don't want to blurt out and say that's not human skin. / This is, thought Sue, actually quite good. She remembered falling and being caught in the springy cradle that Ash had made of his body.

'Even the skin that wraps us up and keeps us apart from one

another: even that seal around us is so much the same, so much in common. It is not just that such a lot of us is water. Not just our DNA, almost all of it shared with other animals.'

And 60% with a banana, thought Philip as Sue began to feel that she was having an idea.

'All our means of sensing, of touch. All wanting to connect.'

There's a lot that's being left out here, Philip's mind uttered like an examiner, such as for instance: disease, carnivorism, aggression.

'So I say to you: sense the rhythms of the earth. Allow them to enter into you. Live according to their prompting. Notice the trill-ing of the turtle dove and let it lift your spirits. Enjoy the zigzag flight of the fly. Make yourself delicately responsive, like leaves bobbing in the wind.'

Sue thought: this is definitely giving me something.

'Here behind me I have nothing special. Except that in another sense they are the most special things in the world. Because every-thing is the most special thing in the world. In Finland, through the long months of the winter, everything is white. The sea is frozen white; the ground is covered in snow. The people there can't bear it. So they keep little pots of grass on their windowsills so they have something green and living to look at. All of nature is reduced to this littlest of plants. That is what I have for you here. Merely a blade of grass. In each little pot, a blade of grass. Or sometimes two or three because sometimes they can't be separated without damage. And I would like to pass them round now. I would like each of you to take one. Hold it in front of you like this.'

His hands as though in prayer but open, cupped.

'Imagine it is all there is. Feel its presence. Give it a little blow if you would like, to see it waver and spring back at you. Bring it to your lips and let it touch.'

'I'm out of here,' Philip hissed in the direction of Sue's ear. She didn't turn towards him. All she did was mildly nod her head.

'OK then' – he hissed again more crossly – 'I'll wait for you outside.'

Then he was up, reversing sideways away from his chair into the aisle, turning, making his way with shoulders bowed, with his head bent forwards. He pushed through the shutter doors and was hit by the bright, bright light of the perfectly ordinary, somewhat cloudy day outside.

Sue held her little black round plastic pot which held a rubble of blackish earth with a blade of grass rising out of it. Or rather a stem rising out of it which, after an inch, split: one narrow leaf to the right, one to the left, one continuing to push straight up. How long the ones on either side were, comparatively, three times as long as the one in the middle. Perhaps they were older. You could see that in the stem bit they were wrapped around it. No actually down there they formed a continuous sheath which split where the leaves divided. You could see the sort-of welding that had been done there to support the weight. Strong though, she thought, pressing on a side leaf. Odd that she could exert what must, for the blade of grass, be so much pressure, and barely feel it, despite what Ash had said. Actually she couldn't feel it at all, even with her fingertip which was meant to be so sensitive. She wouldn't know that she was touching it if she wasn't looking at it with her eyes.

The lower part of the stem was red like rhubarb. And right down at the bottom there were other blades branching off, one scrunched and curly, the other straight like the main one only growing at an angle and splitting into two not three. Shadowing the scrunched one was a brownish papery frond. A dead bit? Were they all competing? The main shoot with its impressive tripartite structure brutally trampling the bodies of blades less fortunate than itself? Or were they all a sort of family? Or actually one entity, with this wizened frond a residue of an earlier stage of life, like hair that people had cut off, like the skin we are perpetually moulting.

You could see the spreading leaves were grooved. That must be what made them strong. They must have tubes inside them or be like corrugated cardboard. What was puzzling was why what's his name Ash hadn't just sent them outside to look at bits of grass, lots of them out there. Surely somewhat artificial, this having them in pots, exactly the isolationist attitude he said he was against. But maybe that was the point. Maybe you were meant to feel that. Next he'd be asking them to restore their specimens to the meadow from where they'd been so rudely ripped. Who was it who had seen the universe in a grain of sand? But that wasn't what was happening here. Or at least, maybe that was what Ash wanted but it wasn't what she personally was getting from the experience. Because in order to see the universe in a grain of sand you had to triumph over the grain of sand with your imagination. Explode it or expand it or make it translucent or colour it in. You were valuing it by turning it into something that it isn't. Seeing the universe in a grain of sand is disrespectful to grains of sand! Whereas what she was doing here was just simply carefully looking at this bit of grass and seeing what it was. She was being herself and noting all the ways in which the grass was itself, understanding how it was different from her. That's what wouldn't have happened if Ash had made them go up into the field and try to look at the grass there: there was so much of it. That was the real problem. That was the fact of life it was so hard to cope with. There was so much of it. Especially people. She was done with her blade of grass now but how many people could you really look at and think about and get to know over a lifetime. Maybe fifteen? Maybe not even one. And yet there were billions and billions and billions of them. Of us.

Her mind came back to where she was, in the present, on this chair, in this boat, in the company of these people. There was a noise. She looked across at the open-faced blonde woman. The open-faced blonde woman was holding her pot in front of her face exactly as Ash had directed (Sue's pot was now neglected on her knee). The blonde woman's brown-clad forearms inclined towards her face. The twin forked leaves of her specimen touched her lips. Her glistening stubby tongue slid out between them and one of the leaves sank down upon it. The tongue withdrew between the lips taking the grass-blade with it. The tip of the grass-blade stuck out of the mouth on the side nearest Sue; the stem of it must stick out of the mouth on the other side. There was a movement of the jaw, a bite, she was biting the grass. Why was there no scream, no denunciation? Sucked, the tip of grass disappeared between the lips like a snake's tongue. Ash had his eyes closed, that must be why the open-faced woman escaped scot-free. Ash was sitting calm on the edge of the table, holding his pot of grass like a candle, the single slim blade making a line in front of the cleft of his chin and the middle of his mouth and the tip of his nose. Oh, he was the source of the noise, this perpetual low hum, how could he make it continuous, it was as though the air went in one nostril, vibrated his vocal chords and out the other in a continuous flow. The blade of grass wavered in the current of it. The open-faced blonde woman was stirring, standing, reaching for her coat, shifting sideways, edging out. Sue caught the impulse and rose and tagged along. The elderly couple still sat politely, watchful, waiting for the end. Other people still sat there too, holding their little pots of grass. The shutter doors were swinging, creaking; the open-faced blonde woman was gone. Sue pushed on through, and climbed the stairs. Oh there she was, on the bank already, red coat hurrying away on vehement legs. Sue's mind saw her face again, the blade of grass disappearing into it. The look of naughtiness and satisfaction and surprise.

Where was Philip? He was over there, standing by that patient. The skinned bit of fallen tree-trunk was near them like an enormous bone. Which meant that actually there was a scattering of enormous bones, a . . . what was the word . . . an ossuary of them. Which meant that death in the heart of life was definitely the theme of the day given how the thrusting, enormous, elegant, living tree soared triumphantly above. Where was the child? Something in the way Philip and the patient were standing made her step towards them quickly, made her want to interrupt, to get him to look at her, to say something and have him respond. Philip's face was angled downwards confidentially; the patient's face was looking up in trust, beaming warmth and intentness up at him. Sue was nearly in earshot now: 'Hello,' she said, perkily.

'Will you promise me you'll do that,' Philip was urging.

'We'll think about it,' said the patient. She had an aura of power about her, of something held in reserve. 'We will. Thank you.' She had a strong face, high cheekbones, hooked nose. Almost masculine.

'And let me know if there are any developments?'

Philip was ignoring her and focusing on the patient. He was punishing her because she hadn't joined him in leaving ten minutes earlier.

'Yeh.'

What was it that made that face the face of a woman? Just the eyelashes maybe. Not the thin lips.

'OK. See you then.'

At last he seemed to become aware of her and turned. His face spread into a smile, his eyes were soft. 'Sorry.' They were moving away from the patient and the tree-trunk. 'Had to try to explain something for the second time.'

'Where's the little boy?'

'Up there.' He stopped, turned back. They saw the patient still looking at them, only of course she wasn't the patient exactly because the patient was her child. Philip waved. Then he pointed. There was a little black figure standing high, high up.

'Wow.'

The light from the sky behind him must be blurring his edges, making him look slighter than he really is.

'He does the first bit with a rope.'

She could see the rope dangling from a low thick horizontal branch.

'After that he just swarms up.'

Her gaze tried to find the way up through the steep branches.

'That's partly what made me want to speak to the mother.'

He must lever himself, feet going up a branch, hands splayed against the trunk to keep the pressure.

'Did I tell you about them in the autumn, the kid with ADHD? Some of my first patients. When I started to have my suspicions about Adam Hibbert.'

'Too quick to hand out medicines.'

'Yeh, basically, and I raised it at a practice meeting, remember, and got my head bitten off? Because he'd prescribed ritalin to this kid himself rather than passing him on to a clinic and the guidelines are completely clear you shouldn't do that.'

They were wandering along, the greenish river flowing more speedily on their left, the landscape open all around. In the distance beyond the river was the little low-lying agglomeration of The Willows with, behind it, the more massy presence of the town.

Although now, he was thinking, maybe it's a bit more complicated . . .

While in the distance to the right was hazy greyish higher ground, fields, with darker patches of woodland. There was blue sky now, the cloud had disintegrated into puffs, the sun was warm on their cheeks through the chill air and sparkled on the muddy river and here and there on wet bits of the ground.

'So' – he carried on – 'I talked it over with her and said it was entirely reasonable to want to come off the drug. That the dose seemed to me probably too high. And that they should go to the clinic for an expert opinion but also so that a support structure could be put in place. There are parenting skills that can be taught or reinforced. And also really importantly behavioural therapy for the child. Because if the drug isn't controlling his behaviour then he's got to learn how to do it for himself.'

You could see the earth was juicy with winter rain. You could see how everything was ready to go shooting up when the heat of the sun switched on. Well crocuses had already, of course, and snowdrops. There must be buds everywhere, waiting to go whoosh. When, what would it be, when the photons went piling in there, bang bang bang bang bang, lots of little explosions, cruise missiles, or actually more like rain, when a raindrop falls on water and bounces up again bigger and the whole gleaming surface of the water wobbles from its energy. There would be a rain of light on all these plants, setting off the chemistry and they would all go whoosh.

'But they never bloody went. That's what I realised today. They just stopped taking the medication. They responded to what I said, which was very carefully measured, by just stopping taking it. Which wasn't what I said at all.'

'Yeh but . . .'

But Philip was surging on:

'You can see what the kid's like now. It might be OK when he's out here but I dread to think how he behaves in school. Clearly she's involved with that idiot in the boat and they're all let's be natural, medicines are poison.'

'He wasn't quite that bad.'

'Yes he was. Let's all join hands and say "Om." Try forming a warm loving relationship with a killer whale. Or MRSA.'

'I don't think that was . . .'

'I know some of what he said was fine. What we all agree about. Use less energy. Go for more nice walks. What I can't stand is when you go from that to a whole anti-science thing, like when he said that all the enormous endeavour that's being done by scientists across the world didn't really matter, what we need to do is learn to love a blade of grass.'

'My blade of grass was really cute.'

'That attitude leads to the anti-MMR movement which leads to children dying. I just can't stand it.'

They were a little way away from one another now. Sue was looking into his face with a concerned, tilted head, appraising eyes. Her gaze slid off him to the ground.

'Sorry,' he said. And then: 'Shall we get a drink?' The pub sign was just ahead and a path turned off, leading beyond railings to a squat, old building, probably a farmhouse to begin with.

'OK,' she said, blankly.

'Sorry: I need a drink,' he said. They turned off into the garden behind the railing, hands in their pockets, side by side.

Once they had stepped into the shadowy interior where a few people sat here and there, and had said hello to the sprightly barman or landlord, and ordered a pint of dry cider and – 'why not?' – a G&T – 'actually make that a double' – and had said what a nice day it was and 'just going for a walk'; and had, taking their drinks, stepped back out into the sunny chill and chosen a table near the base of a tall, bedraggled pine, they each hooked one leg, then the other, into the conjoined bench-and-table contraption, ending up opposite each other with their knees only about 6 inches distant, their noses a foot-and-a-half apart. He lifted the large cold cylinder and drank, feeling his tongue channel the prickly liquid back to where, gulp after gulp, his mylohyoid contracted and relaxed, his soft palate lifted and fell. She raised her slim, chilly glass and sipped, feeling the sweet, sticky glitter of the liquid fizzle on her tongue.

'So was it an Art thing,' he said, wanting to reach out a tendril towards her, to begin to build a bridge, 'that made you want to go to this' – hippy airhead, he thought, but instead said: 'Ash event?'

'Sort of,' she said. Then she thought: sod it why not? There was an image inside her of him talking to that mother and it had a sort of buzzing around it which resolved into words such as: in a way it's lovely that you get so anxious about your patients but you could also listen to me a bit more. And: I've got a stressful job too. So she thought: sod it, just tell him, and if he makes a scene who cares? And so she said: 'You know the Elton Barfitt exhibition.' She saw uncertainty in his eyes and added: 'In the autumn. Exactly when you were stressing about Janet Stone and Albert and Adam Hibbert and drug company incentives and the conspiracy to prescribe everyone too much medicine. We had a crisis at work then, the artist we'd planned to exhibit, Abm Al Ahmed, pulled out, and we had to conjure up a new show out of nothing.'

'Of course I remember. Sorry. Charlotte had the idea of going to those really radical androgynous artists who don't normally show in galleries.'

'Elton Barfitt.'

'Yeh and you were pretty excited about it.'

She was feeling softer towards him now and spoke more gently. 'That's right. Only it turned out Elton Barfitt didn't want to do a show.'

'I thought you said they did?'

'No I didn't. You said something like "how'd it go" and I just said "it went" and you didn't ask any more so I left it.'

They both thought back to that time. She coming in late, turning, shutting the front door behind her quietly. He slobbing on the sofa, telly on, checking this and that on his phone. She standing in the doorway, undoing the belt of her short black raincoat. Her mouth moving, saying something; he looking up, responding. He standing and moving towards her and reaching out and drawing her into his arms, feeling her chin on his shoulder, kissing her forehead. His sleepiness. Her energy and frustration, the need she felt to find a route to calm and bed, silently, to make a space around what had happened, put it away in a cupboard so she would have at least a chance of sleep. The next morning she had been in a rush as usual and he had been thinking of the day ahead.

'I got the impression,' he said, 'you didn't want to talk about it.'

'Maybe I didn't. But I'm telling you now. What actually happened was that Elton Barfitt said no.'

'Oh,' he said. 'I'm sorry.' He looked straight across at her face which was looking questioningly into his. 'So,' he carried on: 'What's going to . . . ?'

'I don't know.'

'What does Omar . . . ?'

She looked down for a bit. She stroked the side of her glass with her index finger. Then she looked up frankly and said: 'Omar doesn't know.'

'Doesn't know what to do either?'

'No. He doesn't know that Elton Barfitt said no.'

'What?'

'Charlotte told him they said yes.'

'What? She's fucking weird that woman! Why did she tell him that?'

Sue felt she wanted to downplay it in the face of his astonishment. She said: 'To buy time?'

Then she found she wanted to say more. 'Charlotte, basically Charlotte couldn't believe it. She couldn't bring herself to accept that it was true. So, well then also she said that it wouldn't make any difference. Since Omar wanted to keep himself out of the whole transaction there was no danger he'd find out and, because that was the case' – she was repeating the argument that Charlotte had put to her – 'a bit of a delay would make no difference. Because the only alternative was for the gallery to go dark. And Charlotte absolutely doesn't want that. And neither do I.'

She was looking at him defensively now, wondering if he had understood.

'But to misrepresent them to your boss . . .'

She felt a scratch of irritation inside her, nails on slate.

'And,' he said: 'Isn't there, shouldn't there be publicity? I mean,' he said, 'if Omar thinks there's going to be a show then he'll want to publicise it; and you can't publicise it without them finding out.'

Sue said: 'That's just it. Charlotte told him that the show had to be kept secret. For the time being.'

'How's that gonna . . . ?'

'I know. I really don't know how she pulled it across him. But the argument was' – she laid it out carefully– 'that, because Elton Barfitt haven't exhibited in a gallery before, they want to make this one a surprise. So that what we are to do is keep that summer slot as to-be-announced. And then – oh, I think she said that the announcement was itself going to be part of the event, or something.'

'And he bought it?'

'I know,' she said. And then: 'I think what Charlotte thinks is going to happen is that Elton Barfitt are going to change their mind. I don't know why she thinks that: they seemed very determined to me.'

'OK.'

'So I'm pretty sure, she hasn't told me this, but I'm pretty sure her plan is, sometime soon, now we've left it for a bit, to go back and ask them again, make a last-minute appeal.'

'Get on her knees and beg.'

'Yup' – Sue was feeling cheerier now – 'because, you know what she's like, she's got this obsessive idea that she's got a sort of special understanding with them, if only she could make them see it.'

'But' – something was occurring to Philip: 'It's been, what' – he thought about it – 'nearly three months since you had that meeting.'

'I know, and so . . . I'm not really sure how realistic that plan is.' Sue's eyes were wandering around the garden. 'Hence' – she conjured up a smile – 'Plan B. Which is, well, what we'd always said officially between ourselves, or unofficially-officially, was that we also needed to work out an alternative. Because actually – well this is what I think, but Charlotte's not so sure – actually Omar was open to alternatives when we had our crisis meeting back in October. But because I hadn't had enough time I couldn't pitch anything in the right way to persuade him. But what I hope is that if I get the chance, with Charlotte's help, really to put together a killer proposal, then, in a month or two, Charlotte can say: Look Elton Barfitt have pulled out too – sorry! – and we can hit him with this alternative, and he might actually let me do it. So that's the possibility I'm' – she had a sudden falling feeling – 'holding on to.'

'OK,' he said, trying to be encouraging: 'That's good. That's something. I mean' – he said, trying harder – 'that's the sort of thing you've wanted, isn't it: that's what you've felt frustrated at not being able to do?'

'Yes that's right, and even if this comes to nothing,' she said, 'just having to think about it . . . well, actually just having to think about it is exhilarating.'

'So that's why you brought me to sit through Ash?'

'Yeh, pretty much. What I was thinking. Well, you know, it's the sort of thing I always think. I want there not to be an Artist with a capital A because that stops people really seeing, really sensing what's in front of them.'

'Yeh because they're . . .'

'They get caught up in the personality, in the body of work. They want to be told what the artist is trying to do.'

'Instead of just looking for themselves.'

'Yeh, so anyway, I wanted to do something, do you remember once we had a conversation about EEGs, and ECGs?'

' . . .'

'In the car once. There'd been a crash.'

Philip remembered.

'So what I'd been thinking anyway,' Sue pressed on, 'was that I wanted to do something with those. Amplified heartbeats. Projections of EEGs. So that people become aware of themselves in a new way. Do you see what I mean? So that they are the audience, but they are also the artwork.'

'OK.'

'But I was worried that might seem a bit narrow. A bit, well, it's obviously inward-looking, isn't it – but I wanted also to try to do something about sensation, about how things come into us the whole time. About this weird way' – and suddenly it really did seem weird, suddenly her head seemed to stretch and stretch, only it wouldn't stretch enough, it wouldn't go transparent – 'this weird way that everything gets into us. You know, we are in the world; but it is also in us. What we see with our eyes, it is in us. What we hear on the radio, goes into our heads. It's amazing. I mean' – she grinned, chuckled, let her voice tumble downwards from the heights of wonder it had soared to – 'it's also obvious. It's everyday. But it's still amazing.'

Philip was looking at her attentively, admiringly.

'So actually I think Ash has given me some ideas.'

'You wanna be careful, though.'

'Yup.'

'It was a bit, well, pious, wasn't it?'

'Yeh I know, but still basically . . .'

'And some of it was frankly wrong. Like the picture he said was human skin, it wasn't human skin at all!'

'Wasn't it?'

'No it was a vegetable. A cabbage or something. It was outrageous.'

'But the point he was making didn't really depend on . . .'

'I'm just saying, be careful with it, be careful what you take from him.'

'Yeh sure.' She felt a gap was opening again between them. 'Anyway,' she said: 'I'm letting it settle. I'll see what's left. It's all still pretty fluid. And it may not work. And even if it does come together Omar may not like it. And then anyway he may see through Charlotte, and if he does that then I'll be implicated too and I don't know how that'll play out. I simply don't know.' There was a sudden change of feeling in her cheeks, the seeping sensation of tears about to come. 'I mean it could . . . I just don't know.'

'You should have told me.'

'Well, I am telling you. I dunno, I didn't . . . it wasn't . . . I didn't really know what there was to tell.'

'Well you could have shared your worry about it. You know that's what' – he reached a hand across towards one of hers, took it – 'that's what . . .' He smiled. He was looking sentimentally into her eyes.

'Yeh yeh,' she said, her unhappiness evaporating: 'I've told you now.'

He was already – worriedly, indulgently – imagining the worst: her coming home, denounced and sacked. He would be there for her. He would take her in his arms. They could both live on his income, easily. He would be solid and she would lean on him.

'Anyway, fuck it,' she said. 'The whole thing is basically angled against everything Omar believes in so if he doesn't like it, he doesn't like it.'

She saw Omar's face going green, inflating, becoming

translucent it was so stretched, until: pop! it had gone, and then the gallery was next to start, going bulbous, growing apple – melon – watermelon – boom – at which flames went up, the punkest possible hairstyle of flames, iridescent strands shooting, arcing, the flames now darkening, becoming turbid, flexing like muscles, tawny like the mane of a lion. And away from it all she walked, alone. She saw herself, a tiny figure, dressed in black, the explosive light behind her. The edges of her squeezed and blurred by the light like that boy she had seen against the sky.

'But maybe,' she said 'he won't get it. Maybe . . . it'll all . . . be . . . fine.'

She was swinging off the bench, standing up bouncily; she spun so she was facing towards him: 'Dunno!'

She took a step backwards away from him. Feeling pulled away from him by the work and the uncertainty that lay ahead she sent a smile out towards him, trying to lasso him with well-meaningness and warmth. 'Come on!' – she cried.

He began levering himself out of the bench-and-table. He put his thumb inside his pint glass, pressed it against the sticky surface as he stretched his fingers down towards her little glass of ex-G&T. But on the edge of his field of vision he could see her still walking backwards away from him, so he decided not to take the glasses back in. He left them on the table and trotted after her. Catching up with her he reached for her hand, and their shoulders bumped, and for a moment his arm was around her, and then they were holding hands again.

They made their way out through the gate and shortcutted through a clump of apple trees where the ground was tussocky.

Then they were on the path beside the river again, the landscape open all around, the sky beginning to tinge with evening as the look of the world darkened and flattened: it was as though the atmosphere were sucking its colours from the ground. Along the river, light puddled and wobbled in a million metamorphic pools on the oily-looking water. The birds had quietened and there was no breeze; only the gentle oceanic roar of the ring-road a mile away. They came to a lock, wider than the one upstream, with a narrow weir beside it where the river poured shiningly in a fast unchanging arc which broke into bubbles and squabbles and swirls and splashes at its foot. Chill prickles of spray touched their cheeks as they crossed the wide flat iron bridge above it.

'This was the line of a railway!' – Philip announced.

'Was it?'

'Look at it.'

Sue saw the banked-up path that continued from the bridge ahead of them through the meadow.

'It goes to where the railway is now. There must have been points there.' He turned. 'And look behind us it carries on beyond that fence.' He turned back. 'You can see it's got a very shallow gradient. Right from the beginning of the meadow it's beginning to rise to get enough height for this bridge.'

'A viaduct.'

'It must have been a branch line going somewhere. It must have been abolished by what's his name in the 60s, Beech.'

'Beeching.'

'Yeh when all that network was abolished.'

'And they built Spaghetti Junction instead.'

115

The two of them stepped from the bridge onto the long grav-
elly and grassy causeway. Gloom gathered upon the low flat land
on either side. Half a mile in front was the edge of the town, with
The Willows clustered along it to the left. In the sky ahead of
them a layer of mole-grey stratocumulus blocked the sun. Twin
solitary little figures, they walked on. Now, in the sky ahead, the
sun a hundred and forty-nine million miles away let its shocking
orange lip drop beneath the line of cloud eleven miles away. And
then amazingly quickly the whole blobby sun was there in front
of them, persimmon-red, looming above the tiny houses. It
seemed on pause; and yet by the time they had crossed the modern
railway and turned left down Helium Avenue it was gone, leaving
an umber and ochre slick that could be glimpsed through the
chinks between the houses, and a blueish brightness high up in
the middle of the sky.

Kitsch, Sue was thinking. No room for kitsch in Ash's world.
Because this is indeed ghastly. She was taking in once more, as so
many times before, the line of too-narrow mock-Victorian semis
with too-little windows and too-uniform brickwork and too-tidy
arrangements of flowerbeds and enormous pots where inappropriate plants like palm and eucalyptus grew. It is fake. It is all wrong.
And yet it is also kind of lovable. You can step back from it and look
at it and think: so much good will has gone into this disaster. Be
charitable. Take the intention, not the deed. No, that's not right:
take the intention plus the way it has gone wrong. Relish the
wrong note.

Maybe it is a bit too concrete, Philip was thinking. Maybe it is a
little bit of Dubai in middle England. But people have got to have

houses. What I don't think he took enough account of is things like insulation and, OK, it's probably artificial materials but without it we would all be worse off. And the planet would be. It's like penicillin. Miraculous discovery. Miraculous drug. Or something simple like just having your appendix out. So straightforward. Who would want to live in a world where you couldn't do that?

But maybe now we shouldn't, Sue was thinking. Because of the environmental emergency actually maybe now we shouldn't find enjoyment in the amazing American ancient gas-guzzling car with shark fins, or those ridiculous completely kitsch SUVs that are 30% too big for human habitation. Maybe we should abandon irony. Look at it all with simple horror. Because now there is no time for forgiveness. The what's it called, the tolerance, the space in which to be tolerant, has disappeared.

They were at their front door. They opened it, and went in, and set about getting ready for the party at George Emory's. Yikes was that the time already? So Sue quickly showered and Philip splashed water on his face and Sue gave some attention to her hair and did a bit of make-up while Philip pulled on trousers and a shirt, really the sort of clothes he would wear to work, only with no tie, and perhaps the shirt was a little brighter, as, meanwhile, Sue shimmied her way into a bias-cut black crêpe slip-dress and reached behind her head to clip on a necklace of marble-sized shiny steel balls. He did like it when she dolled herself up, allowed herself to perform her femininity, as she put it, though he could see why the crisp androgynous trousers and tops were better for day to day – when in fact there was also a frisson in knowing that under the no-nonsense outfits was the beautiful tender woman's body that only he was allowed to hold; but still – as she came towards him in her bare feet, put a hand flat on his chest and bobbed up on tiptoe to peck a kiss on his cheek, and as he let his hand slide down the declivity of her back so that his fingertips rested on the nub of her coccyx, he couldn't help feeling that it was really lovely when she flaunted herself a little, it titillated him. In his mind an image flashed up of her lying contentedly in Ash's arms; but then she was levering herself into some unusually formal shoes, and looking at him and reiterating in her mind her established thought that she did actually quite like the way he had no interest in style; that all he was aiming for, and succeeding in getting, was a look of being courteously smart. Now the taxi was hooting and they were downstairs, coats, out of the box of their house and, after a moment of being in the open, into the box of the car. Smoothly and slowly the taxi drove, to use less petrol Philip thought, as Sue looked out at the black-and-white world tinged amber by the streetlights. Through the centre of the old town they were conveyed along the one-way system and around gyratories until, before long, they were out into the more real dark of the countryside. Here there was speed and braking and turns and dips and rises until they were into the village where there were streetlights again.

'Any idea where it is?' asked the driver.

'It's the rectory so I suppose near the church.'

There was the church on higher ground. It had a square castellated tower. Oh and look, there were balloons at the gate in the old stone wall here, how sweet. 'This must be it.' So they were out in the air again, chillier now, and crunching along a gravel driveway behind dark evergreen bushes. It was a tall fat house with George's long grey car parked in front of the steep-roofed porch. Victorian presumably. They must have built a new rectory then.

Philip reached for Sue, draped his arm across her back so that her shoulder came in under his armpit as he hugged her to him: he kissed her on the side of her head and she with her fingers squeezed his hip-bone on the other side of him. Then he had pulled the bell and they were standing somewhat formally apart from one another. The door swung open and there was, not George Emory, but a girl. Pale pink twinset, black mini-skirt, thick black tights. 'Hello,' she said. Blonde bob.

'I'm Philip Newell, George's colleague. This is Sue.' She must be early twenties.

'George is fussing in the kitchen.' Slightly raised eyebrows. Pencilled. A warm look in her round face. 'Do come in.'

Their feet rang on the flagstones. There was space above them and around them.

'Let me take your coats.'

Through an open door to the right was the room where the party seemed mainly to be. The low light of twinkling candles, the swell and fade of conversation, the sporadic chink of a bottle on a glass or a glass on a plate. The young woman took their coats in one of her arms and, with the other, pushed open a door on the left. Among the shadows inside was a desk where other coats lay harvested.

'I'm Tasha by the way.'

Beyond it were bookshelves that went right up to the ceiling.

'Thanks.'

They turned and moved into the room where the people were.

Tasha went off through the room and out of a door in a different corner to get them drinks. It was a long room going from the front to the back of the house.

'Who was she?' Sue asked.

Big enough for a grand piano to squat at the far end in front of French windows.

'I guess we've a choice of lover or daughter.'

There was a dangly cut-glass chandelier in the middle of the ceiling. There was a complicated cornice.

Tasha brought their drinks. Sue had noticed what seemed to be a really quite good turn-of-the-century painting over the mantelpiece. A landscape with the blank, white, dominant wall of a farmhouse off centre. Couldn't be James Orr? No, surely an imitator. Philip had noticed Sushma and Jackie and David clumped in a corner. Sushma and Jackie had their shoulders to the rest of the room. Their heads turned out to look and then turned back to comment. They shifted, smiled as he and Sue moved towards them.

'No Amanda?' – he asked.

'She's always late,' said Jackie.

'Usually arrives . . .' said Sushma.

'Usually arrives just as everyone else is leaving,' said Jackie.

'Like at the Christmas party, do you remember?' – said Sushma: 'Only got there half way through.'

'When the rest of us were already totally wasted,' said Jackie.

'Especially Dr Kaiser,' said Sushma, mildly.

'How does she get to work on time in the morning?' – Philip managed to contribute.

'She has six alarm clocks,' David put in authoritatively in his soft voice with wide, ironic eyes. 'And a wake-up call. And a cockerel in her back garden.'

'She lives in a flat.'

'Her balcony then.'

'This is Sue,' said Philip; 'and this,' he said to Sue as she glanced from one to the other warmly, 'is three quarters of the back office.'

'And front office,' said Sushma.

'Front and back office,' put in David, bluntly.

'Or SWAT team as we like to call them,' said Philip.

'We do our best to keep the rabble in order,' said Sushma.

'The doctors, that is,' said Jackie.

'Well,' Sue ventured: 'You've made Philip feel really at home.'

'Oh that's no problem,' said Sushma.

'He's a sweetie,' said Jackie.

'Unlike some others we could mention,' said David.

'Philip!' – a voice came booming. Philip turned. Of course it was George.

'Welcome,' announced George. 'And you must be . . .' – turning to Sue.

'Sue,' she said.

'That's right, Sue,' George answered as though confirming it. 'Great man,' he said, looking at Philip; 'and great woman.' Philip saw David wince and felt a smile inside.

'May I?' George was topping up their glasses.

'What a lovely house,' said Sue.

'Thank you.'

'I love that painting. Is it anything to do with the Glasgow School?' – she asked. 'It's not James Orr, is it?'

'Do you know I don't know what it is,' he said, turning, looking it up and down. 'It belonged to my late wife. She was the one with taste. With an eye for . . .' Suddenly he was at a loss. 'Well, with an eye, I suppose. I just . . .' His eyes were aiming past them all, over David's shoulder. 'Anyway,' he said. 'Must circulate. Topping people up. Do make yourselves at home.'

He lumbered away to another group of people where they heard his rich voice rise, 'surely not?', and saw his arm lift to hold the bottle high up, mock-threateningly on display.

The office threesome seemed to have recombined. Philip and Sue were standing a step away from them. How many people were in the room? Four, seven, twelve, seventeen, plus them nineteen, oh and then twenty-two.

'The men,' Sue said, 'are all fat and the women are all thin.'

'Except me.'

She twinkled at him, not replying.

'I think it's partly the cut of their jackets.' Apart from them, and of course Sushma and Jackie, and David, oh and the girl who had opened the door, everyone was of George's generation. Or rather the men were and the women were generally younger. The men wore tweedy jackets and grey flannel trousers – except for the one over there who is in bright yellow cords. The women are in pastel dresses which pull in or are belted round their waists. The men's hair is grey; the women's hair is not. Oh, but there are a younger couple, dressed in black. And there is . . . ' Come and meet Sara,' Philip said.

Sara was in a group, listening and nodding. Philip touched her on the upper arm. She turned and her face warmed, taking them both in. And then they were all three chatting happily, about living where they were, and commuting, and the pressures of the job, and Sue's work. Sara was asking about public funding and visitor numbers and then onwards to ethnicity; at which Sue explained, as she often did, that the difficulty was with the institution, with the place that was cut out in society for art to occupy, and therefore how people looked at it and indeed what kind of people came into the gallery in the first place. That while there was obviously lots of art that was very alert to ethnicity and provocative about it, Ofili for instance or Al Ahmed, it was true that it tended to get anaesthe-tised as soon as it was put on display in the big, institutional space, frankly very often the dead space, of the gallery. And it was the same with people working there. So that even though Omar, obvi-ously, counted as ethnic minority he had actually turned into a pretty conservative figure, culturally speaking – and probably he'd been forced to go that way because of the pressures put on him by the institution.

It does make a difference not drinking alcohol, Philip thought, noticing the green juice in Sara's glass, to the sort of thing you want to talk about. Listen to.

'There is still a lot of prejudice, I think, in this country,' Sara was saying. 'People know they should not say things, know they shouldn't behave like that. I admit there is the BNP but on the whole people do know. Still, there is hidden prejudice. But it comes out when they visit the doctor.'

'Because we are like confessors,' Philip said.

'Yes, there is that,' Sara said, welcoming the thought as though she had not heard it before.

'Though partly it is a generational thing,' Philip said. 'Our older patients really grew up in a different world.'

'I just don't think that's really an excuse,' said Sue.

'I smile sometimes because, with me,' said Sara, 'patients who don't know me, first of all they think they are going to see a man, because I am a doctor, and then they think I am going to be European because of my name. Actually all the fascists choose me! When they come in I see the shock in their eyes. Sometimes they gulp and try to carry on. Say if there is a sexual problem. We get to the moment when I say: so are you going to get your dong out then? Actually that's not what I say, I say: if you'd like to lie on the couch I'll need to take a look. They simply say no.' There was amusement in her voice but also an edge of contempt. 'Or their faces seize up. Like they are in short circuit, you know as if they are trying to say something but can't? So I say: in that case I cannot help you. And they absolutely don't mind. The infection will spread but they don't mind. Compared to how terrible it would be if an Asian woman touched their willie! Because obviously it would shrivel up. Dry up and collapse into powder. They would crawl off and die in the corner rather than that.'

She was declaiming now and Sue and Philip were her audience.

'Actually those ones I tell to go out and make an appointment with another doctor, for instance nice Dr Newell. But there are other ones who walk in and suddenly forget what is the matter with them. You can see it happening between when they open the door and when they sit down. Their poor little minds are racing. Maybe they say: I have got a pain in my shoulder. So I sit them down and check the flexion and rotation. There is no problem. They say: it's gone now, it's completely disappeared. Good, I say. I smile sweetly. I tell them that if they have any more excruciating shoulder pain they should come back. They never come back.'

'Isn't that pretty depressing?' said Sue.

'In a way,' said Sara. 'Yes in a way it is. But also,' she carried on, 'it braces me. Because it shows I matter, you know, that it matters that it's me who is there doing that job. Just by being me I make, only a little bit, but a little bit of a difference.'

'Dr Kaiser.' It was a small man in a tight red v-neck jumper. 'And you must be Dr Newell.' The small man held out his hand. 'Graham Epsom, kiss.'

'Kiss?' Philip said, shaking it.

'Clinical and Integration Solutions.'

Oh, CIS.

'Exciting times,' said Graham Epsom.

'Egypt?' – said Sue.

'Well yes that too of course.' Graham Epsom smiled at her but did not say hello. 'I was thinking more of the advent of GP commissioning.'

'Graham,' said Sara Kaiser, 'is one of the people who are going to make millions on the back of it.'

'We are only here to facilitate,' said Graham. 'You have skills in the consulting room. We have skills in systems management. If we are really going to run with this fantastic opportunity, really going to deliver radically improved outcomes for patients, then the two skill-sets need to work together. Because at the moment they don't. It must be very frustrating for you' – he turned to Philip again – 'to at the moment make your referrals and sometimes they get lost, there are long delays, sometimes they even get rejected.'

'I find it works pretty well in fact,' said Philip. 'In fact the only difficulties I've had are caused by factors which, so far as I understand it, are going to get worse under the new system.'

'Well in fact . . .' Graham Epsom was starting to say.

'Like for instance, I make a perfectly straightforward referral and it gets rejected. I make a referral based on the clinical evidence. Using my skill as a doctor. And it gets rejected by a manager. Who probably isn't a qualified doctor. And who absolutely certainly has not seen my patient.'

'That's exactly what the new system is designed to resolve.'

'No because . . .'

'Would you mind telling me' – Graham Epsom was setting himself up as the expert – 'what condition it was?'

'Cataract,' said Philip, hostility rigidifying inside him. 'In an elderly patient. It didn't meet the mathematical criteria for sight-loss but it was causing intense distress. Stopping her watching television, for instance: she said the blurriness was making her feel dizzy and sick. Absolutely crystal-clear case for surgery. It was rejected! And the nod and the wink said try again when it's got worse. So . . .'

He was aware that Sue and Sara had moved away. He could hear Sara's voice behind him saying '. . . the demonisation of the Muslim Brotherhood . . .'

'. . . so it doesn't save anyone any money in the long run. It makes an elderly lady suffer more, for longer. And it's only done because of an accountant who wants to balance this month's books.'

'Well, actually it's done because of the severe limitations on the public finances. It's done because there isn't enough money to pay for everything that it would be nice to do.'

'This isn't something it would be nice . . .'

'But let's leave that aside.' Graham Epsom was being airy once again. 'To get back to your point. Once you've got control of your own budget, you can make that sort of decision for yourself.'

'I don't want to have to make that sort of decision. I want to be able to help the patient. I don't want to be thinking the whole time: is this cost effective?'

'Well maybe you should because what thinking is this cost effective actually means is: is this in the best interests of all my patients as a whole. OK? What your position ends up as is: I'd spend my whole budget just to help this one patient who happens to be sitting here before me. And then what about the next one?'

'It's such a long way from that,' said Philip wearily. 'It's a straightforward, cheap operation. They do it in villages in Africa.'

But here was George again with the raised bottle of champagne. 'Recruiting?'

'Your young colleague is totally unreconstructed,' said Graham Epsom.

'Uncorrupted, you mean,' said George Emory, topping up the glasses. 'Graham,' he said to Philip, 'is a necessary evil.'

'Maybe I'm . . .'

'The system is changing. I completely agree with what I am sure you have been saying, that all we want to do is treat our patients. Mr Epsom is going to leave us free to do just that. Aren't you Graham.'

'And make sure you earn some decent money in the process.'

'I don't . . .'

But George was saying: 'It's nearly time for the fireworks.'

Fireworks?

George pressed on: 'Could I ask you both to help? I have been meaning to invest in one of those computerised systems the Australians are so good at but for the moment it's slave labour. Sorry.' He looked from one to the other of them appealingly. Then: 'I've got helmets.'

He turned and found his way through to a door at the back of the room. Graham Epsom followed; and Philip followed him. Oh, but here was Amanda who must just have arrived. They were in a back hallway with the kitchen beyond it. He could see Sue in there, pale in the bright light, talking to one of the couple dressed in black. He stepped out into the chill and the darkness.

'They're going out to do the fireworks,' said the young woman.

'Fireworks?' said Sue.

'Every year, ever since . . . you know this is the anniversary of when mum died?'

'No I didn't, I'm sorry, I didn't know.' Sue felt the need to add: 'I hadn't met George before this evening.'

'He doesn't tell people, doesn't want to be morbid.' She put a weight on that word, sort of twisted it. She must have had quite a lot to drink. 'But that's why we have to have the fireworks.'

The voice was higher now, spiralling. 'When mum died I was six and Tasha was eight. And dad faced, I can understand it now, the terrible problem of what to do on the anniversary. So we did some remembering, and all that. Visited the horrible garden of rest. And then we came back and had fireworks. He must have got them cheap left over from Guy Fawkes. There were the two of us little girls, and him, having fireworks. And crying. There were the explosions up in the air, the white and the red and the green and the gold, and the sparkles came down, and do you see because I was looking up at it through tear-filled eyes they all mixed together and it was like . . . it was like the whole universe was crying too.'

'It must have been very hard.'

'It was. Still is to be honest. Though I know it's a bit pathetic to say so after a decade.'

'No.'

'Tasha's better at it than me. She gets on with things. She's better at helping dad. But with me it's like, once mum was taken away from us why shouldn't everything else be? You can never trust anyone. And also you can never trust any thing. Which means, you can never really be happy. Even after all this time. Because you know there might be termites eating away at it from underneath and then – bang! – the whole floor you are standing on will disappear.'

She was standing leaning against the edge of the worktop. She had been looking down as though focusing on Sue's uncomfortable shoes. But now she raised her head, stared into Sue's face with her watery, red-rimmed eyes, then looked away, across through the open door, then back towards the dark window where all she could probably see was the two of them and the kitchen reflected. Her head moved slowly then came to a juddery halt. Now she was reaching for her glass. She started to raise it but put it back.

'Dad feels the same way. I know this and I don't think Tasha does. That's why dad and me are closer to one another even though Tasha is nicer to him. It's what makes him so big. Not big physically though he is' – she admitted – 'fatter than he used to be. But the way he asserts himself. With that loud voice. The way he's got' – here her accent shifted a bit to something Essexey – 'so plummy. It's like he's persuading himself everything is more real than it is, more solid. Like he's persuading himself he's still here.'

Her voice was sliding and she seemed about to sob: Sue reached out, held her shoulder.

'It's alright,' the young woman said. 'Because he blames himself' – she was carrying on the story – 'for not having spotted it in time.'

'What did she – what was it?'

'Breast cancer. The usual,' she added harshly. 'But treatments weren't so good back then. And anyway' – she was speaking fiercely now – 'it wasn't his fault. He can't screen his whole family for everything the whole time just because he's a doctor. But because he's a doctor he won't accept there was nothing he could have done. And because he won't accept there was nothing he could have done he lives with blaming himself. And because he blames himself he does this larger than . . .'

But here was George Emory, clashing the tines of a fork against a wine glass, calling 'Fireworks! Fireworks!' to the tune of 'roll-up, roll-up'. People in the room across the way were murmuring, stir-ring, picking up or putting down their glasses, reaching for handbags, saying 'Do we need coats?' Slowly, sporadically, they made their way out through the narrow back door and found chairs or places to stand on the stone terrace outside. Sue and George's younger daughter came out last.

In front of them, beyond the groups of watching people, the greyish space of the lawn. Crouching shadows detached themselves from the surrounding shadow and moved and then dissolved back into the surrounding shadow once more. Philip must be one of them, which? It was like freeze-frame when they moved; your brain must be struggling to make sense of the exiguous signals from your eyes. Beyond the greyishness, the real absorbent black of a wall of trees. Above, of course, the sky. As Sue looked, her eyes focused or sharpened or whatever it was they did with the, that's it, cones giving way to rods. Mistiness receded and cold, unimaginably distant points of light emerged. Though actually if you really looked, if you really gave your mind up to it, you could possibly start to see how far away they really were.

A figure was coming forward on the shadow-lawn. George, his big body. 'Ladies and gentlemen,' he said; 'it's childish of me I know. But I do like fireworks. Especially . . .' – he let the word hang in the air – 'in February. When we are the only people in the whole country, probably the whole world' (pause) 'to be having them.' There was a rustle of applause.

Now the voice from the shadows became more grave. 'Those of you who know me well, also know, that fireworks this evening are a hallowed ritual. We send winter scampering away, shivering. Scare it off down into its burrow. And we welcome the glorious spring.'

His daughter was bending towards Sue's ear, murmuring: 'He never tells the truth.'

'In one moment' – George was concluding – 'the mayhem will begin!'

More claps.

The misty figures were moving among the shadows of the lawn. Then they were still. You had to hold the positions of last-seen movement in your mind to persuade yourself you knew where they were. A flame. A pause, and then the familiar, surprising, sudden whoosh! – the watching heads rotating upwards to try to follow its trajectory. The moment of waiting silence and then: bang, bright white points of light expanding through the sky, luminous join-the-dots for, what might it be, a chrysanthemum; only now they had become little lines of light, or was that her vision tiring of them, no longer seeing them properly? Or on the other hand perhaps getting used to them, seeing them right for the first time? Sue shut her eyes and the little lines were still there inside them, moving within her at the same speed as they must be moving outside; when she opened her eyes would they coincide? She opened her eyes and the sky was black.

Only: bang, a green explosion! And bang, a red! And clatter clatter clatter a cacophony of spattering gold! What it all did in fact was shut out the terrifying distance of the stars. The billions and billions of them, billions and billions of miles away. Here were these man-made sparkles at a distance of a hundred metres and they were brighter, they were loud.

Wieiah, wieaih, waieaih, vertiginously whirling, whining worms!

So what it said was: concentrate on what is near. Be thrilled and moved by what is near. That was what they were meant to convey to the little mourning girls. Here are these lights which are so beautiful. They soar and fade and die away, and that is sad. But look, here is another one. And each one is an individual. Each one can be remembered.

Wahay, a release of wriggling whistling incandescent spermy globs!

Whereas actually if you think of how many people there really are in the world they are more like the billions of distant unimaginable stars.

So Sue thought. Or so Sue thought to begin with. But soon the sparkles and splurts of light, the kerchings and kerbooms, the splats and peonies and diadems and scattered pearls, the rhythm of it all, and the pleasant smell, came into her body and smoothed the thoughts away. Ker-bang, the gallery was exploding again, and ta-trang, Palm Jumeirah erupted into a million, beautiful, all-but immaterial sparks, and ger-whoosh, Philip was spurting hotly on her tummy, and wa-la-la-la she and Charlotte and Elton Barfitt and Omar Olagunju were morris dancing merrily clanging tambourines. These were the traces that the reaction of potassium nitrate, sulphur and carbon released in her mind as bang! they produced nitrogen and carbon dioxide gases and potassium sulphide.

As carbon and oxygen formed vroom! carbon dioxide and energy so that

$V(t = 0)$ = whoosh!

. . . and $NaNO_3$ jigged with $BaCl^+$

. . . until $V(t = t_1)$ = rising, cresting, until

Boom! – so that x(t) = weilahlulay!

and $\sin \theta \cos \varphi$, v, $(t -$

wowee and

$$\frac{vo2\ \sin \alpha \cos \alpha}{2G} = \quad \text{slowing so beautifully,}$$

t –, fading so T) cos gently,

so quietly,

light, G $(t - \text{fading to T})^2/ 2$ nothing,

dying away.

So physics and chemistry performed their destiny while, on the wet cheeks of the younger daughter of George and the late Mrs Emory, the blurry, reflected colours shone.

FORTY-SEVEN HOURS IN APRIL

As Philip pulled open the surgery door and stepped out into the warmish, breezy air, he had to crease his eyes against the light; and when Charlotte pushed open the door of her flat, Sue, following her in, admired the afternoon sunbeams angled through high windows.

Philip was holding a folded piece of paper, for, on his way out, Jackie had called: 'This came for you'; and Sue carried a little grey holdall which she dumped on the floor before pressing on into the ample living-dining-kitchen area: 'What a nice place.'

Having walked a bit, Philip saw that attractive pub on the other side of the road and thought, sod it, why not, even if I do bump into a patient, for there was a terrace with tables on it lit by the sun. Meanwhile, Charlotte was saying: 'You can sleep on the sofa' which was squashy and wide 'or else . . . double up with me: the bed's quite big.'

As Philip got his pint of lager from the bar, Charlotte was looking into her tall grey fridge and calling out: 'White wine?' And as Philip found a place, dragging one of the chairs away from its table so that, when he sat, he could rest his head against the softened brick of the pub wall, Sue stood on Charlotte's little balcony looking down at the canal and along to the plaza where the bars were and across to the similar flats opposite.

Philip hooked his thumb under the sellotape that held the folded paper shut, and yanked as Sue came in and went to her bag and rootled until she found a notebook and pen. Philip gave up yanking and instead began to tear carefully along the edge of the sellotape as Sue sat at Charlotte's circular glass table, reaching for her goblet and dropping the notebook in front of her with a bang.

The handwriting on the folded paper was jagged, big. There were two sheets, in fact. He lifted one and scanned to the bottom of the other for the signature. Janet Stone. Right. A little spurt of adrenalin from his internal carburettor. He took a pull of his pint and settled back to read as Sue was saying 'So here we are.'

'Yup,' said Charlotte briskly.

'And it was a final, definite no?'

'Yup,' said Charlotte, as though she were thinking it over: 'A . . . final . . . definite . . . no.' And then, quickly, callously: 'Elton Barfitt – who are they?'

Philip realised with relief that Janet was telling him that Albert had in fact been to the behavioural therapist, and that she had in fact been to the support group, and things were going OK. Not that there weren't still bad days. To tell the truth, every day was a struggle. But she felt she could cope. And she felt it was worth it.

Because Albert was still her little boy. Not a zombie. When you pushed them even the school admitted it was nice for him to be lively so long as it didn't get out of bounds. So you were right to be firm with me, Dr Newell. And I'm sorry if I didn't show respect.

Sue meanwhile was saying: 'So it's plan B.'

'Yup,' said Charlotte.

'You think we've got a chance? – that Omar, if we pull something really good together, there's a chance he'll give us the go-ahead?'

'I hope so,' said Charlotte, suddenly turning quiet and wan. She was looking out through the French windows: 'All we can do is try. So what I say' – she brought her attention back into the room, glanced at Sue, spoke vehemently – 'is: you'd better have some good ideas, girl.'

Sue didn't know how to reply.

'What we'll do,' said Charlotte, methodical now, 'is get the thing together, see how it looks – then work out how to handle it.'

Sue wondered: 'Will there be a budget?'

'Same pot as for Al Ahmed.'

'I thought that was ring-fenced for . . .'

'Oh, it's alright. Anyway if there's a problem I can always cover it. Let's not worry about it.'

'You can cover it?'

'Little rich girl,' Charlotte said. 'But it's not going to come to that. Anyway' – she called out teasingly – 'you're married to a doctor!'

'Not married.'

'No but . . .'

'What's that got to do with it?' Sue was suddenly prickling with irritation. 'Charlotte, we're talking about work. An exhibition in a public gallery. I mean, we're not meant to have to contribute, I mean we shouldn't.' It really was a bizarre suggestion.

'No, OK, OK. I was just saying. Just offering.'

'Sure. No . . . thank you,' said Sue, softening. Then: 'So you have money from your parents?'

'Yup. Well, sometimes. From my dad. He bought me this.' Charlotte gestured around her with a queenly wave. Then she shrugged her shoulders, grimaced. 'They've got too much of it. It's' – she looked up smilingly – 'a social duty.'

At which Sue said: 'Nice duty.' And then: 'Shall we start?'

In the sun 53½ miles away Philip was remembering Janet's wrought-up face, pink, eyes bulging asymmetrically, worried into rage. He was thinking that you could see the similarities between the mother's behaviour and the child's. I could have cured her with a pill too, got her to drop a lorazepam, job done. Only that's hardly a good long-term solution any more than ritalin is for Albert. He remembered talking her down, repeating to her what she had said to him that first time she had come for a consultation. Listening patiently as she had spat back in a twisted voice, 'I may have said that then but look what's happened now. I can't have him coming to harm. I'm not gonna risk it.' And using that fear to get her finally to cross the dreaded threshold of the hospital and see the psych and set up a proper programme of care. Which now, yippee, they were properly engaged in.

The ethanol from his sweet, white beer was now osmosing through his intestine and permeating much of his body, wreaking its twinkly magic on his gamma-aminobutyric acid receptors. Given that, and the Friday evening feeling, and the good news, and the lovely warm spring sun, it all now seemed to him quite pleasant and even mildly amusing. Albert on the school roof walking the ridge tiles like a tightrope. The worried representations from the head teacher and social services. George and Sara thankfully supportive at the practice meeting. And even the thing he had kept secret from them, the thing he really probably ought not to have done . . . Though actually, no, surely it was secure – surely the bits all slotted into place unshakeably?

Janet had explained that Albert was scared stiff that Ash, his father, was about to leave again. Because they had been at the boat the night before and Ash had been talking of moving on. So the exploit on the roof must have been an eruption of anguish, a way of crying out to his dad, Stay! Stay! Which meant the therapeutic challenge shifted. Now they were at a stage where Albert's behaviour was manageable so long as Ash was there. Philip had seen for himself the boy's happiness – as well as the mother's happiness – when he had been to that eco-diatribe a couple of months ago. But Ash was clearly not the sort of person who could be persuaded to stay long-term. The challenge now was to strengthen Albert's better behaviour so it could survive the shock of Ash's departure, whenever that eventually came.

So really you could understand why Janet had wanted him to speak to Ash. To which of course he had replied that it really absolutely was not in his remit; that it was something her social worker might possibly be able to do, draw the father into the conversation. To which she had replied that Ash was not going to speak to no social worker, he was against that structure of mind control. At which he, Philip, had said that there wasn't much chance Ash would talk to him then either. But then she said that he, Philip, was about the only person Ash would talk to because he knew that he, Philip, had been there to experience the Birth of the Earth (I hope he didn't notice my expression, Philip thought). And still Philip had said no because an unsolicited visit to someone associated with a patient was completely beyond the boundaries of what was acceptable. And she had said: in that case we won't go see the specialist.

'This is blackmail,' he remembered himself objecting.

'No,' she had replied, looking at him blankly, her eyes suddenly like plastic, impossible to see through: 'It's just there's no point.'

And then he had said that maybe there was a way of doing it. Yes, the thing to do was for her and Albert to be out at the boat. And to call the surgery from there asking for a visit. She could say she was very worried about Albert, that he wasn't responding to questions, something like that. That he was twitching uncontrollably. That they were temporarily resident on the boat and she wasn't able to get him to the surgery. He, Philip, would come as he would to any patient stuck at home. And then he could talk the matter through with Ash and her together, as parents.

He sees the disciplinary panel of the GMC. A line of men with greying hair and concerned expressions. Staring at him more in sorrow than in anger. 'You have conspired with a patient' the chair intones, 'to lie to a receptionist, to make an appointment under false pretences, so as to enable you to intervene in a domestic situation in blatant contravention of good practice.' The chairman reaches out towards the big red button set in the desk in front of him. Bang! – Philip is sent shooting up through a hole in the roof, rotating, somersaulting, spiralling, flailing, until, grrn, he hits the gritty plain of outer darkness. His teeth are smashed, his mouth is crammed with sand.

Now he found that he could smile at that nightmare vision; but back then . . . He saw himself through twilight, lying in bed, rigid, eyes open, reiterating the pros and cons, scanning the consequences while Sue slept tranquilly beside him. Whereas actually, he told himself confidently now, with this letter in his hand, and the ethanol in his bloodstream, and the sun on his cheeks, all that had happened was that he had acted with initiative to promote health. He had put the good of the patient above any puny personal considerations. It was a bloody good bit of doctoring.

And compared to what Sue had got involved with at the gallery! Though in fact, now he reflected on it, perhaps Charlotte's gamble – no, let's be frank – her downright bloody lie, was what gave him the idea, or at least helped him have it. Made him realise it was possible to do that kind of thing. Would Sue be . . . he hoped Sue would be alright this weekend. Because Charlotte was clearly rather a complicated woman. Probably worse than Janet. And without the excuse of a difficult child. Just 100% ego. Just: who should be centre stage? – well, me of course. Look out for no. 1.

Sue's smile. Sue's searching eyes. She formed a blurry presence in his mind, though with bits of her body in sharper focus. A pale right shoulder, the delicate clavicle like the bone of a bird. His fingertips touching her cheek. Her searching hazel eyes looking down on him as he lay. Her head lying dozy on his chest. He delved for his phone and thumbed:

'Go for it, my sweet creative curator,' Sue read, and smiled. Then she turned her attention once more to Charlotte who had a sheet of A3 paper spread in front of her, half blackened with scribbles and lines.

'So what you've given me,' Charlotte was saying, chairman-like, 'is sense, sensation. Being connected to lots of different things. Global. Community. Environmental.'

'We need a space' – Sue was thinking it out – 'like the inside of our heads. Dark, bodily. And there'll be openings. Screens. Not just two of them, like eyes, because actually our eyes are channels for lots of different streams.'

'Like a TV.'

'Yeh because in our lives there is: telly, computer, phone . . . and then also, in parallel, there's the rest of the world that's not actually on a screen. Our eyes are insect eyes.'

'Since everything is mediatised now.'

'But that's the thing – that's what I want to get beyond. That's what the Elton Barfitt show was going to say and I'm just not sure it's right. I know you love them but I don't think it's quite right.'

'No, no: I'm open. Anyway' – Charlotte put on an ogre's voice – 'I absolutely hate them now.'

'Right.' Sue grinned at her. 'So what I think is, we keep hold of the body, we make people aware of the body, like I was saying before. Like I said' – she was remembering – 'right back in the meeting with Omar when Al Ahmed cancelled. So we have this dark organic space with maybe a heartbeat.'

'OK.'

'And coming into it we have images.' She was thinking of Charlton Heston. She was thinking of the man in the blue overalls with the moustache who looked like Charlton Heston: 'Not kitsch ones,' she said. 'Really good ones.'

'To show that the Société du Spectacle' – Charlotte said the French words cockneyishly, half-ironically – 'is not in fact all spectacle.'

Sue felt a scrape of irritation. Too trite! 'Or at least,' she said, 'it isn't always. It's just it is possible, sometimes, for an image to really hit you, bite you.'

'So,' said Charlotte: 'I'm imagining a bank of screens in our dark bodily place.'

'Yeh,' said Sue.

'And on them?'

'Images. Live streams.'

'Yeh but what sort?'

'Well for instance' – something surprising was appearing in Sue's mind: 'Do you remember that coffee pot, or did you see about it, that coffee pot in some lab, from right back at the beginning of the internet, of webcams, so they could all see when it was full?'

'I heard about it.'

'It's actually a really strong image. It's haunting. It was just something on the web, but it's got staying power. It's tiny. Black and white, so really shades of grey. And what you've got is this bulbous technological shape intruding from the right. If you don't know what it is, you're thinking, like spaceship, test-tube, bit of a power station maybe. Or it's referencing surveillance cameras with something threatening coming out of the shadows. And it's got this ancient look. The graininess. What it adds up to is something visually almost tactile. So for instance we could re-create that.'

'Is it environmental, though? Or global?'

'Yeh, coffee's global. Course it is.' Sue paused, smiling, as Charlotte saw the point. 'And, it gets into your body. Completely affects you. Messes with your nerves. It's like there's a physical connection between your heart and bloody Colombia.'

'So speaks the abstinent one,' said Charlotte.

Sue was remembering when Philip pointed the coffee machine thing out to her. That's right, when he was moaning about his conditions of work, the rabbit-hutch of a room and how even the coffee was terrible. This, by contrast, he had said, pulling up the image, was a workplace where they gave proper recognition to coffee. And she had said: 'You could always just stop.' And he had answered: 'Nope, I need an addiction. It keeps me closer to my patients.'

Philip had opted for a second pint of the sticky beer that had come 258 miles by lorry and boat to reach him from a village near Leuven in Flemish Brabant. He had got what he wanted from Ash, i.e. Ash had agreed to stay longer, to give them a couple of months to work with. But he was definitely a troubling figure. Splinter in a toe. Philip saw him again sitting on an upturned tea-box in the boat. Albert had been fidgety, of course he had been: but he was so obviously attached to his dad. He was playing a game of shifting wooden tiles around in a frame to make pictures, that was it, and looking up every now and then to check his dad's expression. Like a dog, if you took away the negative aspects of that comparison.

And the dad seemed attached to his boy too. Every now and then he would catch his gaze and smile back and you could see Albert getting a shot of happiness from that, of calm. But still there was something very reserved about Ash. Yes, it was as though he was receiving homage, and giving . . . what was the word, largesse. And the reason for that was that he thought of himself as being in fact insanely important. Because he didn't think of himself as fundamentally belonging to his child, or as fundamentally being in a relationship. He thought of himself as belonging to the whole wide world.

There was a screech of chairs. Some people were easing their way around the big table between him and the shallow front wall, beyond which, at a lower level, was the road. It was really nice the way the sun sank along the channel of that other road that forked off, bang along the middle of it, along the dotted line, so that its rays would stay focused on him warmingly as long as they possibly could. Like that channel in the original *Star Wars* the fighters have to zoom along to zap the pleasure spot. Or actually in fact more like those prehistoric temples. Like Stonehenge, lined up for the sun to shine a ray between its stones. For some reason. Though when was this building . . . ? He turned to look up more searchingly over the frontage of the pub that he had glanced at many times before. Must be early nineteenth century. You don't think of people building sun terraces back then.

'Well I've got absolutely nothing to report,' Philip heard someone saying at that bigger table, a guy, though you couldn't really see anything of him with the sun behind him. Just silhouettes.

'Same job. Still no girlfriend. I'm the one who's keeping it . . .'

'Keeping it ree-al,' came a growling, Americanised voice from one of the others.

'Keeping it . . .' he hesitated until he found: 'keeping it shit, more like.'

'Do you teach any 6th-form classes?'

'Yeh.'

'There you are then.'

Philip was thinking about Ash again. No job. Certainly no maintenance being paid to Janet. But he must live very cheaply. Probably he had someone somewhere drawing social security for him illegally by proxy. Justify it by the intensely important work he was doing for the salvation of humankind.

'Or Key Stage Two. You're like: "Hello ladees!"'

'Get out of it.'

What rankled was the way Ash had made him feel like a, well frankly like a beggar. What he, Philip, had been talking through with him were perfectly straightforward measures for the benefit of his child. How to avoid having to medicate Albert, or at least, in the worst-case scenario, keeping the medication at the lowest possible dose. How to help him get the most out of school. Etc. Which had made the air of patronage pretty hard to bear. Philip blushed at the memory, despite the continuing effects of the sticky beer; the proliferation of relaxing alpha waves along his nerves. You would say something to Ash and he would receive it graciously. It would go into him like a stone into a pool. And then there would be silence. While his lordship weighed the suggestion against numerous massive cosmic considerations. Janet, meanwhile, sat waiting on a little wickerwork sofa, leaning into it, her arm stretched out along its back. Albert played with his game on the floor. Until, after some time, Ash graciously pronounced. At the root of it, Philip decided, was fucking meditation. Because in fact, when you thought about it, being the one who meditates is an immensely powerful position. You are in contact with numinous forces. You are simply more important than everyone else. It's religion in a nutshell. Because you don't only think, but actually know, or rather think you know; no, are certain you know (what are the words for this? – you are certain you know even though what you are certain you know is obviously claptrap) that people are not what they seem, not what science shows them to be. You happen amazingly to have privileged information to the effect that we are all parachuted onto the world for a brief instant from some super duper other place. And what's it like, exactly, that other place? Oh, we can't say anything except that it's really, really special. Any evidence, at all, of any kind, even a tiny smidgen of evidence, just a speck, a quark of evidence, that will stand up to any rational inspection? Certainly not, how vulgar of you to ask. How simplistic.

Philip was aware of his thoughts bulging and swaying as the ethanol began to mess with his synapses. Getting a bit irritable too from low blood sugar. Eat soon. But he wanted to press his line of reasoning to a conclusion. Because obviously Ash wasn't against the natural world like those other religious nutters. He was the opposite of Mother Teresa. But by making the world itself spiritual he ended up just as bad. Because it meant that you simply weren't facing up to the problem. Because obviously it was a complete fantasy that everyone was going to start living on carbon-neutral canal boats and eating organic pulses. And by going around saying that that was what should happen you were diverting attention from what really needed to happen, i.e. properly thought-through, evidence-based scientific solutions. Which could be so beautiful. Because they could be so clever. That was what was really human. Rather than this mumbo-jumbo about spirituality which basically came down to feelings of light-headedness induced by psychosomatically lowered blood pressure and not eating enough. It was the same thing that was so exciting about being a doctor. Using your intelligence to understand what was wrong with someone, and mend it. Of course there were dangers. Of course you have to keep in mind that people are not machines, that the cure sometimes can be worse than the disease, that hospital intervention especially could strike some patients as industrial. But he was aware of all that. Lots of doctors were. No one was more sensitive than he was, than young Dr Philip Newell was, to the shortcomings of technological medicine. That was what his handling of Albert and Janet, and, sod him, Ash, was all about. But you had to hold on to the benefits as well. Because they were, frankly, magic. Just look at everyday extraordinary things like salbutamol or MMR or ibuprofen. Show those to a medieval person, or in fact somebody pre-war. They'd think you were an angel.

The sun had gone now. The pint was nearly gone too. All the shadows had disappeared, or rather it was as if they had got drawn up over the houses and trees and cars and street signs which had themselves now become shadowy, greyish. Now Philip could see the bunch of lads across from him, one with neat short hair and glasses, one with a pony-tail; one in a suit and tie; another in dusty industrial trousers – maybe a plumber? – and thick boots.

'I turned up at work with no database training,' pony-tail was saying: 'And I didn't blow it up. Flew it by the seat of my pants!'

The air felt suddenly chilly. Time to go.

'It was the most beautiful scene in, like, cinematic history!'

He wondered how Sue was doing. Checked his phone: nothing there.

'There's plenty of more interesting stuff than tattoos, in all fairness.'

Pick up a takeaway on the way home? No there was enough in the fridge. Easier to have pasta with something. Bit of telly. Earlyish night because it was his turn for Saturday morning surgery. Followed by a quick beyond-the-call-of-duty visit to Grace Hanworth, check her pain relief for the weekend. Because it didn't seem right to leave her at the mercy of the out-of-hours people in what was very probably her last few weeks alive. Anyway, he owed her. They'd had some very interesting conversations. So sharp and pragmatic. Seeing what the best thing to do was and advocating it. Absolutely no sentimentality. Ha! – he said to himself suddenly – get her together with Ash the father of Albert. She'd knock the nonsense out of him! Because in a way they had some similar attitudes, but it was the development of them, the quality of reasoning that was so different. Philip saw himself wheeling her on a trolley across the bumpy meadow to Ash's boat, her yellow, wizened face wobbling, her pale eyes focused intently somewhere in the sky. And then when they got there she would sit up at ninety degrees and hold forth. And Ash would be blown backwards by the force of her words until, splodge, he slipped over the muddy verge of the river. Now, that was a happy thought. Chirpily, Philip trotted down the hard, dry terrace steps, and set off along the solid pavement.

Meanwhile Charlotte was saying: 'And the screens need to be . . .'

'We need to get hold of a load of old-fashioned box TVs.' Sue had now moved from the table. She had paced Charlotte's blue and beige striped rug and was perched on the fat, rounded arm of one of the cream Habitat-or-equivalent armchairs. 'There must be millions of them around.'

Somewhere in the spaceless space of Sue's mind was an idea of herself, little, cross-legged in front of the enormous wooden room with its enormous, curving, plate-glass grey window.

'If they haven't all been smashed up,' said Charlotte.

At the rounded corners of the curving window the grey darkened to black. She must have been, what, five? – four? Now she was standing in front of the enormous room and her face was at the height of the middle of it. Three maybe. Morph became a hole in the table and someone vanished into it.

'Remember how different they were from what we have now, how heavy they were, how much they took up space?'

Her mother curled up on the baggy chair behind her. Its flowery swirls.

'They were like' – said Charlotte.

The two of them, the curtains drawn, shafts of warm light where the dust sparkled. The two of them cosy with their attention on the screen.

'It was like having a power station in the middle of the sitting room,' Sue pressed on. 'When you switched it off there was something solid still there, an enormous magical machine still there. You could bash into it. Whereas now . . .'

Though now her mother was still there, that whole scene was pretty much still there, just as it had always been.

'Now they basically disappear,' said Charlotte, glancing at her flatscreen which was over the mantelpiece like a mirror.

Well, not actually always.

'Click the remote: the whole world vanishes. As if it had never been.'

Because her mother had gone out into the world to get her, Sue. And then she had brought her back and kept her safe in the den where they had been together.

'But with great big old-fashioned tellies we'll maybe get people to see how new that is, and strange.'

From which afterwards she seemed never really to have wanted . . .

'The image'll be fuzzier,' said Charlotte.

. . . to move, not really. Except to the supermarket and then back . . .

'And actually' – Charlotte was continuing – 'there may be some technical difficulty as well because I'm not sure . . .'

. . . to the wonderful place . . .

'We can get Stuart to sort that,' said Sue.

. . . where the images were.

'It's a digital / analogue thing,' Charlotte explained.

There was a pause. The surge of energy seemed to have dropped. The light had gone from the room. Sue leaned forward off her perch and stepped towards the table to fill up her glass from the bottle there. Charlotte moved around switching on spotlights and standard lamps.

'We can always go out,' she said.

'Let's just' – Sue sat in one of the squashy chairs: 'Let's just get to the end of this bit, provisionally.'

'So there's something we can draw a line under.'

'And then go out.'

Charlotte gathered up the scattered bits of paper and sat on the sofa opposite. 'The TVs,' she said.

'Older the better,' Sue said. 'You know, wooden casings.' Her voice was abrupt. She was speaking bullet points. 'All stacked up in a wall, like the mosaic of screens at the start of the news. Streams from all over the world. Because we are connected to everywhere, even though sometimes . . .'

'It's bewildering,' offered Charlotte.

'. . . we don't even know what the place we're connected to is. So what we're gonna do, what we're gonna do is give the punters a – what are they called, tic-tac-toe thing, slidey jigsaw puzzle thing, with names of locations, and they can stand in front of the screens and try to make them match up with the names of the places. Which will make them realise they can't do it.'

'Or maybe some of the time . . .'

'That's right, that's better: some of the time they can and some of the time they can't. Because . . .'

'Because that's what it's like,' Charlotte concluded.

Damn that glibness, thought Sue, suddenly savage. But then, actually – she said to herself, calm suddenly spreading through her

– this was how it had to be, thinking the thing out. You put the impulse, the feeling, provisionally into words. Which always, always felt unsatisfactory. But it had to be done. Because it had to. And then you pushed through the words and out the other side: you escaped from the words into the show: using the words allowed you to get the feeling out of words and into the object or the event; into the piece of art. And that was when the ideas and feelings could grow again and flower and flourish and be alive. That was the real thing to hold onto.

'And the actual locations of the webcams,' said Charlotte.

'Can we leave them to tomorrow?' said Sue, slumping back in her chair, depositing her goblet on the glass-topped table beside it.

'I'd say' – said Charlotte, appraisingly – 'you've done enough, and are allowed' – her voice became more jovial – 'a short break! Let's get you out of here!'

'Before I go to sleep.'

'Which is absolutely definitely not allowed.' Charlotte went and stood before her, legs braced, hands held out.

Pee, phones, money, glance in the mirror; and then the two young women were away into the still-warmish evening air.

Philip's mind was somewhat enlivened by his walk back through the still-warmish evening air, down Turnpike Lane, along Helium Avenue, across Elysium Crescent and along Parnassus Row to Eden Grove. Empty without Sue here, he thought as, having pushed open the front door, he stepped in onto the mat and rubbed his shoes on it. Quiet, he thought, as the door slammed behind him. The shock-waves of that impact seemed to spread through the silent space as he turned right into the kitchen-living room. He chucked his jacket on the faux-leather sofa and noticed the slithery sound of it. The fridge started up its periodic irritating buzz as though to say hello.

I'll just do melted blue cheese, he thought, as he filled a pan with water and set it on the hob (the water whirled and chattered; the pan-base clanked). He noticed his foot was on something on the lino and stooped to look – a chunk of toast-crust from this morning – and picked it up. The lid of the swing-bin made a donkey-ish squeak. Yes there was Stilton and half a packet of rocket in the fridge: good. He stood, propping his bum against the edge of the worktop, waiting for the water beneath the lid of the pan to start its breezy roar. I wonder what Sue. He checked his phone again: still nothing. Shall I call? No definitely not. He knew that was one of the stress-points between them, his need for reassurance, for a continuous everyday keeping in touch, versus her need to be trusted, to be left, whenever she felt like it, alone. He was like, what, like a satellite maintaining radio contact. Or maybe he was like a little duckling going peep-peep-peep to its mother. But he didn't know what she was like, apart from like herself. Her face was there, suddenly, filling his field of vision. Like a rock face on Mount Rushmore only soft, pale, round as a drop of dew. There was a scat-tering of freckles across her little snub nose. Her eyebrows were made of distinct separate hairs like black wires and you could see the waxy skin beneath. It was the same at the top of her forehead where her real hair began. She was looking at him with that expres-sion that was so her. What could he say about it? It was: affectionate. No in fact it was OK to say that it was loving. Because when she looked at him like that her hands would be reaching out towards him, touching him at the top of his arm or gently on the side of his neck beneath his ear. It had wonder in it. No, that wasn't quite right. Puzzlement would be better. Because it was amused as well. It seemed to say to him both: I love you, and: what a strange creature you are. And that reservation was what so tore him up sometimes. Tore him up in a way that was love, he knew that. Because love was an emotional pain that was also a pleasure. But the tearing was also something else, also something that was just pain, on top of the pain that was part of love. Because it made him always know, or think he knew, that she could drift, whenever she felt like it, out of reach. There was something conditional, was there something conditional in the way she looked at him? Whereas he was attached to her unreservedly. Like a bee having stung her. Like a tree with its roots grown deep.

The pan-lid rattled and he reached for the spaghetti. He held it upright in his fist, a bundle of rods. Then let it drop, thud, to the bottom of the pan, at which the rods fanned out like . . . maybe like a cut stook of straw. The bits in the water would soften and fatten and the rest would tumble in. He tapped the sticking-out ends with a wooden spoon. Still quite firm. He checked his phone again. For Chrissake Philip, if there had been a message it would have made its noise, just leave it, she is busy working on her thing, or she is having a drink with Charlotte, she is a human being and can do stuff, leave it.

He walked away from the cooker to help change his thought. Ash smiled smugly at him: no please not Ash. He sat in a squashy chair, leaned his head against the back of it. In a moment he would get up and crumble the cheese. The humiliation of Andrew Lansley, yes let's go with that. What was the tune, Andrew Lansley greedy, Andrew Lansley tosser, da-da-da-da-da-da-la-da. He saw the rapper's fingers flicking. That CIS guy too. Graham thingummy. He must be uneasy. Funny not to have known of him at that party in Feb because now he was sensitised he saw CIS everywhere, aiming to facilitate the transition, supply the expertise that health professonals themselves could not be expected to have. Do the dirty work and take the profit. Which showed you something about George.

He stood up, went across to the cooker, stirred the boiling water with the pasta in it, set a little non-stick pan on the hob, knob of butter, splash of milk, reached for the cheese.

He saw a succession of images of George. Bottle in hand at that party / presiding firmly at the practice meeting / crouched in the dark by a firework / sitting solicitously in the waiting room talking gently to an OAP who had completely forgotten where she was and why. The sequence ran again more quickly. No he was, could be, a caring doctor. But he also had the air, always, wherever he was, of being in charge, of having some executive decision to arrive at. And therefore a brusqueness and impatience. So that you never felt he was really hearing you or seeing you, never quite sensing you fully, but instead processing the information so that he could then do what needed to be done and move on.

Philip was crumbling the cheese into the oily mixture, prodding it with the tip of a wooden spoon.

Or maybe actually that was unfair. Maybe that was inevitably the stance of being the senior partner. Experience. How experience always looked to someone who was, let's face it, young and still a bit naive. Because of course George would have seen a lot of stuff before.

Nearly ready now.

And also maybe Sue was right that the early death of his wife was at the root of it. Of course in those circs you would grow a carapace. And expand so you seemed to fill all the available space. He had had to be the whole world to his little girls. He had had to be solid.

Philip lifted the heavy pan and drained it sending puffs and swirls of clammy steam into the air around his face.

Although the thing about that sort of explanation was that you could run it in any direction. I.e. if George had ended up completely different you could still point to the same cause.

He tipped the yukky-looking cheesy gunk in among the heap of spaghetti.

Though in that case you could probably assume the cause was having its effect on different pre-existing material. So that it would still be the cause, even though it provoked a different sequence of reactions and led to a different character precipitated at the end.

Philip turned, put the plate on the table, sat. As he did so, the person in his mind switched. It was his father who sat across from him. His father's face red, eyes panicking, breath rasping, the chest tight, solidified, not working, the air not coming in. Philip winced, his eyes watered, the fork in his hand put the readied mouthful back down on the plate.

His own heart was jolting and there was reflux in his throat. He should have . . . but then Sue's voice cut in: 'You did tell him. I saw you telling him. You worried about him a lot. You said: "Just pop along to your GP and get it checked up." You can't order him.'

And in fact, he told himself, perhaps it was a good thing. Because otherwise, if nothing had happened now, then later it could have been the big one straight away. Whereas this really was going to get him to change his behaviour as no amount of nagging could. Or it ought to.

He saw his mother moving around neatly. Her careful arrangements. The reading-up she was doing on healthy diets. The little verdant meals put in front of his father. The watching for his reaction with concerned eyes. A little myocardial infarction went a long way.

He should ring them.

He was able to eat again. He twirled the oily cables and forked them in. The clingy sauce slithered down the sides of his papillae to where the taste buds responded, sending excitation along fibres to the brain. Bitter, and a touch of sour, and sweet. Smell played a crucial part in the perception of taste. And in fact what about texture which was also pretty damn important.

Dad would be on aspirin and dipyridamole and quinapril and something like glyceryl trinitrate which, did you know, is the same stuff, 100% the same stuff as nitroglycerine the explosive? And a statin of course, to combat the low density lipoprotein which was being endlessly noxiously pumped into the bloodstream by digestion of meals like especially for instance this one he was consuming now. The cheese ending up as in fact something pretty much like cheese again to look at though it would probably be a. slimier and b. harder to the touch. Calcified desposits lumped together with fibrous layers and lipid-rich regions, clagging the blood vessels until an amazingly tiny way through was left – that was what was surprising, how completely narrow they could get before the patient noticed any ill-effects. Until for instance a slimy dark frogspawn clot or fool's-gold nugget came tumbling, boulder along rapids, until, thud, it lodged, a plug, immoveable, the pressure on the one side only fixing it more strongly while on the other side, sudden emptiness, just nothing, nothing getting through, the muscle struggling to contract, spasming, leaking lactic acid, alarms blaring, red lights flashing, a submarine with power failure, sinking, not enough to breathe, everyone will die.

Unless, kerching! The thrombolysis goes zapping in and chips away at the clot until, whoosh, the blood can go spurting through again and there is his dad once more. His dad can continue as a human being. As opposed to not. As opposed to cooling, and solidifying, and becoming food in its turn for, well the pancreatic bacteria for instance, which are probably the first to have a nibble. Hang on, they say, something's up. And then: wahay! Ere we go ere we go ere we go. Which will almost certainly be happening to Grace Hanworth in the next couple of weeks.

Jesus, how callous you can be as a doctor! Philip chewed, reached for his glass, drank. Even you; even already.

Only actually in fact it wasn't callousness. It was knowing what was going on; properly knowing what was really going on. And the question then was how you negotiated between that and other people. Being tactful while also truthful: that was the conundrum.

The funny thing was how, these days, stuff came from all over the place and ended up in a single human body. Which he kept on noticing after hearing Sue talk about her ideas for her possible show. Like take for instance what he'd just been eating. Wine from Australia, Stilton from – where was that from, Somerset maybe? Milk from not far away, he hoped. Pasta, now was that really still made in Italy? He got up to see if it said on the packet. Yeh, here it was, grown and packed in Italy – but for a company with an address in Liverpool. What else? What about the pepper? Where the hell did that come from? India? Indonesia? And had got here by what invisible process of global circulation, wagon, presumably, and lorry, and . . . no in fact presumably a basket first, somebody's hand picking it and tossing it into an enormous basket secured by a band over the person's forehead. Maybe. Unless that was a fantasy. Unless it was all mechanised now even wherever it came from. So: hand and basket, then maybe lorry, then maybe train, then ship, then lorry, then warehouse, then lorry, then Tesco. Or planes? Which were probably too expensive but what does he know?

So you took all that and put in in your mouth. You chewed and mixed it with secretions and turned it into a bolus which was sent down your throat by the amazingly complex action of swallowing, followed by a Mexican he meant a peristaltic wave which sent it to the stomach. Having been mixed with hydrochloric acid, etc. etc., the bolus became chyme which little-by-little was released into the slo-mo helter skelter of the small intestine. Where molecules of carbohydrate and fat and protein were absorbed. And sent scurrying round the body by a circulation system that he this time did know something about. And the molecules were used for, well, everything really. Except the ones that got stuck on the way as atherosclerosis. Which hardened and narrowed and impeded until bang! – that was the end of you. Unless you were one of the lucky ones, like dad.

He was sitting at the heavy, sharp-edged pine table. Ahead of him, the dark, shiny sofa and the squishy chairs. Above the mantel-piece a delicate artwork, courtesy of Sue. Who was now . . . well, let's hope it's going OK. Let's hope it's going brilliantly. Because it was completely brave, what she was trying to do. A complete putting-herself-at-risk. An act of self-definition. Whereas the thing about being a doctor was that that was what you were. People said: I'm going to the GP. And very often they didn't in fact know what your name was. Who is your doctor, Sushma would ask, and they wouldn't know! To them your name was just: GP.

You could imagine GPs all having names that began with G and P like what was that chain of pubs where they did that? His name would be . . . Gerald . . . Partridge. George of course had one half of it already. He would be George . . . Plum.

Whereas if you went to an Art show you knew damn well exactly who it was you were looking at, that was the whole point, even if Sue said it shouldn't be. The individuality. Which of course in a doctor you actually wouldn't want. You wouldn't want to be able to say: only Newell could have diagnosed that IBS. Observe the inimitable flourish with which he inflates the cuff of the sphyg-momanometer. Such delicate tact in the palpation of a shoulder.

Unless Lansley got his way of course. In which case they would all be boasting their distinctiveness. Branding themselves. Or at least the hospitals would be. Ha, the good old bad old District Infirmary. Offering everything you would expect from a two-and-a-half star hospital of county-wide renown. Complimentary tap-water available on request (don't forget to bring your own cup to benefit from this service!). We believe in offering you the fullest possible liberty to take or forget to take your medicine. Our nurses will leave you almost wholly undisturbed.

Although in fact, he thought, as he got up, turning, gathering his plate etc. to dump them in the sink, he was still him. There was the as-it-were uniform of the profession: the skills they all learned and performed reliably. And then there was the way you wore that uniform which did actually matter quite a lot. He was a different doctor from George, different again from Sara, different from Isobel and Paul. And a lot different from Adam Hibbert. It was just that it happened bit by bit. You expressed yourself in little things, each day, within the fixed contraints. A nudge here, a bit of initiative there. As he was doing majorly with Janet and Albert, for instance, and would do again no doubt with Grace Hanworth tomorrow.

Nearly 11. Still nothing from Sue; for as he had been looking in the fridge she had walked out with Charlotte along a canal front-age created in the mid-1980s by one of the privately funded regeneration schemes so typical of those years; and as his pasta water had boiled the two young women had arrived at the bar of a fairly standard place that called itself 'The Sitting Room', with 'Everyone Back to Ours!' scrawled on the doors to differentiate itself from the other fairly standard places all around; and as he sat, forking food into his mouth and thinking of his father, Sue and Charlotte were sitting with cocktails waiting for their salads and a side-order of chips to share.

'I like it here,' Charlotte was saying, 'because it's so utterly basic.' Sue looked around and heard the music of was it Cheryl or Nicole?

– and saw sturdy wooden chairs at sturdy wooden tables; worn floorboards; loungy areas with shiny sofas that were in fact just like the one at home or rather in the rented house at The Willows; a fish-tank room divider; a long bar with spirit bottles glittering behind it.

'Because if you go next door but one to, say, Armando's, they want you to think you're doing something special. They want you to feel you have to speak genteelly and quietly and pick more delicately at their food. But when this whole area was built twenty years ago it must have been just, like, lot 53 along from lot 51 which was this one. They must have both been labelled "Hospitality and Catering" which just means places to eat and drink. And what I like about here, is, that's what it is. Because so much of the rest of my life isn't. Isn't basic. Isn't . . . if I say it isn't honest I don't mean what you think I mean. Don't worry, I'll explain. I'll explain! So that when I come here, and just eat, and . . . drink, and get the chance to have a really good natter, I really appreciate it. Because' – she was draining her glass: 'Do you ever have the feeling of becoming someone, or having become someone, you don't really want to be?'

'I don't,' said Sue, feeling like the target for something; 'not really.'

'Shall we move on to wine?'

'Yeh I'll get it. White?'

'No let me.'

'You got the cocktails.'

'But this is my . . .'

'No I can do it. I mean I do feel frustrated sometimes,' Sue said, standing, moving away with a look that said we'll carry this on in a minute. She waited assertively at the bar, ignoring some fat guy on a stool who was shifting his bulk, he must be looking at her, his mouth half open, getting ready, she knew, to say something if she glanced at him; only she didn't: she got the bottle and the glasses and turned away from that fat guy, who was now – ha ha – deflating, and went back to Charlotte, and sat, and poured, and said:

'But I do basically think of myself as being the person I want to be.'

'It goes back to my upbringing,' Charlotte said. 'Of course,' she added, in louder groaning tones. Then she carried on more quietly, in explanation: 'It was a house in the country. Fields around it. I had ponies, for Chrissake. I went to gymkhanas. I had two big brothers and climbed trees with them. I was my parents' little flower. Dad was working in the city and sometimes he was away. But not very often because he'd done that thing of making his pile and basically semi-retiring. Mum didn't work but she was busy with, oh, church fêtes, being a volunteer for the RSPCA. There was a woman from the village who looked after me when my parents weren't there. And she was pretty indulgent. So what I mean is: it was so secure. It was like Paradise, really, in that everything was thought of and arranged.'

'And also pretty nice, it sounds like.'

'Yes. I can't deny that it was.' Charlotte leaned forward, lifted her glass, drank. Then she propped her elbows on the table and rested her chin on her folded hands. Her wide, plump face was angled downwards and a veil of straight blonde hair fell across. 'Then' – her eyes were focused on the bottle in front of her – 'I went away to school and that was basically much the same. I mean bigger, obviously. But the feeling of security, and of everything being organised, and of a channel to follow, you know, a kind of person you were meant to become – that was what was still the same.'

'And what' – Sue asked brightly, making an effort to be sympathetic – 'was that kind of person?'

'Oh.' She looked up at Sue through the dangling strands. 'A healthy attitude to life.' She moved her eyes away again, focused in mid-air as on an autocue. 'Active, but also feminine. Particular in one's tastes, but never making a fuss. Able to appreciate the finer things, but not reliant on them. As at home on safari as in the Ritz. Having a social conscience, of course; but not allowing it to blot out everything that's good in the world.' She was sounding sententious now: 'A thoroughly modern girl. The values of ladyship, adapted to the challenges of today.'

'Gosh.'

'It really was like that. So anyway, then I went to Brookes to do History of Art' – but now their food was being put down on the table, the waitress asking if there was anything else, the two of them unwrapping knives and forks from the real cloth napkins. They dug in.

'Which went along,' Charlotte carried on through her munching, 'just as you'd expect. Until one day . . .' she said dramatically.

It really was quite charming, this turn into self-parody Charlotte took from time to time. It was actually what made her bearable.

'We were doing a studio visit for a module on contemporary art in practice. There was this artist there whose work was all about repetition. She had a little sandpit. She was sitting in front of it cross-legged, reaching forward: I remember being amazed by how lithe she was, how far she could reach, she was rocked forward so as to be balanced really on just her knees and toes. Anyway she had a camera rigged up above it on a tripod pointing down. What she was doing was basically just doodling in the sand. After each doodle she'd take a shot. She had a remote for the camera so she could do that without getting up. And I was standing in the doorway, watching her.'

Charlotte took another mouthful of food and glug of wine. The place was louder: the music had toughened up a bit – Rihanna – and people were shouting above it.

'I really felt,' Charlotte enunciated clearly and firmly, 'that I was with her, you know, that I was understanding her. I could see how the work was referencing Jackson Pollock and that it was all about being less grandiose. Each doodle in the sand erased or disrupted the one before. The marks made by the artist were transient. What was being recorded by the camera was the erasure of something just as much as the creation of something. The one entailed the other. You know it seemed to me' – she said, starting to sound a bit indignant – 'really strong work. I was standing there, rooting for it.' She looked around her, harassed. 'Let's go outside. I can't shout this. We've paid for this haven't we? Let's go outside.'

So they did. As Philip was dumping his plate in the sink and checking his phone and turning and walking through the room and switching off the light and climbing upstairs to bed, the two women went out onto a balcony over the canal. It was warmish still; or rather, the surprising warmth of the day was still in the process of fading before the chill of deepening night. The sky was clear black; a bulbous – no, what was the right word – gibbous moon shone bright above and picked out swirls and circles on the water. Even through the orangey haze of the city lights, a few stars and planets shone.

'This is embarrassing,' said Charlotte. The two women were leaning on a railing, looking down into the water, or across it, or to one or other side. 'All she did was glance at me. If she'd said something it might have been different – I could have replied. If she'd said something enquiring I could have given her my response to the work. If she'd said something rude, even then you know I could have said something rude back, I could have asserted myself, I would have been strong in the feeling of being me, you know, in combat. But it was such' – the water slapped suddenly loudly against the wall beneath – 'a little thing.' She paused and they listened to the water sluicing and rippling. 'Just a glance,' she said as though airily. And then, determinedly: 'The glance said that I was negligible, and irritating, and not worth speaking to, and basically an intrusion. No actually, as well, more than that: that I was obviously a type she knew through and through already and so totally wasn't worth bothering about.'

'Maybe,' Sue ventured, 'that wasn't what the glance actually said. Maybe that was just how it seemed to you.'

'I know, I'm sure I over-interpreted. But what you need to ask then is: what was causing the over-interpretation? Do you see? I'm not saying this unknown artist could suddenly magically see through me. What I'm saying is what matters is what I made of it, how it struck me. And it released this completely different . . .'

'From someone who was probably having a bad day and not thinking about you at all.'

'Yeh, I know, I know. But it nagged at me. It . . . gnawed me. It was like an illness spreading through me until every bit of me was rotten. Or actually, no. I was the same me, I was clearly the same me: but I just looked different to myself – changed from duck to rabbit, or, I dunno, swan to ugly duckling.'

'A perspective that suddenly switches, from sticking out to sinking in.'

'Yes I suppose. Yes that's quite a good image for it.'

'Contour lines that could be going either way.'

'It was really surprising. As I looked back into my memory, everything was different. Even, for instance right back to even when I was a little girl. It was my birthday. There was a table of food. I had gathered a whole heap of it in front of myself. A whole slag heap of jam roly-poly, and chocolate muffins, and . . . And I was sitting there grinning, and it seemed to me, it must have seemed to me at the time and it kept on seeming to me when I looked back, I mean it used to, that everyone around was smiling indulgently. But now when I remember it' – her voice was cold – 'the faces are strained. They are the faces of people who are putting up with an insufferable little brat. And the terrible thing is, after that glance from the woman at the sandpit, that's how my whole life looked. It was really' – her voice was fracturing into a breathy, sad laugh – 'a bit of a shock.'

'Gosh.'

'Do you see' – her voice was shrill, about to weep – 'all the smiles that had been happy, became ironic. What was cosy, became cloying. Everything I'd achieved seemed flat. Days of happy activity turned into just basically mechanical ways of passing the time. Can you imagine' – she was speaking more calmly now – 'how strange that is: to look into your memory and find that all the colours have changed from harmonious to blaring, grating. You know I'm not' – she was taking deep breaths, her head back, looking up into the height of the sky – 'fat, I haven't ever been.'

Though you are quite big-boned, Sue couldn't avoid saying to herself.

'But now when I looked back into my memory, in all the vignettes there, you know in all the little scenes from plays that make a memory, I'm this enormous oily blob. So, I suppose, that' – now at last she was breaking down, her face scrunching up, the tears starting to come – 'was an episode of depression.'

She had stopped speaking, stopped being able to. She was leaning on the railing, looking concentratedly downwards, holding herself in. Sue could feel that Charlotte felt like just collapsing, just howling, whirling, spattering, dissolving. But Charlotte stood there, leaning out, massy and still, quite still. Sue reached her arm across nervously, touched the edge of Charlotte's shoulder blade, rubbed forward along the bumps of the backbone, moved further up to probe the top of the neck, the back of the base of the skull. Charlotte leaned backwards into the pressure of Sue's hand. Then Charlotte was leaning towards her, turning, and the two women were in a hug, Charlotte's arms under Sue's arms, her hands gripping her back; Sue's arms around Charlotte's, one hand still at the nape of the neck, the other patting the back of her ribcage. Then they came apart.

'Thanks,' Charlotte was saying.

'Oh it's,' said Sue.

'Are you cold?' said Charlotte.

'No I'm alright,' said Sue.

The balcony was an oblong box sticking out from the wall of the bar: one side was the French windows; railings formed the other three. Now Charlotte had her back to one of the shorter sides, leaning on the railing. Sue was opposite. The balcony had become the corral where the conversation was going to continue to its end.

'I got through it. I spent' – there was that breathy, blackly humorous tone in her voice again – 'about a month in a darkened room. I worked out that you can't magically change into another person. No that's not right,' she said, faster, louder, in scorn of herself; 'that doesn't have to be worked out. That's obvious. What I mean is' – she was speaking more quietly now, wearily – 'I accepted that I couldn't magically turn into another person. So I just let myself carry on. While, while sort of standing a bit to one side. I inhabit,' she declared, 'an invisible helium balloon that floats' – she lifted her hand to half a metre above and to the side of her head – 'about up here. And that's what's' – the voice fell again – 'I don't know . . . did you ever look at me and think: how automatic she is! You know, how, sort of into the job, absorbed into the artworld, you know, just a person with wholly predictable responses?'

'No.' Sue didn't know what else to say. Until: 'Anyway these last few months, with Elton Barfitt and everything, you haven't been like that at all. If anything you've been a bit . . . out there.'

'I know. That's completely it. Because Elton Barfitt really call to

170

me. Because in a sense I'm doing the same as them. Or, you know, the same as Orlan, or Gilbert and George. Except Elton Barfitt are the ones who most appeal to me. Because of their vehemence. Their hostility. The way they seem so powerful. They are obviously performing an identity, and it is powerful. Whereas I am trapped into performing an identity. And it feels weak, so weak. And nobody knows about it' – now her face was stretching sideways, like rubber, like a clown's – 'and the idea for the exhibition they described to us, it was so, it so touched me, and I really wanted to be involved with it, I really thought' – the tears had come again – 'that it would help.'

Sue was holding her hand. She said: 'I know about it. Now. And maybe – look. Do you know what we can do? This show we're going to do, we're going to try to do together. Let's, why don't we try and connect that to what you're talking about, just as Elton Barfitt connected. Make your analysis, your self-analysis, a source of it, or part of it, of what it's about. Because what you've been saying really connects with, I think could really connect with, the way it's coming together.'

'Do you think?' said Charlotte, jolting, half-hiccuping.

'Yeh,' said Sue, squeezing her fingers. 'Let's try, anyway. Let's try tomorrow.'

'Yeh, let's.' Charlotte's hand came away from Sue's. 'Thank you,' she said, dragging her fingers under her nose, then wiping them on her trousers, then pressing the tips of them to her cheek, forehead, other cheek.

And then she carried on, sounding lighter after so much declaration: 'In some ways it's been quite convenient. No shame, you see. All I do, me personally, is raise an eyebrow. As Charlotte' (her voice put inverted commas around the name) 'I've shagged a lot of people. Having Charlotte here' – there was something manic in her voice now – 'is convenient for venting Charlotte's dark desires.' Then: 'I was Charlotte when I shagged Omar.' She let the words float away from her into the air over the water, knowing they would shock.

'I didn't know you'd . . .'

'It was a long . . .'

'I'd assumed he was gay.'

'So did I at the time. I was pretty pleased with myself. But it turns out he swings both ways: always has done. So it wasn't' – she spoke through a sardonic grin – 'a great achievement after all.'

Sue didn't say anything; and this not-saying-anything took on the quality of a question.

'Oh,' Charlotte answered, 'I was young. About where you are now. Recently started the job. And I thought: what would Charlotte do? So we did, Charlotte and I. Omar just took it as a droit de . . . thingy, you know, His Lordship's Right. He clicked his fingers a couple of times afterwards and Charlotte came running, as she would. But it wasn't anything really. We never mentioned it.'

'So you don't feel any particular . . . loyalty towards him?' – Sue asked. She was suddenly worrying about the project.

'God no. Obviously not. The opposite. Anyway' – Charlotte had her hands in her jacket pockets now, shoulders raised so her body was straight up and down – 'it was nothing.'

Then she softened and said, mildly, appearing to be losing energy:

'Do you know, the funny thing is I probably feel most enjoyably alienated from myself – because that's the word for it, isn't it, that's the cod-psychological diagnosis – I mostly enjoy it quietly in the evenings. When Charlotte comes home to Charlotte's flat. You must have noticed that,' she pitched at Sue, suddenly vehement, 'what a Charlotte flat I live in?'

'Well I did . . .'

'It's completely conventionally cosy. Nothing idiosyncratic in it at all. Charlotte comes in. Puts on something like Dido. Has a low-fat ready meal from M&S. Watches a bit of telly. You know, just totally fits in to her magnolia and taupe interior. And I find it really very restful to be associated with her.'

'OK.' said Sue.

'Yes,' said Charlotte. And then: 'Well, anyway . . .' And then: 'Who knows – after our show it all may change.' And then, pertly: 'Shall we go?'

'OK,' said Sue.

So the two women stepped back into the noisy bar which was getting towards the end of its late evening. They stepped out again onto the pavement that had been constructed by a workgang consisting of Des Davies (56), Kwaku Owusu (26), Bebe Phipps (40) and Damon Keer (19) using a Probst laying machine to lay bricks that were edged with nibs to create a permeable surface so that the large expanse of pavement would remain safe even on the wettest days. Not that it was at all wet as the two women walked on, between the two-hundred and forty-three-year-old canal and the twenty-seven-year-old retail and residential apartment units by which it was now lined. On they walked, in the midst of that great city of roughly 997,000 inhabitants lodged in 327,961 households; a population of many and varying ethnicities, younger, on the whole, than the national average, and equally divided between the male and female sex. Christian, Muslim, No Religion, Sikh, Hindu, Religion Not Stated, Buddhist, Jewish, Other were the religions professed by the population of this city. On they walked, Sue and Charlotte, covering only 843 yards of the 2,967 miles of pavement that this city contained, and passing under only 27 of its 94,603 streetlights. Among its 93.4 square miles they trod only that narrow shortish line, plus the variable distance they could see on either side: 12.7 metres across pavement and wall and canal and wall and pavement to the front door of what was actually a Georgian lock-keeper's cottage opposite; 138 yards over a bridge along a road where streetlamps and traffic lights and Belisha beacons winked and shone. All around them many, many people were awake; and more were sleeping. All around them were the sounds of cars and radios and hairdryers and flushing loos and central-heating boilers and computer cooling systems and singing and conversation and sneezing and breathing, all of which added up to less noise than by day and so seemed to Charlotte and Sue to count as quiet. All around them, through wires and cables and circuit boards and switches and resistors, electricity sped and slowed and was stopped and flowed again.

53.5 miles away, as the two women climbed the steps to Charlotte's apartment, Philip slept in the unconsciousness of slow-wave sleep; and, as they moved purposefully here and there, Sue brushing and cleansing, Charlotte getting out the spare duvet, he slept on. As Sue snuggled down on the squishy sofa, and felt the scratchiness of the matted texture of its mixed linen, acrylic and polyester fabric through the sheet that veiled it, Philip rocked his head on the luxury micro-fibre pillow: a guttural breath emerged from his half-open mouth. As Sue's mind slowed, as she wondered how much of what Charlotte had splurged at her was true, or rather – well, there had to be some distance, didn't there, beween that confession, that story Charlotte had told about herself, and what being her was actually like. A lot of distance – as Sue's thoughts wandered in this vein, Philip slept in the unconsciousness of slow-wave sleep; and, as she felt thirsty, and rose, and poured a glass of water, and drank, and re-filled, and brought the glass back and placed it on the carpet near her head, and snuggled down once more, as all that happened, he slept on. As Sue's mind slowed again, she thought of her mother who was, well at this time of night she was probably asleep, or trying to be, but who at most other times would be sitting alertly, watching telly, monitoring News at Ten and Question Time and Panorama and News at 6 and Channel 4 News at 7, keeping herself to herself, keeping an eye on things. Which was so – well it would have been hurtful / it was hurtful / it would have been hurtful if it were not so very her, the way she had seemed to say when Sue had gone off to uni: OK you are an adult now, I must not cling. And had kept to that resolution unwaveringly. So that although she gladly received bulletins she never . . . but now Sue's mind was caught by a gleam of imagined moon on the canal which must, after passing through suburban and industrial outskirts, and miles and miles of fields, and doubtless traversing other towns as well, come out at Kidney Meadow, or at least maybe there was a junction so you'd have to take the right turning.

She saw herself and Philip hand in hand. Meanwhile, at last, Philip dreamed: Sue's face emerging from the shadows, vanishing / Sue's face floating up through the night sky towards the moon / a path lay ahead of him over an upland and as he scrunched along it, footfall by footfall, there on the path ahead of him was a pebble in the form of the face of Janet Stone; and as these images flew through his mind, Sue was remembering the weight of his body, the solidity of his shoulders, for even though he wasn't what you'd call a big man it was still lovely to have the mass of him there, when he was there, lovely to have the restless mass of him next to her, to notice as it settled bit by bit to sleep; or to sink into sleep herself while that body, Philip's body, was still alert beside her. Bit by bit she imagined herself back into that bed she shared with him in that house (rented for the year) in The Willows. She placed a hand on the duvet. She attached an arm to it. She connected the arm to shoulder and neck, and joined the neck to her head which she laid gently on the pillow. She imagined another shoulder and arm ensemble hidden by the duvet. One by one she envisaged torso, hips, thighs, calves, feet; and as she did so they materialised under the duvet, plumping it up. There she was; and as the last bit of her arrived her mind dropped into sleep. She slept; he slept. She dreamed: Philip behind a desk, in a white coat, attentive / the two of them sitting side by side on the fat, horizontal branch of a tree. He slept. She slept. He . . .

. . . jolted awake to 'Steel knife / In my windpipe' Eminem strangled shout from the clock radio, what the, Jesus the harshest beep-beep-beep would be preferable to that, don't they ever think, when they do their playlists, that people might actually be woken

176

up by what they play? He reached out, switched it off, and lay back for a last resentful moment in bed; as he did so, she was sleeping. On she slept while he hoicked himself up, washed, dressed, had coffee and toast and marmite and an apple and then was out – oh, of course, the car was at the practice – taking the familiar route along Parnassus, through Elysium Crescent and Felicity Place and out through Lily Walk towards his work. As his hand pushed at the wire-glass window of the practice door, she slept. As he greeted Jackie and went through to the Little Ease – i.e. consulting room – that he had borrowed from Dr Adam Hibbert, and readied himself for the first patient of the morning, she began to dream: an enormous ball of wool, the two of them, Sue and Philip, being wrapped in it, two little wooden dolls being wrapped around, around, around.

Saturday morning surgery was a mix of the brave and the anxious. The brave were people with long-term conditions who were still at work and so could not attend the usual weekday consultations. They took the pre-booked appointments which filled up weeks ahead. The anxious were usually parents who rang as soon as the line opened in the morning. I am speaking on behalf of my daughter who, well, who says she needs the morning-after pill and I know it is available at the chemist but I think it would be very helpful if she could be talked to by a proper professional. My little boy is ten weeks old and he's had a cold and now there's something wrong with his breathing. It's terribly fast. His chest never goes out properly, it just goes in, in, in with each new breath. His temperature is a hundred and two. For real emergencies people dialled 999. So Philip rather enjoyed his tri-weekly Saturday duty, even though of course it cut into the weekend. There was a lot of humanity in this sort of doctoring. Since he was the only GP present the practice lost its weekday feel of crowd control. In fact, this was about the only time he felt able to give completely undivided attention to each patient. Plus, it was all over in three hours.

After which today, of course, there would be Grace Hanworth.

As Philip outlined for a patient a holistic approach to the management of IBS, explaining that it was a process in which medication, diet and more general lifestyle adjustments all had a part to play, Sue slept a dreamless sleep. As Philip tested the peak flow of a chronic asthma sufferer who was taking steroids in the wake of a recent acute attack, Sue opened her eyes to brightness, closed them again, turned over to bury her face in the cushion, and realised that she was not at home but at Charlotte's on a sofa. As Philip treated himself to a quick cup of coffee, Sue gave up trying to sink back to sleep, swung herself upright, blinked, and blearily wondered whether Charlotte had green tea. As he sank back into his chair, she rose; as he buzzed for the next patient she opened a cupboard to begin to look. As she found what she was seeking, only bags but at least basically the right stuff, he was beginning to catch up with Jason Armour, a regular attendee who had MS which was as yet progressing only slowly, thank god, though obviously there was only one way it could go.

Sue sat at the glass table. She watched the lines of light that came in through the slatted blinds and lost their focus in the dusty air / her mother in the little flat in Stoke. Sue reached across and pulled towards her Charlotte's A3 sheets of paper. Leaving the cup steaming on the table, she let her eyes wander over the loops and lines and apostrophes and squiggles and dots and underlinings that

Charlotte had inscribed. Then she reached across again and pulled towards her her notebook and her pen. Clean sheet. She started a column of ideas, copying and adding in her lumpy, mechanical handwriting.

Geiger counter – Japan.

Flood measuring thingy.

Thermometer? / weather station??

Glacier.

An eye.

She heard again Ash's soft, compelling voice; felt again the exhilaration as she fell. But there was a difference between his photo of an eyeball which was analytical and the video stream she had in mind which would be observant, which would show the eye budging as it looked, which would notice the eyelashes twitching, which would be alive.

She saw again the man like Charlton Heston, like Charlton Heston in . . . what was it, that dark film, that Welles film *Touch of Evil*.

They could, obviously they would work out how to arrange the images once they had the images themselves. And of course the TV sets themselves. For instance: a thermometer was like a glacier because both got longer and shorter with the temperature, although in opposite ways. It might be good to put them side by side; or it might be too obvious.

Something to do with acid rain: Taj Mahal?

Or actually maybe better would be tears on the face of the Buddha, of some enormous stone Buddha like those ones that were blown up in Afghanistan but there must be others.

The surface of a river.

Which would display an organic and yet stifling algal bloom; or what was the name of that one Charlotte mentioned that got filled with detergent bubbles or fertiliser run-off bubbles, really horrid, glitteringly overflowing with them like bubble bath. Sue looked for the name through the swirls, the razor wire, the jungle undergrowth of Charlotte's writing. It seemed not to be there.

'Why don't we try and connect that . . .' – Sue remembered herself saying; 'make your self-analysis a part of it.' But actually it was really important they stay focused on the concept because the show was not about individual expression, it wasn't about therapy: it was about . . . well, it was about creating an impersonal sensory environment that lots of different people could inhabit as their own. So she hoped when Charlotte got up she wouldn't . . . Sue was now feeling some trepidation about what might happen when Charlotte arose.

Blades of grass.

Something underwater: coral reef.

Some half-dead reef with a few, what are they, polyps, still clinging on, still popping their little fluffy noses out, hanging their colourful laundry out to flutter in the currents.

But now there was a thud from behind the bedroom door, and a moving-about, and the door opening, and here was Charlotte in a pink-puce silk or satin dressing gown that gleamed intermittently in the shadowy light.

Charlotte said: 'Coffee.' Then she moved through the room towards the windows. Passing Sue, she dropped a hand onto her shoulder, squeezed it. Then she was pulling at the blinds, letting the sun rush in.

'Another surprisingly hot day, looks like' – she said.

'End of the world,' said Sue.

'Oh well,' said Charlotte, in that thin, bright tone of hers.

It's funny, Sue thought, how sleepiness shows in the face. Why is it, when you wake up, your skin is puffy and your eyes are shrunken and pink? Charlotte had the Warhol look, the colour-planes of her head not wholly coalescing with its lines.

Now Charlotte was fiddling with the Italian coffee thingy, unscrewing it. 'I've been thinking,' she began to say . . . but her voice stopped and she switched on the tap, let the pot fill gurglingly up. Then she screwed the top bit on, and set the contraption cooking on the hob as Philip, 53.5 miles away, put his computer to sleep, went out, locked the door of Little Ease, and walked along the quiet corridor and through the empty waiting room.

'Good weekend!' – he said to Jackie who was doing something in reception: she sent an echo back to him. Soon she too would leave and the building would enter upon forty-three and three-quarter hours of emptiness during which some small proportion of the particles in the air would sink to the floor, chair-cushions, desk-tops, keyboards, monitors, glossy magazines and even the plastic toys in the children's corner of the waiting room; during which the earth in the plant pots will dry a little; during which whatever the process is that will eventually make the brown gloss paint flake from the somehow chemically incompatible doors will proceed a little further towards its end.

Another surprisingly hot day, thought Philip, clicking the car unlocked. Not exactly environmental to drive three hundred yards but he needed his kit with him just in case. Though almost certainly, he thought, as he eased the Golf out of the narrow practice car-park, there would be nothing to do except maybe adjust the dose of painkiller and anti-nausea. He saw Grace Hanworth's face, the skin marbled and shiny across the high bones, wrinkled and soft elsewhere where the flesh had subsided. Yellower and yellower every-day but there was no point trying to do anything about that now. As if – he braked for traffic lights – she'd let him! He heard again her quiet decisive 'no' after he had outlined the benefits of chemo for the metastasis in her liver. He smiled as the rhythm of the exchange came back into his mind, his measured, detailed, guardedly optimistic proposal, designed to take her concerns fully into account while also almost certainly extending her life which had to be a good thing surely? Followed by her stone-like, what was the word, lapidary 'no'. Nothing to discuss. I am my own person. I am not going to give myself up to being repeatedly half-poisoned. I am not interested in experiencing chemically induced physical distress – the distress I am already suffering is enough. I am not going, to that extent, and for that reason, to turn myself into a guinea-pig and be experimented on by experts.

'It wouldn't be an experiment.'

'Can they guarantee it would work? Are they in a position to say: this amount of treatment will give you that degree of remission for these many months and weeks and days? No they are not. It is all in terms of probabilitites. And that is always so, is it not, in your profession? You always think in terms of likely benefit in balance with degrees of risk. In that case, every course of treatment is an experiment. There is always the possibility that it will not work. There is always a chance it will go wrong. Which means that you'

– she had pressed on, in her precise, clipped voice, not looking at him but seeming to see in front of her the line of thought that she was following to its conclusion – 'you doctors are in the position of adventurers and we patients figure as the virgin land you are struggling to bring under your control. I have no wish to be a subject of your empire.' Only then had she looked across at him with her ungraspable expression which seemed at once cold, and triumphant, and mischievous, and warm.

It had been even worse – now he was looking for somewhere to park – when he'd suggested she might spend some days in a hospice so that her hypercalcaemia could be treated with diuresis and IV pamidronate. She'd been really irritated with him that time: positively hissing. She'd have thought he might have known her well enough by then to realise that she wanted to stay at home. That she was concentrating on her own decline and did not wish to be exposed to new people in a new environment. That she did not wish to be subjected, etc. etc. – so that she would rather die than leave her home. That phrase for once not being an overstatement. Because in this case he pretty much could guarantee that it would work: the intravenous treatment really was just like having something done to your car, oil change, new clutch; and it really could not happen safely outside an institution.

Although, he reflected, as, parked, he turned the key and the engine stopped, the oral bisphosphonates he had ended up prescribing instead had done a perfectly good job. At least, good enough in the circs. He sat for a moment, breathing in, feeling his chest expand, his shoulders drop. Treating her really had been an education. Because she had an informed, distinctive view set up in opposition to his, no in balance with his. A fully articulated set of wants and values. With no qualms about asserting them. Whereas so often he was dealing with a bundle of uncertainty and fear. All sorts of emotions, and a lot of them. That was it: usually there was this sort of miasma of undefined emotion for which, as he diagnosed what was going on in the body, he also had to find a voice on the patient's behalf, make a channel. Janet Stone was the great example of that, the other week, suddenly crashing, suddenly turning away from everything they had gained up to that point. He had had to sort of rebuild her software, remind her of the decision she had made, of the path she was on, of what she stood for. Whereas Mrs Hanworth was solid. She had it all worked out.

Or at least, he took a moment more to say to himself before he opened the car door, she seems to. You could imagine a psychological argument saying that all this assertiveness was a mask for deep anxiety and distress underneath. But you could make that argument about anyone. And as a GP – he simultaneously pulled the catch and pushed the door, performed the everyday awkward movement of levering himself out of the car and up onto the pavement – as a GP you had to take people – he bent and reached in for his case and pulled it out and straightened and pushed the door shut – you had to take people as they presented themselves – he was walking along the pavement; he clicked the key and heard the car lock behind him.

Push open her wooden gate, take four steps up the little garden path. How quaint, it again seemed to him, the gothic arch above the doorway. But rather lovely, the care that must have gone into constructing it. Having rung, he stepped back to look at the old, patterned brick. It continued down into the terraced front garden, or front patch would be a better word for it. Mrs Hanworth must have done that, or someone: it wouldn't have been original. Every feature given a dark outline. A circular central flowerbed from which a rose bush rose, its shiny reddish leaves beginning to unfurl. And an oblong one behind the low front wall where tufty lavender bushes grew.

Here was someone opening the front door. Pink cheeks, a yellow V-neck stretched over an expansive stomach. The man filled the doorway, his balding head grazing the top of it, the edges of his torso spreading nearly to its sides. Oh yes, it was her son. Close to retirement himself.

'Dr Newell,' said this man, Mr Hanworth, as he must probably be called. He walked welcomingly backwards through the narrow corridor of the hallway. Philip stepped in, occupying the space progressively as it was vacated. The trick with a home visit, as always with being a doctor really, was to be mild, attentive, very much the professional. Put your personality on the back burner so they didn't have the sense of being visited by you as an individual, but by a medical presence. Which diminished this awkwardness of greeting – and the greater awkwardness of barging into people's homes, their private places.

Mr Hanworth had backed into the sitting room. 'The nurse,' he started to say through the doorway to Philip who was still in the hall, 'has gone out for a bit. I said she might as well have some time off. She'll be back at 6.'

'That's fine.' Philip passed his case from his right to his left hand

and let it rest on the second-from-bottom stair. 'How has she been?'

'You mean my mother?'

'Mm.'

'I suppose,' Mr Hanworth said, his head turning to one side and down, his face seeming to sag, 'much the same.' Then his face lifted back up and he looked at Philip frankly, beleaguered, bravely: 'By which I mean she has carried on on the same downward slope. Weaker. Spends more time in bed. She doesn't come downstairs now but then I think that was already the case last week.'

There was a breathiness in his speech; you noticed him pausing for breath between each statement. Probably COPD. You could see he must have smoked when he was younger – perhaps the weight came on with stopping. Funny the signs of illness in someone who was talking about illness. Sad.

'With some of these things' – Mr Hanworth was carrying on – 'you can't tell whether it's that she can't, or that she doesn't want to.'

'Often it goes together.'

'For instance, she used to like sitting in her chair in the window upstairs, looking out at the street. Or watching the trees, birds, you know, whatever was going on outside. She could rest her head and she seemed' – he hesitated, looking for the right word before choosing: 'comfortable there. Sometimes I'd go up and she'd have gone off to sleep. Or be just sitting there, eyes open, completely' – again the hesitation – 'vacant. Which seemed – you know, nice. But now even that has come to be too much. She just doesn't want to do it. And I don't know' – he pressed on, working back around towards his point – 'whether it's because it's become physically painful to sit there or because she's lost interest.'

'Does she say she is in more pain?'

'No' – he lengthened the word amusedly, pooh-poohing the idea. 'You probably know what she's like. That's not the sort of thing she very much wants to admit.'

'No. But I think, as time goes on, she may well do so more, I mean she may well find she needs increased pain relief. When that happens it's very easy to adjust the dose.'

'Yes,' the man said, a serious expression coming back into his face. 'Received and understood.'

'And she's been taking her medication regularly?' Which was to say, 20mg zomorph twice a day, with oramorph top-up as required; metoclopramide 10mg 8-hourly, docusate sodium 5ml 8-hourly: really the minimum conceivable.

'Yes absolutely. The nurse has been most efficient.'

'No side effects?'

'No, or, well . . .' he said awkwardly, sidling closer, lowering his voice: 'She had – an episode of incontinence a couple of days ago. The nurse was very good about it. Now we've got a rubber sheet underneath. But since then she's stopped eating more or less completely and I'm worried that that might be why. Because it's obviously not very dignified and no one would want to . . . Do you see what I mean? If she's lost her appetite, that's one thing. But I wouldn't want her to feel she had to stop herself eating. You know, deprive herself.' He looked at Dr Newell in supplication.

'Was it' – Philip said calmly – 'wee or pooh?' God these stupid baby words.

'Number two,' the fat man said briskly.

'How about her drinking, is she still taking liquids?' If you keep the voice gentle and concerned, your expression kind and thoughtful, then these questions don't sound so much like an interrogation.

'Yes, I think so. Or maybe' – the man's eyes turned, looked past Philip to the corner of the room – 'not so much. I confess I haven't really been keeping very strict track of it.'

Well the nurse certainly ought to have done. 'OK – but you should now,' said Philip. 'Drinking is more important than eating. If she doesn't stay hydrated it'll cause her some distress. But going back to that episode the other day . . .' It was really a bit awkward, this consultation going on in the hallway, or half in the hallway. Philip kept his voice low so that it wouldn't reach upstairs to where Grace Hanworth was. 'It may help if we reduce the docusate, you know the laxative, to just once in the morning and once in the evening. I mean, she needs to keep taking it to counteract the effect of the morphine which – well, it has a tendency to just block up the gut completely, which can be very uncomfortable. Especially, obviously with the kind of cancer that she has. But we can take the dose down a little bit. And the other thing' – this was stating the obvious – 'is to be sure she is confident about how to go to the loo.'

'Oh, she can still get to the loo.'

'Yes but she may be finding it harder, especially if, as you said, she's not getting up to sit in a chair any more.'

The man took this consideration on board.

'The nurse is the person who will be able to help with this. As Mrs Hanworth finds she wants to spend more time in bed, and eventually . . . not get out of bed at all . . . she'll need a commode, and eventually perhaps an adult diaper. But the nurse will be able to talk this process through with you.'

'I'd be obliged,' the fat man said throatily, 'if you didn't mention this to mother.'

'No.'

'She wouldn't want to talk about it.'

'No.'

'Or to know that I had mentioned it to you.'

'Of course.'

There was a moment of reflection. Had everything been gone through?

'Oh, and about her eating,' Philip remembered. 'It's important not to feel she has to keep eating. Not to be upset' – he looked into the man's wobbling eyes – 'when her appetite declines. Because that is part of what happens in the process of . . . in the last days of life. There is a . . . a quietening, if you like, of the body and of the spirit both at the same time. A settling down. A getting ready to withdraw. All we can do, Mr Hanworth' – Philip ventured the name and found it was the right one – 'is . . . well, what I mean is that, as a doctor' – he was about to speak more decisively, to share the view he had arrived at really mainly as a result of observing Grace Hanworth over the last few months: 'I understand what is going on medically. But holistically, by which I mean thinking about the whole person, it is a mystery. It really is amazing to me how, very often, everything declines, no in fact' – he saw that Mr Hanworth was listening gratefully – '"declines" does not feel like the right word. Everything develops in such a way that a death feels like the conclusion of a life. And when that happens . . . when we are in the presence of that mystery, it really is OK to trust your feelings. Your intuitions. So if you feel your mother is in discomfort, she probably is. And probably, by trusting your feelings, you can see how to help her even if she's not saying anything – by raising her a bit in the bed, or drawing the curtain to make some shadow, or maybe to let in more light. But, equally, if you feel that she is peaceful, then she probably is that too. And it's OK, then, to relax, and maybe just sit, and spend some time with her.'

Bit of a sermon. But it seemed to have gone over alright.

'That's very true,' Mr Hanworth was saying. 'Thank you. Let's go on up.'

At which, as Philip followed Mr Hanworth up the stairs, Charlotte, 53.5 miles away, was saying: 'How about Tahrir Square?'

'That,' said Sue encouragingly, 'is a very interesting idea.' Because it would make the leap to actual politics. Although . . .

'Because that is life, isn't it, if anything is,' said Charlotte: 'That is flaring up. Better than a flood. Better than grass. And if what we're doing with our video-streams is connecting the observer to all sorts of pressure points round the planet, making them think about how their nerve system can extend to lots of places that are kind of out of their control or beyond their knowledge, then . . .'

'No, you're right,' said Sue. 'It's a great idea.' Because actually to have something mainstream. Because, actually, given that the other images were all going to be of nowhere-places, or mainly; of ordinary places that you couldn't immediately identify. Because, given that, it would be good to have something iconic as a contrast, or rather to make people think: what *are* these other places? I know what that one is so what are these? I know that that one is really important so how are these ones important? No, it would be good. 'It really is. Do you think we can get it?'

'Oh, I'm sure. I mean they had it on the news so there must be . . . actually I think I, don't exactly know someone . . .'

'Like with Elton Barfitt?'

Charlotte looked startled. Then she smiled. Then she said in soaring tones, 'No seriously!'

'But also if we can't we could try other squares, Bahrain, Tunisia, because in a way it's not that square itself but that kind of square.'

But Charlotte was standing now, stretching: 'Agreed.'

Philip was standing in Grace Hanworth's bedroom. There was a single bed sticking out into the middle of the space. How strange it looked: monastic. Mrs Hanworth's feet, beneath a sheet beneath a blanket beneath a pale pink tufted cotton bedspread, pointed towards a bay window from which light came pouring down upon them. Upon her. There was a pile of pillows, four or five of them, with her upper body propped against them. Its boniness showed through the ivory, shirt-like top of her night-dress. Her head lay back. It was the colour of amber. Her sparse, silvery hair had been neatly trimmed and brushed. No obvious danger signs.

The floorboards creaked as Mr Hanworth went round to the other side of the bed. He was leaning over her. His hands were on his bent knees, propping his bulk. He looked up at Philip. 'Shall we wake her?'

'I think she may wake gently in a minute anyway. The slight disturbance of our being here.'

'OK I'll – damn.' It was the telephone. 'I'd probably better . . .'

Philip moved closer to the bed to let Mr Hanworth squeeze past behind him.

Philip stayed standing by the bed. He listened for her breath. It was strange, the process of listening, how the sound seemed to get louder when you found it. There was the out-breath, strong. A pause. The in-breath, weaker. Rhythm a bit off kilter but no sign of difficulty. He concentrated his mind on the sound once more. No, no congestion. No hint of a gurgle.

He looked around the airy room which he had been in several times but only seen glancingly because he had always been concentrating on Mrs Hanworth. The rectangular bay window, the armchair where she liked to sit. The swirly bluey-greenish Morris-pattern wallpaper. Gnarled leaves like arthritic hands reaching out, fat buds like : . . well, like something. Like sea anemones.

Really at this stage it was just about seeing how she felt. He knew and she knew what was happening. No doubt about that. So it was all about keeping her comfortable. Or in fact in the particular case of Mrs Hanworth – he smiled to himself, half-exasperated, half-admiring – making a compromise between her wish to experience the progress of her disease and the blunt fact that if she was left just to feel it, at this stage, to really feel what it was doing to her, the pain and also other causes of discomfort, for instance, nausea, would be overwhelming.

The chair was oldish, elegant. Square and sturdy and upright. Upholstered in faded, velvety green. There was a table in front of it, wooden, rectangular. Practical. You could sit at the chair and have a meal on it – perhaps Grace had been doing that. Though in the middle of it was a little metal bust of someone. But obviously that could easily be moved.

Feeling awkward just standing there he took the few steps over to the window and turned the chair towards the bed. He would sit and watch Mrs Hanworth and listen to her breathing. For once in his life there was no rush. It was Saturday; and Sue was away until at least the evening, maybe tomorrow. If Mrs Hanworth didn't wake he would ask Mr Hanworth to rouse her gently when he came back from the phone.

The mirror over the fireplace had an interesting wooden frame. It had narrow columns going up on either side, supporting little shelves and hooks. Keys dangled there, and other things. Philip could see the key-thing for bleeding radiators, and a Swiss-army penknife. On one shelf was a pile of what appeared to be old post-cards. He wanted to get up and take a closer look but didn't feel he should.

Because basically he agreed with a lot of what she had been saying to him. Because basically you did want people to be more self-reliant. You wanted them not to come running along to the doctor at the first sneeze. And then you wanted to be able to have a sensible discussion. You didn't want them to put them-selves at your mercy like lumps of meat, as if it were none of their business what was wrong with them and what was done about it. Throwing all the responsibility onto him. With all the pressure that put on him, and frankly also this was the state of mind that bred litigation.

But the fact remained that, as things were, people weren't. On the whole they weren't self-reliant. They wanted diagnosing and they wanted to be told what to do. However much he tried to, for instance, outline alternatives. Almost always it was: you know best, doc: whatever you think is best.

Except when they got it into their heads they absolutely had to have a particular medicine, for instance antibiotics, which might be wholly inappropriate. But, in fact, that sort of pig-headedness was just a different version of the same thing. This, well, this basically turning away from themselves. This not wanting to look at themselves as whole creatures, i.e. including their bodies – or in fact primarily their bodies – and really under-stand what was going on.

So: what could you do when people were so much like that? Not just abandon them. Not kick them out. The problem with Grace Hanworth's point of view was that it ignored these people. It was all about what people should be like and not at all about how they were.

Still, it was definitely interesting to talk to someone who had been there right back at the creation of the NHS, and involved with it. He really hadn't known there had been such a strong movement back then to take power away from doctors and put the emphasis on prevention. 'But Bevan' – he heard again the shock in Grace's voice – 'simply lay down on his back and let the British Medical Association march over him. We were left with the same old oppressive structure where ordinary people weren't allowed to understand anything for themselves. The idea was: they would be left to live their lives unhealthily, fall ill, and then hand themselves over to an expert to be cured. Or maybe not cured. Either way, there were still to be experts on the one hand, and plebs on the other, and no uncertainty as to which was which. Because daddy,' – she finished sarcastically, 'knows best.' It really was . . . well, it was very her, these harsh denunciations coming out of the careful, tidy body, the slim, alert face. He saw her again sitting on the orange chair in the practice, energised by the effort of making it in to see him, when she had still been able to. And probably irritated by the people in the waiting room: too many of them, not ill enough. When she started speaking she was genteel and clipped, just the way that you'd expect from how she looked. But as she went on this sort of roar came through from underneath.

It was strange to have her voice in his mind while what his ears were hearing was her breathing. The strong, contemptuous breath out. The pause. A bit too long, that pause. And then the little uphill inhalation. A limping breath. As though she wanted it out of her more than she wanted it in.

Was it time . . . but something had changed. The sound of the breathing had dropped away and the head was stirring. Philip saw the eyelids open as the head was still laid on its side.

'Hello Mrs Hanworth,' he said. It might feel threatening if he got up and moved into her field of vision before she was fully awake so he would wait for her to turn her eyes to him.

She lay still, looking at . . . probably looking at nothing, to be honest, just registering the light.

He was about to say again, 'Mrs . . .' but now the head had rolled around and the eyes were looking at him. The head lifted itself upright. Mrs Hanworth was doing something with her arms, pushing herself into the pillows. Should he go to help? – no; she seemed OK, seemed comfortable. Still strong enough to manage that.

He leaned forward in the chair ready to converse. He could stand and move closer once she had properly grasped that he was there. Awkward that Mr Hanworth was still downstairs.

Ah, she had seen him. She was focusing on him, about to speak.

Loudly she said: 'Gordon, you know how uneasy it makes me feel.'

What . . . ?

'Have you seen Slansky? Have you looked at the pictures? Do you believe it?'

. . . ?

'Have you read' – the voice was quieter now – 'the confession?'

OK this is probably delirium.

'I am *not*' – she shouted – 'betraying anything. I am trying to work out the truth.'

Though it's not exactly wandering, her speech. He wouldn't call it muddled. Her cold eyes were staring at him. Her voice was enraged but her body was completely still.

'So, according to you, it is bourgeois to try to find the truth?'

It was as if he, Philip, were a body-block or whatever it was called in a movie when they filmed people's bodies and then a computer printed a different identity onto them, a monster or a ghost.

'What I am saying is that if you read with your eyes, and think with your brain, you will find that it does not connect.'

Though there is something a bit odd in the way she is speaking, a sort of sing-song.

'Think of his life of struggle for the Party. Why would he throw all that away? Throw it away for what?'

Still, probably better not interrupt, Philip thought. Better let it run its course.

'Look at the attack on Otto Sling. Two years ago, they accused Sling of conspiring against Slansky. Now they say they are associates!'

Philip became aware of Mr Hanworth filling the doorway.

'Do you know what it puts me in mind of?'

Philip looked up at Mr Hanworth and, with their eyes and facial expressions, the two men signalled helplessness, the need, for the moment, to do nothing, only listen.

'It puts me in mind of Julius and Ethel Rosenberg.'

Whom he had heard of, vaguely.

'That too was a show trial. There too there was hysteria cultivated by the State and channelled for its own purposes.'

That's right they were Americans from, when was it – 60s? – 50s? Meant to be spies.

'But now look at the differences. The Rosenbergs seemed so calm. They were unyielding. Why? Because they were guilty! Because they knew that what they were facing was justice, even if, I *know*' – she barked the word – 'even if it was the wrong justice of a Capitalist State.'

Yes, and they were executed.

'They had strength because of what they had done.'

But didn't it come out afterwards they were innocent?

'And now recall what happened to us.'

To her?

'The fabricated suspicion. The assumption of guilt. We couldn't do anything against it because they had no need of proof. Which meant they were not vulnerable to disproof. We were being used. We too were victims of a State neurosis.'

It could be the morphine causing this. Or it could be dehydration. Or she could be hypoxic. Although again she did not seem restless nor confused. More concentrated on the wrong thing.

'Now look at Slansky, Gordon. Really look at him.'

Her morphine dose was still comparatively low.

'I know it is the Party doing this to him. I know it is not the Americans, and not the imperialist British government. But that doesn't mean it's right.'

Mr Hanworth was still standing there. Neither of them must speak because, as Mrs Hanworth saw it, they were not in the room. The room was dominated by her vision.

'Gordon, when I look at Slansky' – the voice was trembling with assertiveness – 'I see us.'

After a moment she pressed on rhythmically: 'He is slumped. He leans, with his weight on the policeman next to him. He has shrunk. He is kinked. As though someone has kicked him in the side. And no doubt that is what they did. Again and again and again. And worse. Or else' – now the voice slows somewhat – 'he stands with his head bowed. Trying to recede into the distance. An array of microphones is pointing at him. They are like missiles. He says what they want him to say. Because the world has changed. Around him everything has altered, new colours and new shapes. What was up was down and what was down was up. More than anything else in the world, he wants to find a place in it. Even if that place is labelled: traitor.'

That last word seemed to be an end. It cracked like a dropped plate. Mrs Hanworth stopped, her mouth part open, her eyes still looking towards Philip but no longer focused.

'Mother?'

Nothing.

'Mother?' – Mr Hanworth stepped towards her.

Her head moved, and then her eyes moved, wandering through the room and then finding him, her son. She looked with shock, and then bewilderment, and then a terrible spreading disappointment. The energy went out of her body and she sank back a little into the pillows. Her face slackened. Her eyes were shut now. She must have not known, she must have been wholly in the moment she was remembering. And then suddenly she must have come to, suddenly leapt half a century forwards and found herself elderly, bed-bound, tired, in pain, remembered she was dying.

The first thing to do would be assess how she was now, how she would be in a few minutes. If she was compos mentis it would mean she wasn't hypoxic.

Her eyes were closed still and her breathing was audible again. The long breath out, the pause, the quick breath in.

'Mother, are you alright?' Mr Hanworth had sat on the side of the bed, tipping the end of the mattress towards him. Mrs Hanworth's feet beneath the covers were at an angle.

'Do you remember where you are?'

From where he was sitting, useless, Philip could not see Mrs Hanworth's face.

'It's me, Friedrich.'

Philip didn't catch the words with which Mrs Hanworth replied, but he heard the impatient tone.

'Good, good,' said Friedrich or was it Frederick placatingly. Philip looked at the yellow jersey stretched across his pillowed shoulders.

'The doctor's here.' Then Friedrich or Frederick Hanworth stood and turned, backing towards the door.

'I'll leave you to it.'

Now Philip stood, took two steps slowly towards the bed. Mrs Hanworth was looking at him with wary, weary eyes.

'Sit,' she said, in a whispering voice, glancing at the flattened patch Mr Hanworth had vacated.

'So,' said Philip gently, perched side-saddle on the bed, 'how are things?'

'I thought,' she whispered, puzzling it over: 'I thought I was talking to Gordon, my husband' – now the voice was blurring – 'ex-husband.'

'Mmm.'

'That was really' – she was gulping, or trying to gulp: her mouth was dry. Philip looked to the bedside table for a glass of water, yes there was one, and a jug. He lifted the glass towards her, made a platform under the base of it with his fingers as she drank. 'Really a bit of a surprise.' Her eyes were fixed on his face. Her eyes were trembling, watering. 'I mean the coming to. The coming back to here. Horrible.' Her eyelids lowered. Her head shook a little from side to side.

Her eyes were still down. He watched the little greyish wisps of lashes.

'Have you been . . .' he started to enquire, but she was saying quietly, raspingly:

'I am not going to do it any more.'

'Has it happened before?'

'I don't mean that.' He was about to speak but she pushed on: 'The pain is worse.'

'I can increase . . .'

'I could tell you it is so very bad. I could say, doctor, doctor, the agony! I could make my mind wander more, much more, pretend it was wandering. I could howl. I could have hallucinations, more hallucinations. I could be restless, never settle, be at risk of falling out of bed. And you' – now she was looking up at him with direct eyes, appealingly – 'you would set up a contraption to administer the morphine automatically by syringe and I would get you to increase the dose. Or maybe' – she was still looking at him and the eyes went cold, went stony – 'I could do it myself.'

So this was . . . So she was . . . His heart was jumping and there was a panic reaction in his throat but he tried to look back calmly, tried to fill his face with friendliness. He put on his gentlest voice. 'I cannot set up, or authorise, a syringe driver for pain control unless' – he was using official words to show that, for all his human sympathy, he had no choice but to go by the book – 'I'm satisfied you need it. For instance, if you're not able to take the medication in another form, or if you have break-through pain the oramorph can't stop, or if you are in the very last stages of life and in distress.'

'I am in distress,' she said. She was looking past him, at the window. There was harshness in her voice, weariness. 'What I wanted to happen has come to an end. Now it is eating away at me. Not just eating my body. Eating away at me. What will happen . . .' – she was tiring, it was getting harder for her to speak – 'is I know where I am less and less. I will know who I am' – the eyes came back from the window: now she was looking along the thin line of herself towards her feet – 'less and less. I will be at everybody's mercy. I can't' – her neck was tensed, her lips drawn back from her yellow teeth – 'bear it.

'So,' she carried on, turning to him with a strange sudden jauntiness, a sudden ease: 'Let's do it now. Why don't you set up the syringe driver. Fill it full. And when you are far away I will have a miraculous surge of manic energy and plunge the plunger home.'

He sat there. It was easier now she had said that. Clearer. The request was simply there in the room between them and they could look at it. He kept on projecting gentleness and warmth. Because when they looked at it, when she looked at it, she would see it was impossible. He had stated the rules he had to follow and anyway she knew the arguments. They both knew the arguments both ways. What he should do is simply, calmly try to be a firm and caring presence, try to help her like that, hope that that would help.

The energy seemed to fade from the air as the moments passed. Her face was slackening again, sinking back into the pillow. Her eyes were closed. A twitch went across the lids. Pain.

'I wasn't,' she said blurrily, ' a very good mother to Friedrich.'

She opened her eyes slowly to see that he was there still, and closed them again slowly, lizard-like. 'Or the girls. They have hardly been to see me. But Friedrich stays. He has taken' – there was restlessness in her now, impatience – 'all this time off.'

'Well that shows he's a good son. He doesn't want to lose you. Not before he has to.'

She seemed not to hear. She was very still. Her head was lying atop the pillows at an odd, acute angle. Like the head of an artist's wooden dummy that had been posed to seem to ask a question. But her eyes were shut and her attention seemed to have turned away from everything outside her.

Then her mouth opened slightly and breath was coming out. Then it seemed impeded; the breath rasped. There was a gurgle at the back of the throat. The eyes opened and she lifted her head, trying to lean forward. Philip reached his arm around her, slid his flat hand down between her spine and the pillow, eased her further upright. She coughed a weak, congested cough. Then calm again. She was balanced upright, resting with the tiniest pressure against Philip's arm.

'Shall I help turn you onto one side?'

She wobbled her head in assent. Still with one hand at her back, Philip reached his other hand across and tugged a pillow down at an angle towards the edge of the bed. He threw another to the floor, leaving a pile of two at the bed's head. Slowly he let her lie back and tip over as her shoulder abutted on the angled pillow. Now her head was on its side, her cheek on the other pillows; but her torso was twisted, her hips and legs still lying flat.

'Can you turn your hips and legs?'

She didn't respond. So strange after her alertness a moment ago. 'Shall I?' Again the mild assent.

He walked around to the other side of the bed. He knelt beside it. He reached under the covers with his right arm, his hand flat. His fingertip touched the side of one of her buttocks and he pressed the back of his hand down into the warm mattress to slide it under. Now his hand and wrist were all the way through and his fingertips curled up to touch the edge of her hip bone. Really there should be a draw sheet but he would leave that to Mr Hanworth and the nurse to arrange later when Mrs Hanworth had had a rest. He reached down with his left arm so that its wrist and hand lay across her lower legs. Then, gently gently, he raised his right forearm-and-wrist-and-hand like a single rigid lever, and simultaneously pulled the lower legs backwards with his hooked left hand and wrist. She went over beautifully.

'I think you might be more comfortable with a pillow under your ankles. Shall we try?'

No movement but a feeling of consent.

So he reached along for the pillow that had been cast to the floor, and, raising the bird-like, bird-light ankles with his left hand, slid it under. Then he stood and went around the bed to where he had been before.

She lay quiet with perhaps a hint of a smile around her mouth.

An eye opened and she looked up at him.

'I had wanted,' she said, moving the part of her mouth that was not hindered by the pillow, 'to see the blossom.'

She watched him a bit longer with the one eye that he could see. Then the one eye closed.

She spoke again: 'It bursts out amazingly.' A moment's pause. 'But it only lasts about a week.'

'Maybe when it comes out,' he said, 'we can lift you so you can see it.'

'It is,' she said, 'such profligacy.'

Then she settled into quietness again. He listened. The long breath out; the quick breath in.

'Try to keep drinking,' he said. 'Just a little bit. Don't let yourself dry out.'

They sat together in the quietness of her breathing.

And then: 'I'll leave you now,' he said. 'I'll see you next week.'

'Mmm.' As he stood, her head stirred. 'Oh Dr Newell,' she called out, in a voice that was suddenly clearer. 'Do you see Lenin in the window?'

He looked, bewildered.

'Could you bring him nearer, here.' With her eyes she indicated the bedside cabinet.

Oh, she meant the little bust on the table. He went over, picked it up between fingers and thumb. Surprisingly heavy. He put it on the bedside cabinet, a bit above the level of her face.

'Thank you,' she said. 'I'll wake up and see him looking down at me.' Eyes shut again, she smiled. 'So stern.'

'Have a good rest Mrs Hanworth.' Philip was standing by the door now. 'See you next week.' Over the creaking floorboards of the little landing he made his way out, and down the creaking stairs.

The door was open on the left into the sitting room. Philip put his head through to look: there was Mr Hanworth in an upright chair by the empty fireplace. His knees made right angles and his arms were laid along the arms of the chair and he was looking straight ahead.

'Mr Hanworth,' said Philip, moving into the room.

The head turned and Mr Hanworth was looking up at him. The worried eyes looked out from above the flabby red cheeks.

'I didn't get to talk to her as much as I would have liked. She's sleeping again now.'

No response from Friedrich Hanworth.

'That . . . episode. It may just have been a very vivid memory. Or it may have been what we call a confusional state, or delirium. In a way the definition doesn't really matter. What matters,' he continued, 'is how your mother feels, that she should not be in distress.'

He simply sat there listening.

'It's important to help her to keep taking liquids. Not force her, but make sure she's never left thirsty.'

Still no response.

'If she is in pain or seems distressed, you must ring the practice number.'

'She thought she was talking to my father.' There were streaks on Mr Hanworth's mottled cheeks. 'That was the argument, I'm almost sure that was one of the arguments' – his head was nodding, he was piecing the thing out – 'that made them break up. I was only very young then. I didn't know what it was about. I remember the tones of voice. I was in bed and I remember the arguing voices coming from below, and not being able to make out what was said. So it was strange to hear the actual words just now.'

'Can I ask,' Philip said, 'what was it, I mean who was, was it Slansky?'

'He was a communist. He was one of the accused in the show trials of the 1950s. In Czechoslovakia. My mother saw through it all, at the time, unlike my father. Unlike pretty much everyone else on the left. It ended with her splitting from the Party – you know she was in the British Communist Party? And splitting from my dad.'

Friedrich Hanworth had been talking to the air but now he turned again to Philip.

'I held it against her. We all did. It was quite a hard life. She went out to work. She had been in the civil service before I was born, they both were, but they had left, or had to leave, because of belonging to the Party. So she worked as a teacher. It was lonely for us kids. Now, looking back, I think she recognised that, and was sorry for it, and sort of insulated herself against it. That was why she was so, well, not cold exactly, but . . . stern. Oh I know I shouldn't be talking to you like this, Dr Newell, it's not your job to listen . . .'

'No that's alright, I don't mind.'

'I did react against it. I went and got a good capitalist job, and became well-off, and had a bourgeois family, lived comfortably. Enjoyed everything she so much disapproved of and had fought against. That created some estrangement, as you can imagine. But now, when I look back. Well, Dr Newell, you get to my stage of life, and you can look back more calmly and understand. And now I do that, well: I very much admire her.'

'And you are wanting to show that now in your care for her.'

'Yes,' Mr Hanworth said solidly, accepting that he had been understood.

'Are you feeling that your mother isn't allowing you to do that as much as you would like?'

'Perhaps. Yes. It is that, yes.'

'She' – gosh it was strange to be saying what he was about to, to this blustery, jovial, elderly man – 'knows. She knows you love her. You are showing it. And she does love you back. Of course she does.'

The man was gritting his teeth, sucking his cheeks in, biting back tears, nodding his head.

'Yup,' he blurted. 'I hope that's right.'

'But I should really . . .' said Philip.

'Yes of course,' said Mr Hanworth, at last rising, heaving himself up out of his chair, advancing towards Philip. He took Philip's hand between both of his, shook it, kept it in his grasp, looked achingly into Philip's eyes, said 'Thank you.' Then he let go, and Philip was able to back out through the doorway, and walk along the passage, and open the front door, and step through it into the warm air of the world outside. The bright light came darting at his eyes and he narrowed his lids against it. The street was fluorescent white; the trees were purple and pink. Then gradually, as his pupils adjusted, things settled back into their ordinary colours. It was just a bright spring day.

Philip pulled the car door clunk shut beside him. He was enclosed by metal in the still flat air. He let his head lean against the headrest. He wanted his mind to go blank. His mind was a grey sheet. His mind was a shadowy empty bucket. Except for that little, floating nugget of colour and energy that was Sue, that dragonfly. Which now metamorphosed into a face, making the lip muscles of his own face tense in response, his cheeks plump up. But her face had no substance. When he tried to look at it with his so-called mind's eye he couldn't, it kept on twitching away. He tried chasing it for a moment: it jumped here and there away from him in the Tardis-like endless black space of the back of his skull.

His eyes opened. He reached for his laptop and made a record of the visit. He pulled out his phone and left a message for the nurse.

Job done. Now for the weekend.

But he sat there still, not wanting to move off yet, not knowing anyway where to go, how to get out of the professional mood, the stance of listening and assessing and diagnosing and uttering words appropriate to the context. The armour of it, the structure. The rigidity. The being expected to give a definitive response. And, even more surprisingly, the being able to do it. Being the person who knew.

He let his head fall backwards and shut his eyes once more. If it was a weekday he would just stay in role, there would be another visit to drive off to, probably, then return to the practice for afternoon surgery, then end of the day, back home, beer, Sue, cooking, telly or going out. He breathed in deeply, slowly. He opened his eyes, looked at his watch: Christ two o'clock already. But of course – he shut his eyes again – that absolutely didn't matter. He breathed out, slowly and long. What should he, well there was always the idea of going to a garden centre or plant shop, brighten up the back patio. He stretched his neck upwards, let his shoulders drop. Since it seemed to have absolutely no plant life at all. Except for the strange little standard bay tree in the middle like a gobstopper on a stick. Which was entirely surrounded by stone-imitation concrete slabs. Except for the brick-walled raised bed along the back edge of the smallish rectangle. Which seemed to have nothing in it except gravel. Not even a weed. Not even earth.

Oh, that was it, they would have been filled with gravel to stop anything growing: they were designed as flowerbeds but then presumably the landlord filled them up with gravel because obviously you can't trust tenants to do any gardening. Which was perhaps no doubt largely true.

So he could do that, but . . .

As his professional role fell away from him, as he relaxed, feelings and images came in its place. The vulnerability beneath the shell. All the visit to Grace Hanworth reappeared in his mind but not running at the same speed and volume, nor quite the same colours, nor even exactly the same order. Shouldn't he have told Mr Hanworth that Grace had asked him, in effect, to kill her? Shouldn't he have attempted a more thorough diagnosis after her hallucination? It was as though the sequence of time were a ribbon that rippled and folded back on itself. Should he have spoken in that personal way to Mr Hanworth? Shouldn't he have interrupted Grace's delusional monologue, which might have left her not so upset and tired, which might have . . .

The holograms in his mind sped backwards and forwards illustrating different chains of cause and effect. Mr Hanworth would be embarrassed at having been spoken to so intimately, he would ask to see a different doctor. The nails of Philip's fingers clawed up a fistful of the fabric of his trousers over his thigh as he realised that he, Philip, would have to explain to George why that was, why, in the closing weeks of his mother's life, Mr Hanworth had taken the unusual, nay, extraordinary step of asking a different doctor to step in. There was nausea in his chest and such a bad, dragging feeling in his mind, a terrible oiliness coating everything stiflingly. Worse, worse, Grace's delusion would turn out to be caused by something obvious, some incompatibility between her drugs, which would immediately be spotted by the out-of-hours doctor who would be called when it happened again this afternoon, only by then it would be too late, too late. Philip ungripped his fingers from the trouser fabric and reached for the button on the door and pressed so the window wound down for a count of 1, 2, 3, then stopped it, felt the breeze creeping in, caressing him, was lightened by the new expansiveness of sound and the fresher air.

Breathe. Calm.

Because she was on a perfectly standard regimen of drugs. Really nothing dangerous in the least. Because he had responded humanly to Mr Hanworth, in a way that was wholly common sense and nowhere near in breach of the guidelines. Because he had respected his patient's confidentiality, as he was obliged to. Because he had been honest and compassionate. He had exercised his professional judgment. He had recognised the special value of human life.

So it was alright.

So he could go and buy some plants.

Because obviously it was upsetting, it was someone dying.

And actually there ought to be a place to get a sandwich at the garden centre: he really needed to eat.

It was Grace Hanworth dying, whom he had really got to know quite well. And like. Who had in fact become a pretty important figure for him.

There had been nothing from Sue since the text he had found when he woke up saying that it was going OK, that she hoped to be back this evening. That she was missing him.

Because everyone thought that being a doctor was about curing people, i.e. saving life. Whereas it was also quite a lot about going in the opposite direction, about easing people into death.

So he texted back to say that he was going to buy some plants and could she think of any kind she wanted?

And the horrible thing was that he was going to get used to it. As he was already pretty used to it in fact when someone was dead already, when he didn't know them and just had to certify the irreversible onset of apnoea and unconsciousness in the absence of the circulation. Though that too had been a shock the first time he had had to do it. To be the one whose signature said: this life has come to an end.

Should he go home and change into jeans and then go out again or just go as he was?

So that, officially, the person was still alive until he, Philip Newell, had signed his name.

Go as he was and change when he got home.

The name of Death was Dr Philip Newell.

He turned the key, dabbed the accelerator. Vroom.

So that it was OK for him to be upset, today, about Grace Hanworth.

He reversed a bit, turned the wheel, went forward a bit, turned the wheel the other way, reversed a bit, turned the wheel back again, wait, wait, and: now – out into a hiatus in the flow of traffic.

Because in fact it would be upsetting if he wasn't. If he wasn't upset. The upsetting thing would be not to be upset.

He indicated right, slowed. Tricky mini-roundabout, go almost all the way round so that you have done a 'V' almost doubling back on yourself.

But in the future he would be. Be not upset. In the future if he felt sympathetic towards a patient like Grace Hanworth and established quite a warm relationship with her as bit by bit, under his care, she died, bit by bit, painfully, with inevitably some indignity, despite everything everyone could do, she died, kicking against it, in fear, despite her courage, despite her selfless convictions.

You went straight over at the lights, and kept on, and then the garden place was there at the edge of town.

When that happened he would not be upset. He would be functional. It would be all in a day's work, like an undertaker.

Brake! Jesus, what was that, a dog, what was a dog . . . can't people control their bloody dogs! It went streaking across like a . . . like the mechanical rabbit on a track that greyhounds chase at greyhound races.

But then probably he wouldn't have developed a warm, sympathetic, interested relationship with the future Grace Hanworth in the first place. She would have been just another patient, a creature to be treated, dealt with. Which was exactly what she, the present Grace Hanworth, the real Grace Hanworth, was so sensitive about – she was so sensitive to being thought of like that, so anxious not to be. But the future Philip Newell would have turned into a sort of automaton, like in sci-fi – was it in Star Trek? – a computerised medical machine who would provide a uniformly excellent standard of care without any interference from the feelings, who would not be even a little bit sickened by the smell of shit, frankly, all-but whited out by the smell of disinfectant; who would not be unnerved by the feel of her frail flesh under the thin cotton of her nightie, the rickety backbone, the deflated buttock that he had had no choice but to slide his hand under; who would not be at all sent reeling by the pine-yellow face looking up at him, asking for a sudden death, asking to be spared what lay ahead, the greater sickness and the sharper pain, the – so strange it must be, the awareness of everything progressively not working, the limbs heavy, unresponsive, you try to lift your arm and it will not lift, the fingers cold, the toes cold, the coldness spreading upwards, inwards, your skin greying, flaking, your heart reluctant, your lungs taking in less oxygen each breath and in any case your body isn't asking for it, the peristaltic movement of your intestines slowing, stopping, so that your last meal simply sits there because you have no need for energy, no need for food; all this is happening and you are turning into basically a slab of meat and bone and gristle, only perhaps you don't realise it because you, the real you, the mental you, is going to pieces too, this is what Grace was aware of, because the nerves aren't working properly and so the brain isn't working properly, the chemistry will have gone off-kilter, the synapses not sparking properly, the voltage-gated sodium channels creaking on their hinges so that the messages just don't flow at pretty much the speed of light any more exactly where they are wanted but jam up, congeal, so that you get areas of stiffness, of blockage, your limbs don't respond, they may be going cold but you don't in fact know they are going cold, there is just a numbness so that if you look and see them you are surprised to see them there, because in the brain the same thing is happening at a cellular level, basically, because what had been a magical, unimaginably multitudinous web of connections is sagging, disjoining, so that you just can't remember, or worse than that, you don't know that there is anything to remember – the person who, for example, had been your son becomes a stranger, you have no sense of ever having had a son at all, and by the same token, you can't process new material, you can't place yourself in relation to what is around you, because you are like rotten fabric that just so easily rips, or like a wet-through card-board box left out for the recycling that when you pick it up separates into the different layers of itself or pulls apart in soggy lumps, isolated areas of flailing chemical activity which perhaps throw up images into your mind, only your mind is too strong a way of putting it because there will just be images floating some-where and the terrible thing will be that some of them are memories and some of them are fears and some of them are prob-ably nothing to do with you at all, not in any way that matters, they are maybe the cheapest possible trashy things put into your mind by the morphine, Ronald McDonald maybe, he is dancing around with his red banana grin and you are watching him, only again it is an understatement to say that You are watching, because there is no You apart from Ronald McDonald or the magic roundabout, let's say the magic roundabout, that would be better,

Dougal and Zebedee and Dylan, that would be better, that wouldn't be so bad at all.

He was crying.

He had better pull over because you can't drive with tears running down your cheeks it is not good for your reactions.

The garden centre was just there, he could almost see it but still, he had better pull over.

Don't fucking hoot at me you pillock I did indicate I am just pulling over, I just need to pull over.

There; and as Philip came to rest, not entirely parallel with the pavement but still out of the run of the traffic, Sue was saying: 'So what do you think?'

And, as Philip put his thumb and index finger on the key and turned it so that the car went still and quiet, Sue was saying: 'Do you think it's good enough to put to Omar?'

And as Philip sobbed a little, and then stopped sobbing, his cheeks and eyes feeling plumped and tender, Sue was saying: 'You think he would?'

With Philip, the stillness and quiet were entering into him, not consoling him exactly but somehow making him, too, stop; helping his mind, too, come to rest.

With Sue and Charlotte, sitting in the open air, upon grass, in a small park in the middle of the city, where there was a really great playground if you were a kid, all walkways, and climbing walls, and firemen's poles, and colourful nylon rope netting and a fountain-pool thing, a wide, shallow dish of granite, probably fifty feet across and perhaps only one inch deep at the deepest part, so that the granite shone and the sky mixed with the stone, the blue with the grey, the clouds with the granulation; with Sue and Charlotte the space and sunshine stimulated their thoughts, especially since all around, at the edges of the little park, the grass rose in brick-edged terraces like paddy fields with, beyond them, a fence in wavy, anodised steel and, beyond that, the winding distinctive streets of a carefully planned new development, really much better than The Willows, frankly modern, the houses higgledy-piggledy, flat-roofed, with balconies to bring the inside out and big square windows to let the outside in, and beyond that, the busy streets of the rest of the city. They were in an artificial oasis, a bit of nature gated and on display.

To Philip, the sense of just sitting there, enclosed and quiet, was increased by the vibrations of other cars passing by. To Sue and Charlotte, the noise of the rather distant busy streets came echoingly as something not unpleasant, almost the murmur of the sea, almost the susurrus of breathing, were it not for the periodic chainsaw rasp of motorbikes, or were they angry bees?

So, as Philip, more together now, looked in his wing-mirror and touched the accelerator and moved out, Charlotte was saying, 'But he's not gonna let us do it as ourselves.'

'Why do you . . .'

'Sue, he talked to me,' Charlotte said flatly. 'He talked to me and he said . . .' She looked awkwardly across the park. 'He talked to me and he said that it was Elton Barfitt or nothing.'

Sue's body was wax.

'That's why I couldn't, really couldn't tell him they'd said no.'

Wax melting; feathers in the breeze, fluttering, falling.

'I didn't want to tell you because I knew you were so attached to . . . well, what we've been doing. I hoped there'd be some give, something would change.'

In Sue's head there was a single, continuous, high-pitched sound.

'But it hasn't, except . . . Sue?' – Charlotte called the name more perkily. 'There is a way of doing it, I think there is a way of doing it.'

'Is there.'

'Listen. We just don't' – she spoke slowly – 'ever tell him they said no.'

'Charlotte, Jesus!'

'No, but listen,' said Charlotte.

'It's not. A bloody. Game!' – said Sue. 'Why can't we' – she was speaking shrilly, breathily – 'Just . . . be . . . straightforward.' Tears were threatening to come.

'Listen,' said Charlotte gently. Charlotte reached out and held Sue's knee. 'Sue?' – she said, looking enquiringly into her eyes.

Sue calmed a little.

'Listen.' Charlotte became methodical. 'We can tell him that they are doing the show but that they need it to be anonymous. Top secret. So that – do you see?'

'No I don't.'

'He is the only person who thinks it is by them. Do you see? All anyone else knows is that it is an anonymous show. With some secret high-profile artist behind it but basically an anonymous show.'

Though maybe. Though maybe actually . . .

'So he can tell himself he's got a big name artist behind it,' said

Charlotte, as Philip at last turned into the car park for the garden centre.

'So we could still do our thing,' said Sue, observing the new possibility, gauging it. 'But,' she then said, 'we'll have to make him think all the instructions come from them.'

'Yeh but we can,' said Charlotte, mildly. 'They are conceptual artists. They'll be doing, I mean he'll think they're doing, the completely usual thing of just sending a blueprint that the poor curators have to build.'

Philip slammed the car door and walked towards the building where large grey and black placards announced: 'Specialist Compost', 'Sands and Grits'. He aimed right, towards the entrance, past a table of British Grown Hanging Basket Plants, 4 for £10, Petunia, Geranium, Mecardonium. The colours of Lego.

'I don't mind writing the instructions,' said Charlotte. 'I'm' – an operatic flourish – 'practised in deception.'

Inside, there were large, long, display areas, edged with low concrete walls. Concrete paths went between them. Behind each concrete wall were plants, their roots in plastic pots, their stems strapped to bamboo canes. They were separated according to type (for instance: Herbaceous Perennials) and arrayed, within each type, in alphabetical order of their Latin names.

Sue said: 'There'll have to be a contract.'

Philip walked along the rank of Shrubs – Colourful Foliage And Flowers, Ideal For New Gardens And Gap-Filling. He saw some lilies that were a plastic orange colour and some fuchsias with their flowers that were like earrings.

To which Charlotte replied more grimly: 'In for a penny.'

None of this is right, thought Philip. This is completely the wrong sort of place. What I want is something wild. Weeds. Maybe I can ask to buy some weeds. Maybe somewhere they have a heap of weeds they have removed from in among these hothouse specimens: maybe I can get a heap of those and take them home and scatter them. Because this, he said to himself, pausing for a moment doubtfully to eye a clump of whispery bamboo, is not at all right.

'In future years,' said Charlotte, 'when it all comes out, it'll be like, a real thing, it'll be part of it.'

'Part of that loosening, that unravelling of identity that was such a vital artistic movement of those times,' said Sue, quoting an imaginary future history.

On their stretch of grass in the middle of that city, Sue looked up, and Charlotte looked down. The two women, eye to eye, grinned. Happiness and resolve sparked back and forth between them. It could really . . . could it really? It was so dangerous. It was so wicked. But, sod it, she couldn't, how could she continue as she was? She saw the gallery as a weighty, huge, marmoreal edifice, a Doric temple guarded by an enormous statue of . . . herself.

'So let's go back,' said Charlotte, shifting to her knees in the process of getting up, 'and I'll write the first email from . . . E. B.!'

'Plus the small matter of the other two rooms of the gallery,' said Sue, lifting herself into a crouch.

'Fuck. I'd forgotten,' said Charlotte: 'I'd . . . completely . . . forgotten . . . the other two rooms of the gallery.'

Philip, striding back towards the entrance, had his attention caught by an octagonal raised area of little plants. No flowers! Little greyish leaves. Oh, and some shiny bright green ample ones. And . . . oh, they were herbs of course. He bent to read the labels: Thyme Gold; Chives; Rosemary; Mint. He rubbed a leaf between thumb and forefinger, smelled. At least they would be useful, at least there was a point to them.

Sue and Charlotte moved off over the grass towards the gate, Sue's hands in the pockets of her jeans, Charlotte's arms stretched out on either side. They veered away from one another, then came back close. Head down, one of them pushed the black-painted steel gate open. Harmoniously the two of them passed through.

Having decided against the herbs, Philip found that the entrance to the garden centre was not also the exit and turned back. You had to go down a zigzag of ramps and into a prefab building. Where in fact there was a café. He hesitated between his hunger and his desire to escape.

Charlotte abruptly asserted: 'You must really love him.'

'Why do you say that?'

'Well don't you?'

'Yes, I do.'

Philip chose bacon and lettuce with obviously too much mayonnaise, and an apple, and a genuine filter coffee.

'But why, what's made you say that all of a sudden?' Sue was blushing.

'The commute. The fact that you work here but don't live here.' They were walking down a steep slope, their feet jabbing into the pavement. They were not thinking about what they had so recently agreed; not thinking about everything that lay before them. 'I was thinking,' Charlotte continued, 'that now you are here, this weekend . . . I was thinking how relaxed that is, how creative, how' – she lifted her shoulders and forearms in a shrug, looked sideways at Sue with an open, daffy face – 'how fun. But every day instead you get on the train for, what, an hour? and go back to a place where there can't really be much going on.'

Philip was sitting on a solid pine chair at a shiny, round pine table. He lifted his slim sandwich and bit it, leaving a serrated half-moon cut-out in the gooey white bread.

'It's not that bad,' said Sue. 'It doesn't . . . I don't think of it like that.' Her hands were in the pockets of her little grey jacket and she was looking ahead, eyes focused on the pavement five yards in front of her. She was striding forward with a knotted brow. 'I dunno, what can I say? It's how I am, how we are. I mean . . .' – they turned and were suddenly along the edge of a dual carriageway where cars howled past. She raised her voice: 'To me, you make a commitment to someone, I mean, something clicks inside you – and that's that. It's not about weighing up pros and cons. And after that, after that click, you see the world from inside the person you have become. Do you see what I mean? So it doesn't look to me the way it looks to you – you know, something that might have this or that inconvenience. It just is.'

'And there's the doctor's salary.'

'Oh yeh, yeh,' said Sue, mock-aggressively. 'That makes all the difference. That's really the most important thing for me.'

They were turning into a quieter street. They were climbing now, into the fringes of the businessey and light-industrial bit of town. To their right, a somewhat shabby black-glass cube with builders' fencing clamped around it. Grass pushed up between the mauve bricks of its concourse floor.

'I don't think you should psychologise everything,' Sue was saying, 'any more than you should, you know, make it all pragmatic, practical. But it does suit the person I am. You know I've always wanted to be a bit outside the art world, keep a perspective on it? Phil helps me do that. You know the story' – she pressed on – 'of me?'

'No.'

'OK, why not?' – Sue asked the converted warehouse buildings around them. 'So, me mam' – her voice took on a different accent – 'wan'ed a kid, but didn wan' a man. So she went on a trip – to Spain on account of the fact that there are . . . loads of hot guys there. And had . . . The Time Of Her Life. And came back pregnant. And that was me. So growing up in Stoke it was just the two of us. Against the world. Which you can make of,' Sue concluded, suddenly feeling she had said enough, 'what you will.'

On his way out, Philip's gaze snagged on a stand of bright little packets of seeds. He stopped and turned and stooped to scan the paper envelopes that dangled in rows from blunt chrome hooks. There were all the artificial blooms he had disliked outside. But wait, there was a picture of a meadow with what, clover? poppies? windswept bedraggled ordinary flowers. And here was a packet of interesting wild grasses. And here another meadow. And there, why not, some sunflowers, so blatant they would be fun. This was the thing to do, to buy these seeds, and plant them, and OK the flowerbeds would be empty for a while, for weeks probably, but then the little seedlings would begin to sprout and he would nurse them.

Average Contents 1100 seeds, he read on the back of the two inch by four inch packet he held between his finger and thumb. Amazing. Yes he would plant them and nurse them and there would be a whole little meadow of wildish living things in the raised bed at the end of the concrete patio behind the brick box of the little rented house. With four packets spliced between his fingers he walked jauntily to the checkout and paid and walked jauntily out to the car and got in and reversed and turned and pushed out into the traffic, the thousands of seeds reposing on the passenger seat beside him. On he drove, and then paused at some lights; and on, and paused at some more lights, and then he was making the tight turn around the mini-roundabout and on past Grace Hanworth's house which had a long grey car like George Emory's parked in front of it.

Like George Emory's. Philip glanced in the mirror and indicated and pulled to the right and stopped. He twisted round, making his neck ache as he forced his head around to be able to see. He could see a stretch of low, gleaming grey fuselage and a top corner of the windscreen. He sat back straight. He reached up and angled the rear-view mirror so that he could see the scene again in miniature. He was calm. He felt his energy sapping, some depressive movement in his brain, for instance maybe a little reduction in norepinephrine. No jolt of adrenalin. Because all that was happening was that what he had worried about before was coming true. Because something had gone wrong, because they had called and complained and turned to George as a proper doctor. Because.

There was tension around his throat and his lacrimal glands were undergoing stimulation.

But maybe.

Maybe it wasn't George's car. Could he reverse to better see? No he could not. Could he get out and saunter casually across and look for – what? A slew of drug company leaflets across the back seat maybe. Or packets of fireworks! No he would recognise it anyway, he saw the car again as he had seen it in the practice car park, a rare car, old, a black number plate with silvery lettering, what was the make? – yes, a Bristol, with burgundy leather, and a walnut instrument panel and, that was right, a sea of papers in the passenger side footwell, and little silvery handles for winding the windows, and a pale accumulation of dust across the mottled dark plastic of the top of the dashboard.

He saw all this; and then he saw himself self-consciously walking across the road, blushingly looking to left and right, his steps stretched out on Pink-Panther tiptoe; and then he heard a rasping voice shout 'Dr Newell!' and saw himself freeze, and shrivel, and scurry away into a corner where he would turn around and around, curl up foetally, and half-bury himself in a mound of slimy leaves.

So it was not a good idea to try to saunter unnoticed across the road. Because to show concern would be to betray he thought something was wrong. It would be basically a confession of guilt. So what he should do instead is drive around the block, and back, and slow when he was passing the car that might be George's, slow, and glance, and see what he could see.

So he straightened his mirror and turned the key and touched the accelerator and checked the mirror and pulled out and went a little way forward and indicated left and slowed and turned. And drove and turned again. And then he was describing the 'V' again around the awkward mini-roundabout; and here he was approaching George's car again, i.e. the car that might possibly be George's. Black number plates with silvery lettering. He slowed some more. Burgundy leather. But there was someone behind him and he could hardly stop: what if the someone behind him hooted and George Emory looked out of Grace Hanworth's window?

If it was George Emory.

If it was his car.

In any case, he told himself as he drove on now smoothly, drably, there is nothing to be done. Only thing to be done is to sit mum. Pretend that nothing is happening until it does. Unless for instance he could go online and find out exactly how many Bristols of that model existed in grey with burgundy trim and calculate the odds of one of them (i.e. not Dr Emory's) being there on this given street at this given moment. Or maybe you could track the number plate, he looked in his mind and there it was, GPK 24F, you could go online and doubtless have to pay someone to track the number plate.

But Christ, Philip, what would be the fucking point of that?!

Still driving, he slammed his hand down, jabbing his thumb-joint onto the wheel, ouch – and the car is swerving to the right, pull it back, keep straight, stay calm, just go along calmly, gently, gently, right here, straight on, over the bridge, right along Helium, through Parnassus, along Elysium to home. There is nothing he can do. There is no point trying to do anything. Anything he did would make absolutely no difference. The only thing to do is to stay passive. Because in any case maybe it is nothing at all. Maybe

Dr George Emory left his car there to go to the shops which are not more than a couple of hundred yards away. Maybe he had broken down! Maybe he's having an affair with someone in the house next door!! Maybe he was visiting friends. Christ Philip will you just . . . calm . . . down.

Sue, meanwhile, was on the scratchy sofa, sitting cross-legged, holding herself upright against its sag. Charlotte was in one of the soft armchairs, crouching, her laptop unfolded on her knees.

'Look I've basically got a concept for the other two rooms,' said Sue, 'so why don't I tell it you and you can say what you think.'

'OK.'

'The first room, you walk in, and it's just a sitting room. An average sitting room. Like this one, in fact – bearing in mind what you said last night. Or also like the one in Phil's and my house: a completely average room. And the way we get it . . .' – she pushed on over something Charlotte had been about to say – 'is to get people to bring in their own furniture, do you see, that way we tick our community box, we put ads in the local papers, put flyers out, inviting people to send in photos of likely bits of furniture. And then we do some home visits and pick the best.'

'It could be upsetting for those who don't get picked,' said Charlotte: 'I mean, if Charlotte's sofa were rejected she'd get very cross.'

'Yeh, yeh.'

'No but seriously.'

Sue looked up, looked across. Charlotte was indeed serious.

'It does need careful handling. We talk about appropriateness. We send them invitations to the private view, and . . . no, actually. Brilliant!' Sue had uncrossed her legs and was leaning forward, her forearms resting on her knees, her hands gripped into a double fist. She was bouncing her clasped hands as though weighing something. She was staring at them as though they held the answer.

'We use the photos in the next room, we . . . I'll tell you about it in a minute.'

Charlotte nodded and looked pleased and gave her attention back to her laptop with a wrinkled brow.

'Going back to the first room,' Sue said: 'People will walk into it. And won't know what to do. It will be familiar. And it will be strange. They won't know if they're allowed to sit down. They won't know whether to feel at home. Most of all, I think, it'll feel like a stage set. It'll make them self-conscious.'

Philip was standing at the kitchen end of the ground floor of 12 Eden Grove. He was looking through the window at the patio with its barren beds. He breathed in deeply. He breathed out until his lungs were shrivelled, squeezed. Then he looked at the window with its grubby streaks and blotches. He moved both shoulders forwards so that the trapezius muscles tensed. And then he let them relax.

Then he took a glass from the draining board and reached out and lifted the lever of the tap so that a sinewy column of silvery water all at once appeared. He broke the column with the glass and splashed himself and decided not to mind. Lifting his wet hand in its damp sleeve to his mouth, he drank, feeling the chill slide down his oesophagus and pool in his stomach.

Do not think about Grace Hanworth or George Emory.

The lino was sticky underfoot. The pans and plate and cutlery from yesterday were slimy in the sink. Philip's breakfast plate was crummy on the table. The air was tinged with marmite. A heap of unironed clothes slumped on the shiny sofa. Philip stood, surrounded.

Do not think of . . .

And then he thought: the thing to do is clear up, spend the available time before Sue gets back doing that. Which will please her. So that she will walk in and smile. No, probably she would walk in and smile in any case, so what he meant was: she will walk in and smile and after that she will look around and be pleased. And then he can tell her about . . .

Do not think of.

She can smoothe his troubled brow and, what the heck, they can go out, have some drinks, have a good time, laugh.

Though she dammit hasn't texted yet. Though the fact that she hasn't texted yet probably means she is in fact coming back this evening. Though with Sue you can never be sure. And with Sue you must never ever ask.

To ask is to nag.

He clinked his glass down on the aluminium edge of the sink. He looked again out through the grimy window. He felt the obstruction of the seed packets in his left trouser pocket and so stepped sideways and reached for the handle of the kitchen door, lifting it up to unlock and down to unlatch and easing the door halfway open so that he could edge through into the warmish outdoor air. He stood and looked, past the gobstopper bay-tree, at the waist-high brick-edged bed that was covered in gravel. He pulled the seed packets crackling out of his pocket and laid them on the round metal table that was beside him with its two matching chairs. He stepped forward and ran his fingers over the layer of rough gravel, no, bigger than that, really little stones, pebbles. He bunched his fingers into a point and pushed them down between the stones, or tried to: he pulled some of the stones backwards and tried to jab his fingers further in before the stones slipped back into the declivity he was trying to make. The tips of his fingers smarted and their nails were bashed.

He went back into the kitchen and trundled open the cutlery door and selected a spoon. At the back of the sink was a mug from which kitchen utensils splayed: he rootled among them for a spatula. Having returned outside he tried the spatula first. It at once bent 90°. The spoon was more effective. But after, what, three or four minutes of concentrated effort, only a little patch of earth was cleared and there was only a little mound of stones beside it.

The layer of pebbles was two inches thick and the surface area was one yard by four.

Where would he put them all? In a heap? In a rubbish sack? But he couldn't chuck them because probably they were part of the estate there was probably a clause in the contract stating explicitly that no grain of gravel should be removed from this premium rented property on pain of a penalty having to be paid.

Which would be too ridiculous.

He would have to go back to the garden centre and get a tub or a long window box thing to store the pebbles in and also above all a trowel and/or small spade.

Which would mean that he would have to go back past Grace Hanworth's house which would mean that he would have to think of.

Having checked his watch he stepped back inside and shut the door and rinsed his hands under the tap and shook and dried them.

Perhaps he could take a different route, he thought as he made his way through the house to the front door. But that would be no good because the act of avoiding being prompted to think of it would prompt him to think of it all the more.

So he got in the car and drove along Elysium, then through Parnassus and along Helium then left and, his heart pounding, over the bridge and, pounding, left again, following the pounding familiar route, until he pounding, pounding, approached Grace pounding Han-pound-worth-pounding's house where an ambulance was parked outside, its blue lights blinking sleepily, casting and withdrawing their sad tint from the cars and pavement and hedges and the walls of the houses, including Grace Hanworth's house.

Philip pulled in to the left.

George Emory's Bristol had gone and in its place was a police car.

From where he was, Philip could see most of the front door of Grace Hanworth's house beyond the low wall and the lavender bushes. And he could see the front gate, and the whole of the ambulance, and a bit of the side of the police car which was behind it.

He watched.

As he was watching, Sue was saying: 'In the long corridor room, the second room, we get at the fact that there are simply millions of sitting rooms across the country, across the world. So, people have walked in and been in that first room, and then, next, whoosh! – it suddenly multiplies, and shrinks, and flattens, so we have a million photographs of sitting rooms along the left-hand wall.'

'I'm not . . .'

'Well maybe not a million. But . . . how long is it?'

'Say 12 metres?'

'OK, say it's 12 metres by a height of 3 metres. And each photo is 10 cm × 5 cm, that's 120 x 60 = . . .'

'7,200.'

'But anyway, loads: it needs to feel like lots and lots and . . . lots. Maybe the photos could be a bit smaller but we can try out different sizes, see what works. Something bigger than a postage stamp but smaller than a postcard.'

'So like a whole wallpaper pattern of sitting rooms.'

'Yeh that's right, it would be lovely if it could be seamless, a seamless array of flattened, displaced rooms, an army of them.'

'Yup.'

'Sometimes it's the first room of the gallery multiplied.'

'Right.'

'And some of them are of sitting rooms where the furniture didn't get chosen for the first room – do you see? That can be the prize, the carrot: that you get your place up on the wall, in among all the others.'

'Yeh, good.'

'Then also there are rooms from around the world, of obviously different ethnicities, all muddled together. I mean I think there should be a' – Sue waited for the right word – 'preponderance of western rooms because that's the mindset we're in, that's people's assumption. But eating away at that assumption, eating away at the' – she guffawed – 'hegemony of the western sitting room are other ways of doing it.'

'Which we can get from the web.'

'Or like also launch a global appeal. Twitter it. See what comes in.'

As Philip watched, Grace Hanworth's front door yawned open and a man in black stepped out. He had his back to Philip as he was turning to pull the door shut behind him. His shoulders were bulky and his black jacket was belted. The policeman took two strides along the path, swinging his chequer-banded cap up on to his head as he did so. He yanked the gate open, stepped through and closed it carefully behind him. He disappeared behind the ambulance. Must be going to his car. Would sit there, would be sitting there, making notes. Would be radioing someone. Why?

Because he, Philip, had committed some catastrophic.

No he had not. He ran the scene through in his mind again, again, back and forth, as he had run it through before, only slower now, in greyer colours, bored almost, because there really was only the slight possible wrong emphasis to be concerned about socially, and probably not even that, but when it came to the actual doctoring, the medicine, then no. Because actually the point was he had simply and clearly refused to do the thing that was against the law.

So maybe George.

Because George's car had been there and so maybe George.

High-handed George Emory who blusters and knows best. Jovial Dr Emory who is so generous with the pills and the syringe. Who would go padding up the stairs all rotund and pampered and gently, gently open the door and squeeze his way through it and sit attentively with his concerned, sinister smile on the edge of Grace Hanworth's bed and think that it was actually down to him, actually in his power to decide to agree to what she asked. The calmative, too calmative syringe. The excess morphine permeating the body, further stimulating μ-opioid receptors so as to produce extreme relaxation and calm. There is not even a memory of pain. The breathing slowing, the breathing less and less, quieter and quieter, the chest not stirring, the lungs settling into stillness, no little breeze across the lips. No doubt relying on the fact that morphine concentrations in the blood post-mortem are notoriously difficult to interpret given patients' variable reactions to the drug, which was why careful titration was so crucial in treatment. So that he, Philip, would have to testify as to the really pretty low dose, considering, that Grace Hanworth was still on. But anyway that would be in the records. Unless even now Dr Emory was altering the records. But the police were there! The police were there! So that what must have happened was that Mr Hanworth must have got wind of it and walked in on him or just been suspicious afterwards. And dialled 999. So that it was all up now for Dr Emory, it was all over. Scandal for the practice. No good for his, Philip's, job prospects next year although presumably in fact he might be able to just carry on here, if Dr Emory was struck off and if the practice were able to continue. Dr Emory turned into a chess piece in his mind and was taken by a knight's move and lifted from the board.

'On the other side,' Sue was saying, 'it's names. The whole wall covered with printed names. Like the phone book only without the numbers. Or like the names on a war memorial only these will be the names of living people, so far as we know. And again some of them will be people from the local community – that can be another lure to get involved. Others will be random names from across the world. The space is the same as for the photos on the opposite wall and if we do, what 10 names per photo. Or 5 maybe. That's 70,000 names. Or 35,000 names. Or something in between.'

She was sitting back now, happy, expounding, on the home straight, the thing was making sense.

'So the punters walk into the first room.'

'The stage set,' said Charlotte.

'The room pretty much like theirs, the every-room, their sort of space. And then they walk into the second gallery and – boom. So many rooms and so many people. Made miniature and flattened into photos and names.'

'The unimaginable multiplicity of people.'

'And monotony.'

'Where does sameness stop? – and difference start?'

'Then on from that into the last room.'

'The command centre.'

'Well, the place where you can stand and take stock. Reach out with your mind and vision, and notice . . .'

As Philip watched, the front door opened once again. Nothing emerged. But then something began to nose out. At about chest height. Black. Next, the person carrying it. Who was wearing a green uniform. Who was stepping sideways with his or her back to Philip. And then swung round so that you could see the expanse of what was carried, infer the undulant form of the body within the bag, the nape of the neck supported by the right upper arm of the squat man in green who was the bearer, the crook of the knees over his left upper arm, and his hands clasped under the edge of what must be the hip, the same hip that Philip had touched before through cotton.

With his burden, the man stopped at the wooden gate. Until another man in green came out behind him, and edged past, and reached a leg over the lavender, squashing it a bit, and tipped himself then over the lavender and the low wall onto the pavement, so that he could open the wooden gate and let the other man with his burden through. And then opened the back of the ambulance and pulled out the light, wheeled aluminium stretcher. Upon which the body in its bag was laid. After which the two men lifted the stretcher and body in its bag into the ambulance. And hopped out again, one of them shutting the doors while the other went around to the front. Then the one who had shut the doors went round to the front as well, and got in. At which the engine of the ambulance started, the brake lights shone, the reversing light shone, the ambulance nudged back, the reversing light went off; and then the ambulance had pulled out into the flow of traffic and was gone, carrying within it, within a bag, the body of Grace Hanworth who had –

– and strangely Philip then smelled the smell of her room as he had been in it earlier that day, dusty, acrid, cosy, sweet; and saw himself again kneeling at her bedside reaching under her to lift; and heard her say one of the first things he had ever heard her say: that she felt as though she were trying to hold herself; that she was slipping through the fingers of her own hands.

'Are you alright,' Sue was saying anxiously, 'to do the email?' She suddenly saw, black in front of her, the enormity of what they were about to enter into.

'Yeh, totally,' said Charlotte. 'Do you want to . . . ?'

'It's just I really should go back to Philip.'

'Oh,' said Charlotte. 'So you're not . . .'

'If that's alright? – If you're alright to . . .'

'Yes,' said Charlotte, 'I am OK to do the email. Don't you worry about that.'

So, as Sue gathered up her bag and checked the time and hauled on her jacket, Philip sat in his silver VW Golf looking at where the ambulance had been; and, as Sue stood for a moment in front of Charlotte, and was hugged by her, and said earnestly – 'Charlotte: thanks,' Philip still sat in his silver VW Golf looking at where the ambulance had been; and as Sue bounced down Charlotte's stairs and lit out towards the station Philip saw the curtains being pulled across Grace Hanworth's window and, a minute or two later, also across the front window downstairs; and as Sue hurried through the booming space of the station Philip was looking at nothing in particular; but when Sue, as the train pulled out, texted him to say that she was on her way, he was beginning to emerge from the mesmeric effect of all that he had seen; so that when the text buzzed into his phone he was able to reach and grasp and lift and read and even feel the ghost of a smile within the muscles of his lips. Sue travelled through black-brown fields which were dotted with little sprays of violent green, and Philip at last felt able to move, to start the car and slowly, slowly drive along the road and all the way around the irritating mini-roundabout and back the way he had come. So that, as Philip came to a halt in the designated parking space outside 12 Eden Grove, Sue was reaching through an opened window to turn the stiff outside handle of her carriage door; and, as Philip still sat in the car outside 12 Eden Grove, waiting, Sue, striding home, was getting to the end of the lane of old houses by the station and was about to begin the asphalt pathway between chicken-wire fences; and, as Philip waited still, she neared, and neared some more, until, turning into the courtyard of Eden Grove, she saw the silver Golf parked outside the house that was theirs (rented) for the arc of the year, and saw a moment later that there was someone sitting inside it, that there was Philip sitting inside it; so that he watched her seeing him and breaking into a trot as she came towards him; so that when she had tapped on the window, worried, smiling, and he had pressed the button to wind it down, her face was pink and flurried, whereas his was grey and numb; and then she opened the door; and he rose out of it, and in a half-hug the two of them walked on towards their temporary home.

TWENTY-NINE HOURS IN JULY

The sun made starbursts here and there on the black glass front of the building in which, on the fourth floor, the coroner's court was housed. The sun brightened the wet pedestrian concourse where people in summer clothes passed among the sapling beeches and through stark lines of shadow. On the shallow steps leading up to the two revolving doors that gave entrance to the building lingered three men in suits, Dr George Emory, Dr Philip Newell and Mr Hanworth, and two women in dark dresses, Mr Hanworth's sisters.

'It shows,' friendly, authoritative Dr Emory was saying in his resounding voice, 'what a very distinctive woman your mother was, an amazing woman.'

'It was a privilege,' added Dr Newell, who was very much in a supporting role, 'to . . . to look after her in her final months.'

'Well,' gasped Mr Hanworth, 'it's over now. It really is.' He looked to his slim younger sisters for confirmation. One of them, with a wide countenance, and cropped hair, a relaxed-looking person standing slouchingly in flat shoes, smiled brightly back. The other, in a prim, belted, dark blue dress, gave a brisk nod: her chin-length straight grey hair flapped across her face.

'Closure,' said Dr Emory persuasively, looking at each one of them in turn. And then: 'Well' – he glanced at Philip, 'we'd better be going.'

After the handshakes and farewells the two doctors were walking past shopfronts, French Connection, Swarovski Crystal, M&S, their reflections mingling with bikini-clad dummies and panoramas of ideal beaches. George Emory shuffled along doggedly, head down, his jacket still on and buttoned despite the warmth. Philip had loosened his collar and flung his jacket over his shoulder: he walked with a lolloping stride. They did not speak. Until:

'Let's go in here,' said George Emory. It was a café-bar with aluminium chairs and tables. It seemed a decent distance from the court.

'No point going back to the practice,' George Emory urged. It was 4.45.

So in they went and George ordered a Campari soda and Philip a double whisky because, God knows, he could do with one. They sat indoors where it was cooler. Light pooled and blurred in the uneven plate-glass window. People passing stretched and wobbled.

'I didn't realise,' George said, 'how stressed you were until I saw you in there, saw you walk in. You should have seen yourself!' He chortled but then stopped the chortle and made his face look sympathetic.

'I hadn't slept.'

'But it went OK, it went fine.'

'Oh I knew it was just a formality. I mean, deep down I knew that. But I couldn't stop worrying that, I dunno, one of them would stand up and denounce me.'

'The one in blue seemed more cross with her mother.'

'Yeh, didn't she.'

'It was like,' George said, 'the whole thing had been done to inconvenience her, one of a long line of embarrassments that her mother had caused her throughout her life.'

'When she said "It's exactly"' – Philip imitated her impatient intonation – '"the sort of thing she would do."'

'It's quite remarkable, though, isn't it,' said George, 'that none of them had the faintest idea.'

'You mean of what was in the . . .'

'Yes, so you could hardly be suspected of it.'

'Christ, it felt like I was suspected of it when the fucking police-man came round the next day,' Philip said. He gulped some more of the whisky and felt the prickly warmth of it slip down his throat. 'So first he said the cyanide was in the statuette of Lenin and then he said could I supply any information on how the statuette had been moved to her bedside table. "Because in this sort of situation it is very important to establish whether there has been an acces-sory to the act," he said – and, you know, gave me a look. And then he informed me that, according to Mr Hanworth, the statuette had been "situated on the table in the window" and "could I throw any light on the matter?" So I said I moved it. When I said that' – Philip jerked his head up and to the side and glimpsed a triangle of blue sky between the roofs of the high buildings opposite – 'I felt that I had done it, I felt that I had killed her, because if I hadn't moved the thing she wouldn't have, she might not have . . .'

'If you hadn't moved it,' George Emory said firmly, 'she would have got up and got it for herself.'

'I know but still it was me who did it.' Philip felt that he was shrieking but his voice came out very quiet. 'These fingers picked it up and moved it. And then ten minutes later she was in fucking convulsions, presumably.'

'She was the one who did it,' said George Emory heavily. 'She had it planned. She had kept that poison by her for sixty years. Think of that! It was part of her, that it was there and she could use it. I don't know what she was involved with in the forties, or fifties. Who knows? Whether she was ever in real danger. But that feeling, that feeling of power, of being able to step out of it all when things became too – objectionable: that stayed with her. It was as if – George's voice was wondering – 'she was a sort of secret agent in the heart of life. So that when' – the voice was brisker again – 'she faced the ultimate betrayal, the one we all face, terminal illness, she had her escape route just there, nice and simple. Unlike the poor devils who have to go to Switzerland. She's an example to us all.'

'What I still don't understand,' Philip said, calmer now, 'is why, if she knew that, she knew she had the poison there, why she did the whole thing about trying to get me to give her a morphine overdose. I know the coroner took it as evidence of her settled inclination towards suicide but it's weirder than that. It's like she wanted to get me into trouble.'

'That's part of it,' said George, sure of the answer. 'It's part of her being' – he put on a laborious French accent – '*un agent provocateur.*

242

I've known her for twenty years, had known her for twenty years. She needled me pretty much non-stop. Some of it was utter hogwash – doctors are tyrants who turn their patients into slaves – you probably heard some of it yourself.'

'Yeh but some of it made sense.'

'Ha!' – George grinned, leaning back. With his fingers he patted the edge of the table. 'I thought you'd think that,' he said, gleefully. 'When I suggested she go to see you I thought that's how it'd be, that you'd hit it off.'

'Thanks.' Philip's tone was indeterminate.

'No but think about it.' George was suddenly intent and quiet. 'When she started to need a doctor it obviously couldn't be me because I was friends with her. Which left you and Sara. And I didn't think she and Sara would get on.'

'No.'

'And then I thought about you, and I thought, first, that she'd enjoy trying to provoke you, and then that you might find her interesting. Because I know I said it was hogwash a moment ago but actually she did have quite a well developed analysis, didn't she? The problem was it was completely unrealistic.'

'What's odd though is that, well,' said Philip, setting about getting the thing clear: 'her ideas were pretty much formed in the nineteen-forties, weren't they, and fifties. And yet they are still relevant now, or in a way they are more relevant. Like patients using the doctor less, taking more responsibility for their own well-being. Oh, I know in a sense it's old-fashioned. Stiff upper lip, grin and bear it. Given her politics I'm surprised how much of that attitude there is in her, was in her.'

'Two things explain it,' said George, with certainty: 'Age and class.'

'But here's the thing – with the internet, it makes more sense. Because with the internet, everybody suddenly knows a lot more.'

'No,' said George, with a surprising up-and-down intonation as though he were telling off a child: 'No they don't.' And then more plainly: 'They have more information. Which is absolutely not the same thing. Especially when most of it is wrong.'

'No but for instance,' said Philip, unbowed: 'a man I saw yesterday. Perfectly ordinary bloke, I'd say he worked as a builder. Came in and sat down and said: "I think I'm at risk of prostate cancer and I need a DRE and a test for PSA." That's what he said, "DRE" and "PSA". And it turned out he was completely right, his interpretation of his symptoms was completely right. So I turned him round in five minutes. Whereas before, well, the consultation would have taken longer, there'd have been a lot of hurdles to jump. But more than that, he probably wouldn't have realised there was anything wrong in the first place, not until it was too late, till he was pretty much unable to pee.'

'Yeh but how many' – George had heard it all before – 'compare how many times that happens with the number of times you have to say to people, I'm sorry, essence of rhubarb is not going to cure your cataracts. Or' – he gestured in the air to grab another example – 'by all means apply feng shui to your bathroom but don't expect it to have any effect on your arthritis. It's ten to one Philip, it really is. And then' – he was miming exasperation – 'you finish your diagnosis and they resist you. They brandish a printout. They say: "But doctor, it says here . . ." Just because they found it on a computer screen they take it as gospel.'

'OK,' said Philip, shrugging, lifting his voice a little, admitting that there were two sides. 'Still, I think' – emphasising the 'I' – 'that it's more good than bad.'

'Whereas I think' – George echoed his intonation – 'people should accept the doctor knows best. That's why we went through seven years of training, for heaven's sake. That's why we spend our whole time looking at sick people and working out what's wrong with them. It counts for something. And you should realise that too' – he said, getting up, going to the bar for another drink – 'what's wrong,' he said loudly over his shoulder, and then turning so that he was walking slowly backwards: 'what's wrong with actually knowing something, with having expertise? Why's that something to be ashamed of, all of a sudden?'

As the sound of George's voice took whatever little time it took to travel through the air towards him, and down his external auditory meatus, and strike his tympanic membrane which agitated his ossicles which vibrated his cochlea, so that the hair cells of the organ of Corti translated this physical wave into chemical-electrical nerve impulses which the brain then could somehow understand, Philip was thinking of Janet Stone. Of the fact that in her case there was actually some truth to what George was saying. Bearing in mind that the whole thing, with her and Albert, was the management of a complex scenario so as to achieve a beneficial outcome. I.e. not worrying too much about whether this or that in itself did or did not have any actual therapeutic effect. Because in this sort of case, where everything was so fuzzy and entangled, where the physical blurred into the psychological which was influenced by the social, the question of what counted as an actual effect was, frankly, impossible to answer. You just had to sit there patiently and focus on the individual concerned. Listen to what they were saying, even if some of it was rubbish. And then nudge them in the direction that was most likely to do them good.

When it came down to it, his role was, on the one hand, to encourage Janet to stick with the parenting tactics she had finally consented to learn; while also helping both of them to keep seeing the benefits of the CBT that Albert was being put through; while also getting input from the SENCO at school; and monitoring the recommendations of the dietician; and staying in touch with the hospital specialist – i.e., to keep this whole complex structure of approved care more or less in place; and on the other hand also to stop Janet getting sidetracked by the stuff she kept reading about online. But in fact there too the trick was to listen to her with respect, i.e. crucially not present yourself as the One Who Knows Everything in the way George thinks you should. Take for instance Synaptol, the natural homeopathic remedy concocted in an oligotherapeutic base. I.e. basically just water. Dual-action symptomatic relief designed to lead your family back to daily wellness. I.e. absolute complete and utter wank. Still, when she tells you about it, you listen. Because she quite reasonably wants to feel she is contributing to the way forward, and also importantly because she wants to find something that connects to her sources of identity and understanding of the world, all of which are in the mystico-natural bucket, the Ash-bucket, haha. So you listen with an attitude of careful attention, and you say "it can't do any harm to try" – and you get her trust. So that when she is tempted by something worse, like neural feedback, she comes and asks you about it, rather than keeping it secret, and believes you when you say it's absolutely pointless. As though ADHD kids can be helped by playing more computer games – everyone knows they are good at playing computer games. Neural feedback is a perfect example of the phenomenon of the techno-placebo whereby people think that if they are connected to a computer with wires then it has to be doing them good. The ADHD kid has too many theta waves and if you replace them with beta waves then bingo, it's much better. Absolute Star Trek mumbo-jumbo. Pure magical thinking. Because an EEG on its own is a terribly blunt instrument. Because the whole question of how the recorded trace relates to what is really going on in the brain is unimaginably complex; as is the whole other question of how it relates to people's behaviour.

Though actually it didn't take much to put Janet off that one: not really her sort of thing. It was just because it existed that she felt anxious: is this something we should try? And probably it wouldn't have done any actual harm. It's the cost that is criminal. Absolutely something that Janet shouldn't be made to feel she had to struggle to afford.

Though anyway, Philip ended up thinking as George came back with two fresh drinks, Albert's doing pretty well. The whole rickety structure of different bits and bobs, all coming together and focusing on him and making him feel safe and loved and important – it was all working pretty well.

'So how's Graham Epsom?' – asked Philip, as George raised his glass and said 'Cheers!'

'Oh, he's alright,' said George, accenting the 'he' as though Graham Epsom would always be alright, there would never be any doubt about that.

'Not set back by the changes to the bill, the future forum, the health and well-being boards and all that?'

'It's Stalinist,' said George. 'What I can't stomach is that the whole idea was to set us free so we could do more good more effectively; and in fact it's ended up now as an enormous amount more bureaucracy . . .' Philip's phone was buzzing. 'And this has happened,' George carried on as Philip looked to see if it was Sue, 'because of our own campaigning. It would be much better' – he blustered – 'if it had been left the way it was.'

It was Janet.

'Well,' Philip said, tapping Decline, 'you know' – he brought his attention back to George who was in front of him – 'you know that's my opinion.' Philip sat squarely on ground he had staked out many times before.

But he was also thinking: Christ, what can she be calling me for now?

'But, yeh' – George went back to the question he had been asked – 'Graham's OK. He does systems and data, so for him, well, the more complicated it is, the more he'll be in demand.'

It was really getting too much – Philip was thinking – ever since he'd gone out to see the three of them on the barge . . .

'But for me, and Sara and Adam and Isobel and Paul,' George was continuing, 'it's going to be intensely frustrating. It was going to be tricky enough getting together with eighteen other practices as it was.'

. . . he'd stupidly given her his private number and now, every little thing, she called him . . .

'But now we have to form a Clinical Commissioning Group including representatives from blah blah blah it's too boring.'

. . . and he couldn't tell her to fuck off because she had this hold over him . . .

'And run everything past the Commissioning Senate while taking account of the NHS Commissioning Board and doffing our hats to Monitor.'

. . . it was like blackmail . . .

'Can you believe it, "Monitor!" You couldn't make it up.'

'I know,' said Philip.

'But Graham' – George's eyes were focused on the table top where his fingers were pinched together – 'What Graham's after is the data. Basically because he thinks he can make money out of it.'

'He can't sell people's records?!' Philip locked back into the conversation.

'No, it's all pseudonymised. This is one of the big things. Proper pseudonymised data about conditions and treatments and outcomes. I think it's very exciting. That's why I give Graham the time of day. Because this is real knowledge about people and their illnesses. This shows us what's really going on. And it means we can properly target whole populations, not just the patients who happen to come to see us. It means we can make a real difference.'

'Medicine on an industrial scale,' said Philip, mildly. He saw Janet's vehement worried face. All it was, was probably that Albert had had a bit of a tantrum. She'd only need some reassurance.

'Oh for Chrissake Philip. You really need to get beyond this old way of thinking about it as one person being nice to another person.' George was exasperated. 'How many of your patients do you see a day?'

'About 30.' Philip's feelings softened as he imagined the calming tones of his own wise voice solving the problem . . .

'Of whom about half are ones you see all the time and . . . for heaven's sake, you know how it adds up.'

. . . telling her it would be fine, making the stress vanish from her eyes . . .

'About half of our patients we never even see.'

. . . she just needed to carry on with the agreed programme of management.

'We never reach them.'

'Right.' Philip's phone pinged as a message arrived. Irritation gripped his throat again. He didn't look.

'And that doesn't mean there's nothing wrong with them. It doesn't mean they're not in need of help.' George was messianic, unstoppable. 'Then factor in ethnicity. Who are the people most at risk of peripheral arterial disease? The black population. Who are the people most at risk of CFS? The Pakistani population. Who are the groups least likely to go to see their GP? Those ethnic groups, among others. What do we do about it? As a single GP you can do absolutely sod all. But as a consortium' – his voice rose into upland calm – 'then you can put in place targetted measures to reach a whole population and really make a difference. Save more lives.'

'All I know,' said Philip in an empty voice, 'is that I went into this job as a human being, wanting to help other human beings.

And what that means' – his voice rose to cover George's interjection – 'is one human being talking to another. Listening to them. Viewing them as a whole person. Because' – he stopped. Astonishingly a feeling of being about to cry was gathering around his eyes. 'Because . . . that . . . matters. Looking at the person in front of you as one person. As an individual. As . . . a unique person. In a particular body. And a' – for some reason he was smiling through his unhappiness – 'particular smell, and clothes, and voice . . .' he was trailing off but as George seemed about to speak he again spoke over him: 'No, here's what I want to say. The fact of being a person, who does the crazy stuff we do, who is there, ready to listen to anyone who walks in, to give them the time of day, treat them as someone who isn't a fucking number' – he spat the word – 'but' (quietly) 'a person with dignity. That's worthwhile. It's about being human.'

'No. That's right,' said George. 'Fair enough. I didn't mean to. Anyway, let's leave it.'

He rattled the little rounded remainders of ice-cubes in his glass.

'What I meant' – George was hauling together some joviality – 'to do was say: sorry. I mean I hope I've said it before but I wasn't sure I'd said it clearly enough. I didn't know that Grace was going to be as much of a . . . problem patient as she turned out to be. I'm sorry it landed on you the way it did.'

'Oh that's alright.' At the bottom of Philip's glass was a viscous pool.

'How are things' – said George – 'looking for next year?'

'Oh,' said Philip, with mild surprise. 'I'm just gonna do some locums. With Sue, it's not entirely clear what her situation is going to be next year, where she's going to be. So I'll wait to see about that.'

'She's been living with you here this year has she?'

'Yes, that's right,' said Philip. 'I owe her. Anyway.' Philip drained his glass: 'Time to go. I'd better go.' But he sat there still.

'Yes you're right,' said George, looking at his watch and then rising, smiling. 'I'll see you Monday.'

'I just need to make a call,' said Philip, pulling out his phone and tapping Messages.

'Philip,' said George, turning back towards him in the doorway and staging a significant pause: 'You are a good doctor.'

Philip lifted his head from the one-line message and saw George's broad, well-meaning body dark against the bright light of the street where buses lumbered and people hurried past. Then he looked back at the one line which said:

'Albert gone. Help me! Help!'

As Philip thumbed the message to call back, Sue, 54 miles away, was contemplating the stack of glass-fronted wooden, laminate and grey plastic boxes. They were a bit higgledy-piggledy and the wall of them was curved but that worked, it was good, because it was a bit like a bank of surveillance monitors but also a bit like a pile of stuff you might find in a junk shop. So it mingled those references which was exactly what she wanted.

As Philip stood, making the light aluminium chair scrape on the floor-tiles, Sue was thinking: there is something almost Serra about the way it dominates the space.

Not all the streams were running at that moment but, as Philip stepped out into the early-evening summer brightness of the street,

Sue was watching Tahrir Square, one screen down and one to the right from the top left corner of the display. It was amazing, flooded with people again, clotted with banners, flags, tents and an enormous, numinous sheet of plastic which must have been for shade before the dusk began to gather, as it was gathering now, creeping in among the people, softening them into a mass of shadow. Above, blobby streetlamps hovered in the air. Whereas yesterday the square had been fulfilling its prescribed function, cars circulating and dividing, hunkered down and crawling, business as usual, noses to the ground. People sitting obediently in their cars, separated into different channels by dotted lines and following the arrows around the gyratory with its ornamental planting. Now all that structuration had disappeared again beneath – what? – human beings, and a litter of basically just cardboard and plastic and cloth. So random and fragile. And you could crush it with a . . .

Except they weren't crushed. They were there again, not letting go, keeping up the pressure about something or other, for instance putting ex-President Mubarak on trial. So somehow, was it somehow the fragility that had made them strong? Say, right back at the beginning, if they had had proper defences, if they had been armed – then they would have had to be crushed, but, as it was, nobody had been able to bring themselves to drive a tank over this efflorescence of life that was so fragile and breakable and – alive.

Sue's eyes skipped across the wall of tellies to other images. The looped video of an eye (middle of the top row), framed in close-up and slightly side-on so that you saw the fluffy eyelashes and the crinkled skin and the gleaming alertness of pupil and iris, twitching as the light changed. The undulant, iridescent river surface (right-hand corner, one up from the bottom) where orangey late-afternoon light rippled and spread, a bit like the head-lights in Tahrir Square, a bit like the shine on the iris. The clutter of grasses and flowers – poppies, clover – from Philip's flowerbed that was going to appear on the screen just below the river as soon as he switched his laptop on again tomorrow morning. Which he was going to be able to do with a smile, hurrah, since his court thing had gone so well. Even though it was always obviously going to, or rather, always obviously ought to – only of course he had been worried about it, how could he not be given the, well frankly the trauma that had started it off. But still he did understand she had to be here today, not there with him: he could see she had no choice.

Actually it was bollocks that nobody would drive a tank over that efflorescence of life. Because they had done since, and were doing, in Bahrain, Syria. Had always done, throughout world history. Or sometimes had and sometimes hadn't. What made the difference? Well, of course you could do political analyses, median income, level of education, etc., but that wouldn't quite get to it. Sue was sure you could do an analysis, say in theory you did an analysis of two places and found them to be absolutely identical, both on the tipping point of revolution. And what would happen then is that one would go and the other wouldn't. You would never be able to put your finger on what made the difference. Because it would come down to, maybe it would come down to just one thing, just one soldier deciding not to shoot, or one colonel deciding not to give an order. And what would be the explanation for that? Maybe just a feeling that one person had.

And where would that feeling come from? From everywhere. From a face he had seen in the crowd that morning, or from something his mother had said to him fifteen years before, or from a bit of grit getting stuck beneath his eyelid, or because he was tired, or because somebody he knew had died recently and he was grieving, or because he had not been given a promotion, or because he had stubbed his toe on the leg of his desk, or because he had eaten a specially juicy plum at breakfast, or some specially bracing olives, or because he had heard a raven croaking or seen a swallow, high-up, turning in the sky. Or actually, possibly, just conceivably from some secret, deeply held, rationally worked-out, principled position which only at that moment was getting the chance to come to light.

But then the thing was that that decision wasn't much, wasn't anything really, by itself: – only if it contributed to a feeling someone else had, and someone else, and someone different, and another person, and someone else. Etc. Or not. At any point the line of dominoes or the one grass brushing against another, the one tumbling stone knocking into another, could stop, the impetus not be transferred. Like say a stick – she brought her unfocused eyes to focus on the oleaginous river surface which was darker now – floating down the river, and snagging on a bit of the bank, and then another stick snagging on it, and another, etc. etc. Holding there tremblingly with the water pushing against it. And either they would build a barrier, one fortuitously cantilevered against another which aleatorily buttressed a third, etc; or they would not. Either they would be stronger or the water would be stronger, and break them with the surprising weight of its inertia, and disperse them and chase them and scatter them and sweep them away and cast them up here or there along the muddy bank.

'Sorted,' said springy, efficent Stuart, appearing from behind the pile of televisions where he had been working on something to do with the digital to analogue converters, as Sue would put it; or, as he would put it, trying to reduce the stochastic quantisation noise that was inevitably produced by the conversion of digital data back into an analogue signal, i.e. in this case actual video. Obviously Sue had wanted some fuzziness so as to foreground the materiality of the image; but not so much that it became an irritant. The consequent fine-tuning was now complete.

'Huge thanks,' she said, smiling at him frankly.

'I'll be in early tomorrow,' he said, tensely, responsibly. 'Let me just run through, the ones that need sparking tomorrow are: your Philip's bits of grass, Hsin-Yu's face of the Buddha in China, which is gonna switch to infrared at 2 pm, and our own one focused on the pavement outside, the footfalls coming in and out, which I'll set up – but for those other two, I've got the web addresses, I just need you to make sure the webcams go live when they're meant to.'

'I will,' said Sue.

'Tomorrow,' he said, stomping workmanlike out through the gallery, not looking to left or right, his shoulders hunched, hands in his pockets, heading off home.

Sue was so happy. Being on the brink of something good – no, being on the brink of something that was as likely as you could get to be really good, to really do something. Because you couldn't be sure that it was actually doing something until you saw it going to work on people, saw how they reacted. And probably even then there was inevitably always a bit of disappointment because it never had quite the impact you would like. But that was the danger, that was the excitement; and now, here, at this moment, before the slide of the unavoidable slight disappointment, when you could tell yourself that this time it was going to be simply brill, this time there was going to be no unavoidable slight disappointment at all: this had to be the best. Because actually – here was the funny thing. You wouldn't want there not to be the disappointment. Because what the disappointment showed was the work going out into actual people's lives who never reacted quite as you expected, quite as you would like. But, here's the point: you wouldn't actually want them to react as you expected! You wouldn't like them to react as you would like! Still, while she understood that intellectually, really held to it as a principle of audience empowerment, she nevertheless felt it, lived it, each time as an unavoidable slight disappointment. Which was why this minute of being on the brink of it was the best.

In black jeans and a black T-shirt, her uniform for the work of physically constructing an exhibition, she turned and walked back through the gallery, her trainers chirruping on the polished floor.

Now she was in the narrower space with the names on one wall and the photos on the other. What was fun about this was that, each time you walked through, you could zoom in on a different sitting room and/or a different clutch of names. With her arms out like wings she banked suddenly low down to the right. Japanese. Pale, symmetrical, nowhere to sit, except the floor, or rather those thick woven mats. Paper sliding walls. So calm. And actually really fiercely different. Because, though the look had been made familiar by

Heals and by Habitat, R.I.P, the reality of it, when you actually
properly looked at it, actually imagined your way into it, tried to
imagine being a person who would actually enjoy being in that
space, could actually relax there (if 'relax' was in any way the right
word) then it hit you. There was nowhere to bloody sit! There was
nothing to bloody do!

Sue unbent her body, took a step back, spun round and zoomed
in on a name:

Carmen Dell'Aversano

Of whom she knew nothing. Her eyes flicked down:

Habib Musa Farah

Ditto. And across:

Charles Proddow

Ditto. And down again:

Shyni Varghese

Ditto. No recognition. Just letters. She defocused her eyes and
disengaged her body, stepping back, turning, looking at nothing in
particular. In her was a feeling of thwartedness and, circling around
it, stalking it, tugging at it was vertigo because of – well because of
the simple fact that these were little black letters on a white wall,
and they went to make up names, and each name was the name of
a person who had a body and a pulse and eyes and a whole way of
being in the world, an apprehension of the world, and she, Sue,
knew nothing of them, would never know anything of them except
these names which she had happened to point her eyes at; and they
were worse than nothing because they gave you a feeling of how
much was missing, as though the person had been abducted and all
that was left was this name which wasn't in fact really anything left,

as such, because what it showed was the missingness more than the person. That was why it was so good that the wall looked like a wall of commemoration even though these were people who were alive, so far as she knew, or at least so far as she had known during the process of compilation which had finished, what, a week ago. So maybe one or two of them – she eyed the wall again – no longer were. But almost all of them would be and that was why it was so odd, so strong, to represent them in this way, because it brought an emptiness into the heart of life. Because although in a sense it was obvious, yes, that was right, she should revel in this, she should be proud of it – the fact that what the show was saying, if you summed it up, was completely fucking obvious. So, despite the fact that what it said was completely fucking obvious, the way these obvious facts about being a person, now, in our world, where we are so aware of so much else, of so many other people, without being genuinely connected to them; the way these obvious facts were presented in this show really did, she hoped, really would, she hoped, make them strike people in a new way. Which was after all what Art was for: to take the obvious and ram people's faces into it so that it hurt, so that they actually saw it, felt it, rather than being trite about it, rather than turning their faces away.

Here was Shirley with the V-shaped fluffy push-along floor cleaning thingy having a last trawl through for dust and litter.

Though she wondered, actually, how real that Japanese sitting room really was. Because the thing about the others, pretty much all of them, was that they were messy and scuffed, etc. – and part of the power (she hoped) of the display was in that messiness, because people were so used to seeing idealised photographs of things in

259

e.g. interiors magazines that it was actually a shock to see an array of photographs of rooms that people actually lived in. But she did wonder whether the Japanese room really was that, or whether it was more of an ideal, even for them. More of a museum piece. Still, never mind, it had its place, and that aspect of it, that question which it raised, was part of what that photo brought to the collage. Plus the really startling thing, the really real thing, that it was one of so few rooms to differ from the standard model. She had been first surprised and then dispirited, in researching this piece, to discover that there actually was a global hegemony of the three-piece suite. Even most of the African examples had one, like for instance there was a Nigerian one in blue leather in what was obviously a pretty impoverished dwelling but which had still been invaded by this western apparatus for sitting on. So that, well, there was nothing to say about it, really. You had to get over being dispirited and open your eyes and look. Because that is just the way things are.

She felt flatter now as she wandered through to the first room. Anxious. Very tired. Not anxious about the Elton Barfitt connection or actually non-connection any more: that seemed to have gone dead as an issue since Charlotte had talked it through with Omar one last time a couple of weeks ago. Since when he had been calm and accepting, withdrawn almost. Like the fact that today, the day before the opening, he simply was not here. Well, I suppose that was making the point that it was her show, hers and Charlotte's; and that he was concentrating on his own baby, Art and Language, opening in Oct . . . No, it was more just anticipation tipping into anti-climax before the climax had even happened. What if no one liked it? What if the press rubbished it? Because obviously Omar was right: it was a risk to run something without a name attached to it. If not the name of an Artist, then the name of a Movement or a Group. And if no one . . . but, come on Sue, what is this? – that was the whole idea; that had always been the whole idea. Words from the press release appeared like subtitles in her mind:

'Human culture is the artist whose selected works are featured in this exhibition.'

'Because nature, nowadays, is culture too.'

'What are the boundaries of your habitat? Where, finally, do you belong?'

But here are the glass doors swinging open and here is Caro, lovely Caro bustling through. 'Are you alright?' – Caro said, when she saw Sue and focused on her, stopping, her eyes widening a little.

'Oh just tired,' said Sue. 'Overexcited, probably.' Sue saw that she was near the blocky white sofa that was the centrepiece of the staged sitting room. She edged past the corner of the heavy, dark-wood, pseudo-Moroccan coffee table and let herself slump.

Odd, though, that doing that, doing that simple thing, on this ordinary sofa, felt different. Just because the sofa was in this space. Even with no one here yet, or rather no public here yet, to watch. You couldn't just sit; you had to pay attention to the fact that you were sitting. You were yourself and you were part of the artwork both at once.

Sue allowed the feeling of strangeness to prickle along her arms, to tense her toes, to sidle along the upper surface of her thighs. No, sod it, it was good, it was strong, it was something she should be proud of.

Caro was perching on the edge of the wickerwork bucket chair that was situated to the right of the sofa as you looked at the scene from the front which was the way in. 'We're all set in the shop,' she said too loudly; and then she smirked and seemed to want to shrink into herself as the sound echoed briefly around.

And that was good, too, dammit: how they had done the merchandise so as to be an extension of the show not a trivialisation of it, definitely not a slew of sentimental souvenirs. The punters could buy postcards that were exactly the same as the photos of the sitting rooms in the second gallery. And they could buy the catalogue which gave extra information, esp. the sources of those photos, plus of the streams in the third gallery, plus of the furniture in the first including the sofa she was sitting on now. So that having had the experience they could access information about the origins of the experience. Having been in the place they could see maps of the other places to which this place was connected, i.e. which it extended into and so which weren't exactly 'other' after all. And that shift from experience to information would be made available for them to think about. So that the evanescence and the power, the bewilderment of the experience would be the stronger, hopefully, because of that contrast.

So, for instance, Sue knew that the thing she was slumped in, the white cotton-and-polyester-covered sofa, had been transported a distance of 1.37 miles to the gallery on the back of a seven-year-old Toyota pickup. Source address: 27 Turing Crescent. Generous owners Cyrus and Sheila Jilla, retired.

Whereas the wickerwork bucket chair where Caro perched had been carried to the gallery in the arms of Rory Hardwick from his student room in Lyell Building, Hewlett Street (though of course the rattan for the wicker had voyaged a long way before that from a plantation somewhere, like for instance maybe South Kaliman-tan).

While between them was a tall lamp converted from a late Victorian hatstand by one Ed Homburg in 1932 and passed on by him to his son Richard and passed on by him to his daughter Angharad who had driven it 10.7 miles to the gallery in her mauve Renault Clio from her little terraced cottage at 4, Mill Buildings, Eldham.

Opposite was that modernist classic-or-cliché, the Marcel Breuer 'Club Chair' constructed from steel tubes and leatherette straps and transported by X a distance of Y miles from Z location. Then there was the pseudo-Moroccan coffee table, which had been, etc. And a low, square stool-cum-occasional-table, covered with a piece of pale blue crochet lace manufactured in Gurmandi, Punjab and brought to the UK by S.V.S. Phaneendra forty-one years before. There was a pouffe. There was a big, grubby, reddish, bobbly woollen rug. There was a heap of newspapers with different titles and dates on the pseudo-Moroccan table. And a prominent women's magazine. And the *TV Times*. And a Panasonic 37-inch flatscreen TV with Virgin box. And a ball of pink wool. And a small toy car. And some sheets of paper covered with kiddies' scribbles done by Darren and Ada Polonsky, aged two and a half and four and a quarter. There was a woven plastic waste-paper basket whose contents included, among snot-stuck tissues and a bent Pepsi can, the thoroughly bitten-round, brown, dry core of an apple which enclosed the tiny shrivelled carcass of a maggot. There was dust.

There was a stray segment of orange Hot Wheels track. There were two dirty coffee cups and a whisky glass in which a gluey liquid pooled. There was a round aquamarine crystal paperweight full of air bubbles. There was the half-life-size wooden statuette of a mallard duck. Full details of the source locations of all these constituent parts of the work, together with grateful acknowledgment to their owners, can be found in the accompanying catalogue, price £14.99.

Oh but Sue was sleepy now. Allowing herself to relax.

'It's a shame,' Caro said, 'Charlotte had to duck out earlier, missing this last calm before the storm.'

'It was only trapped wind,' said Sue: 'She'll be up again tomorrow.'

'Ouch that can be so painful,' said Caro, making her whole body wince.

Then, when Sue said nothing, Caro added blankly: 'Poor thing.'

Then, when Sue still said nothing, Caro said: 'Look. Shall I help you up? I'll walk you along to Charlotte's, OK?'

'We've probably both been overdoing it,' said Sue, gratefully, holding up her arms.

'It's,' said Caro, grasping Sue's wrists, leaning backwards, 'gonna be a triumph.'

As the two women eased, one after the other, along the edge of the pseudo-Moroccan coffee table, Philip, 54 miles away, eased along the sharper edge of the square, pine, shiny coffee table that was among the furnishings of the little house in Eden Grove that was his and Sue's (rented) for the circle of the year. He let himself slump into the bagginess of the leatherette sofa which squeaked and crackled on receiving him. He reached out to place his phone on the table and then leaned forward to look at it. Nothing.

Of course there was fucking nothing because if there had been something it would have made a noise.

In his mind he slammed his hand on the table and rose and strode around the room but in his body he did nothing, just stayed there sitting worriedly.

And anyway of course there was nothing because it was, what, two hours since they had agreed the most likely thing was that Albert had gone on the boat with Ash whose phone was suspiciously switched off. So probably he had gone with Ash's knowledge i.e. basically been kidnapped. Or else, just possibly, he might have stowed away, though Janet did not want to contemplate that scenario because it meant that Albert preferred his father to her.

'No,' Philip had blurted: 'No it doesn't. He's not thinking. It's a panic reaction. He wants to grab the parent who's leaving, that's all. If it was you leaving he'd grab you.'

If you – the words had continued in his mind – were the one playing games, the one Albert knew he could not rely on, instead of someone who had always been there for him, always wanted the best for him above all else.

And Janet had called the police who would send cars to the places where roads crossed the canal and only if that yielded nothing launch the helicopter – while she herself went along the towpath on her bike which might take fucking ages because, say Ash and Albert had left at 3.15, i.e. 5 hours ago, and bikes and boats went at roughly the same speed, it would take her 5 hours or more to catch him, assuming he stopped for the night; and if he didn't then she never would.

While he, Philip, did nothing. While he, Philip, waited here to hear. Because, please take note, he was not the uncle or fairy god-father or St George or a friend he was just the doctor who must not get over-involved, must not get even more over-involved even in this crisis, no especially in this crisis, when in any case there was nothing useful he could do. Janet and Albert's friendship network were alerted and searching, and the police were, and Janet herself was in hot pursuit. He really must get rid of the feeling that he was involved, that he was responsible even. Because it was his duty to maintain professional detachment, and what was more it was in Albert and Janet's best interests for him to do that, because, without it, his judgment would not be unbiased, without it he would not be able to trust his judgment, no one would.

Sympathy and understanding were OK; sympathy and under-standing were necessary. But there was a line between them and getting involved.

What is that line exactly, can you show me that line? – a mild voice asked in his head politely.

Fuck off it's completely fucking obvious and this is it right here a great big thick white line right here with a no entry sign and danger of falling off a cliff.

Philip's mind went blurry and his balance swooned and he tipped and his shoulder went into the soft seat cushion. His cheek was on the slippery leatherette. What can I . . . ? What can I . . . ? – his mind was whimpering.

You can, Dr Newell told himself, try to rest because you have not had enough sleep. You should, Dr Newell told himself, drink water because there is too much alcohol in your bloodstream for you to function effectively.

As he stood and edged, once more, along the shiny soft frontage of the sofa cushions, Sue and Caro were stepping out of the lift and moving towards Charlotte's pale blue front door. Caro pressed the bell and they stood in the over-bright light of the brick-lined hallway. Then Sue made a fist and flailed her arm and rapped and rapped. After a while Sue slipped her right hand into her right front pocket, and then her left hand into her left front pocket, and then her right hand into her right back pocket, and then her left hand into her left back pocket where she found the key which she conveyed into her other hand which pushed it into the lock and turned it.

'I'll leave you here,' said Caro as the door swung open. 'Are you alright?'

'Huge thanks,' said Sue, turning, reaching out to grasp Caro's shoulder for a moment, then turning back and going into the shadowy apartment.

'Charlotte?' – she called, pointlessly.

So what? So maybe she had got better and gone out to get some supper, or maybe she had gone to the chemist.

Food.

As Sue moved waveringly through the grainy light towards the kitchen end of Charlotte's living space, Philip, having gulped two half-pints of water and brought a third back with him and placed it on the pine coffee table, and having slumped once more into the shiny sofa, clicked on the remote.

'But if I did find him, what good would that do?' – someone was saying plaintively, a sad bloke in a pub. 'He'll have his own life now . . .'

Jesus Christ. Philip pressed channel + . That must have been *East Enders*.

'You put them' – it was some old bloke in a greenhouse – 'around the stems.' There were tall growing plants and the presenter was taking handfuls of big heart-shaped green leaves and stuffing them in around the bottoms of the stalks. 'As they decay all the goodness goes out of them and goes down into the soil . . .'

Jesus Christ. Philip pressed sleep.

He checked his phone again: of course nothing.

He must . . .

He swung his legs round and up and slithered a bit so that he was lying on the slippery sofa with the back of his head on one of its arms and his Achilles tendons resting tenderly on the edge of the other.

He closed his eyes.

He breathed in long and noisily through his nose.

Out whisperingly through his nose.

Janet on her bike, legs pumping, the gravel of the towpath crunching, the river curving silverily ahead of her, darkness under the trees and spreading out along the fields. Darkness lapping at the path.

Albert standing atop the barge, his arms lifted high, the pale light of the draining sky sparkling in his eyes.

Albert swirling in black water, tumbling in a weir, no in the gush of water at the bottom of a deep lock, his cold flesh white, his dead flesh white. His eyes white. Thin, fish-bone limbs.

Philip was ballasted with unhappiness, it was as though the lower perimeter of his body were dissolving with unhappiness, as though he were gluily disappearing into the sofa with unhappiness.

He must think of something else.

He must pull his thoughts back and think of something else.

Sue was there for him to think of.

Because tomorrow was Sue's big day – Christ, now it was a different panic sticking in his throat, how had he forgotten? – but in fact there was nothing he had forgotten, it was tomorrow, all he had to remember was to remember to be out there on the patio at nine with the laptop and webcam. Unreel the extension wire, bought specially, out from the kitchen socket to the patio table, plug in the laptop, plug in the camera, point the camera at the bed of wild flowers and grasses which had indeed grown as he had hoped, first peppering the ground with points of green, then opening minuscule leaves and shooting out minuscule strands; then stretching up and unfurling and stretching some more and budding until eventually one bud split, then another, then another, so that now there was a thicket of swaying but resilient shoots and leaves, and a scattering of flowers: poppy and clover and cornflower and buttercup and some others but he could not remember the names. The crucial thing was to keep the laptop safe from rain since the forecast was for more of this monsoon-like weather, hot but showery. There was the patio umbrella but since he was not absolutely sure it was completely waterproof maybe the thing to do was to put something else over the laptop as well, for instance was there a plastic box in the kitchen cupboard? – or else perhaps a pan.

Yes it would be fine, it would be fine, he would be able to

accomplish this thing for Sue and actually it was lovely – a smiley feeling rose from his tummy, somehow, into his cheeks – to be able to be part of her show, to be one of the few vulnerable, actually live contributions, because he could wholly understand how important it was to her that some at least of the streams should be live, i.e. at risk of going wrong, given that so many of them had turned out disappointingly to have to be pre-recorded. As indeed on the following days this stream from their back patio was going to be shown as recorded video because obviously he couldn't spend every day out here with an umbrella and even if they were able to set the laptop up somewhere securely safe and dry he bloody needed it for work.

There was paleness in the patio beyond the window at the kitchen end. The usual saffron gleam came through the milky panes of the front door and stretched a little through the open inner door towards where Philip lay. Otherwise the room was gloomy: the human being and the furniture were hazy lumps of black.

The phone still buzzeth not.

Should he text Sue? No. She would – he thought – be concentrated, not wanting to be distracted even for a second, even by him, fine-tuning, issuing intructions here and there, sorting the last things out; although really, as it happened, at that particular moment she was in fact snuggling on Charlotte's sofa, feeling the scratchy fabric against her bare thighs through the sheet. Much better now. Just basically a blood-sugar low which a bit of ryvita and cottage cheese had totally sorted out. A jolt of happiness went through her because: tomorrow was the day! The whole amazing gamble had completely come off, and Omar could go fuck himself and the whole stifling Savile-Row-suited art world could completely go fuck themselves because she had pulled it off, she and Charlotte had pulled it off, this magic show that basically took bits of the world, bits of people's lives, bits of the amazing interesting art that was in the world and people's lives, and jigsawed them together into something that was basically just very hard-hitting and unusual.

Hooray! Hip-hip-hooray! She was a crowd of gleeful people chanting, that was it, she was Tahrir Square! – even though to look at from the outside she was just a slight young woman lying foetally on a sofa in the gloom.

Elton Barfitt. The twin plastinated figures appeared in her mind mouthing words she could not hear. The twin plastinated figures sitting on their twin thrones were sucked backwards and up into the endlessly huge and yet incomprehensibly also totally flat space inside her mind, and up and up, higher and higher and further and further until they were just a midge in the top right-hand corner of infinity.

Because it had worked. Once tomorrow had happened it would have worked. Because after that there was nothing Omar could do: he could hardly go public saying 'Ahem, actually this show does have an Artist, or rather pair of Artists, or rather a composite two-and-yet-one Artist, after all.' And anyway obviously he couldn't because it wasn't true.

Because she and Charlotte had lied, because she and Charlotte had constructed a whole elaborate electronic network of deceit.

Which had enabled them to mislead their boss and basically misuse public funds.

So what they needed was somebody, or rather what she should

do afterwards was become expert in computer hacking so she could go into their system and basically delete the whole email paperchase like Murdoch had had done at News International.

No, absolutely not! No! No!

Because Omar had approved the show and the funds were for the show and the show was what it was whatever name attached to it.

Which was the whole point so – No!– nothing needed to be deleted and actually it would be better if it all came out.

Because let's imagine – Sue said to herself one final time – the worst-case scenario. Omar goes nuclear. Charlotte and I are not only denounced and sacked but actually taken to court. Well, what then? What would that trial be about? It would be about the value of authorship in art, the tyranny of authorship in art, the bizarre endurance of the author for what were obviously brazenly commercial reasons despite everything we know about textuality and the multiplicity of the self and the postmodern condition. It would be a trial of ideas! It would be a place where she could stand up and speak out what she believed! It would be like *Sensation* in New York, no it would be like something better than that, it would be like the Whistler trial from the nineteenth century, a pot of paint in the public's face vs. the knowledge of a lifetime. I.e a webcam image in the public's face vs. the way things really are! Well, maybe not quite those words but certainly versus something. So that the trial would become part of the artwork too, part of her campaign. Because for Chrissake freedom fighters went to court, eco-activists went to court the whole time, like for instance Ash she was sure he must have a string of minor convictions so why didn't artists too, or only rarely? OK maybe taggers did but who else in this fundamentally cosy white middle-and-upper-class subsidised world?

Eh? Eh?

So she would. Her toes were stretching taut and her thighs were squeezing tight and her heart was drumming with happiness.

Though actually what she needed to do now, what she really needed to do now, was try to relax, to calm, to relax, to soften, to stretch, to soften, to float, to find a way to sleep.

Because tomorrow was really going to be a lovely day.

Because it was all ready it was all done! – Only Hsin-Yu's and Stuart's and Philip's cameras to hook up tomorrow and that was as it should be, that was part of the aleatory character of the piece.

And it was lovely that Philip was going to be involved because he was so lovely.

It was lovely that Philip had said he wanted to be involved, had just stepped up like that to solve a problem; and she had said: 'You don't have to'; and he had said: 'But I want to'. Because otherwise they might have felt so pulled apart but as it was there was this little connection between them in the middle of the work that was just their little secret. So that, although he would not be there, he would be there.

Because his court thing had gone OK earlier, phew, because she had felt bad, so bad, at not being able to be there for him, but she had had to dedicate herself to the show, he understood that, and now everything was going to be alright.

And then next month they could have a holiday, they could just pick somewhere at random, last minute, and then they would be in a sandy cove with milky, bubbly, sparkly waves lapping at it, or in a sun-dappled Italian olive grove, or actually, why not, just in a little white cottage somewhere in Cornwall or Scotland or Wales, just the two of them, quietly, not connected to anything, or actually rather where they could pretend they were not connected to anything, with nothing to do, but could just be, looking up at the tranquil sky.

The lower slope of a mountain rose behind Sue where she lay; and a flock of sheep-like clouds migrated overhead; and she was just dipping into sleep as Philip, 53.5 miles away, was thinking calmingly to himself that tomorrow evening Sue would be back, and they would sleep entangled in the same warm bed, or maybe not entangled exactly but certainly side by side; and they would wake in the morning together, and doze together, and if they opened the windows nothing would come in and try to get at them except warmth, and they would just lie there with the light and the warmth surrounding them, and nothing else. So that, thinking of dozing in bed with Sue, he dozed on the sofa alone, just at the moment when Sue, 53.5 miles away, was sinking from stage III into stage IV sleep, or would have done were it not that, at that very moment, Charlotte turned the key in the lock, and stepped in, and switched on the light, and said:

'Oh shit' and switched it off again.

But Sue was stirring and opened an eye and panicked as she saw a figure advancing towards her in the darkness but then realised it must only be Charlotte and said:

'Hello?'

'Sorry sorry I didn't mean to wake you up.'

'Are you OK?'

'Oh yeh,' said Charlotte. And then: 'Much better, thanks.' And then: 'I went out for some fresh air.'

'Switch on the light,' said Sue, as Charlotte, in the dark, opened a cupboard for a glass.

Sue manoeuvred herself against the sofa-back and made a zed-bed of her knees beneath the sheet as Charlotte, having switched on the lamp that hung low over the kitchen table, moved round and settled into the sofa beside her. Charlotte laid her head back so that her mouth was open and her eyes stared up. Then she lifted her head forward to its usual angle and turned to Sue and reached out to lay a hand on her knee and said:

'It has been really great. I just wanted to say: it has been really great working with you on this. I have really valued it.' She gripped the knee. She shook it.

'No,' said Sue. 'I mean: thank you. But we've done it together. Actually it feels to me like you did most of it.'

'The organising maybe – but you were the inspiration, you were the one who had the . . . gumption. I don't want to be sentimental but I did want to say it has been a liberation for me, working with you. I forgot myself. It made me feel like, Oh God, but anyway: it made me feel like I was starting again, but starting again the way I should have done in the first place, as, well, the real me.'

'Good,' said Sue: 'Long may it last.'

'Yes,' said Charlotte, maybe a little bit grimly, now looking straight ahead down at the floor.

'Hey,' said Sue, putting a hand on top of Charlotte's hand. 'It's done. It's gonna happen.' Her cheeks squeezed up into a grin.

'Yup,' said Charlotte, maybe a little bit flatly, turning and looking for Sue's eyes. 'Yes it is.' And then: 'I'm sorry I wasn't there this afternoon.'

'Oh, there wasn't anything left to do. And anyway: you couldn't help being ill.'

'No,' said Charlotte in an exhalation as she stood up. 'I couldn't.' And then: 'Big day tomorrow!' She leaned over, braced an arm against the top of the back of the sofa, and touched her lips against Sue's forehead.

Then she walked off towards her bedroom. 'Night,' she said, as she switched off the light.

'Night night.'

As Sue returned to her shadowy mountain, Philip was dozing murmuringly; and, as Sue rolled down the shadowy mountain, Philip was seeing Janet's ghostly face howling; and, as Sue sank into a sea of enveloping, breathable blackness, Philip was seeing Sue's luminous face staring at him solemnly; and, as Sue was in the strange state of dreamless sleep, Philip felt that the solemnly was changing to lovingly, and, as Sue was still in the strange state of dreamless sleep, Philip was shocked awake, grip at his throat, gasping for breath, heart bucking because his phone was buzzing and warbling and when he reached for it the screen said Janet and when he dragged down for Accept and put the phone to his ear her voice said:

'He's not here. He's not here. He's not . . .'

'Janet.'

'He's not here.'

'You're at the boat?'

'I'm at the boat and Albert's not here.'

'Have you searched it?'

'I've searched it. And he's not here.'

Philip saw Janet under the moonlight pushing her way past Ash onto the boat, shouldering her way past Ash down into the cabin, pulling open cupboards, drawers, yanking the mattress off the bed, mattresses off the beds, screaming: where is he?! where is he?! what have you done with him, Ash?! What have you done?!

Or in fact maybe finishing her search and squatting down or kneeling down, letting her mind drain to empty before then after a minute, after thirty seconds, re-gathering her forces, summoning the strength to carry on through a darkness that had now got darker.

'Right.'

'I need you to come and get me.'

'I can't.'

'Philip,' she said, tenderly or was it wheedlingly, 'I can't cycle back.'

'Get a taxi.'

'I could try to get a taxi,' she said, rebuffed. 'I don't know how long it'll take getting here. And if it does get here, I shouldn't think it'll take my bike.' Her voice was rising: 'I would have thought . . .'

'I can't drive,' he said. 'I've had too much to drink.' Although in fact by now he had probably metabolised enough to be OK.

'Oh,' she said. And then: 'Can't have that. Can't have nice Dr Newell taking a risk.'

'I can't,' he said, 'do it.'

Then he said: 'Have you rung the police? . . . The police need to know that you have found Ash's boat and that Albert's not there. And then' – he said – 'maybe they'll be able to take you back.'

'You think,' she said coldly.

'Janet,' he said. 'I am your doctor. If there's anything medical you need from me, then do by all means call.'

'Thanks a lot,' she said.

He said: 'I'm going to put the phone down now.'

She said nothing.

He moved the phone away from his ear and pressed End Call.

He put the phone down on the shiny pine table.

He was sitting hunched forward with his forearms resting along the top of his thighs.

His lowered head was twitching.

His upper body, which was leaning forward, was nudging up a little, and down a little; up a little, and down.

There was a large sticking-plaster stuck across the front of his brain.

He levered his upper body straight and got up and went round to the kitchen surface where there was a bottle of whisky. He pulled out the cork and poured a tumblerfull of whisky and raised it to his mouth and drank; the liquid blocked his throat and he gulped it; it blocked his throat and he gulped it until he was choking on the scratchy liquid and stopped and retched. Then he raised the glass again and sipped a little more.

Now it was true. Now it was completely fucking true.

Then he sat sideways on a kitchen chair with one arm resting on its back and the other arm resting on the table.

Sue stirred, pulling her sheet tight around her as a laugh echoed up from the towpath below.

Philip heard again Janet saying 'can't have nice Dr Newell taking a risk.' Then he saw her face as she said 'we never been to no hospital'; and then he heard himself exclaiming 'but this is black-mail!'

Janet spat on the ground. Philip heard the labial percussion as the slithery glob of saliva left her mouth and tumbled in slow motion through the air, stretching and wobbling and twisting, until splat it hit the pavement and adhered to it, with only a pearl-like droplet, two pearl-like droplets arcing up away from the impact and landing elsewhere in their turn.

Janet took little Albert's hand and the two of them walked away from him and she looked back over her shoulder at him as though he were a threat.

Sue's legs stretched and her head pushed deeper into the cushion.

Philip lifted his head as a goods train started its long rumble along the edge of Eden Grove. Space came into his mind; a land-scape came into his mind. He saw the river winding through an empty landscape with far in the distance a barge upon it like a toothpick. He saw the raised path through Kidney Meadow that must surely once have been the embankment of a railway. He saw the place of giant's bones where Ash had parked his boat; and he saw the great trees black against the cold late-winter sky. High up he saw the little silhouette of Albert, a twig among their enormous suppliant arms.

As Sue corkscrewed round so that her nose was nuzzling into the cushion, Philip was shutting the front door. He went to his car which was beside the little rowan tree in a tube and made the tail-gate swing up. Yes, there was a torch.

And then he was off, along the illuminated, empty streets, his arms swinging, and legs swinging, his trapezius and deltoid and triceps and biceps and sartorius and rectus fermoris and so many other muscles all collaborating to move him smoothly along Parnassus and through Elysium and out along Helium where ornamental planting at the edges of the road served also as a traffic-calming measure. He branched right onto a thin, meandering, nubbly path that led down into the dark. On either side, conglomerates of vegetation: blackberry and hawthorn and nettle and burnet saxifrage and corn buttercups all indiscriminate and entangled, even the gaudy gladiolus unnoticed in the night. Philip flinched at the crackling of something, the scrunching of something; but there are no pumas in England so only a hedgehog maybe or maybe a little squirrel its jaws stretching around . . . um, maybe the little tart beginnings of an apple until, kerrunch, the bite went through the skin.

But now he has gone through the low arch under the railway and is rising a little up onto the grassy plain where meadowsweet and clover and sorrel and fox-tail and mouse-ear and all the rest are blurry and pale beneath the invisible air which is in turn surmounted by the white diffusion filter of the cloud-filled sky. To the left, the embankment angles across. To the right, in the distance, little black broccoli-heads of trees mark the river. He wades through the amalgam of long grass and flowers towards the embankment. Then he is upon it walking faster. The ground keeps on turning out to be higher than it seems to be so each foot meets it with a jolt. He is over the echoing bridge. He is along the river now, among trees. The trees are black, really like cut-outs of nothingness until you focus your eyes upon them when dapple-patterns of leaves appear like down. Between the slender trunks of little trees the path winds on.

Now to the left are thistle and elder and blackberry, from which Philip cannot see that the petals have almost all dropped, leaving fluffy brush-heads on the thistles, and orreries of little green balls on the elder and, on the blackberry, multiple ovaries that have begun to swell, still green and hard but soon to soften and blush.

Now to the right the river leads on through the dark, a path of light surprisingly much brighter than the hazy sky.

A felled trunk lies along the land: is that the one?

No, maybe not because there is another over there and then another.

Remember!

The thing to do will be to go past and then turn back and approach from the right direction and then it will be easier to know.

Philip does. Walks past, rotates, advances slowly, scanning the forms of standing trees and fallen trunks.

This one!

His torch is in his hand and he switches it on and rakes it along the bottom where he had remembered there were half-hidden sandy pits and burrows. He is down on his knees pointing his torch into a tunnel. Only black. Black thickened with floating dust which gathers the light of his torch and blocks it back towards him.

No. But then the other logs may be the same.

He searches them too.

No.

But maybe Albert is so little or can make himself so little that . . . ?

He goes back and kneels and looks again into the tunnel: no.

Obviously there is no point calling out.

He calls out: 'Albert!'

He calls out again searchingly, reassuringly: 'Albert!'

He points his torch up into the tree. The beam bleaches the leaves which alternate grey and paler grey.

There is the rope dangling. Surely not?

He edges around the base of the tree angling the beam up as best he can between the thick forks and branches. He takes two steps back and does the same again; and two steps back and does the same again.

Well, there are places the beam has not probed. There are intractable patches of black.

He stretches out and pulls on the rope. Strong.

But it would be crazy for him to try to climb this tree in this darkness, on the millimetrically tiny chance that . . .

He pulls on the rope again, lifts a foot, braces it against the trunk.

Obviously the sensible thing . . . He turns his eyes to the sky which is bright but that must be with a mixture of the moon behind the clouds and reflected light from the town. He gets out his phone to see the time: 02.47.

Still, obviously the sensible thing is to wait until dawn which must be hardly even an hour away.

He heard: 'can't have nice Dr Newell taking a risk.'

Fuck you! Fuck fuck fuck fuck you!

He throws the rope against the trunk and stumbles backwards from the force of the exertion.

He turns and takes a few steps down towards the river. His feet are on gravel. He looks to the right. Black overhanging bushes cast a deeper blackness on the water beneath. He looks to the left. That comparatively narrow whitened branch reaches out into the water really like a hairless forearm and a thumb.

Behind him is a cut-off stump. Head-height and the same distance wide. Well, if that is a forearm then this is an ankle. He felt sick with disappointment, pointlessness. Stupid, stupid stupid, what was he thinking?

He sat down, his back against the barkless wood, his legs stretched out. He looks out across the river, out across the meadow on the other side. It as though the dark brush-stroke of the land is hovering between the brightness of the water and the paleness of the sky.

So wait.

Wait.

And tomorrow he just needed to get up in time and set the camera and if he dozed off after that it would be OK.

The sky was so strangely white.

His mind faded and then, bang! – his head had fallen back and knocked against the stump. His occipital bone vibrated with a frisson of slight pain.

Knocked.

But of course what happened with these stumps was that the centre rotted. Like bones, like marrow, like when you scraped out the marrow.

In which case . . .

He stood.

He looked.

He couldn't bloody see over the edge.

So he is going to have to . . .

He steps back, throws himself forward, jumps!

The edge of the stump is painfully against his tummy and he is swinging his legs round and up and over. He is sitting. He finds his torch and points it down inside and switches it on:

There is the boy curled up! There is the boy like a baby.

Philip switches the torch off.

He switches it on again.

He points it at the boy's little white face with its snub nose.

The closed eyelashes cast tiny shadows.

Then they stir.

And then the eyes open and the little forearm is brought across the eyes and the face is looking up at him, blinking; and Philip moves the beam away.

He says: 'Hello Albert.'

He says: 'It's me, Dr Newell.' He turns the torch beam into his own face, creases his eyes against it. 'Philip, call me Philip.' Then he tries to place the torch where it will light up both of them.

The boy turns his head back and lays it down as though he wants to sleep again. He is curled up again among soft rotting bits of wood and also there is fungus, and a couple of crisp packets, and a squashed tin can.

'Albert, your mum's been looking for you, we've all been looking for you.'

No reaction from the boy.

'Albert.'

And again: 'Albert will you listen to me?'

Obviously what he should do is call the mother. But Philip does not want to call the mother. Why does he not want to call the mother? Because he does not want to appear this ineffective in her eyes, because he does not want to have to say: there is your child, I cannot get him out of there, can you?

Because what he wants to say is: no, I can find the child you lost and bring him back, I know how to handle Albert. He likes me.

Or anyway, also, the simple fact is it would be better if he, Dr Philip Newell, could think of a way of getting Albert out and getting him back home now because it would be quicker and the boy, who is so thin, might be cold, it must be damp down there among the rotting stuff.

And if he rang Janet now the boy would hear him and that would be it: if Albert knew his mother was coming he would stay there until she came; there would be no chance at all of budging him until she came.

'It's beautiful out here, isn't it,' he said, trying a different line. 'It's a really special place. I can't believe' – he carried on – 'you can climb that enormous tree.'

Albert looked up.

Albert said: 'It's a Railway Poplar. Railway Poplars can grow up to a hundred feet tall! I can get up it because of the bark, I can get my fingers into it, into the cracks. My fingers are really strong!'

'That's amazing. Do you know a lot about trees?'

Albert had lifted his head and his shoulders now, his hand was pushed down into the woody mush and his arm was buttressing his upper body.

'I know the difference between poplars. My dad taught me. He took me on a trip to see a Black Poplar so I could see the difference. The Railway Poplar is a hybrid.'

'Your dad,' said Philip, risking it, 'is a wonderful man.'

Albert was now sitting with his knees up in front of his chest and his arms tight around them. His chin was resting on his knees and his little shoulderblades stuck out at the back.

What Philip wanted to do was veil the world with light. Albert was sitting there hunched as if he were about to be hit. And what Philip wanted to do was soften the world. So that then maybe Albert would come out into it.

'Your dad,' he said, 'loves you more than anyone. And he loves the world. And when he goes off, like he has done now, it is to try to make the world a better place. And do you know why he does that? So it can be a better place for you to live in when you grow up.'

No reaction from Albert but maybe the words are sinking in?

'And your mum loves you more than anyone. Do you know,' Philip said, 'this evening she got on her bike and chased along the river, all the way along until she caught up with your dad in his boat, because she thought you might be there.'

'I wanted to be,' said Albert. 'But when I got here he was gone!'

'He'll come back. Lots of dads have to go off to work. Lots of mums do too. But they come back. Your dad will come back.'

There was no response to that.

'Do you know,' said Philip: 'I don't know how you got down there. I don't think I could.'

'It's easy. You jump' – came the contemptuous reply.

'And if I could get down there I certainly wouldn't be able to get up again. Do you think you can?'

'Course.'

'Really?'

'Course.'

'Are you sure?'

'Course I'm sure.'

'How?'

'Like this!'

It had worked. Albert was sitting on the stump beside him. The two of them were sitting side by side on the tree's edge, where there was no longer any bark, and their feet were dangling down into where there was no longer any heartwood. Albert's pin-like legs and Philip's adult ones.

'I bet you don't know the way home from here,' Philip said. 'I bet you . . . do you know what I bet you? – I bet you five pounds.'

'Alright.'

The boy looked down into the pit of the tree for a moment and then he had swung his legs over and sprung to the ground and was scampering along. He shouted: 'Come on then!'

So the two of them went along, Albert leading and Philip working to keep up. Now they were at the end of the big trees, at the end of the railway poplars, and going in among the scrubby elder and brambles and thistles. Philip pulled out his phone and pressed Janet Stone.

'Hello doctor,' she answered acidly.

'I've found Albert. He's fine.'

A high-pitched sound came through the phone, a shriek or mew.

'He was in Kidney Meadow. By the river. We are walking back together now through the Meadow towards the gate by The Willows.'

'You've found him? I'll come. I'll meet you there. I'll come.' And she was gone.

The little trees with slender trunks.

The rattly bridge.

The causeway.

The causeway stretched out straight before them. It was lighter than the land around. Flints glittered in it. And there at the end of it, under the brightening sky, with the orangey, blurry lights of the town behind, was a figure standing. No, walking towards them. It looked squat among the immensity all around. Albert was scampering faster; and when he saw it was his mother, really was his mother, he was running. The little arms scurried and the little legs scurried and his thin form moved smoothly away from Dr Newell, quite slowly, it seemed, though Albert was running his fastest. And then his little form and the squat figure of Janet Stone became one.

When Philip caught up, Janet Stone said:

'Thanks.' She held out her hand. Her face was reserved, blunt. Anything could break on it and leave it unharmed.

'My pleasure,' he said. His eyes moved over her face, noticing her cheekbones, her eyebrows, her skin which was bright white, her eyes which were looking up at his.

They turned and the three of them walked along for a bit. Once they got to the road, Philip kept left, the side where the entrance to The Willows was, while Janet and Albert went over on to the pavement on the right. So for a minute or two they were moving along on opposite sides of the road. Then Philip turned; and the others kept on; and Philip walked back down Helium and through Elysium and along Parnassus back to Eden Grove. He opened the door and climbed the stairs and took his clothes off and slipped into bed. He checked the alarm. His hard, tender head sank into the soft pillow. Now at the front of his brain there was a lump of plaster of Paris. He had taken ibuprofen but it was still sore. He had drunk water but still his tongue was polystyrene. There was a fizzing in his arms and legs around the muscles: ions dissipating, presumably; and the tissue charging up again with glucose and fat and creatine phosphate. He tried to quieten this interference from his body. In his mind were the shades and forms of Kidney Meadow, the light-diffusion sky, the floating land. The curled-up child in the empty heart of the tree.

As Philip slept, Sue slept.

As Philip rose towards consciousness for a moment when a goods train trundled past, Sue was in the stolidness of deep sleep.

As Philip still slept, Sue's mind stirred and her eyelids flicked open. It was light! She was, yes, she was in Charlotte's sitting room. This was it! Excitement went from her tummy up her spine across her shoulders. Her feet and legs were ready to spring.

She levered herself up in the sofa and looked across to the clock on the cooker.

5.32.

Oh right. She lay back, closed her eyes again. She stretched her arms a little bit to either side and let them go slack. She wanted to get up, and be out, and be doing things: be getting ready, be phoning, rushing, checking. But no one would be there. And anyway she probably couldn't even gain access to the gallery this early. And anyway – she looked into her mind. There really was, apart from the three streams to set going, nothing left to do. And the three streams were wholly provided for, plus there was back-up if any of them failed. Plus if any of them failed and then the back-up failed as well – well, then that would become part of the piece. Because the whole point of the piece was not to be self-sufficient. The whole point was it relied on other people.

Which sometimes worked out perfectly and sometimes didn't quite.

And even when it didn't quite there was still the feeling that it might have done.

Which mattered. Which really did.

Her mind walked through the gallery.

Her mind lifted the roof off the gallery and floated above it watching as people came in and moved around the space, pausing, concentrating as their eyes caught at this or that; drifting on when the object of their attentions released them.

There in the first room were ponderous, gentle Cyrus and Sheila Jilla, surveying their sofa with what seemed, from Sue's aerial viewpoint, to be a feeling of satisfaction. His thinning hair was combed across his shining skull; she wore a broad-brimmed, mauve, lacy summer hat. His shoulders were covered in the beige checks of what was probably a suit; hers in pink silk with shoulder pads. Her hand was on her bag. His toes were in polished, tan half-brogues. They leaned towards each other; spoke. Sheila shrugged her shoulders; Cyrus waved his arm in a gesture of explanation. Oh, but now they were moving on. Now they were opening themselves to the rest of the show: to the second room, and to the third, where twitchy, keen, young, ever-so-slightly-ingratiating Rory Hardwick was standing, skinny and intent, in T-shirt and jeans, holding one of the slidey tic-tac-toe boards, focused on the monitors. He was really concentrating, really trying to do it, to attach the images to the names of their places of origin. He was really trying to do it; and really failing to do it, she was sure from the signs of tension in his shoulders, the angle of his head. Of course he was failing to do it because it couldn't be done; couldn't be done with certainty. And then, yes, there he was giving up, turning away, but turning away (she was sure) with a smile; because he had felt the impact of trying to name and failing to name.

Of not managing to be an Adam.

Happiness went through her. Quiet went through her. The light in the room turned to whiteness in her mind.

She slept.

Here is Charlotte leaning over her. Here is Charlotte putting a hand to her shoulder, pushing it. Sue stirred, woke. It was harder to come out of sleep this time.

'Are you alright?' – asked Charlotte.

'Mmm,' said Sue. And then: 'Yes. Of course. Of course I am.' She was sitting up.

'I've made green tea,' said Charlotte.

'Thank you.'

The two women sat for a moment, Charlotte in her shiny pink dressing gown at the glass table, Sue still on the sofa wrapped in a sheet. Each cupped a hot cup in her two hands, in front of and beneath her chin. Both faces blurred a little as the steam rose up across them.

Then the two women were moving, washing, peeing, dressing, taking a peach from the bowl or making a slice of toast by way of breakfast. They were quite smart but still informal. They went out, and down, and then were walking along the 1980s frontage which adjoined the 1780s canal. They turned right through the concourse with the permeable pavement; past The Sitting Room, Armando's, Swarovski Crystal, Pret, Fat Face, M&S; beneath flats and offices inhabited and worked in by so many other people, until they arrived at the stark form and glass doors of Spike. Charlotte put her key into the wall to open them. The two women walked on in.

Here is the entrance hall, all white. There is the desk. There, ready piled upon it, are the catalogues. Casually lying at an angle next to them is a clipboard upon which Osh, once he has got in, once the day has started and is progressing, will record the names and papers of visiting press.

The two women walk further in. The first room, with the white blocky sofa and the pseudo-Moroccan coffee table and the hatstand-lamp. The second room with the photos and the names. The third . . . and here is Stuart emerging from behind the monitors.

'Those,' he said, 'are the traces you left on the pavement coming in.'

They all looked at a monitor which showed some greyish texture and some lighter, dusty streaks.

Actually you could work out it was a paving slab if you looked carefully and thought about it because you could see the edge and the mortar between it and the next one, a combination that was actually quite recognisable.

But which traces were theirs, or rather how much the two of them had contributed to the multiplicitous dusty record could not be known.

And actually if they could rewind and watch their feet passing through and compare before and after it would still be all-but impossible to tell.

And also, actually, now you could see that this monitor was going to be especially fun because people would look at it and puzzle. And then they would see a momentary foot in the image and go 'aha!' But still they wouldn't know where the stream was from – until maybe they picked up one of the slide-frames and started working through it and saw the address here as one of the locations: maybe then it would click.

Or maybe – think how lovely this would be. Walking back through the gallery they would notice someone's shoe and recognise it as a shoe they had seen three minutes before on the monitor. Then they'd get it. And then, next, they'd realise that their own foot and ankle and sock and shoe had probably been up there too. Which would make them feel differently about walking and being on the ground. Maybe only for a moment but still there'd be a shiver. Surely there would. And maybe they would even, maybe this ideal person would even go back and stand in front of the monitor and stare and stare.

'So now it's just the grass and the Buddha,' said Stuart.

Sue looked at her phone. 9.15.

'I'll text her,' said Charlotte.

Sue pressed Philip.

'Philip,' she cooed when he picked up. 'Sweetie . . . wakey wakey . . .'

'Oh shit, shit,' said Philip, 'sorry I slept through the . . . oh bollocks.' He had seen the time. 'Sorry. I've had quite a bizarre . . . I'll tell you about it.'

'Don't panic,' said Sue. 'There's a bit of time.'

'Sue?' – he said, full of tenderness: 'Good luck. It's gonna be amazing.'

'Yeh maybe,' she said.

Philip lifted his head. He slithered his torso upright and leaned his occipital bone against the wall. Pain.

Nausea.

He shut his eyes. He reached sideways, scrabbling on the bedside table for the ibuprofen then feeling around for the glass of water.

He gulped. He waited a moment.

Safely down into the stomach. Settling there.

What he wanted to do was snuggle back under the sheet and into the microfibre pillow until the jabbing in his head had softened. But what he had to do was get up and go downstairs and sort this thing out. So he got up, dressing gown, glasses, downstairs, coffee on. He knew he shouldn't have a coffee (he was a doctor!) but he had to have a coffee.

He opened the back door. He turned around and bent down to where he had left the extension cord.

Woaa!

He was on his knees. His stomach was spiralling or rather his medulla was being bombarded with afferent impulses originating in the chemoreceptors of the upper GI tract. Stay still. Breathe.

Move . . . ever . . . so . . . gently.

Coffee shouldn't help with this according to the book but in his case it always seemed to.

Having imbibed some coffee he refilled the cup and took it outside and put it on the metal table. He returned into the house and studied the extension cord. With one hand he seized the plug and lifted it and moved it towards the socket on the wall where the toaster was plugged in. He put down the plug of the extension cord. He grasped the plug of the toaster and pulled it. He pulled again.

When the plug of the toaster erupted from the wall the consequent soundwaves battered his tympanic membrane and jangled his ossicles and sent a flock of tin-tacks into his auditory cortex.

Gingerly, he put that plug down and lifted the other one and pushed it in. He turned the grating handle of the spool to unwind the hissing black extension cord. He took the end of it outside and, so as not to bend down, dropped it.

Then he realised it would have been more sensible to lay it on the table.

He gulped some health-giving coffee.

He went back indoors, past the kitchen table, to the sitting-room part of the room. He half kneeled against the soft seat of an armchair so as to lower himself without inclining his head or his torso. He picked up the laptop and its wire and the little webcam and its little wire which was already connected to the computer.

All set up: just plug it in and go.

They had tested it the other day and it had been fine: just plug it in and go.

He turned. Carrying his precious cargo he made his way back outside and laid the computer and the wires and the webcam on the metal table. He would have to drag the table closer to the flowerbed.

Exercising various muscles across the front and around the side of his head, he scrunched up his face. His glasses lifted but his ears would not close.

Well obviously his ears would not close.

Some creatures could close their bloody ears: for sure they could. So why was it not possible for him to close his ears?!

He seized the edge of the table, his fingertips and nails gripping under its rim.

He pulled: the table thundered and the flagstones screeched.

He suffered without complaint.

Now he could half sit on the edge of the flowerbed. He did a first provisional positioning of the webcam. He lifted the lid of the laptop and pressed power on.

He confronted the challenge of the plug. The computer's power cord and plug were on the table. The socket at the end of the extension cord was on the ground.

He relived in his imagination the unbearable about-to-vomit feeling of spiralling stomach and bombarded medulla. He could not bend over and he could not kneel down.

He could always leave the laptop not plugged in? – no he could not leave it not plugged in because the battery life on this machine was terrible.

So he lifted the plug and positioned it as accurately as possible above the socket and dropped it.

It fell.

Now it was all about his feet. In its cork-soled, felt slipper, one foot moved to one side of the plug while the other foot, in its cork-soled, felt slipper, moved to the other side. The slippered feet approached each other. Their edges came into contact with the plug. They exerted pressure on the plug.

In each leg the rectus femoris contracted so that each foot rose and, between them, gripped by them, the plug.

Crane-like, the legs and feet manoeuvred until the plug was above the socket.

The body-mechanism lowered the plug until its nubs were touching the receptor cavities of the socket.

Then the body-mechanism pushed and the right foot slipped and the plug tumbled and it was all to do again.

Philip extracted his feet from the cork-soled, felt slippers. Now he could deploy the more subtle forces of his phalanges and metatarsals and their multiple associated flexors and abductors.

He tried.

One foot, the other foot: squeeze.

The toes against the hard plastic were strangely sensitive.

Lift.

Now the nubs were resting on the rims of the cavities.

Steadying the plug with one foot he gingerly lifted the other until it was resting atop it.

And then he pushed and the nubs went in and a satisfying 'krunnk' echoed around the walled-in, open-top box of the patio and the problem was over.

Now it was going to be easy.

He turned to the laptop. Password. Wait. Click to open Tin Cam; wait. Find Capture: click. Scroll down to Streaming Video. Click.

We are go!

We should be go.

Click Firefox; click Favourites; click The Whole World cam 14. Password.

Which was . . .

Which was . . .

Oh fuck, what was the fucking fucking password!

He was going to have to call Sue.

If he could find his phone he would call Sue.

But hang on because in fact did he really need to check the image had gone live? Because if it hadn't she would call him. In not very long at all she would call him. And he could ask her the password then. Only if the thing wasn't working would she discover that he was so crap as not to have remembered the password. So that actually it was OK to stop now. To have a sit down. To just . . .

It felt like the ibuprofen was maybe having an effect at last because his head seemed gentler.

Leaning there against the wall was a deckchair and it would be so nice just to be sitting in that.

If he could open it.

Of course he can open it: what is this!

So he walked boldly over to the wall and seized the deckchair and bloody well opened it and placed it near the laptop and sat down in it and inclined himself backwards.

His occipital bone was resting on the wooden strut.

He slithered himself downwards so that his head was gently on the canvas. He let it loll sideways.

On the moorland of his consciousness, mist swirled.

Although there was the fine-tuning but actually . . .

He opened his eyes and tipped his head to see the camera on its little tripod.

. . . it was obviously OK because they had a wide field of view and it was pointing at a whole load of grasses and a couple of poppies and some clover and buttercups, and the grasses were leaning this way and that, and the whole point was that it wasn't aesthetically composed but just a bit of the world.

And anyway if Sue didn't like the image she would call as well.

He let his head roll back into resting balance and concentrated on what was happening in his mind, the purple waves of pain receding to reveal tranquil stretches of bleached sand.

The other thing was the weather.

He opened his eyes. Pale sky. Blobs and streaks of cloud.

Looking at them you could see that the greyness was shadow and the whiteness was where the sun was shining on them or through them.

Well, that didn't seem very threatening.

And anyway the thing was that if he was out here in the deck-chair in his dressing gown, then, if it started to rain, he would know. So in fact there wasn't any need for him to put up the umbrella. Or find a plastic bag. Because, just by sitting out here, he would be doing the job. He would be a human rain alarm. Which meant that he could have a nice rest. A lovely gentle long sit-down. Because there was no purple in his mind now, only white. Because the line of land was floating on the river. Because the grass was streaming.

As Philip dipped into sleep, a message, which he didn't hear, pinged into his phone which was by the bed in the house upstairs.

Thnx xxxx, Sue had thumbed. Because now it was all go. The grasses and the face of the Buddha were really a very interesting juxtaposition. Because the one was stone and solid and meant to be impassive, whereas . . .

'It's so good!' Charlotte was exclaiming, walking back from the second room into the third, in her grey, shortish, short-sleeved cotton dress, her big arms forming a W on either side of her, her face scrunched into a grin. She came close, leaned forward, whispered: 'It could actually be by Elton Barfitt!'

What a stupid thing to say. What did she say that for? Sue thought it was understood between them that the whole point was to use the veil of Elton Barfitt to introduce something new. Something that wasn't . . . Oh for Chrissake, of course Charlotte understood that. It was taken for granted in all the planning they had done together.

Perhaps Charlotte meant it as a joke.

Sue looked back at her and smiled mildly.

'Three minutes,' Charlotte said, 'until the doors open!'

She sounded like a ring-master in a circus.

Well, it was exciting. But she, Sue, when she was excited, as she was now, sort of turned in on herself, didn't do histrionics. Sort of felt that there was a beacon sending out light from inside her and rotated her mind to bask in it.

The thing to do now was vacate the gallery. Because the first people in needed to feel that they were the first people in. Needed to feel they were discovering it.

Sue said: 'I'm going up, shall we go upstairs?'

They walked back through, out through the swing doors of the first room.

'Hey Osh!'

'Hey ladies!'

They turned left and climbed the stairs.

As the sun warmed his face, Philip slept.

Sue was logging on; she was about to check her emails. She was listening intently.

Damn the whirr of the computer!

But there they were. There were footsteps like castanets on the pavement. A pause at the door. A change of pitch as the metalled heels stepped onto the polished concrete of the entrance hall. Was it one person or two? Or three? Or more if there were others in for instance trainers.

Now they would be going into the first room. Now they would be staring at the transplanted or recreated or staged or (how would they take it, exactly?) sitting room. They would be wondering if they were allowed to sit.

Moths of happiness went up Sue's chest.

The sun peeped over the trees. Philip's eyelids twitched. The sun beamed into his body. Beneath his dressing gown, sweat-beads budded and spread.

Having dealt with her emails, Sue thought: why not? Go down and take a peek. Drift through. Pretend to be one of the masses.

She pushed back in her Aeron, stood, turned, and walked out past Caro's back and Elmer's back. She stepped quietly down the stairs. As Osh looked up she raised a hand. She paused in front of the inner door. Looking through the glass she saw a chubby man in the middle of the sitting room exhibit. He was looking this way and that, deciding. He revolved. Having made up his mind, he moved towards the Breuer steel and leatherette chair. Having stopped, he rotated. Having rotated, he sat. Patted the arms in a friendly manner, pleased. Then leaned back gingerly as though afraid the whole contraption might collapse.

It didn't.

At which, he crossed his legs. Having gaily crossed his legs, he reached out his right hand to gesture in a francophone style. Then leaned forward. His hands in front of him, fingertips touching, he held forth. He was an interviewee on air.

Carefully, slowly, Sue squeezed the door open, sidled in.

There were no words! His mouth was mouthing but he made no sound.

He saw her. He stopped. He looked puzzled. Looked around him as though there were something he was trying to find. Then he rose and walked on through.

Sue also walked on through. In the second room two people had their attention held by the walls. A sunny, pastoral young woman in a white top and long red skirt and straw hat was angled to the left looking into the photographs. She focused on one and then her head bobbed a bit and then she focused on another. Could it be the woman who had brought the lamp, what was her name?

The woman sensed Sue looking at her, turned her head, smiled, lifted her hand in greeting; and then returned once again to the photos.

Angharad. Angharad with the hatstand. In a hat.

On the right a small man stood. He was wearing a pale jacket and pale trousers and flipflops. Through his glasses he was reading the names. Sue watched as his knees began to bend. His head and therefore his gaze were lowered by an inch. And then another inch.

Was he going to read them all?

She walked on into the darker space of the third room. Tahrir Square still crammed; a white banner stretched between two poles. Philip's grass and flowers, the lip of a poppy wobbling. The streaked, greenish face of the Buddha with its elegant eyebrows. The pavement outside: a foot landed on it and was lifted off.

People were clustered, watching. She let herself lean against the wall. She watched the backs of the heads on the fronts of which were the eyes that were watching the monitors. The heads made a black mountain range that partially obscured the lit-up samples of the world.

Into the open-top box of the patio, the sun shone. Philip's face pinkened. Moisture gathered on his forehead and trickled leftwards down around the orbit of an eye.

Happy, Sue wandered through, back up the stairs, past Caro and Elmer who both looked round and smiled, to her workplace. She sat.

Maybe she should tidy her desk. Piles of paper; piles of catalogues; swan's-nest heaps of this and that; scatterings of paperclips
and pens.

Or maybe actually the thing to do on a day like this was to look
forward. Because there was Art and Language, then Johnson Epp;
but after that it wasn't yet fixed; there were several possibilities. In
her Aeron she rolled forward, reached for her mouse, moved it,
clicked.

Philip's sweat was drying and his skin was deeper pink.

Yes: that outsider art idea, Scottie Wilson and the others, Bart
Powers. She clicked open the file.

In his blood vessels the plasma thickening; in his tissues the
osmolality tailing off.

There was a certain amount you could do via Google.

Uuurghhtfh. His head tipped and an eyelid hauled itself open.

What was it exactly that Elmer had said about dates?

Bright. His eye hurt. He hurt. He felt terrible. A thought levered
itself up out of his salt-mine mind. Must get out of the bright. Must
cool. Must stand. Must drink water.

Though actually now . . . Sue wondered what the time was.

He needed to arrange his weak, sore limbs to make it possible to
stand. Or crawl.

Past two already so she could go out for a sandwich and swing
through the gallery on the way. It was bright outside: looked hot.

OK this is it. Hands on his knees, he tried to stand.

As she came down the stairs into the hall, Sue noticed the white
piece of paper on the clipboard on the desk. She asked: 'No press
yet?'

'No since they're all coming at 6,' said Osh.

'Why are they all coming at 6?'

'Because of the change of plan?' – he spoke as though he were reminding her of something: 'the decision to have a standard press view after all?'

'Whose decision was that?'

'All of yours, I thought.' Osh was looking puzzled: 'Omar told me.'

Omar told you, she didn't say. What was. What was going on? Charlotte.

'Have you seen Charlotte?'

'She's in there.'

So Sue pushed into the gallery and stepped methodically through the space, not seeing the work now, looking for Charlotte. Who was standing by the monitors.

In a teetering voice she said: 'Charlotte? Press view?'

'Oh,' said Charlotte, as though it were something she had forgotten. 'Yes,' she said, in a more melancholy tone.

Sue followed Charlotte as she moved away towards a corner.

'Omar decided' – Charlotte said slowly and quietly – 'it would be better.'

'But it's our . . .'

'Sue,' said Charlotte, looking enquiringly into her eyes: 'I should have told you this before. But I didn't know how.'

Sue waited.

'Omar' – Charlotte sighed the name – 'is going to announce that the show is by Elton Barfitt.'

Sue had the answer to that: 'But it isn't.'

'Well, it could be.'

'But it isn't.'

'And sometimes, ' Charlotte hazarded, 'I wonder if it isn't in a sense really theirs after all. Because if it wasn't for them we wouldn't have . . .'

'Oh fuck off.'

'And if you think about the show they outlined to us, ours is in a sense a development of . . .'

'Rubbish.'

'Physicality. The nature of the image . . .'

'Charlotte, it is not by them.'

'. . . so that if you ask what the origin of the exhibition really is, who the author of it, artist of it really is . . .'

'If Omar says that, then they'll come out and say they've had nothing to do with it. It'll be a disaster!'

Or actually, she was thinking, it'll be a scandal, which isn't the same as a disaster. It'll be a great big explosion. There'll be publicity. She'll have a platform. Yes, this is it: this is going to make the gallery explode. Because, by his own act, Omar is going to self-destruct.

'He says,' Charlotte said, in an oddly sing-song voice. 'He's talked to them and they've agreed to abandon their incognito.'

They've agreed to abandon their incognito. They've to them he's talked and they've. To them agreed to talk and they've abandon. To them he's talked to them and incognito.

'Ask Omar,' said Charlotte. 'You need to talk to Omar.'

By Omar ask is them he says abandon. They've talk. To them is Omar ask is need to talk.

'I'm sorry,' said Charlotte. 'There was nothing.' Charlotte seemed to be starting to cry. 'There was really nothing I could do.'

Charlotte had gone and Sue stood in the gallery. She saw the monitors. A foot appeared and vanished; a geiger counter clicked from 34 to 30; the surface of the river water flickered; the meadow grass . . .

There was no meadow grass.

In place of the meadow grass and the poppy with the flickering lip was something else.

The camera must have tipped.

Sue stepped closer. Sue studied the image.

It was blurry. There was a contour. There was a reddish bit and a brownish bit. From out of the brownish bit a whiteish curve emerged.

She narrowed her eyes.

She opened her eyes and let them wander here and there.

She tried to understand the image.

Then she saw that it was part of a face, the side, between the edge of the eye and the start of the ear. Then she thought that it had to be most probably Philip's face and then she recognised it as his because of the brownness of the hair and the puffy roundness of what she now knew was his earlobe.

So for some reason he had turned the camera on himself.

And the question was how to deal with Omar, because if he's talked to them then they must be claiming that this is their show and why would they do that when it isn't, and, not only that, when they turned down the offer of an exhibition in the first place?

But actually, no, given who they are . . .

Because it was just conceivable that maybe it was exactly the bloody-minded 'playful' sort of thing they would do. To dramatise the question of identity. To ask: where does the being of Elton Barfitt end?

Why would Philip do that? Why would he turn the camera on himself?

If it is the case that Elton Barfitt actually said that. If it wasn't Omar's blustering bravado.

She looked again at the blurry, grainy image on the old-fashioned television. He had not moved.

But Omar wouldn't take that risk. He couldn't make that announcement without having first persuaded them. Nobody could. And especially not Omar.

Still not moved.

Or Charlotte, if it wasn't Charlotte who had somehow . . . or maybe all along. Because she was the one who had done the emails and maybe behind them all along? Maybe E.B. had somehow been behind her all along? Maybe the whole thing was a fucking sick E.B. experiment in which she, Sue, figured as some kind of animal in an experiment with electrodes stuck into her so she could respond to stimuli, so she could be given a series of electric shocks and her interesting reactions could be studied.

She had to think out why he was not moving. She had to clear her mind and make it cold and think out carefully why he was not moving. In her mind she drew a picture of the patio. She positioned the camera. She thought about the meadow grasses and the raised flowerbed with its brick edging and she looked again at the angle of the part of the face that she could see.

She pulled out her phone, pressed Philip.

Ringing ringing.

Divert to voicemail.

She clicked End Call and rang again.

The same.

Now anxiety was wobbling in her stomach and prickling in her throat.

Think it through. The neighbours. She did not know the neighbours' names and so she could not get their numbers.

So she could call someone they knew for instance Sara. And Sara could go round and. And what? Put a ladder against the wall and see? See what? And do? Vault over and pick up Philip under her arm and zoom into the air and fly all the way to the hospital.

No, but she could call 999.

Well but in that case then she, Sue, could also call 999. Because that was what you did in an emergency. Even an emergency you weren't quite sure was an emergency? But she was quite sure! He wasn't moving. He must have fallen. He must have fainted and fallen. He must have had a heart attack and fallen. Robbers must have jumped over the wall and clobbered him so he had fallen. Or shot him so he had fallen. Someone had held a gun to his head, to his sweet, chubby, pale-pink head, to the forehead where the fine brown hair was always so neatly brushed across, and . . .

A black hole appeared in the forehead.

A trace of smoke vanished into the air.

Calm. Be calm.

It was not that, not necessarily exactly that. But it was something. It was still an emergency. Just because she had had to reason it out didn't mean it wasn't real.

And then she could go and deal with Omar.

She would have to go out to call because the people.

But she had to be able to see.

So, watching the screen, she stepped backwards, and then crabwise, always watching the screen, until she hit the wall and could hunker down in the shadows of the corner and call. And explain. And expostulate. And explain again. And shout, insofar as it was possible to shout while keeping your voice lowered so as not to disturb the punters in the gallery. And, with icy intensity, explain once more the situation. And then say:

'Thank you. Thank you.'

And then: 'Please do.'

So that, as Sue walked off through the gallery to talk to Omar, an ambulance left its station and set about nee-nawing through the streets.

So that, as Sue paused in her workspace to gather her thoughts, the ambulance was taking a right into The Willows.

And, as Sue knocked, just a formality, before brusquely pushing her way into Omar's office, two paramedics in green overalls propped a ladder against a wall.

'Omar,' she was saying frankly, 'the show is not by Elton Barfitt.'

To which he answered: 'I'm sorry?'

A paramedic was kneeling next to Philip, feeling for his pulse, tenderly lifting his head away from the brick edge to assess the gravity of the gash.

'It's my show. I mean, Charlotte and I curated the show. There's no Artist behind it.'

'Sue?' – said Omar, 'are you alright?'

'I don't know whether you are in on the deception, or whether Charlotte has deceived you, or whether Elton Barfitt are deceiving both of you. But the fact is Charlotte and I have done this show. It is nothing whatsoever to do with Elton Barfitt.'

'Sue, I spoke to them about it yesterday.'

'They were lying.'

'Sue,' he said more shrilly: 'They signed a contract, months ago. Over the intervening period they have sent us numerous instructions via email, listing every detail of this exhibition which we, which you and Charlotte, have put together according to their stipulation.'

'Charlotte signed the contract. Charlotte faked the emails.'

'Sue, I repeat, I spoke to them about it yesterday.' He was looking at her with sorrow and with maybe also a teeter of unease.

As Philip was being laid on his side in the recovery position, one leg bent across the other, its toes hooked behind the other's calf, Sue was saying: 'I can prove, I'm sure technicians can prove the origin of those emails. And it was not, I can tell you it was not, on any computer belonging to Elton Barfitt.'

'Sue,' said Omar carefully, 'you've been working very hard, I know you have. And I think it possible the stress has been too much for you.'

Swab the wound. Gently guide the lips together. Press one end of a suture strip and pull across. And again. And again. And again. And again. And again. Now lay the gauze padding over.

Stick down with microporous tape. Wrap the bandage round, around, around.

The show! – Sue wanted to scream – Is not by Elton Barfitt! It is not! Not! Not!

'I know' – Omar was saying – 'how much you were attached to the idea of this exhibition being anonymous. I am aware of your analysis, and I respect it. But I think' – Omar raised a hand, bunched his fingers – 'that people create these works. Individual artists. Geniuses, if you like. And since they did the work, why not let them take the credit?'

Now try again to wake him. Call loudly. Give him a little shake. Pinch an earlobe hard.

'So I visited Elton Barfitt. I put that argument to them. And they agreed.'

The thing to do was not to scream. The thing to do was try to find an angle. Try to find the piece of evidence or the argument that would persuade.

Philip was being scooped onto a stretcher by the two men who were on their knees. They laid him on his side, with a pillow carefully positioned to support his wounded skull. That done, they strapped him in.

'And, to be pragmatic, Sue, it's very much better for the gallery.'

The two men in green lifted Philip and set about walking through the house to the front door.

'When I rang the arts desks to tell them that The Whole World was in fact by a major artist whom I would name to them at the press view, they were very much more interested than they had been before. I think you'll agree' – he raised his eyebrows again, tipped his head back – 'there was not a tremendous amount of interest before?'

'It was alright,' Sue protested automatically.

'But hardly . . . mega.'

Oh god, as though the level of press interest were what mattered.

As the ambulance moved off, Philip's eyes were opening and shutting and he was moaning: water, water.

There was no way through. Sue's mind scurried this way and that: bounced off this and rebounded onto that, the emails, the careful, oh-so-careful covering of tracks that she had done with Charlotte and that now was being turned against them, against her. Because whatever Charlotte had done she could not be relied on. Whatever Charlotte had done she would not back her up.

Which meant that Elton Barfitt were utterly and oh so casually able to appropriate all this work done by so many different people.

Philip was managing to sip some liquid.

It was just so unjust.

He was emerging from the faint-compounded-by-concussion. He looked around him woozily and everything was blurred. But this must be an . . . he must be in an . . .

So fucking wrong.

There must have been a crash.

Such a fucking lie. So fucking fucking wrong.

'Sue,' he called out in a whisper.

The car must be a write-off. It was smashed. It had hit the side of a bridge. They had been on their way back from his parents' house when . . .

He could not remember.

'Sue,' he whisperingly howled.

'It's alright mate,' a blunt voice said. 'You had a tumble. Knocked your head. Try to stay quiet now. Try to keep sipping.'

'OK,' said Sue: 'You win.'

'Do think,' said Omar, 'of taking some time off. Do think of visiting a doctor.'

Sue said: 'That's good advice Omar. Thank you.'

As Philip was trundled over the smooth floor and under the bright lights of A&E, Sue was standing at her desk. Trash it? Clear out never to return? Go into the press view and shout the truth. Stand outside on a soapbox and declaim. Torch the place, use semtex, send the whole institution fireworking up and shattering into a million whistling iridescent shards.

But ohmigod, but how was Philip?

She checked her phone. She speed-walked through the office and she gambolled down the stairs and she hurried through rooms one and two.

The edge of the wall. Stained – she looked closer: blood? Some strands of grass and a poppy bent across. So there was . . . So there had been . . .

So at least something had now happened. So at least the ambulance had probably . . .

She pressed Philip: ring ring: voicemail.

Strangely thrilled now, as well as worried, she stepped back. She surveyed the stack of old TVs. There was Tahrir Square. There, in the strange grisaille of infrared, was the damaged face of the Buddha. There was the beautiful, mercurial surface of a river; and there was the bloodstained wall.

She saw or thought she saw a railway line. She saw or thought she saw Philip wrapped in a blanket and strapped to a stretcher. The scribble of a twig floated away from her across a reflection of the sky.

She walked out. Out between the photos and the names; out past the blocky white sofa, and the hatstand lamp.

'Bye Osh,' she called.

The inner gallery doors swung shut behind her; the outer doors swung out into the world.

Where Betty and Ken Newell were sitting, one on each side of their picture window in their cream and fuchsia sitting room, looking out at clumps of white, white cloud and intersecting contrails which dappled and scratched the exhilarating summer sky.

Where Dr George Emory, in the practice, in his consulting room which was actually quite comfortable and spacious, having despatched his 19th patient of the day, was turning to his screen to remind himself of the name of the next.

Where Janet Stone, in a playground, near the shadow of an old brick wall, among other parents – mums, mainly – waited for Albert to come running towards her out of school over uneven tarmac ridged by the roots of a huge willow whose mourning boughs leaned over a little climbing frame and slide.

Where, lying back on a double-width chaise longue, in the light of a full-height, half-moon window which made the floor of polished concrete gleam, Elton Barfitt felt their Crème de la Mer re-animating face-mask do its lovely permeating thing, readying them to rise, and dress, and manifest themselves at Spike, where they would preside over the press view of The Whole World, courteously.

Where sweaty Dr Adam Hibbert, bored of months of heat, proud of what he felt he had achieved but missing England and the fact that, well, you can just sit down and have a pint there, scrolled through his calendar: not so many hard days left now till his return.

Where Dr Sara Kaiser was sitting with Sushma and David in the back office, among the revolving filing-towers of old paper notes, talking through the planned structure of collaboration with the other practices in the Clinical Commissioning Group that was soon to be given the green light.

Where, standing in his mother's shadowy, cleared house, or rather the house that had been his mother's, with a candyfloss of roses outside the open window, and eddies of lavender breezing through it, Friedrich Hanworth watched dust float wanderingly in rays of light.

And where Sue now walked through streets of the city, among people she did not know, past windows and walls and doors and lamp-posts and a letter box, past bent tin cans, and squashed and swollen cardboard boxes, and imperishable, recently aseptic tetra-paks made in Wrexham, and polystyrene coffee cups from Xi'an and their imperishable plastic lids; past Sarny Heaven she walked, over five-decade-old concrete pavement between whose non-slip slabs the cracked, old-fashioned mortar gave roothold to clumps of moss and tufts of *poa annua* while, in the shelter of a litter bin, procumbent pearlwort spread and dandelions and Canadian horseweed soared; she walked through air, among phone signals and wireless networks, and lacings of nitrogen dioxide and traces of ozone, and drifting specks of this and that, and scraps of music and rillets of conversation and the traffic's companionable roar; beneath the swooping flights of swifts she walked, towards the triangle of parkland through which she would stride, making pigeons blunderingly scatter, to the junction which she would cross to reach the station whence she would travel through fields that were pale with wheat or yellow with oil-seed rape that had been treated with pyrethroids and nourished with Foliar N, past woods where bats in daily torpor dangle, where foxes doze among mealy shards of bark and shreds of leaves, where pheasants are bred in cages for the slaughter, and where azotobacter and acromobacter flourish and woodlice scurry and earwigs writhe; through all this, and more, her way would take her, to the place where Philip lay: a windowless, bright area in a building on a hill by a large fast road which led towards The Willows, where their house was (rented) for the circle of the year, in Eden Grove, near a line of ash trees and a scattering of elders with, beyond them, Kidney Meadow, where the grass, and buttercups, and flax, and all the rest of it were drying in the sun; and where the endless, un-translucent river flowed.

ACKNOWLEDGMENTS

Thank you Kate; and thank you Mark, my brother.

Thank you Helen and Erica and Peter.

Thank you Audrey, Don, Katja, Margaret, Martin and Tania.

I have drawn information and inspiration from the following sources. Chantal Simon, Hazel Everitt and Tony Kendrick (eds), *The Oxford Handbook of General Practice*, 2nd edition with corrections, 2007; Gillian Pocock and Christopher D. Richards, *The Human Body: An Introduction for the Biomedical and Health Sciences*, 2009; Horace Bolingbrook Woodward, *Stanford's Geological Atlas of Great Britain*, 1904; T. B. Johnston and J. Whillis (eds), *Gray's Anatomy: Descriptive and Applied*, 30th edition, 1949; Sarah Simblet, *Anatomy for the Artist*, 2001 and *Botany for the Artist*, 2010; James Lovelock, *The Revenge of Gaia*, 2006; Richard Mabey, *Flora Britannica*, 1997; Mark Cocker and Richard Mabey, *Birds Britannica*, 2005; Owen Johnson and David Moore, *Tree Guide*, 2004; Lars Svensson, Peter J. Grant, Killian Mullarney and Dan

Zetterström, *Bird Guide*, 1999; Richard Fitter, Alastair Fitter and Marjorie Blamey, *Wild Flowers of Britain & Northern Europe*, 5th edition, 1996; pulsetoday.co.uk; M. Fagot, B. de Cauwer, A. Beeldens, E. Boonen, R. Bulcke and D. Reheul, 'Weed Flora in Paved Areas in Relation to Environment, Pavement Characteristics and Weed Control', *Weed Research: An International Journal of Weed Biology, Ecology and Vegetation Management*, 51 (2011), 650–60; Christopher Green and Kit Chee, *Understanding ADHD*, 2nd edition, 1997; *Wikipedia*; Richard Hamblyn, *The Cloud Book*, 2008; airquality.co.uk/bulletin.php; cancerhelp.cancerresearchuk.org; macmillan.org.uk; Paulus P. Shelby, *Cotton Production in Tennessee* (utcrops.com: PDF); healthyalternatives.com/attention-deficitdisorder.html; *Delirium: Diagnosis, Prevention and Management*, NICE Quick Reference Guide, July 2010 (PDF); Noreen Branson, *History of the Communist Party in Britain, 1941–51*, 1997; John Callaghan, *Cold War, Crisis and Conflict: The History of the Communist Party of Great Britain, 1951–68*, 2003; H. Brandenberger and Robert A. A. Maes (eds), *Analytical Toxicology: For Clinical, Forensic, and Pharmaceutical Chemists*, 1997; S. Kerrigan, D. Honey and G. Baker, 'Postmortem Morphine Concentrations Following Use of a Continuous Infusion Pump', *Journal of Analytical Toxicology*, 28. 6 (September 2004), 529–32; J. S. Rodwell, *British Plant Communities, Vol. 3: Grasslands and Montane Communities*, 1992; Joseph Engelberg, 'On the Dynamics of Dying', *Integrative Psychological and Behavioral Science*, 32. 2 (April–June 1997), 143–48.

A NOTE ON THE AUTHOR

Matthew Reynolds is the author of *Designs for a Happy Home: A Novel in Ten Interiors*. He also works as a critic and scholar, in which vein he has written *The Poetry of Translation*, *The Realms of Verse*, and many essays in the *LRB* and elsewhere. He spent time in London, Cambridge, Pisa and Paris before settling in Oxford where he teaches at the university and is a fellow of St Anne's College.